RAVES FOR CHARLEE JACOB AND
THIS SYMBIOTIC FASCINATION!

"A stunning and provocative debut. *This Symbiotic Fascination* kicks out all the stops!"
—Edward Lee, author of *Succubi* and *Coven*

"Charlee Jacob is a fantastic talent and she stands out among other writers of the gruesome."
—*Masters of Terror*

"It's rare that a writer can make me cringe or actually frighten me, but Charlee Jacob does it."
—*Deathrealm*

"Charlee Jacob is without doubt becoming the Queen of Hardcore Horror."
—*Delirium*

"Charlee Jacob is one of the finest new horror writers around."
—*Shivers*

"Original, thought-provoking, Charlee Jacob is one of the best in the business."
—*Deadlines*

"A chilling, provocative, and often vicious account of the psychotic/supernatural creatures given rise from pain and loneliness."
—Tom Piccirilli, author of *A Lower Deep*

"Charlee Jacob is the Goddess of GrueSex!"
—*Scream*

This Symbiotic
Fascination

Chapter One

It was just out of habit that Arcan Tyler followed the pretty woman.

For old time's sake.

He told himself that he absolutely wouldn't hurt her. Wouldn't touch her.

But the animals in him kept his feet moving long after the failure of his initial efforts to turn away to go down a different street, away from their *pushing* and the urges.

"Keep close," hissed the cat inside him. "Maybe she'll veer soon into an alley brain pan."

"Look how dry her thighs are in the moonlight," the wolf pointed out, slavering, penis rising engorged in blue jeans 'til it hurt. The denim seams pressed like the ridges of a woman's pelvis.

A snail trail of silvery drool exited Arcan's mouth at the sharp corner of his lips and slipped down his chin. In the right illumination—red fibrillating strobe, dusky candles on a wall, the scarlet numbers glowing on a clock radio in a blackened bedroom—it would resemble a trickle of stolen blood.

Salty, rusty metal, FINE blood, the ghoul giggled.

"Look how wet her breasts are in the moonlight," the wolf growled. "Like lactating teats on a doe. Run her to earth!"

"Erotocupcakes," the ghoul said, *pushing* hard. Pushing Arcan to run her down. "Look wet, like they've been PEELED."

Arcan resisted with everything in him. His guts pulled him after her with eyes glued to the sway of her very round apple ass. His teeth chattered in that tiny mincing way of cats imprisoned behind windows watching birds through glass. His loins were coming alive with the scorching. He could smell her in the air.

"Fuck you," Arcan whispered to the animals.

A command. An order from the man. He was a man.

He put his hands to his face. If it had begun to shift even a fraction, he would rip it off, skin hanging through his fingers.

"Fuck off." Arcan said with more confidence.

And he congratulated himself on another nightly miracle as he managed to come to a dead stop on the sidewalk. As he began slowly to rotate to face the opposite direction.

Until he saw the very ugly little man hop out from the shadows and speak to the pretty woman. He came out like the cuckoo darts out of the clock, like the bouncing crow from the children's old cartoons. (Like an erection through a broken zipper.)

Arcan paused, looking back across his shoulder, something catching his attention about the manner in which that crumpled skeleton of a man *moved*. The familiar feral combined with the knotting coiling and uncoiling of a snake and the prissy oiled shiver of a rodent shaking from the fleas in its fur.

He has animals inside him, too, Arcan thought.

This Symbiotic Fascination

The woman had been visibly shocked by the queer, homely geek and started to reach into her purse. Pepper gas or mace or gun. Rape whistle. Now she was smiling. Charmed. Batting her eyelashes, moistening her lips with the tip of her tongue. Thighs quivering.

Arcan had twisted back and was trying to open his mouth. He worked at it, screwing the lips and teeth into crazy planes and angles, trying to shout a warning to her. Look out! That guy has THINGS inside him!

Whether Arcan's own spirit animals were putting all their nasty collective force into keeping him silent or he secretly wanted this cosmeticized, wonder-bra'd lilith to get it, (just not by me I don't do that anymore), he wasn't sure.

The ugly man led the woman away by her manicured hand.

Wisps. Gray half-lights and domes of scarred faces did a languid, liquid ooze around Arcan. They wept in the barely audible peep of the ghosts—but that woman wasn't one of them.

She could never be one of them. Arcan would have had to let his creatures have her. Now it was too late. The squat-ugly dick shifter had approached her first.

And these ghosts were of Arcan's victims only. One of them was truly the spirit of a dead woman. The others mere souls stolen by the cat, the wolf, the ghoul. Arcan's by were-proxy.

What would that woman lose to the ugly little man? Only her soul with some choice skin between her thighs, scrapes of punctured uterus, and a half-moon bite of tender breast?

But this latecomer hadn't attacked her, hadn't clubbed her or forced her into the darkness with a weapon. He'd taken her hand.

And there was no way that spongy, hoary, pizza-faced geek had the physical strength required to overpower this woman. He didn't look strong enough to pinch off a piece of readily available intestine.

He shouldn't have been able to smooth her into going for a stroll either, but there they went.

The ghosts around Arcan moaned, partially stretched from the boles of trees that lined the street, hands invoking pain from the walls of the shrouded buildings.

Arcan followed. He'd lost sight of them. He *smelled* the ugly man, not able to recognize that particular scent or combination of beastly scents. He only knew it made his hackles rise.

Arcan discovered the woman's body sprawled in a culvert. Little more than a torso of ravaged flesh, a fish left in the process of filleting. The legs were severed (not severed, *wrenched* out of sockets and then ripped off) and were in the right position below the hips, spread unnaturally wide. The triangle of pubic hair flashing through the shredded dress glittering with loops of a quickly darkening seed. Her pretty face had been mangled to where Arcan couldn't be sure this was the same female of the apple ass. It was a ripe melon someone had scraped with the tines of a fork until the fruit had lost its fresh appeal.

Arcan could still smell the ugly man. Not that he was there anymore. His strange musty spoor was all over her body, an arcane symbol of it ejaculated in hunter graffiti across one rough cement side of the culvert. It marked nearby trees. It stained the bumper of a late model Thunderbird some rich Texas redneck had affixed longhorns to the hood of. It curdled around the slits to a grate.

Arcan's animals sniffed. He trembled, fearing they would want some of what was left of her. Especially the wolf, whose erection had choked him as it grew in his jeans when Arcan had first started to follow her, grinding against denim seams as if against bones.

No, especially the ghoul, gazing with a salivating longing at the juicy loops of white/red flesh on her that still steamed. He struggled to turn, ready to fight them for dominance, for the human right to run away from this.

But they didn't *push*. Not this time. They shuddered flanks, flattened ears back, tucked their vestigial collective tails of ether between their (his) legs. They did not let him run, but they did let him slink away, the roiling stench of a superior beast in their nostrils.

Chapter Two

Menses sunset. It would spread.

A razor thin line of it was red, crisscrossed, a clumsy suicide attempt.

Yeah, she could do that tonight. It beat watching television.

Maybe eventually Tawne would get it right.

Maybe not.

Then she noticed him. Probably because he was at least as ugly as she was.

She was late coming home from work again. Or were the days just getting shorter? They weren't that short yet. The first day of autumn had been just last week.

It was nearly seven. She was supposed to have been off at four. The street was beginning to get dark in patches, making the row of brownstones look threadbare where the avenue dipped to its lowest point. The man stood on the corner as Tawne Delaney drove up in her rustbucket Buick. He was chatting up one of the most elegant women Tawne had ever seen, enough to give the large woman double flashes of annoyance and jealousy. Through the lowered window of her car came the reek of opulent Chanel as the lady hung onto his every word, staring at the ugly little man as if he had diamonds in the craters of his pockmarked face. Both his eyes glittered with cataracts. His warty hand brushed her rouged cheek, and Tawne was surprised the woman's skin didn't visibly crawl.

Tawne smirked as she considered the scene in reverse. Not trying the suicide song again but holding an incredible beefcake under enchantment.

She wondered if the ugly man was drunk. He was looking down the front of the woman's bodice. The lady's chest heaved dramatically. It might be that he simply leaned forward all the time, as crooked as his back was. How did he keep his balance so he didn't fall face first into cleavage?

Tawne yawned. Bimbo alert. She ought to mind her own business. But she couldn't stop watching. Because this guy was really vulva-shriveling ugly and the woman was so gorgeous. It was as comical as it was weird.

He has money, Tawne decided as she watched him pluck figment lint from the expensive dress, cheapfeeling the swell of an eager breast.

The woman pressed her legs together tightly at this. How was he doing this act? With mirrors?

His uneven teeth showed behind his thin lips like buckled concrete, tongue worming behind them covered in ocherous pimples. They were just large taste buds but what had he eaten recently?

The lady leaned against him as he slipped a scarecrow arm around her waist. They walked down the sidewalk together.

Tawne stared open-mouthed as they went past. He glanced at her and their eyes met for two seconds at the most.

Had those silver clouds on his eyes been a mirage? They

17

weren't just green now; they were a heart-stopping emerald.

Tawne gasped as athletic muscles rippled and a smile flickered across cupid's bow lips over straight white teeth.

This was one marvelous man, and she knew she couldn't have missed a nagging detail like that.

The pair strolled away out of a fashion magazine. The woman's shadow was a silhouette of Venus. His shadow was warped and unbalanced, gnomishly hobbled. His shadow was pulling his trousers from the crack of his scraggly ass, which the man Tawne saw as a hunk was not doing.

Tawne frowned at the shadow, shaken from her dreaminess.

Working too many hours lately, babe, she told herself as she squinted after them.

"Ugly dude. Socialite going on a charity date as her good deed of the month. Or high-priced whore with the Visa upfront," she whispered to herself, still jealous but not sure of whom.

They were going away from the last rays of the sunset. Razor streaks in the low western sky poured blood now. The sun would be dead soon. And the night would lower it into its dark grave without a second thought. Easy, the way it was with all of creation's throwaways. And the blood would feed the stars 'til they twinkled.

Tawne wished she had the kind of bucks that guy must have.

She dragged herself wearily up the steps to her brownstone. She grasped the key and tried to focus on the brass angles going right side up into the lock. Trying not to notice her oversized hand, swelling at the end of the wrist crosshatched with scars.

Some bastard told her once that she had a steelworker's hands. It had made her furious. Fit to bust. Another guy at the store had said they were more like a ripper's. That had made her cry, not openly but as soon as she'd been able to get alone.

If Tawne only had bucks she could pay men to stroke the sausages of her fingers, kiss the meaty palms, tongue her sweat claiming it was wine and oh, my how they hungered for more. Gigolos would hang on her every word, pretending to tingle as she plucked imaginary lint from their crotches.

She couldn't do that on what passed for salary in the stock room at Galway's Department Store. She wasn't presentable enough to work out front. One had to be at least a marginal clothes horse to do that. Please. Galway's sold very fine things.

She'd have to win the Texas lottery to afford fine men seeking to ingratiate themselves with a rich—not tall and fat—*Rubenesque* classic beauty such as herself. It would have to be a really big lottery, too, not just the beginning pot of a measly four mil which many gamblers considered beneath them to buy a dollar's chance for.

"So maybe he's going to butcher her. Like the one from two nights ago. Yeah, that's better than being stuck in front of the TV," Tawne said wryly. "It also beats the do-it-yourself kit."

Inside her apartment on the third floor, the television box squatted with its busted screen. Right where she'd put her boot months ago, through pouting Heather Locklear's face. Or was it during some ad showing anorexic models with the flat chests and the pubes of eight-year-olds and big blowjob lips? Didn't matter. She'd been disgusted with all of it. Or heartbroken. Same thing really. Maybe that was the last time she'd slit her wrists, creating blooming sunsets below those ripper hands.

Tawne skipped supper and went straight to the bathroom to shower. She undressed. There was stray packing popcorn in her pants. This made her laugh. "Only thing that'll ever get in my underwear."

No man ever had.

And why? Why, when warty little buggers like the one she'd seen picking up beauties at twilight could find companionship, couldn't she?

She knew the answer but she looked into the full-length mirror for a long time anyway. A glutton for punishment.

It was as if Tawne had been assembled by alchemy. Mercury and sulfur had been mixed to make cinnabar hair, red and heavy. In other than ropy strands the mass might have been beautiful. Her eyes were lead, too gray for use as a lover's speculum and too flinty for quicksilver. Her face and body remained an unmalleable lump comprised of elements and biological invocations that—once assembled, cooked by nature, and chanted over by the Armadels of DNA—still didn't finish into gold. Those deals seldom worked out, did they?

It had always been difficult to be unattractive. Nowadays in the America of skin and skeletal miracles, it was a sin. A crime punishable by death . . . death-by-ugly.

And to top it all off by being a virgin at 37, unable to give it away in the era of bonded close-up smiles, hardbodies in soft spandex, and profligate screwing? Oh, there were sex plagues but everyone knew that beauty was better protection than a condom. But such unsalable flesh as hers transcended sin into pathetic joke. Like the hee-haw that said it was only possible to find a fat woman's love hole by first rolling her in flour and then looking for the wet spot.

It would make anybody go out for blood.

"I hate you, Mister," Tawne said to the ugly man.

Why did she hate him instead of the elegant woman? Wasn't it easier to hate what she couldn't be? No, because the emotion struck toward the woman was futile jealousy. She hated the man because he had no right to that companionship. To any sort of happiness. Not if Tawne couldn't have it, too.

What does he have that I don't? Bucks? Hypnotic powers?

Tawne stepped into the hot sluicing water. She faced it, never turning to do her back. She let it scald her breasts, the ruddy thatch of hair at her untried porthole. She didn't even soap up. She watched the boiling water sear off her nipples in pulpy flakes. It stripped away her flesh, melting it to basic atomic elements. It sloughed down her arms and legs like the pelts from skinned rabbits, unrolling like fuzzy socks, except for the ladles of creamy fat squeezing between the layers of muscle. She shrieked in the burn as what didn't fall off plumped up until it would have to explode. But she reveled in it, too.

She knew this wasn't happening. The water in this old building never got this hot or, if it did, it was only for the first floor residents. No fission for Tawne.

It would be easy to lie down, take a razor and make crimson sunsets glow, blood swirling away cloudy in the torrent.

The last time she tried it, the tub overflowed. The people downstairs saw it coming through their ceiling in bloody gushes. Seth Howe had taken the stairs two steps at a time while Stephanie called 911.

Such good folks. Church-goers. Caring Christians. Not capable for one truly compassionate moment of letting a mortally unhappy woman end her life.

They had even taken Tawne to church with them for a while, after saving her life. She'd looked for answers there but all she got was: Well, God does things for His Own reasons.

Yeah, because He's a mean So-And-So. He can do what He wants to, making this one a gazelle and this one a hog. Must make for some good yucks in Heaven during the slow eons.

Tawne turned off the water, the drain clogged with hair and soap. The landlords never fixed anything. They were painting the walls but paint was cheap, providing a simple cosmetic fix. They had laid new carpet on the stairs. One of them had a relative in the carpet seconds business. Plumbers were expensive.

Electricians, too.

She didn't want the tub overflowing again. She didn't want the concerned Howes dashing upstairs to check on her. To make sure she hadn't slashed herself again, trying to make the sun go down, numb to the razor's edge.

The water gurgled slowly into the drain. It moaned in the pipes. Nowhere to go, after all, but down.

Tawne toweled off, rubbing too hard with the nap, trying to uncover something. The luscious woman who had been hiding for years under all the coarseness.

The one she wished she could make others see.

Tawne curled on her bed, the book she'd been reading fallen next to the pillow. Pages of poetry full of blood and pale people. Transcendence: even if only through death and into the night.

Asleep and in the veils, she still wasn't fooled. No poetry would be magic enough for her to become some breathy porcelain heroine waiting to be swept up by Heathcliff on horseback, racing along the beach under a full moon. She knew exactly what sort of woman merited that: she held few illusions. She never pictured herself in strings of pearls. She would never be offered a ring or receive long-stemmed roses at her door. She'd never even been given a valentine. Did pale people give valentines? She smiled in her sleep. *Sort of.*

Sort of valentines.

She dreamed about men but they were different. They might have hearts pinned to their sleeves, but the hearts were not their own and they had not been won with poetry.

These men rode no fast steeds, drove no jaguars, raced not between stars in light-ships nor posed buff for GQ.

This Symbiotic Fascination

One was in her dream now, howling from the darkness. The one she'd seen there for a long time, since her last suicide attempt and the failed sunsets of her wrists. His eyes glittered in the shadows. She couldn't glimpse the pale face that must go with those beckoning eyes. He couldn't see her because it was too black. This made her more comfortable with her shortcomings. But he was a man of second sight and saw her soul with more clarity than anyone ever saw flesh. He knew the soul was scented with the musk of her need. He wanted her, called to her in a voice not altogether human. It was a voice so deep it shocked the base of her spine, frightening and galvanizing.

She walked to him like she always did, not once stumbling. She heard the rumbling of his breath, smelled wet fields and dangerous alleys about him. She didn't find fault with the premise that suggested that anything and all that came before this moment was ended. It was simple when the anythings and the all amounted to zero. What did she have to give up? Loneliness? Ridicule? Panic?

When Tawne finally reached him and darkness split, his smile was as wide and glittering as the feral bridegroom. The cave was lined in slick red, and there were deflated lumps everywhere which stank of sulfur and rust, not unlike large eyes shriveled into ocular raisins. Those murdered suns had to go somewhere, didn't they?

What did she have to give up?

What she'd give up was absolutely whatever he asked for.

Chapter Three

The cat is out.

He has climbed over the fence and entered through a window, aware of the moonlight on the glass as he slinks in. He's been waiting for the woman to come out of the bathroom and now she does.

She is humming some mindless tune from the radio top 40, and her breath is heavy with cinnamon mouthwash. Her hair is damp from the shower. The sound of the toilet running keeps her from hearing his heart beating. Or perhaps she's just stupid and oblivious. She doesn't even turn on the hall light. She's all too comfortable in her dark house. But that will change.

She looks behind her in time to see his hand reaching out of the shadows. He grabs a fistful of her lingerie, peach and lavender and sheer.

This is always a sublime moment, that of the initial physical contact, coupled with her first realization of his menace. She's been too foolish to feel him there, to sense the wrong on the other side of the bathroom door which has been there all the time she took her shower, brushed her teeth, and emptied her bladder of the white wine he smelled as he slipped through the living room. There had been an invasion into her frilly little world but she hasn't understood it until this instant as she feels the pain of his clutch and sees her doom in his face.

How he exults in this terror of hers. It is a moment ripe with appetite, mercenary, unconfining him at last. The minutes will soon be consecrated with her tears, and each act of brutality will serve to perpetuate a cruel universe. Life is a series of wearing shackles, struggling and bleeding into the blunt links of the chains, of screaming in the feudal bonds, and then of breaking them to pass them on down to others. He knows this is the ultimate truth. This is *his* personal truth. He squeezes her shoulder beneath the fabric, digging his fingers into the tense muscle where a nerve jumps in panic.

She starts to cry out.

He lets her see the knife glint. So long. So sharp.

"One noise and I'll cut you." he promises. "You won't like that much."

No, because she is egotistical, like all of them. She spends more money in a month on cosmetics than many people have to spend on food.

She remains silent, twitchily eyeing the blade, the nerve in her shoulder leaping but trapped. He digs his fingers in until she flinches, twists under his grasp. She squints as the knife's subtle light effects are drawn from the street lamps and the moon through a distant window.

And all the time he is:

Afraid she will yell. People will come running. One loses power in a crowd. Especially in a crowd hungry to castrate him because they can't understand the truth. Ready to destroy his demons because they can't face the ones within themselves . . .

Charlee Jacob

Hoping she will cry out, aching to hear her lips part, mouth open, and thunder issue forth. So he can slice the pretty face, bisect the traitorous coral mouth, carve a luminous blue-glossed eyelid. She'll know who's boss.

Yeah, *scream*, give me a reason to prove it to you.

The ultimate truth of the cat.

But she's silent. Only her heavy breathing gives her away as being alive at all. She would silence even that if she could, because he warned her to be quiet. Only fair to give that warning, isn't it? Give her a chance to obey.

He forces her into the bedroom, makes her take off the filmy nightgown. Her shoulder is already bruising from where he wrenched it to hold her fast in his introduction.

"Tear it into strips," he commands her once she is naked, holding the gown limply in her hands.

She complies, watching him out of the corner of one eye as he perches nearby. His knife moves slightly. He whittles air into obscene shapes.

He ties her to the bed with the strips.

The cat retires.

The wolf comes out.

He does it to her to show her how sterile she is. How static is her delicacy. He beats her down with his fists, comes white slime into her face after forcing his swollen, resentful penis between her dry legs. He breaks a few little bones with his bare hands. He makes sure her eyes are haunted before he finishes.

He makes sure she will never be the same.

He turns her jittery, weak, passive *act* into the genuine article.

He puts a clammy hand between her breasts. Her heartbeat pitter-pats irregularly, hammers, hammers, like his loins did against her fragile cleft, not a pleasing rhythm because it has been shocked. It may never beat properly again.

Well, that is the idea. Shackles are being passed down.

26

Interesting how truth for the cat is the same for the wolf, except in the manner of degree. The wolf is a creature of hunger.

He puts an iron hand between her thighs and grabs a handful of pubic hairs and slippery labia. They are wet with saliva and blood. She cries out from this new pain. But she does it softly, seeing the knife moving. Subtle light and lightning flashes. Fear clogs the throat, fear of worse things.

He wipes the fouled hand across her mouth, hooking viscous fingers over her bruised lips, over the even row of sparkling teeth. There is so much semen on her face he could skip a rock across it.

"Please don't kill me," she whimpers. "You said you wouldn't kill me."

"Did I say you could talk?" he whispers.

The wolf ruts.

Gags her carefully for the worse things to be.

Then he retires to wherever the cat went.

The ghoul comes out.

If the wolf is a creature of hunger, the ghoul is a beast of torture.

He takes bites from her breasts, her thighs, her soft flat stomach in ragged half-moons.

Then he leans close so that her bulging, veined eyes can see him chew and swallow them all.

Oh, she will never forget him.

He's made sure of that.

She'll never be too proud again.

There are disadvantages to womanhood. He has shown her what they are.

The vein in her forehead looks as if it will burst.

She looks as if she knows she can never wake from this horrible dream because the night has become an endless vision.

But it is he who wakes up screaming.

He realizes after a few minutes of panic that he is in the

dark of his own room, and that this was only another nightmare of a memory. When he goes to sleep again there will probably be another.

And another after that one.

He has them most nights. This one was very bad. Worse than most but not as bad as some. He can taste her blood and muscle, still see her freaked-out eyes in the after-image. She is flashburned onto his retinas.

He needs a cigarette.

He gave them up. Quit smoking last year at about the same time he committed the last assault, wasn't it?

Arcan sat up in bed and tried to recall just when that was.

It had been around Christmas and colder than a stone mother's tit offered to a dead baby. He'd worn the old gray leather jacket.

He got up and went to the closet, reaching all the way to the back. His fingers hit the suede and he pulled it out. There was a partial pack of Camels in the inside pocket.

There was a smudge of blood on it. He stared at this for maybe five seconds before blinking it away to focus on trying to scrounge for matches. There were none in the coat but he had some in the kitchen.

Nine months then, since the last time he'd given in to the beasts.

Long enough for that stone mother to bear another kid. Stillborn, of course.

It had been nine months since Carmel Gaines had managed to break away from him, bleeding and screaming out of her mind. She'd leapt from the bed trailing flesh, stumbled to the drawer and pulled out the 38 caliber. He'd been sure he was going to die then. He was frothing at the mouth, cussing her and telling her what he was going to do with that gun once he took it away from her.

. . . you filthy cunt bag of shit bitch scrotum sucking slut gonna put that right up your ass in the fucking twat and pull the trigger watch it come red all the way up between your tits . . .

He jumped across the room after her but she never even aimed it at him.

Oh, no . . . maybe never intending to shoot him.

She put the barrel in her own mouth and bit down . . .

. . . as if the blue steel were his own meat which had been there just three minutes before in wolf pelt and gristle.

She bit down as she pulled the trigger, and the whole back of her head and the roof of her mouth and all kinds of teeth shrapnel and skull dust and gray brain pan pudding went: BBBBLLLAAAAMMMM!!! The ghoul, beast of torture, sneered and disappeared. The wolf, which was a creature of hunger, sniffed but preferred nothing that had not been ruined by himself and so he also vanished. The cat, who was an animal of casual mean curiosity and feared loud noises, never returned to see what happened. They left Arcan shaken, hearing the voice of a child from somewhere in the house, a child who was wakened to the sound of a gun or who might have heard his mother's screams but was too frightened to cry out himself before the gun exploded. The husband wasn't home but the child was coming down the hall. Arcan heard the bare feet running. He quickly locked the door and hurried to escape through the window as the boy began shrieking, beating on the door.

Arcan now took a drag, letting the hot smoke scorch the tender throat that hadn't taken a puff in nine months. It hissed out his nostrils. He coughed but took another puff, slower, deeper.

And remembered sneaking to the funeral. Seeing the four-year-old boy throwing a conniption at her gravesite as the coffin was being lowered in.

The boy's father held his hand tightly and tried to calm him down. The child slipped and almost fell in on top of the coffin. On the lid that had been kept closed for the ceremony, on top of all the thorny roses, orchids and lilies. The loose earth, so carefully sculpted at the sides, was unraveling at the little feet as his daddy pulled him back in time. Then the man held him even tighter as the kid beat and kicked at him, ripping the solemn black suit coat.

The father's own eyes were squeezed shut, letting in no light.

And, yeah, did this one ever forget him? She must have. Must have been the point of the slug. So she would forget permanently.

Arcan wasn't sure why he cared. But the guilt had a sharper edge than anything he'd ever used on any of his victims.

He cared because this woman led his ghosts.

He knew there were lots of them in the house, hanging off the walls, sometimes everywhere he looked. Even when he followed others.

The urge was always there, strong and needing. There was a woman where he worked named Delia who brought growls and whispers to his head every time he thought about her. She was a clothes horse, stuck up like all the pussies that worked out front at Galway's. Weak, despicable succubi that sucked men dry after working them to death as they fluttered their lashes and pranced and oh God, wouldn't want to break a fucking nail. Leaches sucked men but they could be stepped on because they were just worms, right? Which got fat and squirted good under a boot and lord this cigarette was so *good* why had he ever quit?

Arcan discovered he had an erection.

The smoke burned, seared, made him raw all over. His lips were scorched as he drew hard on the Camel. His dick throbbed with every drag, even as he thought about Delia. How good it would feel to give it to that bitch.

When had he quit smoking?

More importantly, *why* had he quit?

Because the last time he'd used the lit cigarette on the woman. On Carmel in patterns of sunbursts and a tri-elliptical atomic symbol and the word cunt with a K. The round blisters had swelled as she struggled in her bonds, eyes growing wilder, belly undulating, bucking, fucking bronco as he tattooed it with daisychains of suppurating sores. He could still smell the flesh as it burned. Taking a drag off the Camel, he tasted the flesh swimming back to him through the tobacco.

It was like meat because it was meat.

Meat put through a fire.

And what survived the fire had to atone for having cheated the ashes.

This wasn't the cat's ultimate truth, nor the wolf's, nor the ghoul's ultimate truth. This was Arcan's alone.

He'd survived the fire of his loins and brain. He would do this no more. There must be atonement. There had to be salvation.

He looked at his fingers gripping the table in the kitchen. His nails had dug into the wood. There were splinters under them. That was what he'd been doing for nine months—hanging on by his fingernails. Fighting his animals.

He thought about the ugly man he'd seen the other night. The woman or what remained of her in the culvert. He'd never done damage like that to any of his victims. Somehow he could taste even her through the cigarette. But atoning for her wasn't his problem. The ghosts hadn't really expected him to save her, had they, as they groaned from their middle realm?

They were rattling chains that bound them to him.

So much for the chains being passed on down.

"Quiet, bitches," he said as he put the cigarette out. But he said it softly, as if the word *bitch* referred to something more elevated than a Lilith. A goddess, maybe.

He trashed the rest of the pack. He went back to bed, fearing and praying for another nightmare.

Chapter Four

Tawne and Arcan were unloading Sony televisions in Galway's Electronics Department. All around them video games flashed and beeped, CD players pounded out bass-high rhythms from rap songs and steel guitars from country hits. Every TV on display was turned on and tuned to the same station—Channel 7. The evening news was on.

Tawne scarcely paid attention as the anchor announced that another woman had been found with her body mutilated. She had been discovered stuffed into a culvert. Identification was being made through dental records. Tawne worked without hearing most of it. She shut it out because it was just one more murder in a city—a world—full of them. If you followed them all, it drove you crazy with fear and grief. Unless you were the sort of person who got off on it. It didn't get Tawne off. Some of it rendered her numb; some of it scared her—thinking of the red swirls down the bathtub drain. But that was self-murder. Mostly the idea of being murdered seemed remote. She looked at her huge hands and knew her own strength. Tawne could defend herself well if any woman could. She could likely defend herself in a battle better than many men could.

The news disturbed Arcan as he also tried to ignore it, although for vastly different reasons. He'd never been one to kill. But what he'd done had always been just one step from. Could he be sure he wasn't the one going out and doing these culvert murders? Could he finally have gone over the edge completely where he couldn't say what he did? Did he have a new alter ego in an ugly little man whom he saw leading women off in some out-of-body experience?

"It wasn't me," he grumbled softly, convinced it wasn't true.

Assuring himself, yes. Saying it to himself, to the cat, the wolf, the ghoul. It wasn't *you*. It wasn't *us*. No ugly squirt in here.

"Huh?" Tawne asked as she stood fulcrum while he swung his end of a console around onto the pedestal. "You say something?"

He smiled thinly and shook his head. "Nothing important."

"We should haul ass," she said. "You know we got those microwaves next."

Arcan began to sing. "We got to install microwave ovens . . ."

She joined in spontaneously. "Custom kitchens . . ."

"Dee—liv—er—aaayyy!" they rang out together.

A few customers grinned at them.

Arcan laughed and repeated the title of the Dire Straits song, "It's money for nothin', all right."

"More like nothin' money." Tawne nodded her head, muscles in her bull neck taut.

He couldn't help admiring the cords in that neck, the strength in those awesome hands of hers. He thought they were really beautiful but didn't want to say so for fear she would take it the wrong way. He knew how sensitive she was about her size. But there was no one else at Galway's he'd rather work with. Tawne could always be depended upon to do her share. Unlike most men, and unlike all the women he'd ever met.

Alan Moravec came onto the news. People were gathering in tight crowds around the sets to watch.

"Today's segment of *Mean Streets* brings us to Shorecross Mall."

This brought more customers over, being the mall where Galway's was to be found. Plus *Mean Streets* was popular. People tuned in hoping to catch their neighbors or enemies in a rank act, hoping like hell it wasn't themselves caught on tape being jerks. Alan Moravec was a video sneak and seemed to have the penultimate knack for finding embarrassing moments. He leered from the screens, smug, certain of attention. The scene shifted from his face to the recorded action which he described as it progressed.

"I scoped out the Shorecross Mall parking lot this afternoon, originally thinking I'd catch someone parking so close you'd need a can opener to get in or maybe scraping a long wound into a fender and taking off. Or taking up three spaces fore and aft for their miserable Cadillac like it was a starship or something. Hey, you know who you are. But there's this Prism. Yeah, see the woman inside? She's changing her kid's diaper in the car. Then—look at that!—she dumps it right out the window and onto the blacktop. That's her face on the zoom. I got a good close-up of her, huh? The steaming diaper. One. *Two*. Ugh! Some people's kids. Let's pull back and show this slob's license number. Wait a sec. Here she's getting out of the car to go into the mall. That's right, step *over* it, nose in the air. My baby didn't do *that*! And even if he *did*, it doesn't *smell!* Right? Take a good look at her because . . . Hey! Lady! You're an asshole!"

It was the line Moravec always closed his segment with. He didn't film Samaritans.

"So remember. I may be watching you. And if I am, the whole city is watching!"

People were chuckling. Milling around the sets.

A woman in the store gasped and cried out, "Oh, my god!" She gripped the handle of the stroller she was pushing until her knuckles were white. "Oh, god!"

Everyone turned in her direction. Including Tawne and Arcan.

It was the bitch with the diaper that Moravec had just shown on the tube.

She glanced around nervously. Yes, everyone was staring and recognizing her. She hid her face behind both hands.

Someone chortled and pointed. "Hey! Lady!"

And the whole electronics section, customers and clerks alike, pointed at her and chimed. "You're an asshole!"

Tawne and Arcan burst out laughing, watching her quickly push the stroller down the aisle past them toward the store's exit, her face as red as a ripe jalapeno pepper. She sobbed noisily.

Everyone in the city had seen. Her friends. Her neighbors. Probably her husband. She'd never live it down. And folks would be calling up the Department of Motor Vehicles to get her name and address from the license number, calling her endlessly all the next day, proclaiming, "Hey! Lady! You're an asshole!" She'd get up in the morning to find a hundred shitty diapers on her front lawn. People would mail them to her in express parcels and crates. Even after someone else became infamous on *Mean Streets*, she would be forever remembered as The Shitty Diaper Woman. Litter Bug and Doo Dumper.

Tawne almost felt sorry for her. She stopped laughing and chewed her lip thoughtfully. It was never nice to get laughed at. She knew how it felt.

"Don't," Arcan said firmly, seeing what she was feeling. "Don't sympathize. She got what she deserved. Someone ought to make her eat it."

Tawne made a face at the thought and suggested. "Couldn't she just wear it around her neck as a penance?"

Penance.

Arcan saw someone.

A familiar face floated in the crowd in Linens and Boudoir.

"Moravec's lucky she can't sue him. What's truer than videotape?" Tawne shook her head as she pried open another Sony crate. The nails popped like knuckles.

Normally they would have uncrated in the back but there was no room. The docks were swamped with coat racks today. And with summer swimwear unsold during clearance being sent back in shame to the manufacturer.

Arcan had seen a woman walking past the bedding displays as if strolling by rows of winding sheets, shrouds flapping in slow motion, drapes for catafalques and curtains for mausoleums. The material had a peculiar texture, as if flesh were stretched and scraped to the transparency of an organdy. As if guts were pulled apart and shredded, then the threads twirled on a spindle 'til very fine, woven to make a grisly silk. And they used to make ornamental mourning-wear from the hair of the dead, didn't they? The woman doing a slow sleepwalk past these morbid chiffons bore a scar down the side of her nose and had a white patch over one eye.

She'd screamed.

Well, he'd warned her not to.

And he'd cut her because she'd screamed.

He'd aimed down with a jab as if plucking a plum from a pie.

A year ago?

What was her name?

He was surprised she didn't have a glass eye. Come to think of it, there had been too much lost. Although he thought the surgeon did a rather nice job on the nose and cheek even if her face was still badly scarred. All the way into the next department, down the aisle, through the crowd that had seemed so alive a few minutes ago and now looked dead to him, Arcan could see the damage he'd done.

Perhaps another four or five operations would fix it.

He froze, watching as the face floated and the dark hair surrounding it drifted. She would disappear for a second, be there the next as lithe as any figure striding past loops of cerements, pausing to finger the stiff gravethreads that must accompany the stacks of pillows for coffins. Then she was gone again in the sea of dead shoppers. From time to time there would be a glimpse of her shoulders above the swell of people. She still moved like a gazelle. It was the first thing he'd ever noticed about her. But it was a crippled (shackled) gazelle, one that has not well escaped a lion.

He shuddered with the image. The illusion of graveyards was gone, replaced by wilderness—a place suitable for gazelle. For cats and wolves and other animals, too.

Elise Reedman. That was her name.

She was the one who started the support group, intended for women who had been his victims. Arcan spied on them once back in June. He'd seen Elise talking about the group on a local cable access show. He'd watched them walking in pairs from their cars to the building. It was in an old business school that rented out the classrooms at night to little groups like this one. All 10 women bore his scars, either in what flesh showed or in their eyes. The special haunted look had been his trademark.

Now he trembled, seeing her only a few aisles over.

Don't let her see me. Please.

If she did see him, would she recognize him?

Maybe not. A lot of these women blotted it from their minds, having memories of their assaults in bits and pieces. The fact they couldn't recall every detail straight was the reason they were given little credibility at rape trials. The poor woman's mind was the best friend of the rapist. Providing the guy hurt them enough to begin with.

Arcan always had.

Elise Reedman had been one beautiful woman, the best

looking of any of his victims. He looked at her now with tears in his eyes for what his animals did to her. All traces of his hatred for her were gone. Most of them anyway. As many as he could successfully repress.

He shuddered, teeth banging together until the fillings vibrated. She could look up and see him and begin to scream. SCREAM.

Until someone ran him down. Pressed his face to the floor and cuffed him. Wrenched his shoulders from their sockets until they exploded, white ball joints exposed through rearranged flesh, veins squeezing around in a ripple. He would chew his tongue to keep from crying out and he'd taste blood. He knew the taste of blood.

"Arcan?"

The vision of Elise Reedman was swimming, unclear as a bad memory. He should step away, slink to the back room of electronics. Hide hide hide hide.

"Arcan, are you okay?"

Tawne put her hand gently but firmly on his arm.

He stared down as current ran through that hand, grounding him back. His shakes melted away into her fingers.

"Arcan?" Tawne looked concerned for him. Not that shifty, false concern that many women professed. No batting of the eyelashes or pouting the lips.

He looked back toward Linens And Boudoir. The face was gone. He looked toward the nearest aisles. Elise hadn't come this way.

Perhaps she'd seen him and fled to find store security.

Or maybe she hadn't seen him at all.

"Yeah. I'm okay," Arcan told Tawne.

"You sure? You sick? Need a break? Because I can finish this."

"No, I'm okay. I thought I saw a ghost," he replied, looking back for Elise one more time before deciding that this was what she must have been.

Chapter Five

The clothes on the Z-rack were expensive, raw silk from the Ellen Tracy fall collection. Not for the squeamish of pocket. Tawne loved the material. Silk worms must have gorged on whipped cream before spinning their cocoons. She constantly used hand lotion as she worked on this merchandise. She rubbed it into her rough skin until it was no longer greasy, wiping the excess on the knees of her jeans. She did this to keep from snagging the delicate fabrics as she checked sku numbers and prices, rehanging on the store's special labeled hangers, padded with foam for further protection.

Definitely not horse blankets, these were made for sleek females with long waxed legs and $50 manicures.

Nothing she could ever wear.

Even with her employee discount, everything Tawne had came from the moderates section of the queen-sized Ladies Department.

Every so often one of the presentable saleswomen in

high heels sauntered in to check on incoming for a special customer. The men in the stock room would stare, checking out the tight buns and the made-up eyes, drooling as if they hadn't seen a woman all day. Tawne always felt the momentary envy, shrugging it off to return to work. Such feelings were self-abusive and pointless.

(Queen-sized. What a misnomer. Think Guinevere wore a size 18 or that Marie Antoinette almost fainted in Paris summers from the friction raised when her thighs rubbed sparks along her pantaloons?)

Delia walked through the swinging doors, sashaying in her health club torso. She was wearing Elizabeth Taylor's *Passion*. On any other saleswoman, the fragrance was a big purple net. On Delia it was a hint of violet dabbed sparingly at the pulse points. Nothing about Delia was overblown. She was the closest thing to a lady that Tawne had ever seen.

"Are these checked in with the sheet yet?" she asked Tawne politely as she examined a gold and cobalt wrap-around dress with a plunging neckline.

Tawne nodded, sniffing casually at the flower mist. She stepped aside to give the other woman room to look at the rack.

"Good. Is it okay if I take this here six and eight to Mrs. Peters?" Delia asked in her deep drawl. She was definitely no Texan as there was no twang. It was soft but precise, a cultured blur that might have been Georgian.

Tawne nodded. "Have at it. We'll deliver the rest soon as it's checked."

"Thanks, sugar." Delia plucked the dresses. She started to leave when a second style caught her eye. She lifted it off the rack. It was a loose-fitting toga dress in speckled fawn. "This style would look real good on you."

Tawne chuckled. "It'd look like shit on me."

"No. This cut would be flattering. The colors suit you. Your skin and hair are definite autumn. If you come by later, you could at least try one on. See how pretty you'd look."

Delia's eyes shone above her smile. None of the other women ever tried to get Tawne in a designer piece. No one else would waste the time. Most of the expensive lines didn't even make clothes in Tawne's size.

"Why bother when I can't afford it anyway?"

"Because it's nice. Don't have to buy it just to slip it on and see it." Delia winked and patted the chunky hand. "Come by later if you change your mind. Okay?"

She turned to leave. Bill Tower whistled low, then rubbed his nose with a nicotine-stained finger. Jerry Shelly swung his head from left to right, mimicking the sway of Delia's practically non-existent behind as it moved away from them.

"Hey there, Miss Peach America. Smellin' somethin' pretty tasty. When are you going to take me out to dinner on some of that fat commission check you draw every week? Show me a good time, I'll show you something good, too."

Tawne rolled her eyes, knowing who made the remark without having to see. She tried not to turn.

Carl Pruitt punched in on the clock, coming onto his shift. And coming onto Delia.

Delia didn't reply. She never did when hooted at. She didn't even flinch. It wasn't possible to tell by her face if she'd even heard.

Carl shrugged, grinning at the guys. "Yeah, she wants it."

Bill winked. "Muscles ain't enough, Carl. Got to have class for a woman like Delia."

"Class don't turn up the heat," Carl replied as he flexed a deeply tanned biceps. He kept the short sleeves of his T-shirts rolled up even shorter so the hard curves of those muscles were always visible.

Tawne tried to picture him in a few years covered with

woody carcinomas, karma for the carelessly vain. Reap what you sow, conceited sun-worshipper. The pale of night won't know that burn.

But she couldn't imagine it. He was too handsome to picture flaws where none existed. Still, he couldn't get to first base with any of the lookers on the Galway selling floor because he was such a jerk.

Carl noticed Tawne ploddingly working the silks and trying to see him without being obvious about it. He knew Tawne would look at him even if Delia wouldn't. She couldn't help it every day when he arrived and opened his big mouth. He fixed her with his famous stare, all indigo eyes and soft blond eyebrows. A fair-haired boy if ever there was one.

Tawne's stomach fluttered, regretting she'd looked and been caught at it. Everything about Carl skewered her, from frayed jeans to meat hook eyes.

"This is for the next batch of sportswear," Carl said, handing her a sheaf of invoices.

"Okay," she replied, feeling as if she had a mouthful of stale peanut butter. She even stumbled over the word. How could anyone stumble over two measly syllables?

Seeing she was flustered, Carl grinned. When she turned away to study the invoices—trying to hide her blush—he swatted her on the butt. She swung back, snarling between grit teeth.

"Don't do that." The paper crumpled in her fist.

"You're beautiful when you're angry. You know that. Ton?"

Bastard, mispronouncing her name all the time. Tawne rhymed with dawn. Why did he have to make with the tired weight jokes?

He strutted off with a swagger full of jock itch. Tawne knew what he was thinking. *Yeah, she wants it.*

She'd overheard him telling it to the other guys in much the same way he'd made the remark about Delia. And about

Bette, Janis and Kim. Except they really laughed when he said it about Tawne. Because it was true.

TON. The infuriating little dick.

Yep, he skewered her and left her twisting in the wind, her insides in gory love knots.

Delia glanced away, embarrassed for her. She looked at the clothes on the rack that Carl had just given Tawne invoices for.

"This the new AK-II collection from the catalog?"

Tawne was barely able to speak for mortification. She swallowed and pointed. "Arcan's checking that in over there."

Delia thanked her and walked over to Arcan. Tawne was awed by the slender legs. Long-stemmed American beauty was the phrase that Tawne's father used to utter when seeing a woman like that. He'd say it with reverence, with a glimmer in his eye and with pride, PRIDE mind you, as if this somehow proved he was a man.

As a child, Tawne couldn't figure out if this proof came from some enigmatic verification process in the woman's beauty or just from the fact he was able to notice. She still didn't know.

She did know this had always hurt her mother from whom Tawne inherited her large frame. Her mother would downcast her eyes, never rebuking her husband for the cruelty. Accepting it as the fate for big women like herself. She could be the bloated fertility symbol but never the goddess.

Not that Tawne resented Delia for this.

Carl started hanging the women's wear while Arcan inventoried them in. Arcan glanced up, rustling the invoices a bit irritably. He tried to suppress it. It was his problem, not Delia's. Carl was muttering some *uhm-mmmmm's* which irritated Arcan more. Carl was a slave who didn't even know it.

"You going to take some of this?" Arcan asked her. It

was why Delia was in the stock room, wasn't it? Why else?

(To taunt the males. To flex and make us drool. To create slaves.)

"If you don't mind. Don't do it special for me though. I can always come back if it's more convenient. I don't want to get into your hair." Delia pronounced it hay-yah. "Mrs. Dellacourt wanted me to snare her sizes soon as they came in so she can be ahead of all her rich friends."

"Go on. It'll be a good sale if she decides she wants each piece," Arcan mumbled, looking down steadfastly and wondering why the hell he was talking to her. Let her take the shit and stop bothering him. Stop expecting him to grovel like his dick was leashed. "I'll remember what you took and add it back to my count when I get to it. It's the next rack anyway."

Delia laughed. "I'm sure she'll want every piece. It must be nice, huh? That's 16, maybe 17 hundred dollars without tax and all for this collection. Maybe 18. But she is the mayor's wife so she's got this image to uphold."

She sighed. "AK-II. Sounds like an assault rifle group, doesn't it? I ought to go call my customers in the NRA. Make 'em look their best for hunting season."

Delia removed a size twelve in the blouse, shell, sweater, skirt, trousers and both long and short jackets. She turned to hang them on the smaller wheeled rack where she'd already put the other items for transport back to her department. She lingered over the long skirt, examining the fabric.

"This is simply gorgeous," she murmured. "Sure hope something's left in my size when it goes on sale."

Arcan looked up after she said *hunting season*. Carl Pruitt was muttering the wolf noises pretenders to the pelt made to prove that their testosterone levels were as high as those of non-slaves like Arcan.

The flash in Arcan's head came unbidden. Of Delia in a close shot with a starkly white rag in her mouth, smudged with lipstick in fuchsia Rorschachs. Mascara ran down both cheeks in rivers and in flood until it looked as if he'd painted half her face black. Making her appear as if she was about to change into a raven.

Arcan's body strained against the crotch of his jeans. The denim had shrunk.

(Black as powder burns. A lot of Carmel Gaine's head had been black after she put the gun in her mouth and pulled the trigger.)

This memory shriveled his erection. He blinked. Delia was unbound, out of his fantasy and absorbed in the skirt she was examining. The silk flowed like water, unchecked in oil paints of yellows, forest greens and rusts over her immaculate fingers. The pattern of autumn woods in the weave rose and shifted, as if Delia's hands were struggling under a pile of fallen leaves, gag in mouth, face smudged, altered and now forever hidden.

For he had put her there and covered her body with leaves in a private spot in the forest. Still slightly struggling. Still trying to crawl away from him after the fact. Face shadowed with patches of black that smelled of equal parts rot and licorice.

The new image brought the erection back. Arcan's lungs stung as he breathed in so hard he was almost hyperventilating.

Carl bent to whisper conspiratorially into his ear, "Wouldn't you like to get into that trim snatch? Wonder if it tastes like tuna or chicken cordon bleu?"

Carl leered. Arcan tasted it. It wasn't fish or chicken. It was two-legged lamb. He closed his eyes, knowing exactly how it chewed. He said tensely, "Fuck off."

Tawne looked up, hearing Carl. Hearing Arcan's warning to him. She wanted to grab Carl by the scruff of the neck. Lift him right off the floor with his sneakers wriggling. Shake him like babies could be shaken to death. Tossed hard enough and the brain came loose from its moorings within the infantile skull, turning it to jelly. Tossed long enough and one could listen at a little ear like at a sea shell, hearing a roar like oceanic waves.

Delia was close enough at the nearby rack to overhear. She ignored it like she always did.

"Naw, man. Fuck her," Carl persisted, breathing huskily into Arcan's ear. "Up the cunt and in the ass."

And the phantoms this conjured up. And the flood of haunting and haunted faces that moved, screamed and pleaded through the fabric of nearby clothes. He knew no one else saw them but this didn't help. Arcan told Carl, "Back off."

Arcan was seeing fireworks in front of his eyes, wheels of sparks that sizzled round cigarette blisters in naked skin.

Carl snickered, relentless. "Tongue in her twat and dick in her mouth."

Arcan swung blindly, his fist connecting as if by magic with Carl's chin. The carefully maintained eighth inch of stylish cowboy stubble parted across the bone. Blood spurted in an arc of a falling star. Lightning seemed to crackle across Arcan's knuckles, aching to strike again. A cat, wolf, ghoul moved in those knuckles.

Carl howled like a kicked dog and flew into a stack of boxes full of end-of-season manufacturer returns. Delia turned in surprise, daintily bringing her thumb to her mouth, dark hair swirling around her face. Her eyes widened when she saw blood gushing over Carl's chin, drenching his shirt. Her eyes were positively luminous when she turned her gaze to Arcan who stood opening and closing the fist he'd used, staring at it as if he half-expected it to change into something else.

Arcan tried to rein in what was left of his temper. He really wasn't happy that he'd been unable to stop that one stupid punch. But he'd warned the little squirm to shut up.

No one at the store had ever seen Arcan angry before. He was always reserved to the point of being icy. But there was something more than merely losing his temper evident in his face. Delia blanched when she saw it. It was scary and it *slid*. The muscles and bones seemed momentarily elastic. Tawne saw it, too, and for only a second flashed back on her dreams, of a man-creature offering her the heart he had pinned to his sleeve.

"Shit holy mother of granola what did you do that for?" Bill exclaimed. He strode over and stepped in front of Arcan so he couldn't scoop Carl up for another punch.

Carl was still crumpled in the nest of boxes. Bill glared at Arcan, protective of his younger drinking buddy. Of course, Bill knew damned well why Arcan had done it. Everybody had heard and should have expected something. Even from Arcan the ice man. Carl often joked that Arcan had buttons to push somewhere. Today he'd found them.

"You stupid asshole," Jerry announced as he and supervisor Jack Bederman came over. Jerry began helping Carl to stand.

Arcan stared steadily into Bill's eyes. He saw only that which he would just as soon destroy, given enough incentive. It would be as easy as knocking down the little creep. Bill pushed him roughly with both hands. Arcan only barely stepped back from this puny show of force. Carl blubbered, dribbling onto the concrete floor, trying to squeeze the edges of his chin back together.

"What did I do to you? It ain't as if she's your woman," Carl whimpered, even though he'd been trying to provoke Arcan. He'd seen a blur, shifting as Arcan swung at him. He didn't know what it was, it being too fast to register as it slid into moon phases. But he thought he'd seen another face beneath the one that Arcan usually wore. Carl gingerly probed the bleeding gash where a fist harder than any he'd encountered in a barroom brawl had landed. "Goddamn, bet this'll scar me for life!"

"What happened here?" Jack Bederman asked.

Tawne spoke up. "It wasn't Arcan's fault. It was Carl's big mouth. Somebody should have washed it out with soap long ago."

Delia stepped forward. "It's true, Jack. It was Carl's fault. He wouldn't let up. You know how he is."

Her eyes melted gratefully all over Arcan. Arcan thought it would make him throw up. (Don't do me any favors.)

Jack cursed when he saw blood across the AK-II line. It was ruined. He wondered how he could take the damages out of both men's paychecks. He shook his head. "It doesn't matter that Carl was being his usual self. You can't go around hitting folks, Arcan. No matter what comes out of his mouth, you got to hold onto yourself. I'm afraid I've got to let you go for this."

Arcan thought, you have no idea how I'm holding onto myself. You have no idea what's holding onto me.

Tawne protested. "That's not fair!"

"What about Carl?" Bill asked.

"He's still got his job. Free speech, I guess. But, Carl, you'd better hope the women in this store don't decide to sue you for sexual harassment." Jack turned back to Arcan. "You'd better punch out. We won't call the cops. I don't recommend you call them either, Carl. Galways doesn't want that kind of publicity."

Carl sulked, spattering blood through his fingers.

Jerry frowned. "I'm gonna call an ambulance though."

Jack nodded. "Okay. You do that."

Bill squinted at Arcan. "Be seein' ya on the street, pal."

Arcan suddenly smiled. "Anytime." It was the wolf smiling, being sure to show as many teeth as possible. Bill flinched.

"Arcan, I'm so sorry," Delia said.

"Let me know if there's anything I can do," Tawne added.

Arcan didn't answer. He was trying to make it outside before he couldn't hold himself in any longer.

Chapter Six

Alan Moravec was set up on the freeway with the videocam mounted onto the special dashboard clamp, hoping to get a plum for *Mean Streets* to air that night. He'd been driving for two hours, aimlessly, watching average jerks cut other drivers off, clumsy fender benders, crazy near-misses, et cetera rudeness. Nothing that qualified as being out of the ordinary. It might do for a Tuesday night segment but this was Friday. He felt he really should leave the audience buzzing over the weekend. This was hopeless. He was getting annoyed with the grind that came with sneaking trips on run-of-the-mill assholes.

He was getting vaguely sick of *Meean Streets* anyway. It could just go so far. It was two or three minutes of schlock. It was one step away from doing weather in a fluorescent tornado suit.

Alan wished just once he could have the chance to see someone doing something really fucked up.

Bizarre. He needed a close encounter of the vicious asshole kind. Chain-swinging, eyeball-sucking, hell-in-leather halters with ground-corpse-obsessions assholes. Veterans-of-foreign-nightmares assholes. Southwest-nuclear-plant ionically-enlarged-genitalia-stomping-toward-Dallas assholes. The next-slob-of-the-apocalypse kind of asshole, a notch or two up from the last real beast to grovel in carrion in a damp cellar.

Then Alan might get his own show. Not just a few seconds of news piddle. And not just cable but network. Opposite *America's Most Wanted* and *Love Those Wacky Rabid Pets*. He could get respect and be taken seriously for once in his life if he could get his hands on some real sneak horror.

Moravec dug a peanut butter cup from the glove compartment. He unwrapped it as he watched the traffic zip by. He wished the camera would catch a good highway sniper, barrel sticking out of a window like the predator part of an alien's poison blowhole. Get an I.D. Maybe see someone toss a hefty sack full of body parts by the wayside. Catch himself the serial killer of the current season.

No, Alan corrected himself, the culvert killer put victims into culverts and pipes, hence the name. He didn't do roadsides or garbage bags. His M.O. was strictly snug, narrow passageways of city rectums which stank of mold and sphincter fudge.

A different one, then, might drive by. In transit from Texarkana maybe. Transporting teenage kibble across the state lines past the immoral purposes stage and into rictal dementia.

But none of this happened. Shame. Folks just zipped. Occasionally clipped. Without a rip. Moravec bit into the peanut butter and sighed. It could be a long day at this rate. Pretty soon the traffic would blur until each car and each ordinary asshole looked identical.

Alan let his thoughts drift to the future he preferred.

If he got his own show, he wouldn't want to do another

Mean Streets thing. He'd want something new. What could he call it?

Witch Hunt? Everyone spying on everyone else, a great non-contact sport for the safer-sex turn of the century. It would create popular paranoia. Who's into those backyard satanist rituals? Who's having sex with kids and kittens? Who's been abducted by aliens, helping Andromedans to do crop circles in a cosmic game of Twister? Who's performing sloppy circumcisions on college boys with their teeth?

There would be cash awards, cars, trips, freezers full of free meat given to neighbors and fellow employees who got the best dirt on friends and family.

I Know What You've Been Up To. The name was too long. It wouldn't fit snugly into a *TV Guide* column.

Nightmares On Main Street. Derivative. He'd want to look more original than that. Originality was the only true hallmark of genius. The rest had only the steroids of plagiarism.

"I'm a renaissance asshole," he said out loud, noisily sucking chocolate from his front teeth.

Moravec watched as a van speeding by him dumped a bag of trash out the window. Aluminum cans bounced, cigarette butts flew in ashy whirlwinds, fast food wrappers flapped. It blew back across the lanes, clattering.

Amateur scum. He shook his head in disgust. Not that it wouldn't be a touch for the Don't-Mess-with-Texas theme, but it was so much like the diaper segment he'd done a couple days ago. *Dull*.

Alan went back into dreams of glory. Should he have beautiful broads as video hostesses? It would be a good way to meet sharp-looking trophies to hang off his famous arm.

He would do that anyway if he had his own show. Better to be original. For hosts he should use crippled dwarves, toxic-spawn mutations lisping with green neon drool, burn

51

victims with microphones pinned to their blackened throats live (though barely) from the ice vat. What better way to introduce great American tragedies than with freaks?

It shrieked TAKE A LOOK AT THIS! It made the audience cringe immediately, hooked on visual-slamming UGLY. They would stay to watch what could possibly top the M.C.

"Ozzie And Harriet Underground. Todd Browning Meets Star Search. Amateur Hour Goes From Ted Mack To Ted Bundy."

A seedy old Firebird with peeling red paint rolled to a stop on the shoulder before a girl who was hitchhiking. Moravec rallied. She was wearing a waitress uniform although she looked barely old enough to be in high school. The skirt was very short and she wore too much makeup. Teenagers. They always made the best bait. Just look at all the cheap chop 'em flicks.

The camera rolled, catching her smile as she bent forward to speak to a greasy-haired man through a rolled down window. Moravec licked his lips. Her skirt was so short, the film picked up the color of her panties when she leaned and her ass stuck out.

"Honey, don't you read the papers?" Alan said, tsking as if lecturing up close. "There are fruits, nuts and sex-crazed Nazi cannibal humpers on the road. This greaseball might be Saucy Jack."

I hope.

Alan drove as close as he could without making it obvious he was trailing as the Firebird went toward the nearest off-ramp. The car took a right at the corner, removing them from the service road. Then they made two lefts.

Would this guy find some lonely spot to rip her clothes off? Produce a knife that glinted nicely in the noonday sun? Her screams captured live (and on Memorex no less) while Alan lackadaisically punched 911 on his car phone?

Let's see. Nine. That's down there somewhere. Uh. One. Oh, what was that third number? Oops, hit the wrong one. Silly me. Have to start all over again.

The hefty bag with the older body parts could be smelling up the trunk even as Crisco Man took this one for a tool and toodle. Didn't her mother tell her not to accept rides or candy from strangers, much less be on a busy thoroughfare actively soliciting them?

This could be exactly what Moravec was waiting for. He would show this with its onset on the road and the chase with the grisly aftermath. Hadn't he tried to save her? These madmen just worked too darned fast.

The station would do a follow-up series on the road dangers of hitching. Not that Alan cared two bits for this drivel, only as long as he got some credit. They could pull out stories from the files sighting past atrocities in *Hard Copy* style. THAT he wouldn't mind narrating.

Oh, would this perv, *could* he possibly slice off her arms?

(Well, that's hardly original, is it, Alan?)

No, but who else had it on tape?

The Firebird pulled into a parking lot at an International House of Pancakes. The girl got out, waved to the driver while trying to get the short skirt to tug back down over her hips after it had ridden up as she slid across the seat. She then hurried inside. The Firebird drove away.

Alan's jaw dropped. Was that it? He just took the little bimbo to work?

Moravec's teeth ground noisily as he shut off the camera and rewound the tape. This greaser picks up a pretty thang in a short skirt on the highway and all he does is give her a lift to the job? What kind of sexless geek was he?

Moravec reluctantly headed back to the highway, irritated, looking at his watch. It was getting close to the time when he ought to be getting to the station to set up his segment. The producers usually insisted on okaying his films before Channel 7 aired them. He hated cutting it close. He didn't want to have to settle for an ersatz tape of a couple of young candyasses dumping out a surgical dumpster at a local abortion clinic. It was a lot ickier than the Shorecross Mall diaper and would be sure to arouse plenty of Pro-Life outrage. Perfectly formed little people in gooey red slime like sardines in a raspberry aspic, sad little umbilicals in shriveled lifelines, some crudely bisected by the scalpel 'til it made a hardened veal-eater cringe. But it was still a childish prank. Actually, it could even have been a Pro-Life prank except that these two were barely pubescent boys in Cannibal Corpse T-shirts, so Alan doubted it. The station would get heavy action from the brats' parents because they were underaged juvies and this could scar their little developments forever.

Touchy. Channel 7 didn't want to play it unless there was absolutely nothing else. And even then they were likely to insist on an environmental tie-in (with that oozy surgical waste issue). It would involve bringing in an investigative reporter accustomed to hard news to assist in refinement. Moravec didn't want to split the screen with anyone and he despised *relevance*.

Then Alan saw the pickup truck pull over to the shoulder. The driver got out and reached back inside, yanking out a whining dog. It was a real beauty. A golden retriever about half grown with champion lines and large intelligent eyes full of trust.

The driver deposited the dog on the shoulder with the cars zooming by and started to get back into his truck. The dog bounded after him, wagging its tail, trying to get back in, too.

Moravec squinted, tensing his hands on the wheel. He swallowed hard. The guy kicked at the retriever with scuffed redneck boots. The pup backed away, cowering on the shoulder as the driver slammed the pickup door and squealed off.

The camera rolled. The license plate number was captured. Also the retriever as it began searching anxiously for a way to get off the highway. Alan had never seen anything look so terrified. Gravel flew from passing cars grazing the rocky shoulder. The dog dodged, backing up as far up to the abutment as the concrete would let it.

"Oh, you prickstein," Moravec muttered, then grinned as he took off after the pickup.

He slowed as he got up to where the dog sat. He could hear the whir of the videocam. *Stop and pick it up, stop, STOP. It'll just take a second . . .*

Shouldn't he? There was a tug somewhere in his chest where Alan assumed a heart sat. But it was an organ he rarely used so he wasn't certain. One thing he was sure of was that he'd never catch up with the pickup if he wasted time on the dog. He wouldn't be able to get the asshole's face on camera, and it would be useless for *Mean Streets* without the positive I.D.

He glanced toward the dog, deliberating quickly.

The pup's brown eyes silently pleaded for him to stop, for someone to stop, seeking an avenue of safety in-between the streaking—almost surreal—images of cars fleeing past it. It would look good if Alan could yank the dog to safety at the last moment. It might save the segment even if he couldn't get a face.

Its tail thumped weakly. The ears flattened with dejection. It bounded, seeing three more feet of space between two cars. It made its decision before Alan did, to leap, and it actually made it through the first two lanes. Its agonized yelp was brief as it went under the wheels of a Ford van in the third.

That was an expensive dog, too. Worth a grand. If it was a purebred, that is, with papers. Alan could have used a dog. Waiting for him at the apartment at night, all thankful and worshipping. Better than a wife.

The tape whirred almost without noise, saving the instant three seconds before Alan might have stopped, six seconds before he'd driven past too far to catch the continuous demise on peripheral.

"Damn, pup, I'm sorry," Alan said, whistling through his teeth. He shook his fist at the driver far ahead of him. "What? Was he peeing on the carpet too often, fella?"

He really felt sorry for it, as car after car went over the body. Well, he had some feelings after all. So lots of guys could relate to violence when done to the lower forms of life: like women and children. But dogs were totems of when men hunted, needing beasts that were guards, pals and willing slaves.

He could see it in the rearview, the motion of tires striking and pushing, making it appear as if its broken bones and squeezed-out fistful of mush were still trying to escape across the busy road. Maybe it was on some level. It made Alan ponder the notion of sudden death, wondering if there was any such thing.

Moravec sped, frantic now to get near enough to the pickup as its driver raced up the freeway. He could hear the truck's radio blaring out shitkicker twang and steel guitars, the noise trailing behind him in the highway wind like a bloody flag. He was a good dozen car lengths behind the guy by the time Alan spotted him. If much traffic came between them. Alan might not be able to get close enough to get the face on tape. Worse, he might lose him completely. If Alan couldn't save the dog, he at least wanted to show the world who this sleaze was.

People were really going to hate this slime when they got a load of this. He'd have to move away, out of the city. Out of Texas. He'd have to have his features surgically altered, if the SPCA didn't alter them for him.

It would be the best thing Alan had caught on film yet. The meanest, nastiest gesture he'd filmed since he got that woman breaking her little girl's nose with a left hook in the lot of a HelterSkelter Food Store. He'd received a citation from The Department Of Human Services for that one. And 50 dollars worth of free groceries.

Alan could hear 'Achy Breaky Heart' like the ultimate in teeny bronco-bopper cow-patty pap at illegal decibels as he twisted and turned the wheel to hustle around cars and into any lane that put him four feet closer to his quarry. Alan never played his own radio while on stake-out. He didn't want to lose any possible subtle audio. Like steel hitting steel, profanity, threats against lives, shrieks of agony. (Dying yelps from half-grown pups.)

Once, Alan saw a pair of dogs—a shepherd and a chow—riding in the back of a truck. It was about a year ago while he was still understudy sportscaster for a local radio station. He'd been driving behind the truck along the service road, watching the dogs get friskier, exhilarated or scared by the whipping wind. They ran back and forth the length of the flat bed, and from side to side, looking out and barking, their black tongues threatening to snap off and fly back into Alan's windshield. The truck went up the highway ramp, accelerating. Alan was still behind. When they hit the asphalt strip at 70 mph, the dogs bailed, leaping one to either side of the vehicle.

The truck slammed on its brakes, and Alan almost rear-ended it slamming on his. The chow didn't hit the asphalt right and was lying on the shoulder with all four legs broken. The shepherd darted into traffic and—well, that's been told once, hasn't it? It was fully grown and the car that hit the shepherd tried to veer and miss it. The dog was knocked a good 30 feet ahead, right under the wheels of another car where it caught, a sharp bone puncturing one of the tires. There wasn't heavy traffic at the time but that car veered into a car in the third lane, which was hit by the one behind it.

The man and woman from the truck climbed out in a hurry. As had Alan to see if he could help. He had to at least be a witness to the pile-up. The lady knelt and carefully lifted the wailing chow in her arms. She wept over it as she screamed at the man, "Joe! You said they wouldn't jump out! You said dogs never jump!"

People were blowing their horns from behind the three tangled cars and the one with the blown tire. The occupants of those cars were climbing out, shaking, slowly walking across the lanes to the truck. Alan watched one man with a purpling goose-egg growing on his forehead from bouncing off the windshield. He was furiously yelling, "Hey! Mister! You're an asshole!"

That's how things got started.

People were blowing their horns right now. At the pickup swerving around everything in sight. And at Alan as he pulled in and out of the holes in traffic trying to catch up with him.

The truck gunned, the frame shuddering slightly, and black smoke blew from the rusted tailpipe. It was back on Alan in two seconds, choking him. He began to hack, tasting oil. The cam was probably picking this up so he refrained from gasping out any epithets even Channel 7 wouldn't air. The FCC may have become lax lately but they weren't gone. More smoke belched out, becoming grayer 'til it went white. The guy must be punching it to get some impurity out of the engine. Alan thought. Or maybe he always drove like a bat out of Texaco hell.

Alan hoped he wouldn't get stopped by some over-zealous highway patrol looking for another notch in the quota. But it would be *fine* if they were to stop the Lassie-killer. Then Alan could pull up with some civic duty crap and give the cops the lowdown, zooming in on the face of this slayer of helpless Rin Tin Tins.

At least Old Yeller had rabies so there was no choice but to kill him.

Suddenly the cowboy flung the truck into the right lane, cutting off an old lady in a vintage Bel-Air. On camera, thank you. He crossed the double white lines to make an exit and was down the ramp. Alan had to do the same if he wanted to keep up. He didn't want to lose this guy to a bunch of wormy side streets. He laid on his horn until the old lady visibly froze, hitting her brakes. Alan swung around her, almost getting clipped when the Bel-Air did a donut. Alan crossed the double whites himself, nearly hitting the guard rail and raced down the ramp. (He'd edit that out before air time.) He watched the pickup which was already a quarter of a mile ahead of him on the access, swinging an almost geometric right angle into a parking lot. A honky tonk bar. Did it figure?

Alan stood on the accelerator, glad that everyone was yielding for once to his right-of-way so he didn't get smashed. He had to make it to that lot before the driver went in. He had to get the face on film before the man entered the bar or Alan would end up with no idea who it was. And he couldn't wait for him to come out again. The guy might be in there drinking way past time to air the segment. What Alan could do then wasn't much. He couldn't just flash a license number. It could be anyone behind the wheel. The owner would swear the truck was stolen for some unknown perp's joyride, then mysteriously returned to his driveway.

I wasn't driving and if you say I was, I'll sue your ass.

Alan turned into the parking lot so fast the car almost flipped. The tires screeched. The guy getting out of the pickup stared balefully at him. But the belligerent slob didn't make the camera. He turned and clomped into the bar, the door swinging shut behind him under a small sign that said:

Red's Stomping Ground

Alan got a good look at the face. So did the camera. Sagebrush mustache, veined nose that must have been broken at least twice, low forehead beneath a fringe of close-cropped curls, color indefinable because it was so dirty.

He switched off the camera and rewound the tape, removing it. He started to pull out of the lot to return to the station when he had an idea.

Alan popped a second tape into the camera, took it off the dashboard, stuck the first tape under his arm, and got out of the car. He walked into the building and casually went up to the bar.

Behind it, a middle-aged woman barely glanced up. Her head stank of hair spray, the sheen of the stone coif oily under overhead lights.

"What can I do fer ya?" she asked around her cigarette. It dropped ashes on the bar which she brushed with the back of her liver-spotted hand.

Alan set the first tape on the counter and pulled a bill from his wallet. She saw the 50 and really looked at him this time. Her eyebrows went up. Alan had seen the television set behind the bar. It was on, baseball play-offs getting a lot of attention from the patrons.

"Yes, ma'am. If you would please. Play this tape on your video recorder for me?"

"What's on it? Porno?" she asked him. She tried to X-ray how much weirdness might be in his bones.

"No porno. Just something worth that 50 to you."

She shrugged and plunked in the tape. The game switched off.

"Hey! We was watchin' that!"

People grumbled loudly over their beers.

"Now you just watch this here. Everybody, watch!" Alan cried out, snapping his fingers. He looked through the crowd, trying to locate the pickup's driver. He didn't see the guy but he nodded with satisfaction when the bar's customers glowered attentively at the set.

Someone snarled. "This better be good, mister."

"I got a bet on this game," said another.

"If'n there ain't some naked tits on there, I'm gonna bust

60

yore brain, boy," threatened someone who looked easily big enough to carry this out with one hand barbed-wired behind him.

Alan chuckled. He promised. "Mister, I guaran-damn-tee ya you're gonna want to bust something."

The tape replayed the pickup pulling onto the shoulder and the redneck kicking the poor retriever onto the road. Its eyes pleaded. God, what a gorgeous shot of that dog's sad face. Man's best friend. Alan snorted with delight.

The dog dodged road gravel.

The dog leaped.

Everyone yelled when the dog was hit.

Alan stepped around to the back of the bar. "Excuse me, please, ma'm," he said to the lady as he hit fast forward to cut out all the traffic chase bullshit. He went to the spot showing the pull into this very bar's parking lot. To show the face of the driver with the scarred boots who had actually kicked that poor animal out onto the highway.

Lord, there was nothin' more heartless in the world, was there?

"Holy shit, that's Zeke," said a man in a green plaid flannel shirt.

Alan turned the camera on to record their reactions as sneak history was being made. He pointed with his free hand as he told them, "And that's him headed out the door. Trying to get away."

The patrons stood and threw their chairs aside with indignation.

The driver stumbled. Two men blocked the door so he couldn't leave. He looked like a terrified—what?—retriever? As if the cars were coming at him from all sides. Would he leap? Would he go under? Alan could feel the camera's vibrations as he filmed.

Somebody said, "How could you do that to a poor doggy, Zeke?"

Another stepped right into his face. "Mister, what kind of man are you?"

"He's an asshole." The lady behind the bar was crying, tears carving canals in her makeup. "He always was an asshole."

"I do believe you need to be taught better," a man in a black Stetson growled as he picked up a beer bottle and broke it against a table. The shard of the jagged neck gleamed wickedly as he waved it menacingly in the driver's face.

They descended on him, dragging him away from the entrance. Alan couldn't see well after this, there were too many people. Too many blows landed from enraged fists and steel-toed boots. The driver screamed, choking over broken teeth, lungs making tinny noises as rearranged ribs poked them, making bubbles and fluted wheezes. There were staccato farts as he emptied his bowels in a refried heap. There were sharp snaps and hearty crunches. This was a marvelously attentive camera. Oh, technology. Crimes and punishments up close and personal.

Alan left the carnage briefly to get a shot of the woman behind the bar. She wept and blew her nose in napkins that bore the logo, cheering the righteous brutality while grimacing with blood lust. Tendrils of mucus sparkled on her lipsticked mouth 'til it looked like fresh blood, as if she'd buried her face in the redneck's caved midsection for a slurp.

He swung back to the huddle. He saw a part as men moved away to grab stuff from the wall decorations to hit Zeke with. Whips and pieces of wagon wheel, rusty spurs and a stuffed coyote. A burly guy in a buckskin jacket bent with a jagged pair of old gelding snippers and not too cleanly severed Zeke's pink testicles. Another was steadily stomping his skull. When the condemned redneck's eyes rolled up to the whites and then fairly floated out of the sockets on a tide of blood, Alan knew he'd gotten what he came for.

Alan quickly removed the first tape from the video machine. He moved rapidly but cautiously toward the rear of the bar, still filming with the second tape as he slipped out the back. He ran to his car, hoping he'd get out of the lot before any of the patrons realized he'd just filmed them committing murder.

Ah, no one had seen a good lynching in a really long time, had they?

Chapter Seven

It didn't seem right working the next day with Arcan gone.
Delia didn't go back to the dock at all. Not even to check
to see if the new Nippon suits had arrived. Tawne realized
she likely didn't want to come into any kind of contact
with Carl. After he'd gotten away with the worst of his
remarks—if you could call having his chin broken getting
away with it (at least he hadn't been fired)—Delia figured
he'd be insufferable.

Carl had taken the rest of the day of the fight off to get
medical attention. He was back the next morning, and sure
enough he was cockier than ever. And he was very resentful
of the fact that Tawne had spoken against him. Any chance
he got, he said something crude to her.

He was coming by with a load of boxes destined for the
shoe department. He had to go right past her so he said.
"Hey, move your fat ass, Moby Dickless."

It might have been the pain killers talking. He must have
been given some sort of prescription. His resewn chin was

covered with a protective cup, the adjoining jaws swollen to twice their usual size (making him look vaguely like a purple Jay Leno). Even under the mass of gauze and surgical tape, Tawne knew it was purple.

Didn't it hurt to talk? Then why did he do it? Why didn't he shut up and cause less pain to everyone around him?

Tawne still swung around at his comment, furious and hurt. Unable to strike out. Which he knew she couldn't do. Who dared hit him now? Not only because he was already injured and it would make her look like the worst sort of pig, but because hitting Carl got people fired. Wasn't that the truth? It made him invincible.

God, this abuse was bad enough from anyone else. But to have it come from someone her loins cried out for—well, what could she say? Her loins were stupid. They had poor taste.

Actually, she thought, my loins have never tasted anything.

Lust was an ignorant beast.

Carl strolled by at lunch time, through the break room. He paused to look down at Tawne's hero sandwich and potato salad. He said quite loudly. "Should you be eating that? Whole lotta calories. Shit, Ton, no fuckin' wonder you're big as a horse."

She left it, going to the employee ladies room to cry for the rest of her break. Looking into the mirror and hating herself. Tawne studied her hands, which were quaking at the moment, curling and uncurling like spiders undergoing strychnine convulsions. She could easily wring Carl's neck with hands like those. She could rip away the bandages, take both sides of the flesh Arcan had so effectively split, and pull them farther apart.

Farther, until she tore Carl's face in half. Then people would see who wasn't so pretty.

What have I done to deserve this? Did I run Auschwitz in a previous life? Was I beautiful and smooth and too proud?

La Belle Dame sans Merci?

Charlee Jacob

She stared at the leaden eyes, the dull and flat red hair. Tawne doubted if she had—in any life upon the cruel wheel—been beautiful. This was a burden she must surely have been carrying forever.

She'd seen shock in the break room as Carl made his comment. No one said anything. Delia watched her go, outrage in her eyes for the larger woman.

Tawne plucked hair out and ran her fingers down the coarse length. It wouldn't be too much longer before gray crept into the red. It didn't take much to break the heart of a homely, aging virgin.

Why did Tawne always have to fall for boy-men like Carl? Who only took pleasure from her in the form of jokes at her expense? Why were good looks more valued than strength or the quality of dreams?

(Long-stemmed American beauties, spoken with reverence, with a sighing penial piety. All the while aware of the thorn it pressed between the breasts of his wife—Tawne's mother—and into the heart where all such barbs of merit were destined to go. Her father always did have great aim. Men might marry a good, plain woman. But then they spent the rest of their lives ogling, continuously drooling and taking off their hats to images—as if they had been robbed of their birthrights.)

Was Tawne a good, plain woman? *She dreamed of feral bridegrooms in subterranean deeps.* Was she a queen-sized fertility symbol, able to deliver forth whole nations from her womb? Then why was she still unclaimed? Plain but not good? Quality of dreams. In her eyes perhaps a nightmare knight stared out to frighten people away from her.

Why couldn't Tawne want someone like Arcan? So strong and self-assured. A silent type. A gentleman and gentle man.

(Because she was no better than the men who prayed to those American roses. She saw the good looks and they

66

triggered a response beyond the brain. If anything proved that people were only animals, this did.)

Carl drove Arcan to that punch. But Arcan hadn't hit him a second time. And it had been evident that he badly wanted to. Yet, the look in Arcan's eyes—scary. She'd never seen that before in anybody. As if what peered out from behind those orbs of soft wet tissue wasn't human.

No, those who people our dreams look out.

Windows to the soul and all that jazz.

Something bad lived in Arcan's house and at that moment had been staring from the windows.

If people were just animals responding a certain way to beauty, how did Arcan's animals respond to it? Not the way others did. Tawne noticed this. His dream people were different.

And had his face actually *moved*? Did it slide as if physical laws concerning shape had dissolved? Did the person in her eyes ever cause Tawne's face to change and she didn't know it? What did it change into? And was this why no man would touch her?

She stared at her face intently in the mirror, looking for the feral bridegroom to peer out from her eyes. Seeking some altering twist in her forehead and cheekbones. There was no one in the eyes and no change in the sad, doughy head.

Delia came into the bathroom. She said softly. "How are you doing?"

"I'm okay," Tawne replied, splashing cold water in her face to make the swelling go down. It always made her furious to cry. It was worse when it happened with other folks around. If strength was Tawne's best quality, then weeping made her appear to have no strength at all.

"I know; it's hard. Especially with a moral miscreant like Carl. The world's full of them." Delia pretended to be fussing with her lipstick. "My mother always taught me that ladies didn't respond to lowlifes like him. That it was beneath our dignity."

Delia laughed, peeking at the big woman from the corner of her eye. As if she knew how old-fashioned this sounded.

"So I grew up never speaking for myself, never striking out. Rarely anyway. Then when I grew older, I realized it was really a sort of self protection that has nothing to do with being a lady or a woman or even female."

Tawne watched her across the long line of identical porcelain sinks.

"Maybe it's cowardice," Delia continued. "But I know it sure can hurt a lot less to realize that people like him don't deserve to get to know you so they certainly don't deserve to get a rise out of you."

Tawne raised a puffy eyebrow. "What you're saying is, I should just not listen?"

"Sounds silly, I'm sure. But you're such a nice gal, Tawne." The southern accent really punched on gal. "And it's unfair for cruds like Carl to upset you. To be able to upset any of us. So, yeah, don't listen. He opens that mouth of his and all it is is noise. And no one but a tone deaf rattlesnake, who's had his shakers cut off so he can't even rattle, is going to think it's music."

Tawne hung her head and chuckled. It was a fair description of both Bill Tower and Jerry Shelly. Maybe it wasn't the best advice in the world, but it was nice to know someone cared.

Delia patted Tawne's arm and winked, then glided out the door to go back to the selling floor.

Tawne returned to the stock room. Carl was yacking it up with his cronies, Bill and Jerry. They watched her walk through the swinging doors. Carl smiled and then winced from the pain of moving his sore facial muscles. The chin cup bobbed irregularly. He knew how much he'd upset her in the break room and it pleased him no end. He was clearly getting maximum mileage out of this. Tawne hadn't noticed before but his clothes weren't even clean. He had food stains all over his shirt, and the supervisor hadn't ordered him home to change.

Carl's indigo eyes glittered until they were the color of blue gun barrels.

"Yeah, she wants it," he said to the others none too softly.

Even Jack Bederman stared hard across the room at him from over a sheath of invoices. Bill and Jerry didn't laugh this time. They looked down at their boots.

Tawne ignored him.

I have dignity, too. Too much to let that tick get under my skin. I don't hear him. He doesn't exist.

Strength, quality of dreams and dignity.

Did a feral bridegroom peer from her eyes, shrouded in shadows? Well, if he did, he wouldn't put up with that shit either. He'd have Carl's heart on his sleeve before you could say vena cava.

Tawne walked out of Galway's and looked out across the parking lot at the waning light in the sky. The street lamps had switched on, turning everything to the curious in-between of purple/white light and lavender/gray shadows. The strip of sunset was cloudy but the setting sun lit no fires; there were no reds or golds there. It was the color of new steel.

People were arriving for evening shows at the Shorecross Cinema. They passed her as they entered the building through the department store's doors. It had been another extra long shift for Tawne. She should have left for home three hours ago. Carl had left at that time, complaining his whole head hurt so he could hardly be expected to work any more.

(Crying shame, that was.)

Bill was let off early to drive Carl home because on all those pain killers Carl wasn't supposed to drive. And Bill was his roommate.

With Arcan gone, that left their normal full time dock crew of five down to two. It was a lot of unpacking and struggling for just Tawne and Jerry to manage.

Jack was actually having to do some of the physical work for a change. This almost made her smile. She didn't feel sorry for Jack. The man—like most company bosses she'd met—didn't have an ounce of real gumption. He considered everything was running smoothly as long as no fists were flying and no blood was getting onto the merchandise.

Tawne was almost to her Buick when she spotted Delia several aisles away unlocking her own car. Delia had been off at six but she'd lingered for a while to shop. She was now laden with her purchases.

Delia wasn't alone. A crooked little man was perched near her elbow.

Chapter Eight

He knew she was there by her perfume, even before she touched him. Of orchids that have been atop a grave in winter, frozen to the turned earth.

She was sitting next to him on the floor. He could feel her too-soft and damp hands moving against his breastbone. She was shaping something wet on his chest. He could feel it as she molded it there, as it began to slide, her fingers reworking and patting it back into place.

Arcan opened his eyes. Carmel Gaines stuck a fist inside her skull, at the back where the exit wound was large enough to put an entire hand. She scooped out a handful of pulverized brains to add to the gray-church she was building on his chest. It was topped with a steeple and a cross that kept stooping, failing to erect. She tapped wormy fingers at its base, up the spine to straighten it. She added blood from her mouth in hopes it would clot to form a reasonable mortar. The smell was of dessert gelatin and spoiled gizzards, snotty oatmeal and rotten orchids.

Charlee Jacob

Arcan shuddered from the clamminess of the church's necrotic building material against his bare chest. It wobbled, walls and roof rippling in the earthquake of his heartbeat. But the structure ultimately held. As he watched, places where she'd poked holes with her fingers to make windows filled with faces. They looked out at him. Tiny faces. All women. Too small to recognize.

Yet he knew who they were, yes.

"There is a sanctuary built upon the heart," Carmel said.

Arcan wondered how she could articulate since she'd put the barrel of a 38 caliber between her lips and pulled the trigger. Since she had no roof to her mouth or back to her throat.

She looked at Arcan with blood-filled eyes and added. "All who have been wounded are welcomed there."

The gray-church's walls fluttered. Chinks appeared. Tiny living things swarmed, chewing into his bare skin. They had the faces of women, *he knew who they were, yes*.

Arcan screamed and swiped it off him. It burst apart like a ripe watermelon head.

He opened his eyes and saw no ghosts. He smelled only wine, hashish and nacho-flavored tortilla chips.

The old bong of rainbow plastic was tipped over. Cabernet sauvignon and black oily *bhang* resin had dribbled out, darkening the mangy '70s salt and pepper shag. The coffee table had become fit for firewood. The lamps lay in broken pottery shards, their bulbs ground to dust.

Arcan remembered the pops the bulbs made as he'd unscrewed them from their sockets and thrown them to the floor. Then he'd ground them under his feet. He'd stalked the dark house, stoned and trying to curse from his smoke-roughened throat as he lifted the then-unlit lamps by their delicate throats or slender bases, striking them against the walls like invading armies dashing out babies brains against surmounted city ramparts.

But he didn't remember leaping onto the coffee table as

if it were his mother's bed, determined to break its back and hers. Nor did he recall going to his real bed and ripping each nocturnally, seminally-spoiled sheet into shreds. Nor of ripping the pillows into a froth of imagined milk and bone bits with his cat-wolf-ghoul teeth.

Each mirror was a keyboard of glass on the floor, tinkling as he now walked down the hall. They were webworks of schizophrenic slivers he dared not look into. He didn't want to see his face—in fragments or from any angle.

His mouth tasted of moss. Of alum and atropine.

From the hashish. He'd read somewhere that medieval Arabs used hashish to make the warriors feel invincible. That they might ride into combat and not feel the spears and swords of infidels. Arcan smoked it that he might ride into the combat of his dreams. But his wounds were many and his ghosts had beaten him. Again.

Had he read it wrong? Had they used hashish to experience Paradise? A paradise they could be bribed with to enter battle ferociously and die in blind obedience to gain? Arcan couldn't imagine a paradise but he'd been fierce last night. He'd raged and torn, broken and . . . *trembled*.

He'd been shaken by a whirlwind of faces. His scars had risen to seem fresh. He'd thought she was there again.

His mother.

She was in the window. Its tall curved glass seemed to miniaturize her when he viewed her from the hallway. As the boy did the housework, he could casually peer down the hall and see her there. She was a cameo silhouette, always in black, always in tears when she looked across the lawn that he couldn't keep up no matter how hard he tried. She wept, looking, hoping to see Arcan's father coming home.

She wore black as if Lucas Tyler had died. But he wasn't dead. He'd only run off with a much younger woman who was only five years older than Arcan was.

73

Charlee Jacob

His mother wouldn't call her a woman. She was that stupid girl. *Seventeen-year-old girls haven't yet earned the right to be called women*, his mother would say. Obviously his mother had earned it. But what it took to acquire this nominal honor was beyond Arcan's twelve-year-old comprehension. Maybe it took childbirth. Or gray hairs. Or a certain number of tears.

"She's a monster. He had a family, and she just ate him up," Deborah Tyler would say. Then she'd whisper, "Lucas, come home. I won't be angry."

He remembered her crying in front of that window. She'd been flitting from room to room in her black chiffon dress today, last night in her black silk nightgown. Nearby were all of Lucas Tyler's framed photographs, decorated with black crepe paper. She fingered each of these lovingly, murmuring. She quoted from Browning.

> "The moth's kiss, first!
> Kiss me as if you made believe
> You were not sure, this eve,
> How my face, your flower, had pursed
> Its petals up; so, here and there
> You brush it, 'til I grow aware

Who wants me, and . . ." she stumbled. "And . . . who wants me?"

She frowned, closed her eyes, touched her forehead, and tried again. This time she quoted Fitzgerald.

> "Ah, my Beloved, fill the Cup that clears
> Today of past Regret and future Fears.
> Tomorrow!—Why. Tomorrow I may be . . .
> I may be . . . ," she faltered again.

Deborah screwed her features into a scowling drama mask, pounding her temples with her fists. She inhaled a ragged lungful and plunged on, trying to quote Burns, rapid as machine gun fire.

> "O my luve's like a red, red rose
> That's newly sprung in June . . ."

She was furious. She'd always been able to remember them before, hadn't she? She could quote chapter and verse from all her favorite classic poems of love as if they were from her personal Bible. She howled in torment, "Lucas!"

Then she put her fist through the window. She crawled into the corner and folded herself up into something with hind legs that seemed to bend the wrong way. She squatted there and pissed right through her dress, a noxious yellow pool that steamed. She snarled, flecks of foam gathering at her lips as she bit at the injured hand with self-loathing. The voice that came out of her was deeper and rough as she said to herself. "Who wants me? Tomorrow I may be a red red rose . . ."

Arcan sighed, knowing he would be in charge of replacing that glass again. As soon as possible. He ran to fetch iodine and bandages for her cut hand.

"Where's your arm band?" she asked when he returned from the medicine cabinet. Her pupils had acquired circles identical in color to the urine puddled on the floor.

He tried not to look at how her legs bent. He knew when he looked twice, it would all be back to normal. It was only an illusion of the non-human, after all.

Whatever the hell passed for *normal* around here.

She even made him wear the arm band to school.

"The kids call me a Nazi," the boy explained. "They think it's a political statement."

Deborah grabbed him by the shoulder and shook him, fingernails too hard and sharp. He might have to bandage himself after he was finished tending to her. "You're to wear that black band, you hear? Just as I wear black. Until Lucas returns alive to us. Do you understand?" Her voice was broken glass, was the hiss of an animal urinating. Then she howled and cradled her injured hand.

Arcan nodded. He must wear it always. Yes, ma'am.

Except at night.

Deborah sat at night, staring into the mirror above her dressing table. All the drapes were drawn to shut out the darkness. She asked her son, "You don't think I'm old, do you, honey?"

Arcan sat on the edge of her bed in his robe, freshly bathed. She'd made him splash on English Leather, a bottle of which she always kept in the medicine cabinet.

"No, Deborah," he replied, even though she did seem very old to him. Even Daynann—the girl his father had run off with—seemed a bit old to him. And Deborah Tyler at 44 was more than twice that.

"Do you think I'm pretty?" she asked him as she took off the top of a shiny tube of lipstick and screwed it to its maximum erection.

"Yes, Deborah," he said solemnly by rote. He wasn't allowed to call her Mother or Momma or any appellation that signified they were parent and child.

"Do you like my hair?" She pulled a tortoiseshell comb through the dark tresses. There was no gray. She dyed the roots faithfully every four weeks before even a trace of silver or iron could appear.

He nodded carefully. "You have pretty hair." He tried not to tremble. He tried not to act as if he knew what came afterward and dreaded it.

"Do you like my eyes?" She opened them wide, batting the naturally long spiders of her lashes. She still affixed false lashes to these until her eyes looked as if they had been trapped in a web and were about to be devoured by black widows acting in tandem.

"You have pretty eyes," he replied, hoping there was no

quaver in his voice to match the flutter in his stomach. If he didn't seem cool and unafraid . . . oh . . . oh . . .

"Do you like my breasts?" Deborah untied the jet satin ribbons which fastened the bodice. She let the top fall open. They sagged and were full of bluish veins, canals of stretch marks where she'd swollen with each pregnancy, and had breastfed Arcan and his two brothers before him. (Both older boys were serving in Vietnam.) She wore too much perfume on her breasts and powdered them with heavy talc to make them appear less sallow.

"You have puh-puh-pretty breasts." he stammered, twitching.

She wheeled and glared at him. Her eyes were bloodshot from crying all day. "Lucas, I've missed you," she hissed like a cat, trying to keep up the pretense of dialogue, used in their nightly script. But she was clearly angered that her boy had faltered.

It showed in her face as it subtly changed into something other than purely human. The flesh across her cheekbones and along her jaws seemed to melt, to flow in gradual ripples like heated wax. Even her scent changed, becoming thick with the secretions of animal glands.

She made him get into the bed and followed him in, after stepping from the black mamba coils of the gown.

"I'll show you how much I've missed you," Deborah purred, kittenish. "You won't leave me for that stupid girl again. You won't want to."

Arcan wept as she scraped her fingernails across him, the triangular tips gouging into even but flooding furrows. He should never have shown his fear and revulsion. Now she'd make him pay for it. She scratched him like a tigress, a she-wolf. He felt those creatures of hers go deep. He tried not to see the angular transformations in her features but he couldn't help it. Inside him, he felt them running over ground in his own veins. In his limbs. In his penis and tongue. Their rank breath gusted through his lungs, and the tattered shreds of their prey sloshed in his stomach. They rolled onto their swollen sides and parted their lathered legs, squeezing, pinching out lumps of bloody fur. All inside him.

As she'd given him life, so her beasts bore his beasts. His were too young to rise up. They shivered and snarled, prowling and sniffing at his orifices to find a way out. They smelled blood but all they had were milk teeth.

Outside, with the flesh and the solid, Deborah was heavy on top of him, hot and panting as she left stripes on his back, on his adolescent chest where no hairs yet grew. Did Grendel's mother do this to her son?

"You won't want to leave me again, will you, Lucas?" She mewled, yapped, bayed, clawing and in mongrel heat. She smothered him. Her long loose hair—matted with his blood—hung in her face.

"No. I won't leave you!" he growled, then howled in creature agony at a sudden intolerable fire.

Arcan was too feeble to tremble now. He was poured out, crippled in the fever. He thought he'd languish in her bed until he died. She knelt beside him, no longer astride, no longer scratching. (Inside, no longer generating monsters.)

Deborah whispered, "You shouldn't have left me the first time, Lucas."

Her voice had lost the lioness, the hairy bitch. It nearly laughed. It almost tittered with derision. It *would* have, had it not been so sibilant.

Her hair fell across him again as she bent to devour him, piece by piece. She chewed and then opened her mouth like a nasty child at table, showing him the mush of himself across her tongue.

Arcan started to get dressed to go to work. Then he recalled the fight with Carl Pruitt. Being fired by Jack Bederman.

"All that damned bitch's fault," he muttered as he tried to make some sense out the wreckage of his house.

This wasn't true and he knew it. Delia never reacted to Carl's assism. She never sought a defender or even made with the pout and sad eyes.

"She cost me my job, that's what she did. Now what am I gonna do?" he said louder.

The truth wasn't a comfort. Rage was always a comfort. Truth left him cold but fury . . . fury warmed, stoked a fire in the head and gut. Some woman was always getting him into trouble. They were weak and crazy. Lazy tits with psychoses attached.

"Make you think they're defenseless so they can lure you into all kinds of traps," Arcan babbled, snarling as he swept broken glass.

Bits and pieces of him reflected in the shards: an eye, a scar on a cheek, a tooth. The button on his fly. As if he'd been torn apart and lay on the floor. And all the king's horses couldn't do a damn thing about it.

Women were flitty and weepy. They were breathy harridans, devious with their long red harpy claws. They lived off a man's liver and spleen while he toiled to keep them in soap opera journals and bubble bath.

Arcan should have belted Delia, not Carl. Carl was only voicing images Arcan already had in his head. Carl was a major wad but he was male. The problem with Carl was that he had no subtlety. His attacks were verbal and up front, indiscriminate. But they kept the sluts on the defensive.

(Except for Tawne Delaney. What Carl did to Tawne was unfair. Tawne was the strongest woman Arcan had ever met. There was never any bullshit where she was concerned.)

No doubt about it, Carl was a mouth. Not able to do any more than deride. The fact that Arcan avenged on a more secretive level only made his fight more real. Less plebeian.

He considered this with a shudder. No, he avenged in the past tense. He didn't avenge, present tense.

He had abused and he had maimed. He wasn't a super-hero IronDong Twisted Knight, Defender of Balls, Nemesis to Evil Bitches Everywhere. He shouldn't glorify it. He shouldn't make it a battle in his mind when it was really only criminal terrorism.

Especially when the ghosts were nearby, leaning from the walls like nyads rising from water. Especially when their scars made his look like paper cuts.

Arcan picked up the bong and took it into the kitchen to clean it. It had belonged to his brother Harry who used to visit sometimes. He hadn't come in almost a year but Arcan still kept his room up. In that one room were all the lights intact, the mirror whole.

Brother Elliot had died in Saigon. Harry had been home in time for their mother's funeral.

Arcan was 16 by then. He'd grown a foot and a half taller than he'd been at 12.

That final night he sat on the edge of her bed, leaning forward on his hands, breathing deeply.

"Do you like my breasts?" Deborah Tyler asked as she looked into the mirror. She was 48, bloated on chocolates and brandy. Her fingernails glittered on her hands and where they reflected in the mirror.

Arcan tried not to look at those nails. He felt raw pain in new and old scratches down his back, across his shoulders, up his stomach, in his scalp. His flesh was tight with lines of scabs that burst open every night and then re-formed, spoiling the sheets with scarlet which never washed out. He didn't dare twitch but he could no longer bear the sight of her. His mouth twisted into a grimace as he struggled to say his line.

Her eyes were fastened on her own image in the glass.

She was mesmerized by it as she looked at some beauty who had disappeared to all others long ago. She saw it through the great furry beasts of her false eyelashes.

Then why did she ask him if she was pretty? If he liked her hair? Her eyes? Her breasts? He'd seen cows with firmer udders.

Before Arcan knew it, this was precisely what he told her.

Deborah swung around, eyes bloodshot from weeping and alcoholism. She was still furious at her husband's abandoning her, and now she must agonize over this last betrayal. She reached out with both hands bent into claws. The nails gleamed, ready to rip into his face. She would take the skin clean off until he couldn't hide what lurked there. Her eyes took on the yellow circles around the pupils. Her shoulders hunched, bunched behind the shoulder blades 'til they were grossly uneven.

She screamed at him. It was nothing articulate. It was a shriek of animal sorrow and ordeal. Her anguish couldn't end until his began.

Arcan gripped her by the wrists and squeezed until she froze. He stared coldly down, refusing to be intimidated by the feral shifting of her features. He was used to it. It held no terror for him anymore.

Deborah was amazed he would stand up to her. Her tortured eyes were too confused to figure out what to do next. It had followed a certain pattern for years.

"No! No more, damn it! Don't you ever touch me again, hag!"

Arcan jerked her from the vanity bench and tossed her to the floor. He stepped forward, on fire, the pelts of animals pressing him from under the skin, hooking their talons through his hands like slipping on gloves.

He wouldn't touch her. She was disgusting. The animals whined, wanted to be fed. Didn't there have to be a first hunt for the young?

81

But he knew this wouldn't be a hunt. It would only be a killing.

Arcan stepped back, wrapping his arms around himself to hold them at bay. He told her, "You make me sick."

"Lucas!" Deborah cried, clutching at her crotch where a stain was spreading darkly. "Lucas, don't go!"

Arcan walked out of her room, dressed quickly in his own, and left the house. He spent the rest of the night drinking coffee and studying in the back booth of a 24-hour pancake house. The sweet smell there made him nauseous. And all the waitresses had red nails.

He returned the next morning. Mornings were safe. Deborah only wept then, not coming out of her room until noon. Dressed in black, crying by the window. Flitting helplessly from one restless perch to another. The worst that could happen would be a broken pane of glass and an outhouse mess on the rug.

He vowed to spend no more nights at home. Fine. He'd keep her house and do the yard work and the book work and the endless whatever work. But he wouldn't let her press her creature lump of flesh against him ever again. Nor call him by his father's name. Nor force him to play his father's role.

Arcan busied himself making breakfast. Then he vacuumed the carpets and dusted down the hall. He paused at her door. There was no noise. There were no wracking sobs, no sounds of tissues tearing and being dropped sogged into the waste can. She wasn't snuffling or gasping with affliction.

This wasn't normal. This was a woman who had never learned to suffer in silence. It was the only reason he rapped his knuckles on the door.

"Deborah?" he called out. There was no answer. "Mom?" he called, deciding it was time she realized a parental connection.

Arcan turned the knob and stepped inside her room.

This Symbiotic Fascination

Deborah was at her dressing table, her gown in folds at her thick waist with the hem pulled up to expose her hips. Arcan wouldn't look there, knowing she had probably masturbated to make up for him not being there. He mustn't look because his animals were leaning forward to press their snouts to the abnormally wide gash. She'd fallen asleep on the velveteen stool.

She'd spilled a bottle of red nail polish. Or 20 bottles of it. Motes of talc floated in it in pinkish clots.

She'd scrawled red on the mirror. *Who wants me?*

Arcan called the police.

The coroner said she'd managed to cut a great deal of the tissue that lined her vagina and was working on one breast with the shears when she bled to death. The man was amazed that shock hadn't stopped her much earlier. The shreds of gummy labia and vulva were carefully set into the trays of a jewelry box.

They first looked sternly at Arcan but the coroner placed the actual time of death as several hours after Arcan had left the premises. He had an alibi from the pancake house. And the woman's medicine cabinet was filled with bottles of prescribed Lithium, the dates going back to 1970, not a single pill taken.

Harry came home four days later to stand with Arcan at graveside as they lowered in Deborah's casket.

Lucas had the nerve to show up. He was stiff when he saw his sons. His posture seemed to say *I told you so. She was crazy. You should have left her like I did.*

Arcan had never before noticed the scars his father bore on his face, running like rite-of-passage tattoos into his scalp. A quick glance would make most people think they were character lines. But the creases were too familiar. He imagined what the body beneath the clothes looked like, with furrows down the back and across the chest like the stripes on a flag.

There was a different young cutie on Lucas's arm. She

had a short skirt up to her butt crack and blonde hair just down to it, straight as three-penny nails. She held on to him, her hip pressed to his. Her mouth was as red as fresh polish, as heart muscle. She was as pale as a Lilith.

And a Lilith was what she was. She drank Lucas Tyler's will as he drank her beauty. They sucked each other's parts for different joys. It made Arcan sick to look at them. What scars had she made and which ones had come from Deborah? No animals peered from Lucas's eyes. Arcan knew his father didn't have the bestial strength to do anything other than leave once the bitch grew too old to chase him. But he was a slave-man and he would forever roam from pelt to pelt. He was dying for his pleasures. He was already dead.

"The real grave is in your eyes," the teenager said softly, staring at his old man.

What sense of duty had even brought Lucas there? Had he come to make sure Deborah was really dead? Or had he come to show her unresting spirit the new girl on his arm?

Who wants you?

If Lucas must be a slave to his passions and have a Lilith, then let it be a young one. So he could at least say to himself, *I'm not dying and I'm not used. I'm virile and strong. I'm getting younger with every heartbeat.*

Harry leaned over. "What did you say, little brother?"

Arcan didn't reply. But he could see the death in his father's eyes, as the female took parts of him even as they stood there. The most disgusting thing was how much Lucas enjoyed being enthralled by this symbiotic fascination.

"I should have hit Delia, not Carl," Arcan said to himself as he soaped the rainbow bong and ran tap water through it.

The water was brown as it came out, flushing the built-up resins away. It wasn't the best way to smoke *bhang*.

Small-bowled hashpipes were better suited for it. And the medieval Mohammedans used to drink it, not smoke it.

But it hadn't worked anyway. It hadn't made him safe in his dreams. He wasn't destined to be invincible or to find Paradise.

The ghosts, hanging close by the walls, gently standing in the hiding folds of the kitchen drapes, shook their heads.

No, Arcan would never be invincible.

Chapter Nine

It was the same ugly guy Tawne had seen several nights ago. He was trying to talk to Delia without much success. True to Delia's aloof charm, she was politely ignoring him. She unlocked the car and began putting her packages into the back seat, all the while refusing even to look at him. She might have appeared stuck up if Tawne didn't know better. Delia's shell of protection was firmly in place at every edge.

Until one small bag slipped from her hand and fell toward the asphalt. Before it hit the ground he'd snatched it. He handed it to Delia with a warped bow, bending stiffly on his knobby knees.

Delia turned a bit to accept it graciously. She blushed, a trifle annoyed but far too much of a lady to tell him to please *just fuck off*.

Their eyes met.

Tawne had to watch. Thinking it couldn't possibly happen twice. That well-bred and unapproachable Delia couldn't fawn over this gnome.

Delia's eyes fluttered. Even several aisles over, Tawne saw her cool expression change to perceptible coquetry. She smiled radiantly, like a beauty queen for a scrutinizing judge, and accepted the fallen package as if it were a crown. She let him touch her hand.

He smiled back over the broken masonry of his teeth, the pockmarks in his face cramped in the elastic furrows created by this grimace. The hairs curling out of his nostrils brushed his flared upper lip. He took Delia's hand and tenderly kissed it.

He began to lead her away.

Tawne was appalled. Even if Delia thought he was the most incredible man she'd ever seen, she wouldn't just go off with him this way. Delia was no singles scene pickup.

But she was going with him.

Hanging onto him like she could practically pull off her clothes in the parking lot and mount him on the tacky macadam.

The man had a power to make her see him as desirable. A power to make her want him. On the spot. On any spot.

He led Delia around to the passenger side of her car and opened the door for her. He went around to the driver's side and got in. Delia never took her eyes off him. He never stopped looking directly at her as he crossed before the front of the car to get to the driver's side. Delia handed him the keys. He started the engine and the shoulder harness belts crept up like serpents to their throats.

Tawne's knees were shaking. She put a hand on the hood of the Buick to steady herself. Was she just going to let him hypnotize Delia and spirit her away like this?

Tawne hurried to get into her car. The old engine didn't start quickly. By the time she got going, there were several cars between them and the exit to the mall. Delia's Lexus in metallic teal went ahead but was stopped at the first light. Tawne was able to shorten car lengths to two by the time she slid to the same light. She was determined to follow. To make sure this freak didn't hurt her friend.

And to watch. This was an admission Tawne made to herself. She wanted to understand how he did what he did.

Tawne remembered briefly meeting his gaze earlier in the week. There was a thunderbolt and he was transformed from an ugly little man into a walking, talking godform of the 20th century.

It had lasted the merest of seconds. Until he swerved his attention away and he was ugly again. He'd smiled wickedly when he did this. He'd known what he was doing, my yes.

Wires had to touch for sparks to be made.

What had happened to the woman in the sequins? Who was to say anything happened to her?

Delia was a friend, wasn't she? The only one Tawne really had other than Arcan. Delia couldn't possibly know what she was doing. Not the way she was acting. Streets intersected and bisected. Traffic continually cut her off but Tawne managed to keep the metallic teal Lexus in sight.

It was enough that she could see as Delia disengaged her belt and slid over on the front seat. She was sitting as close to him as she could get without being in his lap. From the back and 10 car lengths away, the two heads might have been one. Then the sun drowned entirely in those steel clouds and the shadow shifted, blending with solid objects to make a somber uniformity. Tawne couldn't see the interior of the Lexus anymore.

A light turned amber. The Lexus went through it. Tawne was caught behind the red light.

She pounded on the steering wheel and muttered, "God damn."

She fidgeted through the wait, and honked at cars too slow when the light finally turned green again.

"Let's go," Tawne growled. "Are you waiting for a different shade of green or something?"

The first driver gave her the finger. The second deliberately slowed down in front of her. Tawne braked when the asshole suddenly braked. He did it just to piss her off.

Tawne jerked the wheel and jumped up onto the sidewalk. The other driver stared as she maneuvered around him, then sliced back down the curb and clipped his front fender for good measure.

"Chase me if you want to," she told him, grinning. "I'll bet I'm twice your size. I'll beat the crap out of you if you stop me again."

Tawne could see him hopping up and down in his seat, wrangling with the belt to try to get it off so he could jump out of his car and show some righteous indignation. He craned his neck to see her license number. But it had grown too dark outside for that with the dusk hanging between buildings.

Tawne honked again as she bumped back out ahead of him, shaking her fist belligerently. She didn't slow down as she quickened through the next yellow light and turned right, thinking this was the direction the Lexus had taken.

Tawne wasn't worried about anyone witnessing her hitting him and driving off. This shit happened all the time in their city. Folks were getting blasé about violence going on around them but not actually *involving* them. Just like the people in those crime-infested northern towns. Women were getting cut and raped on sidewalks right in front of their apartment houses and nobody even bothered to call the cops as they overheard the desperate screams.

Just look at *Mean Streets*. Lots of assholes out there who didn't give a damn.

She couldn't see Delia's car. She turned her head both ways until she damn near gave herself whiplash, trying to see out the rearview and both side mirrors at the same time. They could have headed any direction once out of her sight even for those few seconds. He might have noticed Tawne was following and recognized her from the other night. It was by sheer luck that Tawne got a glimpse of metallic teal shining under a streetlamp flickering in her right-side mirror. It was an instant's worth. The car was going up the ramp to the highway.

Where was he taking Delia? To some out of the way motel where he could pawn her sudden affection for him into getting his sleazy rocks off? Would he be able to keep his hold over her throughout several hours of sweaty sex or would the vision deflate at some delicate, embarrassing moment of release? Delia would begin to scream. She surely must, after finding herself being plunged into by a man with all the physical appeal of a Seuss grinch with acne. And then what would happen?

It reminded Tawne of a joke she'd overheard Carl telling the guys. About a man who had been falling down drunk, waking up after a night of hot ins-and-outs with this gorgeous doll he'd picked up. Only he found a gross, foul-breathed bestial hag sleeping on his arm. Try as he might, he couldn't get his arm out from under this smelly dog-woman. So he finally chewed his arm off in order to escape. Like a coyote in a trap, chewing off its own leg.

Get it? Har har.

It didn't seem all that funny to her then and now it really made her shudder. If she couldn't catch up with the couple and lost sight of them again, AND if Delia showed up at work on Monday morning struggling to manage with only one arm, would Tawne understand what happened?

Delia would have a haunted look in her eyes. *I have slept with the coyote man.*

It was after seven on Friday night. The highway was pretty busy. Tawne was so far behind them that she barely kept the Lexus in sight at all. But she could see he was staying in the right hand lane.

She maneuvered over into the next lane, getting close

enough to notice that she didn't see Delia anymore. Was Delia on the floor of the car, beaten into submission? Did the spell only work for a short time? Tawne thought of ramming him. She could step on the accelerator enough to do this in about 20 seconds. She'd knock his ass right into the guard rail.

Rescue her friend even if she never found out what the ugly man's secret was.

If she rammed, wouldn't she hurt Delia? Tawne slowed.

Delia's head came up from his lap. She wiped her mouth. Seemed to shiver. Looked long back into his eyes. Smiled.

Tawne thought she would be physically sick. She imagined the ugly man in her huge hands, like a breakable doll with hollow plastic limbs and a rubber chicken neck very twistable.

He signaled, took the off-ramp suddenly. There was nothing out there but the river. Was he taking Delia to the boons? Why did he need such an out of the way place?

Tawne hadn't time to make the exit herself, being in the second lane and unable to merge in traffic in the right even with a quick switch. She'd gone past the exit. She sped up, searching madly for the next ramp. It was an eighth of a mile but she took it. She blared her horn at the fool who didn't want to yield at the bottom of the ramp. She heard his wheels squealing as she peeled in front—up to the turn that would swing her left and back toward the opposite lane on the highway.

So Delia hadn't been clubbed senseless. She'd seemed to be okay.

No, she'd shivered after coming up. (Up for air. Gross!) Eye contact must have been broken. Well, of course it had been broken if Delia had bent to do what Tawne figured she must have bent to do.

The idea of that hairy, pockmarked, corkscrew of a man was grotesque. Some things weren't meant to be ingested.

Some people weren't meant to be ingested. His semen would taste like old death.

Again the picture of Delia, both arms intact but having chewed off her own lips. *I have sucked the coyote man.*

Tawne felt righteous nausea 'til she considered that this might be what men thought when they made sexual jokes about her. Men like Carl.

She climbed back onto the highway for the eighth of a mile, swung back off, went under the overpass, and down the road she'd seen the Lexus take. They were nowhere to be seen.

Tawne began to panic as she drove up the first roadway through groves of post oak and pine trees. Why? It wasn't as if the man had kidnapped Delia. She'd gone with him willingly enough.

Delia wasn't herself. She'd been hypnotized and led away.

There must be a motive for this which wasn't honorable.

He'd already gotten Delia to give him a blowjob. Tawne had seen her head come up. Had watched Delia wipe her mouth.

How else could a very unattractive man like him get women?

Tawne once assumed he had money. But he didn't dress in a wealthy manner and they had taken Delia's car. He could be some homeless Svengali with a serious hard-on.

Then why was he taking her way out here?

Tawne turned from the paved road onto a dirt one, looking for the Lexus. Darkness had been full to night for at least 30 minutes. The sun hadn't only set, it had vanished. There were no city lights out this far. Tawne could see only by the Buick's headlamps, hoping to find the couple by those of Delia's Lexus.

A car passed, throwing gravel and dust. She stared as it came parallel. It wasn't the Lexus but a patrol car. Tawne was tempted to wave the cop down and tell him that she was looking for a friend who might have been kidnapped. Who might be in the process of being raped.

She didn't wave him down. Why? Wasn't she sure of what was going on?

Tawne found herself in a maze of narrow, rutted roads. She smelled the river, occasionally hearing rushing water from some of the streams that snaked through the area, much of it only ankle deep. The rains had been unusually heavy the last three years straight. There were broad patches of land visible from the roads where the standing water had rotted away tree roots until there was nothing left to hold them up anymore. They had fallen into each other, laying scattered, their decaying barks and leaves smelling like a rancid salad.

Tawne frowned as she tried to see between them. Seeing them as spectral figures swooning, overcome by a ghostly smoke.

A lonely hunter was traipsing over the broken ground. He was carrying his rifle as if it were a mop handle. If he wasn't careful, he was going to trip and blow his feet off. Tawne wondered if he was tired or drunk.

"I'm projecting myself onto him," she said aloud as she crept the Buick by. "That's why I think he wants to use that gun on himself."

He barely looked at her as she went by. He was in a hunter's world—or a suicide's world. It was enough for Tawne that he wasn't the ugly man. A few minutes later she heard a blast and knew it was the hunter's rifle. How did she know he hadn't shot an animal? He'd been looking at the ground, not out for prey.

But she wouldn't go back.

I have no time for him . . . I have to rescue Delia.

Tawne caught a glimpse of the moon at a crossroads to her left, cresting the eastern horizon which didn't sport the clouds the western rim had shrouded the sunset with. But the lunar light didn't penetrate the trees. Once she was beyond the intersection, the scant moonlight was digested by the dark.

"I'm lost," she admitted to herself. "Go figure. I've lived in this city all my life. But I've never been out here before."

She'd never had a reason to come. How was this possible when her dreams were filled with shadows and a smell that surely must belong to woods, with caverns and dampness?

"Sheltered life, kid," Tawne said. "NO life, kid."

Now that Tawne had a reason to be out there—Delia needed help—she was lost and couldn't even help herself. Or that hunter with his head blown off back there.

Of course, he might only have shot a deer.

Tawne made a face. It bothered her more to think he might have just blown Bambi to smithereens than to let it ride that he'd murdered himself.

She sighed and searched the trees. They could be anywhere. They might have gone back up to the highway, satisfied they had lost her. Three's a crowd, baby.

I'm not here to rescue Delia. The thought popped unbidden into Tawne's head, (let's be honest for a sec.) *I'm here to see that ugly man. Try to figure out what his power is* (so I can do it, too).

No! She'd come here to help Delia. Sure, she wanted to know how he did what he did. Who wouldn't want to know that?

But she'd come for her friend. Because the ugly man had put a charm on Delia and brought her out here to nowhere. That was wrong. It was dangerous.

How long had it been since they turned off the highway?

When Tawne finally saw the Lexus, the surprised automatic reflex caused her to slam on the brakes. So much mud flew that she had to switch on the wipers before she could again make out the car.

It was parked off the road, under pines which clearly had root damage. The head lights were beaming through the swooning pines. These lights were what Tawne noticed to begin with. If they hadn't been on, she probably never would have located the car.

She parked as well as she could on the narrow road. There was no real shoulder and no decent place for her to pull off. She might have taken the slim passage through the forest that Delia's car had but Tawne was afraid she wouldn't be able to get back out. Especially without having part of the woods crash down on top of the Buick.

She didn't turn off her own lights. Out here she needed all the help she could get.

The ground was too soft. It was like trying to walk over a mantle of overripe plums and long-dead cats. It smelled sour. She also smelled the river strongly. She heard it, moving against an unseen bank. It burbled the low, swirling, clarinet noises of fast water.

There was no one in the Lexus. Both doors were wide open. There was no sign of a struggle. Until Tawne walked into the headlights which blasted off twin shots into the trees and saw drops of blood on the ground.

She gasped, realizing worst fears.

Had Delia snapped out of it? Had she tried to escape so he'd beaten and dragged her off?

Tawne opened her mouth, sucking in a piercing lungful of the cold river air. She started to yell, "Delia?"

Instead, she let the air out in a slow gust and closed her mouth. She followed the trail of blood, stepping as quietly as she could without letting tiptoeing slow her down too much. The drops of blood became heavier, became patches of shiny oil beneath the headlight's beam. They were black on the dark ground not brightened by the glare that passed over it. She smelled a copper/salt stench which sharply contrasted with the sweet rot of wet vegetation and the fungal smell of the river.

Water splashed against concrete. This was where the county had stacked a section of drainage pipe in preparation for installation to help with flooding and erosion. It was eerie, loud and hollow but infinitely liquid. She imagined this was what it sounded like when blood went through one artery but not another because it had been severed.

It was into one of these pipes on the slimy bank that the ugly man was stuffing Delia's body. He would push and cram, stopping to rip in a blur of curves, liquid spewing straight out to fall in a deranged slow motion totally opposite from the speed of his clawing. Hair with blood at the roots erupted into the air like disemboweled hummingbirds. Slivers of flesh, teeth, and an eyeball arced upward, veering out, falling, as if he was doing a visceral juggling act.

(Yet there was no sound but the river, burbling sepulchrally as if flooding a mausoleum. Delia didn't moan or scream. The ugly man didn't breathe raggedly with exertion and insanity. Even when he bent to his work with his mouth open, the teeth didn't clack, reasonably solid flesh didn't rip or cartilage pop.)

Delia's body spasmed arms and legs, back arching, as if she were doing some bizarre victim's dance meant as seductive to savage gods. It was the sort of dance that little girls might have been taught in Neolithic kindergartens where children marked at birth were sent. The teachers wore vulture masks and had had their own vaginas sewn shut with the severed penises of their fathers imprisoned within.

The farthest motes of light from the Lexus showed this scene poorly. The ugly man looked more twisted and bent than before. His cratered face was swollen with each pockmark. He looked as if he'd been stung by hornets.

Tawne refused to believe it could even be Delia. It was only a torn rag. The arms and legs were arms and legs but the clothes were shredded until the woman was nearly scratched naked. Her face was a pulp, as if she'd gone nose-first through plate glass.

This Symbiotic Fascination

Tawne tried to blink and tell herself she'd come upon this scene after he'd killed Delia, that she hadn't stood there frozen and witnessed the weird speed-up/slow-down murder. Tawne's heart sank deep into the pit of her stomach.

She thought of the joke, of Delia chewing off her own arm, her lips. Well, a lot more damage had been done trying to get out from under coyote man.

(Tawne suppressed a horrible giggle which was rising into her throat. The joke was reversed. It was supposed to be the trapped one who was the coyote, chewing off its own member to free itself. But it became irrevocably turned inside out in her head. The self mutilation happened after waking up pinned under the smelly dog woman, the coyote man. It would forever remain this way for Tawne, a joke gone wrong.)

Tawne edged closer. Damn, why did she feel the need to do that? She could see enough from where she stood to know this wasn't a good place to hang around. It was a place where time was a homicidal contortionist and sounds went limp.

Because she wanted to kill him, that's why she stayed.

There was blood on his mouth.

Tawne let out an unfortunate sob. Oh, she really had meant to keep quiet.

He quickly looked up, into the beams of the headlights which only barely reached him. He snarled like a startled animal, lips pulled back to reveal fangs, slender as thorns. Beyond coyote and into shark.

Not a human's mouth. Not even a very ugly human's mouth. It wasn't the mouth of a mammal at all.

He exhaled and it was a deep bell. A horn across water. Sound had begun again.

In his open mouth Tawne could see blood across the gums, coating the tongue. The bell note was a reverberation in scarlet.

Tawne felt instantly weak. His eyes locked onto hers and

97

Charlee Jacob

she saw Max Schreck of the 1922 *Nosferatu, Eine Symphonie Des Grauens*. He was pointy-eared as a bat. He had a possessive claw draped over his victim.

She saw Christopher Lee, red eyes and all, dressed in opera black. He had a possessive pale hand draped over his victim.

She saw Frank Langella, magnetic and sexy. He had a possessive hand draped over his lover.

Somewhere in-between these something with all the finesse of pipe cleaners draped in twisting rotted rat skin flapped. Split-seconds worth, long enough to make her jerk back and forth between the arousal these other images were supposed to invoke. Tawne turned her head, refusing to see any more. He was doing it, making her see what wasn't there. He was running the gamut of theatrical bloodsuckers from eerie and alien to downright succulent. To—whatever that maggoty Gumby thing was.

Don't look at his eyes, she told herself sternly.

He sprang to his feet. Pretty agile for a guy who only hobbled before.

He's going to kill me like he did Delia. I don't want to die, certainly not like that. Why I've scarcely lived yet—so do something . . . something now.

Tawne held her hand over her eyes, shielding them to look at him sideways. Not letting a full connection be made with his face.

"Gee, how did you do that? Teach me," Tawne said as evenly as she could, hoping her voice didn't shake. There were two kinds of desperate here, and she wanted to choose which one she projected.

He stopped in mid-stride, his feet slowly sinking in the muck. His eyes glittered wickedly, a washed-out green but as luminous as swamp gas. Dotted with cataracts.

"You can see I'm not pretty," she said. "How do you make people see what you want them to?"

There was a touch of pain in her voice that Tawne wasn't

convinced was the terror of death. It was that second desperation, virginal and alone. How could she even think of it with poor Delia mangled close by?

"Come here," the ugly man commanded. His voice was high and nasal. It wasn't at all a deep bell or horn across water. "Let me look at you."

You must be crazy. But Tawne didn't know if she meant him or herself. Because her feet were moving, taking her helpless body along with them. To him, a killer who had just mutilated her beautiful friend. To a murderer with blood inside his mouth.

She avoided his eyes as she sidled to within three feet of him. It made her flesh squirm to have him look her over. She wanted to run when he leaned toward her and she smelled the raw breath. Like that of a dog which has just torn a rabbit apart.

"It's a terrible thing, loneliness is," he said.

Chapter Ten

Alan hadn't given himself much time to get to the studio. It was important for him to delay so he lounged around for about an hour. He edited, removing anything which might incriminate him for his reckless driving, wiping his own offensive language—but no one else's. Assholes were always better displayed with obscenities. He made sure when he walked into the station that it was too late for the producers to view the tapes before his segment.

"Hi, guys!" he announced as he strode in with confidence and an enormous grin. He had the two edited tapes under his arm. "I've got the best spontaneous shit you've ever seen."

He'd been monitoring the news as he edited, listening to the police band. No one had yet reported what happened out at Red's Stomping Ground. And Channel 7 ran nothing about it before he went in. He knew it might be a while before it came out, if they hadn't just buried the poor bastard, vowing over a keg of Lone Star and a few buckets of barbecued ribs to keep their silence forever. None of these people involved in the pickup driver's death would want anyone to know.

"Where have you been, Alan?" Barry Martinez shouted, hair caught in-between his fingers from where he'd been tugging it in frustration.

"Do you know what time it is?" Susan Greentree asked as she pointed to her watch. A ridiculous gesture since there was a big clock on the wall behind her moon head, telling everyone what time it was. It was three minutes before magic.

Before Alan Moravec's future would commence.

"Yeah, it's *Mean Streets* time, baby," Alan bellowed back, waving the tapes. "And have I got a story. It's the best thing we've ever done. People'll talk about this for *years*."

The two producers hurried to his side.

"What is it?" Susan asked, peered at the video tapes as if she could intuit what was on them if she stared hard enough.

"It has everything," Alan said, nodding smugly. "It has pathos, drama, human interest, emotion, adventure and is rated PG 13 for violence. If you only see one *Mean Streets* this year . . ."

Barry protested, "Damn. We don't have time to preview it."

Alan waved a hand in the air dismissively. "I know. I know. But I just came from the scene and there was absolutely no time. I'm sorry but, believe me, you're gonna love this."

The pair put their heads together and conversed rapidly for about 10 seconds. Then Susan bit her lip, turning to Alan as she said, "We'll trust your instincts."

Barry agreed with a smidge of hesitation.

They had probably been afraid Alan wouldn't show. They didn't want to have to cancel the *Mean Streets* segment; it was too popular. And they didn't want to have to run the horrid surgical dumpster scene with the bloody fetuses and the two brats in the Cannibal Corpse T-shirts who should have been aborted themselves. But what would they replace it with at this late moment?

Alan had counted on them feeling this way. He'd ticked down the minutes before getting out of his car to come through the door of the station. He hadn't wanted to risk even a chance, however minuscule, that they would be able to deem the contents of the tapes to be inappropriate.

After all, this was *Mean Streets*. It didn't get any meaner or filthier than what he'd taped on the highway and afterward at the bar.

He'd brought the station some great stuff in the past and by god they ought to trust his instincts.

By the time Alan showed the first tape to the television audience and spoke his famous, "Hey, Mister! You're an asshole!" the studio was jumping. Neither Martinez nor Greentree could believe he'd managed to tape anything so vicious. They were both grinning from ear to ear behind the cameras. They pounded each other's backs, hardly able to wait to see what could follow to top it.

Then Alan showed the second tape and said forcefully at the end of it. "Hey, Mister! You *were* an asshole!"

No one was smiling now.

Susan Greentree clutched her chest, reaching into her pocket for what might have been heart pills but only turned out to be acid reflux meds. She said in disbelief, "He got a man murdered, Barry."

"He set it up. Not the dog part, but the bar. And he did it on purpose." Barry Martinez was pulling hair from his head, staring at it as if it might save him. Because he was damned. They were all damned.

The switchboard went epileptic with lights. Phones rang and buzzed indignantly, adrenaline in the wires. There was a lot of outrage pouring in.

"Old-fashioned lynching, wasn't it?" Alan remarked as

he left the stage. "Kind of makes you wonder why it went out of style."

The two producers stared at him with round eyes and open mouths. Everyone was staring at him. The station switched immediately to commercial as the anchors tried to recover themselves.

"That man's family is probably going to sue the station," Martinez finally said, amazed Moravec couldn't have foreseen this.

"The FCC will fine us. They may even yank our license," Greentree whispered, barely able to make any sound at all.

"You could face charges. Alan. *Charges.*" Martinez's voice dropped even lower than hers. "You incited a riot that ended in murder."

A secretary hustled up and blurted, "The other stations have already jumped on it. They're deploring it, calling it dirty tricks news. They're saying he engineered a situation to create a media event."

"Christ!" Martinez jerked out two fistfuls of hair. "Prepare an apology at once. I'll deliver it on the air personally in five minutes."

Alan fumed. "An apology? For what? Doing my job as a reporter? Hell, once I showed the dog thing tonight and people saw what that shit heel did, the whole city would've marched en masse to his house and jerked his butt out to the tallest tree. I just anticipated it. The other stations are jealous as hell."

The two producers turned to him, trembling. Susan's dark skin had gone maroon. Barry's had done the opposite and turned white.

"You're fired, Alan," Susan told him quietly, in a kind of shock.

"Oh, yeah?" He chortled and glanced at Barry to naysay it.

Martinez nodded to back her up. As if there was nothing more to say. So that's right, just get the hell out. In silence. As if they were dreaming this, because nobody could be foolish enough to do this thing. Neither Alan for taping such an abomination nor themselves for letting him run tapes they hadn't previewed.

In a day they would both probably be fired as well.

Alan started to say something like *you can't fire me.*

But he knew that, as the station's news producers, they could.

He started to say something like *you don't dare fire me.*

But Alan knew they didn't dare *not* fire him.

It was one thing to stand up for the rights of a free press and another to be accomplices to murder.

Alan spun on his heel and kicked the door to the hall open.

"You'll be sorry when I'm on prime time, folks," he said. He heard phones ringing all over the station, the voices of operators and secretaries blathering nervously and apologetically into the receivers. "Why do jerks like you even bother to report news when you don't have any more balls than this? Stick to cooking shows for fuck's sake and let the bigger boys show the world as it is!"

Alan slammed the door behind him so hard that the glass in it cracked. But he was scared. It never occurred to him that he could face charges. He wouldn't let himself consider that he should have let it stay put with the first tape, ending with the culprit identification of the redneck's face.

Everyone stared at him in mute disgust as he walked down the hall, past the offices and sound stages. Out the front door. Phones, phones rang everywhere.

"People might be bitchin', but they're talking about it, aren't they?" Alan shouted at someone coming into Channel 7.

Hell, it was probably all they could talk about. And after they came down from the blood high it gave them—pounding their brains toward entertainment overload and aneurysm—they would want more. Because nothing less would ever suffice again.

This Symbiotic Fascination

People used to complain about sex on TV. Now there was sex all over the set. Women bared their breasts on soaps and prime time. Couples made like horny thumper bunnies on every single channel but The Trinity Broadcasting Network.

People used to complain about the language on TV. Now they said fucking near anything. *Hey, Mister! You're an asshole!* Tune in at the right time of evening and it would be *Hey, Mister! You're a fucking asshole.* And after this it would likely be *Hey, Mister! You're a fucking fudge-packing cocksucking rimlicking armadillo-fisting roadkill-slurping asshole!*

People used to complain about gays, interracial couples, incest and teens making out on TV. Now the only taboo was leaving someone out.

Of course, there had always been violence on TV. Since the beginning with unrealistic, smooth moth holes for gunshot wounds on *Gunsmoke*, to the recent spurty decaps on *I Witness Video* and prisoners slowly roasting on gigantic spits on *Saddam Theater Presents*. The screens ran with blood, and the audiences laid supine on their wall-to-wall carpets with their faces up and their mouths open to catch it as it dripped down to them. Could it be any truer than when the first televised execution was held a short time back? The man being fried had his hair catch fire, and his flesh bubbled and ran like so much cheese. Phone-in sales immediately after to local pizza delivery places skyrocketed. Yummy.

They were going to swallow this, too. Like warm sperm. Swallow it, choke some, and want more, tongues out and wagging as if to catch the snowy fallout from Sodom. Because this was nothing more than another baby step forward toward the total embrace of what Alan referred to as America's natural weirdness.

He'd be back. No doubt about it. With his camcorder in one hand and an Emmy in the other. What good was breaking new ground if it wasn't once sacred ground?

At present, though, it seemed like a good idea to get drunk.

Alan didn't bother going back to his apartment. The police might just come a-knockin'. He decided to head for the river outside of town where he could badmouth and dream in private, talking himself out of his fears.

Who would bother looking for him out there? Not anyone who might care. Not even the 20 or so rednecks who might feel—with some tiny brainsplatter of justification—that Alan had trapped them into sneak-butchery. Not the brothers of those rednecks. Not their cousins sworn to vengeance. Not their friends who had just been passing the 10-gallon hat trying to raise bail money.

"Some justification hell," Alan swore to himself, taking a swig from a bottle of Chivas Regal. "They did the deed. I just showed them what he'd done and then sat back. Did I say *git that sucker*? No, I didn't. Did I say *smoke 'im for the lily-livered varmint he is*? No, sir. I didn't. Did I say *please, fellers, would you accommodate a poor struggling journalist and beat the blood and guts out of that man while I get it on tape and be sure to smile*? Shit, no. They did this themselves. I didn't really have any idea that a bar full of boozed-up shitkickers were going to go wild and commit mayhem. How could I possibly have predicted that? Fuck, they might have settled for dragging his ass back to the highway to lick that poor doggy's jelly off the asphalt."

Alan chuckled and took a long pull from the bottle. "Now, *that* would have been something to have on film."

He drove down bumpy back roads, Chivas between his thighs. Alan disdained beer. Beer was for cowpokes and high schoolers trying to prove their manhood. Jack Daniels was for cowpokes and for construction workers who had not quite lost the linings of their stomachs. He had better taste than that. He'd been drinking since he got off the highway and hadn't sweat but once. That had been when he caught sight of a patrol car about 10 minutes ago.

This Symbiotic Fascination

Alan's bladder ached. He needed to pull over and take a piss. Where he was seemed as good a spot as any. There was another car half blocking the narrow road. There was no way to get past it. The headlights were on but he couldn't see a driver. Oh, well, he'd just step outside, unzip, and let 'er rip. If they saw him hangin', fuck 'em. They shouldn't have been hogging the road.

Alan would have to wait for them before he could leave. That, or try to turn around in the cramped ruts with trees close on either side. Not that he was in a hurry. He could just as easily get sauced right here.

He got out of the car and showered the bark of a nearby pine. He looked through the woods and saw a second car parked at least 50 feet into the boons. Its headlights were also on, skewering the darkness less than relentlessly.

Alan heard a scream. It was brief, female, painfully high. It was followed by a gurgle and a growl, the latter definitely relentless. And . . . was that a bell?

He didn't bother to pull himself back in and zip up. He grabbed his camera from the front seat and took off through the trees, slipping on wet leaves and splashing through mirrors of sour, standing water. Toward the other car and its streaming, foggy headlights. Then beyond to where he heard the river moving. And where he heard bodies moving.

A naked man had his face buried between a naked woman's breasts. Alan heard sucking, growling, slavering swallows that made all that fine scotch in his belly threaten to erupt. The woman's eyes were wild as she bucked under her assailant. Their hips were solidly welded, the man's back arching impossibly. He had to be a contortionist to bend so much, joined to her loins as he savagely drank from her chest. Were there no bones in his back?

He sat up, pumping, sweaty, blood smearing both cheeks and his nose. He was the ugliest man Alan had ever seen. He lifted the woman's thighs over his shoulders and there was an audible crack from each. A white ball of bone showed through a rift in one of her legs. Yet at this point, she was only moaning, not screaming anymore. And her hips still ground, tilting up to meet the man's.

The ugly man looked squarely at Alan. And at the camera. He smiled. Alan's vision swam. He went lightheaded.

The man's muscles flexed. A shock of golden hair fell back from a high brow, eyes cobalt even in the dark. The skin was a flawless, luminous linen. He stared back down at the woman under him and bent to . . . kiss . . . her?

His body convulsed as he began to regurgitate the blood he'd swallowed back into her mouth.

Alan's legs gave way as he fell to his knees, dropping the camera into the grass and pine needles. He began to vomit, too, sure the Chivas and the chicken he'd eaten about a half hour earlier were crimson library paste sewn with veins and lathered with an unspeakable gumbo. He shivered down on all fours, unable to stop retching, afraid to see anymore. He hoped the camera on the ground was at least pointed the right way and still filming. Alan couldn't help the woman.

I am a newsman I must remain detached . . .

Everything inside his guts had certainly become detached. *Sympathy heaves.*

Bile scorched up Alan's throat, burning like he'd swallowed a nest of fire ants. His eyes poured as if he was weeping for the woman. Alan heard her choking, trying to scream, heard her attacker coughing it up, lips pressed tightly to hers.

But if Alan was weeping, it was for himself. For he couldn't get up to run away. He couldn't even crawl. Not while his stomach seizured and it seemed as if every morsel he'd eaten since 1965 was coming up.

Moravec disgorged and then fainted.

He opened his eyes to stars seen through spidery branches. He gagged on the smells of his own vomit drying on his chin and mouth. If his stomach weren't already empty, he'd have thrown up again. Instead he had a few dry heaves, then sat up, wiping his face with his sleeve.

The man was gone. The woman's nude body lay on the bank in the mud, face and breasts covered with blood.

Alan reached for the camcorder. He checked it over, afraid it might be broken. And if it was sitting in water, the video would be ruined. Fortunately it hadn't fallen into any of the puddles. It had switched off when hitting the ground but otherwise appeared to be undamaged. So he hoped. He turned it back on and began to film the dead woman in closer detail.

It was evident she was dead. Both legs lay limply, broken and at a somewhat peculiar angle from the hips. Her eyes stared, unseeing, half-popped from their grayish sockets. Her dull red hair lay in a fan around her head, gradually sinking into the dark bank. The wound in-between her breasts and slightly to the left was ringed in serrated crimps and was gory. There was so much blood on her mouth that it looked as if she'd tried to eat her own heart.

Alan could see this organ within the chest wound. See it plain as the night around him. Red and blue and purple and black. Torn. The ventricles were laid bare, raw and practically hollow. He became dizzy and looked away.

He knew he ought to check for a pulse. (Sure! Why, she might be alive this way, Alan!) He couldn't bear the thought of touching her. He could feel her cooling. It was as palpable as the air coming off the river.

The raggedy pieces of flesh in her mouth had come from that heart. This was a fact of which Alan had no doubt. No wonder most people didn't like organ meat. It looked tough as leather. Maybe it was only the way it was etched with acid into lumps.

Of course, she hadn't done this to herself. He didn't have to think it. He knew the truth for he'd seen the man.

The ugly man.

The handsome, golden-haired lion of a man.

109

This second had surely been illusion. Alan's reaction to the scene in puke and hallucination and shock. Yeah, some newsman. Breaker of sacred ground.

He'd seen bodies before. Well, he'd seen a dog wiped out on the highway just that afternoon. He'd seen a man beaten, castrated and kicked to death. Those had been nothing, nothing at all.

But there had never been a corpse like this one. No, not ever.

Reluctantly, he zoomed in on her, feeling weak at poking into her grisly nuances. She'd been a large woman. Not really fat. Big-boned folks called it when they were being kind. Thick with muscle that wasn't hard but which must have been strong. How had a runt like that ugly little guy ever overpowered such a woman? She was six foot two if she was an inch. And she had to have the biggest hands Alan had seen on a female outside the primate house at the Dallas zoo.

Then Alan saw the other one. The one in the pipe. Stuffed like the murder victims in the culverts.

Was it even possible that, now that he'd lost his job with the station, he'd blundered across his career-builder? Fate was warped and destiny was cruel, bless 'em.

Alan carefully walked on the slippery ground to get a better shot of this second victim. The dead woman in the pipe had no face. This was like the other culvert murders but not at all like the dead woman on the bank. Yet it must have been the same maniac who had done them both.

And, he, Alan Moravec, had the killer on tape.

"Hey, Mister," Alan said thickly through the bitter crud in his mouth. He said it completely straight, without humor. "You're an asshole."

He heard a sound. Soft needles and grass being scraped. He shrieked and turned around quickly with the camcorder, sure that the murderer was creeping up behind him.

There was no one. And the large woman's body was gone.

Chapter Eleven

Arcan cleaned up his house, nitpicking for dust and shards of glass, either shooting dark looks at the ghosts or glancing away sharply so he wouldn't have to see them. Trying to find any excuse not to go out and look for another job. Monday morning would be soon enough to have to demean himself before what might be women in charge of hiring. He could not, would not smile at them. It didn't matter that deep down he knew they weren't to blame. He still had too much contempt to swallow. And lately it had become really difficult again to control that mindless hatred, to keep his creatures caged.

Arcan frittered away the day, and had similar designs on the night. He was determined not to get drunk or high. There was no protection to be had in armor created from such substances. He didn't feel like zoning out in front of the TV. Too much of it was devoted to medusas with cleavage. Pretty soon the indecent jokes and matriarchal propaganda brought out either his rage or the fever.

111

He ended up retiring to the spare bedroom. This single place hadn't been damaged a bit during the violent revel of the night before. Not even drunken and doped would Arcan profane this area where Harry had slept during his infrequent visits. Arcan's animals didn't dare enter to shred and shit here. Not because the cat/wolf/ghoul honored Harry. They'd been afraid of him.

Or was it more accurate to say they'd been in awe of Arcan's brother?

Arcan sat on the bed awhile before finally leaning forward to open the top drawer of the dresser. He lifted out the first of two Polaroid's. He hadn't looked at either of these in almost a year. He held the first picture up and squinted at the old photo of Harry, snapped by some other grunt in Southeast Asia.

Harry smiled through layers of black and gray jungle foliage, as if leering through the levels of a camouflaged self. He was gripping some high tech baby-burning weapon in both hands. Acidic sunlight flared off his teeth and dog tags.

There was a peculiar optical illusion in the picture. The way the tropical trees lifted their branches made it seem as if Harry had several pairs of extra limbs. Dancing arms gestured like some Hindu diety of bone bracelets. Centuries before, Indians had brought their gods into the region, hadn't they? Shiva had come pretty far east to be worshipped in the rice paddies and wet jungles.

Shadows from the leaves slid across PFC Harold Tyler's eyes. As if he'd outlined them with kohl.

This brought back a memory. It had happened just after Deborah's funeral . . .

The old man wasn't very pleasant when Harry showed up on the doorstep with Arcan in tow. Lucas was less friendly—if that was possible—after he'd reluctantly let his sons in. He allowed them to sit in cane back chairs, not six feet from where his young mistress curled up on the couch.

And then Harry had the audacity to ask him to take care of little brother Arcan.

Lucas's face turned red across the scarred bridge of his nose.

"He needs you. Arcan's still a minor," Harry explained.

"He has you. You're back from Nam. You take care of him," Lucas protested, fidgeting visibly in the presence of his children.

"I'm being transferred to Okinawa for two years. I can't take him with me. Believe me, I wish I could. Arcan would love the orient."

Lucas snorted. "Delphina wouldn't like it. And I wouldn't feel secure with him in my house. He's got his mother's blood in him. I see it crawling in his face."

The long-haired girl regarded them contemptuously with a sidelong glance. Harry stood up from the chair. He strode over to the sofa. She spread languidly, sly legs folded under her, arms draped across the padded velvet. She looked up coolly as Harry turned his broad back to his father.

Harry growled. "Leave here, bitch. And don't come back."

Except he didn't say it in English, did he?

Yet somehow Delphina understood him very well, yes.

Harry reached down swiftly and snatched her up by both conical breasts. He lifted her right off the sofa by them. The breasts appeared to stretch, blooming elastically out of their natural roundness. He didn't pay an ounce of attention as his father shouted, "Hey!"

(But Lucas didn't come forward an inch to physically restrain his son. The red across his nose spread to both cheeks like a gin blossom, then up to cover his forehead.)

Harry dropped her back to the couch. She screamed painfully, clutching the bruised bosom. She quickly unraveled from the cushions and fled the room sobbing. They could hear her grabbing for things in the bedroom, flinging open drawers from the dresser, banging open the closet. Then she returned, lugging an overstuffed suitcase. She hurried past Harry without looking up at him, shot a whimpering glance at Lucas, and stumbled out of the house, slamming the door behind her.

There was a crystal silence in the room for a moment. Then Harry marched up to Lucas. He was a good foot taller than the aging professor as he glared down at him.

"And what do you see in *my* face?" the soldier demanded to know.

Arcan watched, spellbound in his own stiff chair. He looked from his brother to their father.

No, it most certainly wasn't English Harry was speaking. It was a mixture of raspy files and birdsong. It was a language you heard on the evening news when a correspondent interviewed one of the small yellow people as somebody else translated beneath a waterfall and the avalanching artillery.

Arcan could understand him, that was what was so strange.

Stranger still, Lucas knew what his son was saying. The old man shuddered until his shoulders and knees creaked. He saw Harry's mouth split almost all the way back to pointed ears. The teeth glittered like the sharp points of a whole skyful of suiciding stars.

It didn't resemble anything that Lucas Tyler remembered of Deborah, back in the beginning of their odd, doomed relationship. Back when he'd actually found her sexual transmogrifications (transmongrelfications) to be bewitchingly beastly. Then fucking her made it possible to break the standard taboos of screwing outside one's own species, while still remaining within the sanctified boundaries of legal matrimony.

It wasn't anything Lucas could recall of the inevitable end of their marriage when the mere sight and stench of

Deborah made him feel unclean, made him feel as if he'd lain with a freak. (Which he had.)

How did those shepherds in the fields, cornholing their sheep, *sleep* at night after such monstrous sins? How did those natives in the jungles who buggered diseased monkeys then proceed to *live* with themselves, knowing they'd been partners in such perversity? Lucas had wondered these things after a few years and after a few of her hybrid mongrel gets squirmed in their cradles. Then and only then did Lucas decide it was high time to get moralistic.

—And only commit adultery which must be a lesser sin than bestiality any day.

"I see the same old hell," Lucas retorted, taking a couple of blanching steps backward.

"Not quite the same old hell. I didn't get this from Mother," Harry told him. "I got it from a Cambodian hermaphrodite."

Arcan noticed that Harry got a faraway look in his eyes, haunted. And had they just changed color or did a shadow only filter out the blue, causing the pupils to go black?

"It was part man/part woman/part fox/part night terror. Some other guys in my unit found it hiding in a tumbledown palace or temple or something the locals called Nagas Wat. They dragged it out and shouted at me, 'Hey, Tyler! We know you like some strange knotholes but we bet you a month's pay you won't fuck this moi!' "

Arcan leaned forward in his chair, aware that his animals were stirring in the dens they kept in his solar plexis, anus and scrotum. The red in Lucas's face flowed down his scarred neck, disappearing under the collar of his button-down shirt.

Harry wiped a sheen of drool from his mouth as he continued. "So naturally I had to do it. I had to fuck this Khmer. Let me tell you, it was weird. Two of the grunts held it down so I could mount up. There I was, my dick in its pussy and my hands on its tits. Its own little yellow cock and balls wriggled between us. It bared those betel-black teeth at me defiantly, shouting curses. I slogged in and out but I couldn't come. I was so grossed out, I was going limp. But it did. It came right in my face when I sat up on top of it, like some poisonous jungle mushroom. I passed out from the stink."

"I don't really want to hear any more of this. Shut up. I'm ordering you to shut up about this in my house," Lucas said, barely parting his tight lips to squeeze the words through.

But Harry would not be stopped. Nor would he be ordered by a man who had abandoned his family, and who treated his sons as if they were infected pit bulls.

"When I came to," Harry went on, his lids fluttering a brief show of the whites of his eyes, "some of the guys had skinned the gook alive. They'd hung the long empty piece of it in a mango tree. It was night and when the lopsided moon rose and shined on it, that piece climbed down from the branches. It scuttled off, boneless arms and legs dancing!"

Arcan was still able to feel the concussion of air where the girl had slammed the front door shut. He stared absently at his hand, surprised suddenly to see the fistful of hair he'd grabbed as Delphina rushed past. He'd pulled some out by the roots as it floated by, not even wincing as she shrieked. It was only a couple dozen strands, a yard long and as pale as that moonlight which must have animated the hermaphrodite's flayed pelt. There was blood on the roots from Delphina's scalp. Arcan brought this to his nostrils and sniffed, curiously excited. The animals inside scurried to press behind his nose for the scent. It smelled like his father. It must ultimately have come from Lucas since Arcan doubted that the girl had any blood of her own. All the blood possessed by Liliths was purloined, right? And he'd just set these few drops free.

Arcan smiled and stuffed the strands of hair into his jean's pocket.

"You *will* take your son," Harry commanded in a voice not to be denied. "It won't have to be for long. He'll be 18 soon enough and won't need your cowardice."

Arcan frowned. He didn't want to live with Lucas. Not for a year, not even for a day. He wanted to go with Harry to Okinawa.

The cat ran circles inside him. *Yes! Lots of flesh sold cheap in the far east. You can buy little girls, exotic fetuses in cinnamon oil—no questions asked!*

The wolf licked its balls in anticipation. *Maybe later they'll transfer us to Germany. Wolves in the Black Forest! Soft fraulein clits and kinderchild sausage underbellies. We'll need to eat soon after hunting in the orient. Hungry again after just an hour!*

The ghoul groaned huskily, massaging the activating penis from the inside, masturbating thoughtfully. *Could we visit Hanover if we go to Germany? Where Herr Haarmann buggered and then ate all those boys? Is everything better on a Ritz, fritz?*

It tried to tempt Arcan to masturbate, too. The ache was unbearable. He crossed his legs and folded his hands in his lap.

Go ahead! You know you want to—smell the blood on that Lilith slut's hair and imagine you yanked it from her crotch . . .

Arcan pulled his hands away. He laced his fingers behind his head, rocking back and forth in the chair.

"I *won't*," Lucas declared, spine to the wall. He was shaking badly, aware of how puny he sounded. "I'll never live with another goddam mutant."

Harry roared and swung back an enormous fist to strike him. He paused, punch in mid-air. Then he leaned forward and pinned the older man with both hands.

Arcan tensed, sitting up uncomfortably straight. He felt a coarse bristling as if hair were growing backward under

117

his skin. He held his breath, wondering what Harry was going to do to Lucas. Yet it was a sickening curiosity, a fascination that had nothing to do with concern for their father's safety.

Harry kissed Lucas, smothering him face to face, sticking his tongue deep into his father's shocked mouth. Lucas gurgled and choked.

Arcan's own heart hammered. He might not be tempted to go to his father's defense but he was still frightened. Had Harry ever been violent like this before going to war?

Harry jerked Lucas around, putting him face down snug against the cool plaster. He ripped down Lucas's gabardines and then unzipped the fly on his own uniform. He wrenched the outflung arm 'til his father's hand could be thrust—however awkwardly—between Harry's legs.

Lucas gasped at what swelled and receded there.

"This is for both women mutants and men mutants, Daddy," the soldier whispered, "since I'm both now."

The labia sweating behind cock and balls, Harry snarled and forced himself up Lucas's anus.

Arcan squeezed his eyes shut, waiting for tears. Tears of shame, delirium or frenzy. But the beasts within compelled him to open those eyes again to watch.

Harry released the old man, letting him fall to the floor.

"This probably won't change you," Harry told Lucas, standing over him. "You don't have the blood lines for it. But I reckon it'll put you off your game for a while."

Harry got Arcan up from the chair. The teenager didn't say anything. He was trying to decide if he was sorry for Lucas, or if this was some sort of penance the old man needed to serve after completely abandoning Arcan to Deborah. Had he imagined that female sex lurking behind his brother's dick?

He must have.

Harry was now obviously all man as he ushered Arcan

through the door. There wasn't a speck of anything foreign visible, nor of anything soft.

Harry next took Arcan over to their Uncle Ted's place. This brother of Deborah's had been at her funeral, slowly tearing a wreath of thorny roses to pieces. Tiny droplets of blood had splattered her coffin as he tossed in the remnants of the petals and leaves.

"Boy needs a place to stay," Harry said once they arrived.

Ted just nodded curtly and stepped aside to let them in.

Uncle Ted was a burly bear of a man with a full beard that totally hid his mouth. Actually it concealed the entire lower half of his face. His bushy eyebrows met between his eyes.

After Harry left. Ted asked the boy, "Your mother fuck you up?"

Arcan nodded.

Ted rolled up his sleeves and held up his arms. There were fingernail scars up and down the flesh in ragged schematics and webs. If there hadn't been so much hair on the face, Arcan might have seen the features ripple. But, then again, he might not have seen a thing.

Deborah's brother told him, "She did me, too."

The boy and his uncle never spoke again. Ted left his nephew alone and Arcan left him alone. Ted died in his sleep on Arcan's 18th birthday, apparently strangling on a dream he couldn't swallow.

Chapter Twelve

Tawne walked through the trees, clothes clutched in her fist. She came to herself as if coming down from a sickening drunk. She stopped and turned about. Soft pine needles made an uneven carpet beneath her bare feet. Land water oozed between her toes.

Where the hell was she?

(in the woods by the river there had been a murder or two murders and everything had been red choking red)

But she couldn't see the headlights from Delia's Lexus nor could she find the Buick.

She'd died and risen, right? She'd died and stood back up again. How much simpler it would have been if she'd had the presence of mind at the time to return to her car. She might be home now, and warm instead of walking naked in the dark. She was wet. It took a few minutes for Tawne to realize that most of the wetness was blood.

There was blood between her legs where she'd lost her hymen to the ugly man. It caked down her thighs in streams mixed with river mud. There was a great deal of it on her chest. She gingerly touched the wound he'd made there so he could drink.

"Wow!" Tawne gasped, preparing to shudder and jump with the pain she fully expected. Such gaping, sucking wounds hurt. It was in their very nature to be excruciating.

There was no pain. The gash had closed itself and the bite marks were now only a rose tattoo. The greatest amount of blood was on her face, spread across her cheek-bones, and matted in her hair. It was a musty rag in her mouth, drying in a solid clot down her throat, the convulsive inches of esophagus, past the trapdoor epiglottis.

And what about her legs? She thought she remembered weight and burning heat and bones through her skin. Yet she was walking just fine, thank you. She looked but there was so much crud already down there that she couldn't be sure if there were even scratches where the femur had exploded through the flesh.

He'd said, "It's a terrible thing, loneliness is."

Tawne knew he didn't mean it as a cruel jest. He meant it because he understood better than anyone the ghastliness of life without beauty in a society that respected nothing less.

Tawne had nodded and actually shed tears of empathy for the ugly man. "I hate it," she told him honestly. "I hate me."

"Do you believe that if you can make others love you, you will love yourself?" he asked, arching caterpillar eyebrows. They knitted together obscenely, performing a twisted unnatural act.

She glanced at Delia's corpse, stuffed into the pipe. "She didn't love you. At least, not for long."

"True," he replied, smiling too widely even for a generous human mouth. The result was deliberately sardonic and rictal. Was he trying to frighten her even more than she already was?

Yes, and to see how committed she was to what must certainly be a desperate course of action.

Tawne was asking for the secrets to his power. How desperate did it get?

Was the ugly man thinking about it? Could he actually be thinking about sharing it with her? Out of pity? Out of sympathy because they were both ugly? He knew what that was like. He had to. If he'd ever been human.

Had ever been? Then what was he now if not human? As if Tawne didn't know.

"She didn't love me for long but her kisses were honey. The moments she was mine were condensed from all of her potential for lifelong devotion. How long does romance usually last? How long does love last?" He sighed melodramatically, and a softer light reflected from his terrible eyes. Tawne saw a brooding poet pining for his Lenore.

He became Edgar Allen Poe. He had a high, white forehead and large obsidian mirrors for eyes. Black, wavy hair and a little mustache. She thought even his style of clothes altered to a frock coat and a fancy cravat. But Tawne couldn't look away from his eyes to be sure.

The ugly man blinked, purposefully, and Poe was gone. As if he'd never really been there—which he hadn't.

He smiled again. "Nothing human lasts." The smile was done without the previous rigor mortis flair. Instead it smacked of irony.

The ugly man bent on his crooked knees, studying her until Tawne felt the weight of each year she'd been alone. His gaze bored into her until she recalled in a rush every aching night in which she'd invented lovers in her head and each morning which brought reality to its unresolved peak. How did he do this? How did he know about her?

He nodded as if he'd stripped her and read her life in an augury's remains. Shining liver and entrails in a bowl.

Something else was there. She understood that if she didn't do this, he'd kill her. This was the bottom line. He

was waiting for her to slip up. She could see it in his re-
pulsive face.

She remembered Delia's head coming up from his lap in
the car. Delia's shudder in the dark as she wiped her
mouth. Delia, always kind to her, mutilated and stuffed
into a pipe not so many feet away. Tawne was faint, sure
her knees would buckle. Then what would he do to her?

"Do you—uh—live forever?" she asked so that the
words would give a focus she could steady herself with.

No! She asked because she wanted to know. That was a
part of the deal, wasn't it? She hadn't come here to rescue
a friend. Although it would have been nice if she could
have saved Delia, Tawne had come to find out what his
power was. She had a chance to do it, didn't she? He was
talking to her as if he might share . . .

He might. It was only a game, wasn't it? It was hard to
tell from the ugly man's face. Every gesture he made, each
expression, was exaggerated. As if he'd learned them
watching bad actors.

He laughed, his pockmarked jaws dropping on their sinewy hinges and creaking. They were a snake's jaws, wide
enough to gulp bunnies down whole.

"You're speaking of the fear of death?" the ugly man
chortled. "A moment ago it was fear of being alone. Of
never being touched. Which is it? OR DON'T YOU
KNOW?"

He spoke the last four words in a sonic boom that drilled
holes in Tawne's head. She slammed both fists to her ears
as her skull throbbed.

He was enjoying himself. This was more than just going
for the kill. It was a kind of sick foreplay. Let me rub your
clit, honey, before I tear it out with my bare hands.

"I was only curious," Tawne blurted. It was a bonus feature of the myth, wasn't it? It was bad enough to be unattractive and alone. Did she have to endure growing old
as well?

Charlee Jacob

The ugly man walked a tight circle around her. Tawne didn't like it when he moved behind her. His movements didn't sound normal. He scuttled. She wanted to spin around to keep an eye on him but she didn't dare move. He was making his decision, that's what he was doing. As Tawne had made hers.

She wanted to win a smile with a look, to have acceptance with a stupefying glance that erased all doubts about her desirability.

There was a poem in that book she kept by her bed. 'Immortal Inamorato'. She didn't mean to say it out loud but she did. "Oh, come to these deserted hips, this outcast breast. Befriend my desolation with your stunned embracing. Blood will be our contract."

No wonder she fancied beast men in dark caves.

He touched her shoulder. His breath sounded like gas escaping from a valve. He was back around to facing her.

"They like to say we're all formed in God's image. You seem to be made in the image of Thoth's animal. Do you know what that is?"

Tawne blushed from having said the poem aloud. Maybe he hadn't noticed. Nothing spoke truer about Tawne inside and she didn't want him to know. There was a prose pain in everyone that ought to remain private.

Tawne shook her head. "No, what is it?"

"Thoth is an Egyptian deity with the head of an Ibis. But his animal is a dog-headed ape," the ugly man replied.

She closed her eyes. Derision she could get from any quarter. Why was she putting up with this? Wring his neck and be done with it. Get revenge for Delia. *Escape if you can.*

(How did one strangle an elemental like him?)

Or just escape, she thought. Run. Put this violence as far away as you can. Delia's dead but you don't have to die with her. You weren't that close.

"I seem to be cast as a gremlin. Only the beautiful would

invent an idea like it. I suppose it makes them feel holy but they're really just congratulating themselves, while putting down the rest of the animal kingdom," he said.

Tawne didn't see him as a gremlin.

She opened her eyes and shrugged. "I wouldn't know. I'm not sure I've ever felt holy. Not past a few thrilling moments in an evangelist's tent when I was 12. I expected to turn into a Madonna on the spot. I was very disappointed."

His eyes narrowed until she thought she'd done something wrong.

"If you would have my power to make those you would possess see you as an angel—as a Madonna if you want— then get undressed and submit to me. Blood will be our contract."

Tawne jumped when he said this, an unpleasant jolt of current running along her body. He'd heard her. And it was time.

But this wasn't what she'd imagined. And what had she thought it would be? A gentle bite on the throat and instant karma? She would be transformed into a sex kitten bride of Dracula, devoid of half her weight in the I Lost A Hundred Pounds In One Night On The Undead Diet?

The supernatural in that book of poetry were all beautiful in one way or another. They had an allure that made death seem easy—less stockyard killing floor. Was it because the words added passion to an otherwise deteriorating condition?

(But he was saying *yes*, wasn't he?)

Her mind reeled at the idea of re-creating herself into slender night and voluptuous moon.

And there was a moon overhead as death transformed everyone. For most this meant rot. For her, Tawne would be able to choose her transformation. All it took were a few moments of the distasteful act of sleeping with the coyote man.

Tawne nervously pulled her T-shirt over her head. She unfastened her bra self-consciously, releasing the solemn pink-capped mountains of her breasts to the chilly air.

She hadn't really expected him to agree to this. She'd thought she'd be rejected. As always.

The ugly man also began undressing. His body was covered with tough hair, curly as spring wire. Much of it coiled from the large moles which spotted his scrawny frame like septic patches on a leopard with radiation sickness. His testicles were pimpled and flaccid, grossly uneven. The penis was erect but miserable. Tawne's thumb was bigger and better shaped. This dick looked like a poisonous mushroom.

He gestured for her to lie down on the river bank after she dropped her jeans onto the T-shirt. The mud was a shock to her buttocks, ice along her spine. She let the back of her down in it with the greatest reluctance.

The ugly man knelt and yanked her legs apart, stronger than he looked. *See?* she thought toward Delia's corpse in the pipe, *I couldn't have avenged you anyway and then neither of us would have had anything.*

His loathsome touch froze her very neurons. This, with Delia's body not 20 feet away. This was surely how Tawne must end up, too. Logic, girl! she thought with the pain of it pounding in her head. He was luring her with a lie, taking advantage of her desire to—what?—either do what he did or simply buy time for herself?

Could she really take him if she tried? Her hands were as wide as his whole head. She could take his skull and squeeze it to make the coyote howl.

With him there holding her legs apart that badly wanted to snap shut and be sealed against his greasy harm, she suddenly wanted to fight for her life.

Delia's torso and face were mangled. Yet Tawne had watched him use no weapons as he'd brought his nails down in those swipes that defied space and time. She expected sound to stop except for the river. She screamed just so she could hear a noise and prove to herself that this physical law had not been overturned here as she took what might be her turn at grisly refashioning.

"Look at me and *love*!" he commanded.

She looked. The ugly man's hair softened and became golden like Carl's. His cataracts flashed into indigo and his body muscled. The acne scars were gone as were the moles and the insectile-feeler hairs. He was young and vital, and his erection was the one from her dreams.

Then Tawne loved him. *Yes*, gasped in an epiphany of desire and worship. She thrust her hips up to meet his. The hot spear of her first real orgasm made her scream. She didn't even mind when his kisses on her breasts became sharp. Nor when he jerked her legs up to stretch over his shoulders, and she was sure something split in two directions. It brought him deeper inside her. And the pain that came with it was just another notch upward on the Richter Scale of pleasure.

Tawne set her clothes down and waded into the river to wash herself. Water moccasins glided nearby. Their smooth round tubes of flesh were caresses, not unlike his were at first. None of them bit her. They raised their heads out of the river and opened their cotton mouths only to snap at bugs and at the blood which came off her. Tawne rinsed her mouth and spat out the gore that the ugly man had vomited into her. It curdled as it cooled. The snakes raced for gobs of plasmic chutney until the water churned around her.

Feels like a Jacuzzi of the damned, she thought absently.

Tawne examined herself for changes as she dressed.

Am I dead?

Her body was still mostly firm along the arms and legs. It was a weight lifter's but not the kind that made the cover of Glossy Pecs Monthly. She was more like a smaller version of a sumo wrestler—smaller only because she didn't weigh in at 400 pounds.

There had been no alteration in her shape. Her hips were wide, lunar breasts pale in the moonlight. But no more than before. She spread her hands. There was no webbing between the fingers. There were no ruby talons, no bird-of-prey grace. They were as huge as ever.

She felt along her teeth. Flat in the molars and even at the front. An omnivore's basic choppers. Maybe they changed if she became angry or was threatened or when she got hungry. They would slide out of hiding like switchblades.

Was it a hormone-induced transformation?

Or saliva-induced. Hunger made the mouth water and then she'd have fangs and claws. But hers would be lovely, like a cat's. Not like the coyote man's. She would will it to be so.

Tawne had actually fed for the first time—her own blood back to herself—as he spewed it with his blood, saliva and bile. What secrets were there in these secretions?

She rubbed herself but felt no finer flesh. She touched the angles and hollows of her face and detected nothing more elegant than what she'd had before.

He'd pulled back from her, stinking bloody lumps and acids drooling from his mouth, and he was the ugly man again. He let her broken legs drop but somehow kept her from passing out from the pain. His body was as cold as the mud underneath her and just as clammy. The huge, throbbing blowtorch muscle she'd been riding into hysteria reverted to an icy diddling finger no sexier than if he'd stuck a grubworm between her legs. Or a leech. She wasn't even being fucked by a coyote man. She was being fucked by a sickly maggot.

Suddenly Tawne saw through him as his face and hunched body seemed to disappear into flashes of starlight. They swam together to make a single white diamond.

Delia stood over her sorrowfully. She wore a veil and gown of scarves. Tawne saw that these were merely the bloodless folds of Delia's wounds, thin and dry as tissue paper. They rustled as Delia said, "Oh, Tawne! I hope you're not making a mistake. It's so very hard to be happy."

Then even this faded and Tawne drifted to sleep or to death, hearing only the river like whispers in a churchyard.

"Am I dead?" she asked out loud, seeing nothing about her body that was either re-made or definitely murdered.

She held up her hand but didn't see moonlight passing through it. She shut her eyes and concentrated but felt no shift. No leathery wings sprouted so she could fly away, guided by radar into the night.

A real coyote peered at her suspiciously from the other side of the river. There were several of them, feral eyes glinting. They didn't recognize her so obviously she hadn't become a coyote woman. (Was this a relief?)

"Phooey." Tawne sulked and began walking back to where she hoped to find a road. "I'm not dead."

She was cold. She wanted to go home, slip on her flannel peejays, and get warm with her book. The creatures in love there were more comforting, held out more hope in amorous grue than did an icky jump by an oversexed maggot-dick.

"I guess I should be glad he didn't kill me," Tawne mumbled.

But she did feel cheated.

She stumbled through the woods as if only learning to walk. When she fell over a body on its back in a bed of pine needles, Tawne cursed and rolled off. She turned to see what it was. Some animal perhaps.

"Well, hello," she said. "How come you don't have a face?"

She looked closer at the gaping wound. The neck was a ragged tree stump.

She added, "How come you don't have a head?"

There were burns around it and the smell of gunpowder. She followed the lines to the shoulders, the chest and out-ward to the arms. To the rifle clutched in one hand flung at an almost 90-degree angle from the body.

"I know you," Tawne whispered. "Sort of."

It was the hunter she'd seen earlier. The one she'd been sure was out there to commit suicide.

He'd done that all right.

"I knew it," she said with a whistle through her teeth.

The scent of his cold blood itched in her nostrils. She was surprised she didn't want to get down and lap some of it up.

But she wasn't dead, remember?

Tawne thought she heard a sob. Saw a figure lurking in the trees. It almost made her jump, thinking it was the ugly man coming after her again. But she knew it wasn't. An instinct told her it was only the hunter's soul. And it wasn't sobbing. It was slavering.

In the bushes a small east Texas deer moved, and he went after it. Maybe that's what suicides did.

The deer tried to bound from the bushes. The spirit caught it with both arms but there was no head to bite down with. The deer escaped. Tawne was transfixed, never having seen a ghost before.

(Then what was Delia standing over her? A dream. Just as the act of having her legs stretched to make her cunt more accessible had been a dream. And having her breasts yanked apart and her chest ripped so her heart could be gobbled . . . nothing but a dream.)

Tawne wondered if she should cover the body. She hadn't done anything for Delia's body but she'd wandered away from the site in a trance.

She looked down and felt nothing. It was another casual violence and remote from her. Another senseless act that didn't touch her, *couldn't* touch her.

But she'd felt it at the time she'd been chasing Delia and had seen this hunter traipsing through the trees. The fact he was going to kill himself had been clear enough to her. Those in despair knew one another.

Those in despair died by their own hands or, failing to do it, thus engineered situations so others would do the deed for them.

Tawne had fucked up both ways. She wasn't dead by her own attempts and the ugly man hadn't murdered her either.

No, he left me alive. Meaner that way.

She left the hunter's body and the weeping spirit without a head. She made her way to a road. After following several dirt ones, she eventually had her feet on a paved one. She never did find the one the Buick was parked on. The battery was probably dead anyway because she'd left the headlights blazing. Same with Delia's Lexus.

The asphalt was pitch black going between the trees. She had the sensation of walking over a ribbon of starless space. However, the trees were strangely luminous, and it helped give her some sense of direction.

A car was speeding toward her. Its lights were blinding. She stepped to the shoulder and waved at it.

"Okay, let's see if this works. Not that I actually think anything will happen but maybe they'll find me gorgeous."

She could hear their radio hammering out gyrating bass and percussion to Ax'l Rose's throaty vocals. It streamed from the windows in purple smoke. The car stopped and three drunken boys peered at her over the tops of beer cans.

"Yeah?" asked the driver, a young James Dean look-alike.

Tawne smiled and tried to pose prettily, hoping it would take. She gave a helpless flutter and felt stupid.

"I've had some car trouble. Could you give me a lift?"

Shouldn't she feel something if this was working?

"Wait for the next car. Maybe they can harness you up

131

and have you tow them into town!" the driver smirked, then floored the accelerator and left Tawne shielding her face from flying gravel.

She hated their laughter. It trailed between clashes of loud metal.

"They didn't see Michelle Pfeiffer, that's for sure," she told herself bitterly.

It was Friday night, and the only people out by the river were drunken kids and drunken kids on dates. It was going to be a long walk home.

Tawne heard the distant highway as she'd been able to hear the river. She might make it there in half an hour if she moved briskly. From the highway, it was at least 20 minutes by car to her brownstone. It had taken 15 minutes to follow Delia's car from Shorecross Mall to the river exit. Unless some trucker took pity on her, she would definitely walk all night.

I went through it for nothing. All that groping and insult from his nasty body, the blood and puke. He's laughing his head off wherever he is. Laughing at both Delia and me.

Even ugly men laugh at ugly women like me.

What went wrong? Where was the power she'd been promised in exchange for her degradation?

His terrible eyes.

Another car was coming. Tawne stepped back into shadows. She thought of oblivion. It would be simple to throw herself under its wheels when it came close enough.

"Yeah, step back," she told herself. "Barely let him see you. This time, make eye contact."

That was what the ugly man did.

She stuck out her hand and waved. A slashing appendage of her heavy red hair swung in the air as Tawne tossed it back across her shoulder.

It was a patrol car. She'd seen one earlier and wondered if this could be the same one.

If I'd flagged him down then, Delia might still be alive.

Bullshit.

If I'd flagged him down then, he'd be dead, too.

Tawne almost laughed, sickly and full of regret. And I'd still have my virginity, she thought. And we all know how much I prized that.

The officer rolled down his window.

"Trouble, ma'm?"

She leaned forward enough to put a bit of his light on her face. "Yeah, I've had some trouble. I'm stranded."

She smiled and widened her eyes. His sleepy ones locked with hers. This time Tawne felt an electric surge, as if she were directing the ends of exposed wires into him. As if she were the bare wires herself. She almost expected him to twitch and his hair fry. Fireballs would shoot out his nostrils like they had on that killer she'd seen go to the chair on the TV. This didn't happen.

Think of someone beautiful, slim, melt-in-his-mouth.

Tawne did and the cop smiled back. His face grew slack around the grin like a man opening a centerfold as all but a very small part of him went out of focus.

She stepped from the shadows and the car's headlights bathed her in Shalimar.

"Could you possibly give me a lift?" she said, thinking of the dulcimer voices of other women. Of a woman like Delia, all of chimes and breaths.

"Why, young lady, that's exactly what my job is."

He nodded eagerly and Tawne thought, *Eureka!*

Her head warned her, no . . . don't give in to small victories. Keep your eyes on him.

Tawne moved carefully in front of the patrol car, practically leaning on the hood to get to the passenger side. She'd seen the ugly man do this when getting into Delia's car. At the time it had looked weird. It felt weird now. It had *come hither* written all over it. It might have seemed cheap if it hadn't been necessary.

His eyes on her body were warm fingers, nice on her half-frozen flesh.

"Did you have car trouble?" he asked, fumbling with the steering wheel and the shift because he didn't want to waste a second of getting to look at her for mere mechanical necessities.

Tawne flushed, surprised at this adoration. *Please, don't ever let it end.* She blushed and almost looked away.

No! Don't look away!

"Actually I was with my date. We were supposed to go to a dinner theater but he drove here instead. I punched him in the nose and he kicked me out of the car." Tawne chuckled, figuring this was better than the truth. She didn't want him to take her to the Buick. The battery must be dead by now anyway. And if the headlights for the Lexus were—by some miracle—still on, even faintly, he might go to investigate.

But shouldn't she do something for Delia? Was Tawne just going to leave her like that, butchered and crammed into that narrow pipe? It was such a cold night. Who was to say that the dead didn't feel the chill. (The dead chased deer . . . at least the ones dead by suicide did.)

Delia had been kind to her. She'd cared. Didn't Tawne care?

And what about the hunter? That wasn't a personal concern. He'd received what he'd come for. But Delia hadn't wanted to die.

Oh, and how did Tawne know? Maybe the only people the ugly man could attract were those who wanted to die.

The patrol car reached the highway in minutes. This cop knew his way around the river.

"Could I buy you a cup of coffee?" he asked.

"Thanks. I could use one." Tawne smiled, beauty radiating from her in roentgens. Perhaps she was finally back to that alchemical process, and the lead made it all the way to gold this time. Sex kitten bride of Dracula.

This Symbiotic Fascination

It was hairy as he drove trying to look at her. The patrol car weaved dangerously from one lane to another. Three times they almost hit a concrete divider between the fore and aft sections of the road. He'd jerk the wheel at the last moment, take his eyes from her for nanoseconds, put them back on course, then look at her with puzzlement. Seeing her—what?—as she was? But it was only for a scattered few breaths until she'd lock the image on him again.

It was hazardous to put someone in a dream. No wonder the ugly man had driven when he picked up Delia. The patrol car headed for the concrete, then veered for the hump that would take them spinning off the highway altogether. Tawne tensed, her fingers gripping the seat, still smiling that vacuous beauty contestant smile as her teeth chattered.

Somehow they made it to a roadside diner called Swan's. He parked, got out, and went to open the door for her. He gave her his arm to escort her in.

"Thank you, Officer," she purred, fighting off the urge to kiss the ground.

"Rich," he corrected her.

"Thank you, Rich," Tawne said. "I'm Vicki."

He led her into Swan's and they took a booth near the door. The place was nearly full and none of the back ones were available. He had a back booth look in his eyes, which was close enough to bedroom eyes for her. He sat down opposite Tawne and took her hand. Their knees touched under the table, sending a blast of heat up Tawne's thighs, settling in her vagina in a combination of ache and sizzle. His gaze never wavered. Even when the old waitress came up and slapped him on the back.

"Hey there, Rich!"

Her name tag identified her as ELMA. Her crepe sole shoes sounded like mating gibbons.

When he didn't respond to her hail, the waitress

135

frowned and added, " "Didn't expect you for at least 'nother hour."

Rich winked at Tawne. "Coffee, El."

The waitress raised her eyebrows when Rich didn't look up to acknowledge her. She glanced at Tawne and then back at him.

Plain as a brown paper sack, was what Tawne knew the old lady was thinking as she stiffly asked, "You, honey? Coffee?"

Tawne's control rippled slightly as she glanced at the old lady. She quickly brought her eyes back to Rich's face. "Yes, please."

Peripherally she saw that everyone in the diner was watching.

Rich is known here. Oh, brother. And I know what they think. What's a guy like him doing make puppy faces at a gorilla like her?

Shit, maybe he had a girlfriend. Fuck, maybe he was married and they knew he didn't mess around. Besides his being quite good-looking, which Tawne wasn't, they could tell that she was at least a decade older than he was.

And her clothes were a rumpled mess, and her hair might still have traces of blood and mud in it, and her breath had to stink . . . from what the ugly man had put into it earlier. A beetle crawled out from under the edge of her sleeve. Tawne gulped in embarrassment as it walked across her arm.

Tawne couldn't put this number on all of them, could she?

She brushed off the beetle with an impatient swipe of her hand as Elma returned with a pot. The waitress turned over the cups that were already on the table and leaned forward to pour, deliberately creasing the space between them with her humpbacked figure. Rich leaned away to keep smiling at Tawne as she desperately did the same to keep her eyes locked with his. It was ridiculous.

Elma grunted and waved a hand in front of the cop's face. She croaked, "So who's your friend here, Rich?"

All the faces in the diner watched. People perched on their seats and craned their necks. In the distance Tawne could hear *rode hard and put away wet . . .*

The cop's eyes fluttered as Elma broke the test pattern a little. He seemed confused.

"Uh, Vicki," Tawne told her irritably. "Vicki Frazier."

Elma stared hard at her.

A voice way in the back said: *could pull a plow six ways from Sunday.*

The cook came out of the kitchen and stood at the counter scratching his oily scalp.

A trucker in a down vest was sitting at the counter munching a rare cheeseburger. He sputtered flecks of mustard and blood as he eyed Tawne suspiciously.

Tawne fidgeted. This was horrible. No wonder the ugly man took his women out to the boons. To someplace completely private where he only needed to focus on one person.

Apparently one was all the power could manage.

A man in a Rangers baseball cap called from a rear booth, "Hey, Rich! How's the kid?"

"Huh?" was all the cop could say as he sighed.

"The baby, Rich. You and the missus name him yet?" a petite, frizzy blonde with the man in the cap asked tartly.

So he *was* married. And a new father. Everyone there knew him.

"Oh, yeah, right." Rich nodded vacantly and twinkled his eyes at Tawne.

She shivered, maintaining the eye to eye. The rolling, static charge hummed from her to him. She was terrified. Now what? This was definitely not going as she'd expected. Not that she'd known what to expect.

She'd expected to spend some time finding out what it was like to be treated with admiration. To be seen as desirable. All the trite romantic notions that had always escaped her. Oh, for shallow tenderness and mundane physical attraction.

The trucker with the rare cheeseburger pressed. "So what'd you name him?"

Rich twittered. "Vicki."

"What?"

Several people stood up from their tables.

An ice cube that had spontaneously generated in Tawne's gut took on mass. She wanted to ask him to please take her home now. This was all wrong. Rich was staring at her like a lovestruck adolescent, and she dared not look away. What was in her book? (trapped by you/ I become stone/ debauch my granite belly/ with an indecent fandom/ take the pictures I must pose for)

Damn, there was no poetry in this shit. It was hard work and for what?

Tawne's eyes were going to petrify in their sockets. She feared to even blink.

The radio on Rich's hip began to squawk.

Several folks, including the man in the baseball cap and Elma, walked up to their booth. Tawne's hackles rose without sweat. She couldn't believe she wasn't perspiring this out. For all her mounting discomfort, there was no heat. Not even her bulging eyes burned. They stung as if she faced a strong winter wind but there was no burning and there were no tears.

Just the ice in her gut, frost up and down her body. It moved sluggishly through her veins, through the arteries in glaciers.

"Somethin' ain't right about that gal," the waitress muttered to the others.

"Not exactly his type, is she?" whispered the fuzzy blonde.

"His Caroline's such a looker, too," said the trucker.

"Why would Rich go for a dog like that? Especially one what looks like it needs a flea dip."

Tawne felt sick.

"Hey, Rich." The cook brought a greasy hand down heavily on the cop's shoulder. "Bud? You okay?"

The radio squeeped and farted.

"Answer your dispatcher, Richaroo," Elma spoke to him as she glowered at Tawne with something more than just moral indignation at her homewrecking.

"What are you doin' out with this baboon, honey?" asked the fuzzy blonde. "You with a pretty wife and a bitty baby at home?"

Rich sighed and only looked at Tawne, the toes of his feet nudging hers under the table. He was in the zone if anyone alive had ever been. He acted as if he was on drugs: the opium of love, absinthe of passion. The older narcotics sounded better than the crack cocaine of ardor.

The big man in the Rangers cap shouldered the others aside. "Fuck this," he growled, jerking the cop out of the booth. "I don't know what's goin' on but will you look at us, dammit, Rich?"

The man was as loose as a ragdoll in his hands. He held the cop by his shoulders and gently shook him, raising him to his tiptoes.

The cook glared at Tawne, his face shiny and red. "Just who the hell are you, lady?"

Rich slumped in the big man's hands, groaned, and moved his head from left to right.

Tawne slid out of the booth. The contact was broken but what difference did that make now? This wasn't going as she would have dreamed it. Electricity crackled away. The cop's radio sputtered.

"Rich, you all right?" the frizzy blonde shouted in his face.

He moaned. "Where am I?"

Elma snatched at Tawne's T-shirt. "What'd you do to him?"

Tawne put one large hand on the old lady's wrist to pluck her off. There were snaps and the waitress screamed. Tawne looked down as the bone ends popped through the wizened skin with a spray of scarlet, reminding her of her own legs breaking earlier that night. Why, she'd barely touched her. She'd only meant to disengage the old biddy.

"Hey!" The cook grabbed Tawne by her hair, twisting it. He raised his fist to hit her but she literally beat him to the punch.

"Ow!" She snarled as she struck him. She felt the mass of bone and cartilage pulp. She drew her dripping hand back and watched him crumple. His nose had disappeared with his cheekbones into the cavity her knuckles made. His jaw on the right side hung slack.

The blonde shrieked. Tawne pushed people aside and ran for the door. The trucker pulled Rich's service revolver from its holster as the man in the Rangers cap held the cop up.

He fired as the other patrons in the diner yelled and dove under the tables. Tawne screamed, too, twice as weight slammed her shoulder and back, nearly knocking her onto her face. She kept on her feet, racing through the parking lot and beyond its measly lights into the darkness. There had been no heat or real pain. Only the sensation of force at the end of velocity. She was well into the night before she realized she'd been shot.

In a ditch, shaking from the cold, fingering what looked like slime when the moon was obscured by clouds and looked like blood when the moon swam free, Tawne probed the edges of the exit wounds in her front. She moved her hand back to touch the smaller entry wounds in her back. She poked her fingers into them and wriggled them around. She tried to hurt, tried to feel mortality creeping up on her. There was ruined meat, the edges of

140

nearby bone, soft slickery organs the deeper she went.

(She'd cried out when the bastard yanked her hair. But it hadn't really hurt. She'd cried out because she thought it would but it didn't.)

The wound in her shoulder was already healing. The one lower down had removed a large chunk of her right lung out the front and was going to take longer.

She pulled and plucked and pinched.

Am I dead? she asked herself again.

Tawne laughed. "Hell yes."

And then she shivered again.

Chapter Thirteen

Alan went back to his car to retrieve a pair of gloves. Were there bugs under his clothes? He hated bugs. Tiny squirmy aliens with the nastiest diets. He couldn't keep still. Either insects had invaded him after he fainted in the grass or his flesh was doing the slam-dunk-scooch. He wanted to climb into the driver's seat, rev the engine for some purely rational manmade mechanical noises to fend off the encroaching shudders with, and drive home to the real world.

No, he couldn't go home. The police might visit. The redneck dogkiller-killers might visit, ready to show him who they thought the real asshole was.

Lynching, a longstanding American tradition.

Alan stared longingly at the half bottle of Chivas Regal on the front seat. He almost took a swig to calm his nerves. He needed a fire to suppress the messages his brain was sending him to jump, shiver and scream. Then the nausea in his belly re-asserted itself and he changed his mind. He backed out of the car, gloves on, fear like an icy hand on his penis.

Alan glanced down. He still hadn't zipped up after stopping to take that leak in the first place. It was goosebumped from the autumn chill and dirty from the plunge Alan took onto his face.

There was also a graphic plop of vomit-oatmeal on it. He cringed, shuddering, not able to help wondering if it was his or . . . Had the ugly little man hovered over him while Alan was unconscious, eyeing the cock with hunger until he drooled out some of that pathogenic slobber he'd given to the big woman? Had he maybe even put that pimpled tongue to it?

Alan made a gagging sound in the back of his throat as he swiped at it with a gloved hand to get it off him. It stuck briefly to the leather palm and he damn near broke his wrist trying to jiggle it off. It splattered into the leaves at his feet. Tiny dark skulls of bugs scattered and Alan jumped onto the hood of his car.

He chattered. "Shit, boy, it ain't as if they spontaneously generated out of a spot of sputum. They were down there and it landed on them. Get a grip on yourself."

He looked down at himself again, grumbling at the pun inherent in this comment. He self-consciously stuffed the wayward dick back into his pants and then battened down the hatches. He'd stumbled on one murder *ex post facto* and witnessed another, all but standing there with it in his hand.

He laughed. "No wonder the big woman's corpse hustled off. She probably saw me standing foreskin-in-the-wind and was afraid I'd be up for a bit of necro."

He slumped. That was about as sick as anything he'd ever said. If it was meant to ease his tension, it failed miserably.

He had another flash of both the ugly man and the lady

with the hole between her tits and the bloody spew on her face bending over him. The bone sticking from her broken leg made a nauseating wet sound as it moved in and out of the ruptured flesh of her thigh in a noise so like sex that it completely unsettled Alan. The ugly man was lowering his face to the reporter's penis while the woman bent to give him a sloppy emetic kiss.

Alan had planned to trudge through the woods to the car where the headlights had illumined the grisly scene. The trees loomed tall in their crazy fainting angles. Those lights were far away through the menacing blackness. Who knew where that creepy little killer had gone?

Looming trees. Lurking psychopaths. Close by. Alan was surprised it wasn't also a dark and stormy night. It didn't go at all with what he'd come to believe was reasonably weird for the kind of news he did. Maybe it was just that different in person. No, it was more than that. He'd seen killings in person. Nothing like this. Those were murders committed by humans. Whatever that ugly fart was, he certainly wasn't human. Not with the way he changed how he looked.

And he was out there somewhere, ready to do a third. Why not, when three was the charm? Out there under the trees that didn't stay upright like trees were supposed to. Where there were all kinds of stinging, itchy, poisonous bugs.

Alan stuck his hand down the front of his shirt and scratched.

It had to have been that gross man—or maybe the rock star shapeshifting hunk with the golden hair—who dragged the big woman's body off while Alan was investigating the one stuffed into the pipe. He was hiding, feeling up her huge, blood-sticky breasts as he waited for Alan to be fool enough to return to the woods. Without a weapon. With only gloves in his hands so he could rummage through the Lexus for evidence without leaving fingerprints. And what good were gloves unless Alan wanted to check the killer's prostate? *Turn your head and upchuck some blood.*

Alan took two baby steps from the road. He smelled rotten pine and oak roots. The stagnant puddles that had bred mosquitoes this past summer now shimmered like ink. They were dead things, reflecting only scum in the headlights from the Buick that blocked the road. He felt those bugs dancing prickly waltzes in his clothes again.

He couldn't go to the river. Down there was the entrance to hell. He'd never believed in such a thing as hell before. It was funny how one encounter could change a person's mind.

Alan went around to the driver's side of his own vehicle and pulled out the tire iron he kept under the seat. Its weight in his hand failed to reassure him. It wasn't enough to make him brave.

What if the second woman's corpse was gone by now? What was the creep doing with them as he waited for Alan? Riding them from one set of chilling hips to the other as he changed from one aspect to another? Did he fondle the end of that broken but fully lubricated bone as it moved in and out of the flesh of the big woman's thigh?

Alan crept back to the Buick. On its front seat was a squarish satchel purse, as utilitarian as purses got. There wasn't a shred of ornamentation on it. He snapped it open and pulled out an equally basic billfold. In it was a driver's license with the large woman's photo on it. The one whose bitten breast had moved like a melon filled with brain-disease-carrying fruit worms. He pulled the license from the clear plastic and pocketed it, though he wasn't exactly sure why.

Then Alan scurried to his own car and made as careful a U-turn as he could manage in the narrow roadway. Black limbs reached from the woods to scratch the paint job. Backing into one particular oak left a dent in his bumper.

He screamed as he rammed it, thinking the ugly man had turned into Godzilla and leapt onto the car, determined to ride it back to the river and hell.

"Is there a place around here I can rent a video recorder?" Alan asked the man at the motel desk as he was handed the keys.

There was no chance he'd risk going back to his apartment. But he couldn't stay at the river either.

The guy grinned with stained false teeth, as if he knew what Moravec would be doing tonight. "Sure, right across the street there's an all-night movie joint. They got a great list of hard core. Real meat-jerkers."

Alan nodded. "Uh, thanks."

He turned away from the clerk's own sour buttermilk smell, rising from his crumpled clothes in curdled wafts. The man stank of stiff gray stains in boxer shorts. The idea of this creep crunching microwave pork rinds with one hand while he beat himself off with the other was enough to put Alan off sex forever. If, that is, what he'd seen out by the river hadn't been enough to do it.

Alan was going across the street for the video recorder and nothing else.

In 15 minutes he was in his room, lugging the rented player and the cassette from his camcorder. He switched on the lights and watched the roaches scatter. He'd also stopped at a convenience store for ginger ale and a bottle of double strength antacid. He tried to avoid seeing the black plastic phone by the lumpy bed, guilt being an emotion he could ill-afford. He knew he should call the police to tell them where there were a couple of mangled corpses by the river. But the bodies might both be gone now and then how would he look? Well, he had the tape as proof of a crime.

He even toyed with an inspiration to call the station. Get back in their good graces by telling them, "I taped it all. I

146

have the Culvert Killer's face on film. Exclusive."

It could make him a hero in the city and make people forget about Red's Stomping Ground.

But what about seeing the killer change? From a pizza-faced twerp into a lion-maned beefcake in front of his eyes? Did that tape, too, or was he just drunk? And if it did tape . . . ?

He would be accused of faking it. Because that couldn't have been real. Alan was in enough deep shit over inciting to riot at the redneck bar. His credibility and reputation were zip.

Could the transformation have made it onto the tape?

It couldn't have; it never happened. It was hallucination brought on by a half bottle of great scotch and under-cooked not-so-great chicken. Not to mention the hefty visual shock of rape and blood.

"That wasn't rape," Alan said to himself. "She was enjoying it. At least she appeared to be when I walked up."

Alan chewed about four chalky antacids and washed them down with the ginger ale. It fizzed toward his stomach.

"It wasn't until her lover started puking down her throat that she changed her mind. That would tend to bring anyone out of their reverie."

Enjoying it. With another woman slaughtered nearby? Enjoying it as a man munched through one breast like it was a moonpie?

Alan hooked the rental into the room's TV. It surprised him to see a color set in a place this seedy and to see one that worked so well. The owner probably had a pipeline into stolen shit. Too bad he didn't also have a connection for industrial strength bug zap.

A roach skittered out from under the bed and raced across the toe of Alan's shoe.

"Damn!" Alan cursed as he stomped it. Then he felt queasy and wiped the bottom of his shoe on the carpet.

147

He dropped the bag from the store over it to hide the mess. He thought of an old joke. That cockroaches in Texas came in two sizes: a foot long and then two feet long after you stepped on them.

He slipped the tape into the machine and sat on the edge of the bed. He worked his hands over his knees until the friction raised the hair along his arms.

"Here goes," he whispered, seeing the two bodies swim into focus. The river moved behind them, reminding him of a dark tide of soldier ants. The kind that stripped everything alive of all the tasty damp stuff: fleshy dollops, glossy innards, leafy snotables.

The ugly man pumped, humped, bending forward, a spineless slug fastening his mouth over her chest wound. He sat up and lifted the woman's legs which snapped. Then he looked at Alan and smiled.

Alan tensed, feeling as if he also had no bones in his back. It had turned to stone.

"Oh, god," Alan said between teeth which were clamped shut.

The man's muscles flexed, tendons erupting on his body. The flesh lost the pimples and the spots curling with bristly havalina hair vanished. A golden mane took the place of the scalp caked with dandruff.

"How about that?" Alan mumbled, amazed it had taped. He hadn't hallucinated it. It hadn't been a result of the scotch. That really was hell by the river.

The eyes flashed from cataract green to cobalt.

And then they went white.

Not like eyes rolling up in a seizure, but the white of light across arctic waste. It was simultaneously blinding and cold.

"I don't remember that." Alan said.

The sides of the man's gloriously transformed head popped. The sound recorded. Horns coiled from the skull in bighorn sheep curls. The tipped ends blossomed into black roses, and red bugs with strange heads that looked like tiny black skulls began to swarm from the petaled centers of these.

"Wait! I don't remember *that* either!"

He hadn't fainted yet so Alan would have seen if it had happened that way.

The attacker bent down to the woman and begun to upchuck the blood he'd swallowed back into her mouth.

The scene pitched to stars overhead. This was when Alan was passing out and the camera tumbled, switching off.

The tape went to fuzz and white noise. End of show. End of nightmare. Alan was sweating. It ran under his collar and welded his shirt to his back. It dripped from his nose, and he tasted its salt on his lips. Was that it? What had the camera picked up that he hadn't seen even as he'd been there, with it going on right in front of his eyes?

There was nothing about the large woman's body that he'd tried to tape after he woke up from his faint. There was nothing about the body of the second woman, stuffed into the pipe. The camera must have been damaged after he dropped it. He'd been afraid of that.

Alan ran it again, mopping his face and hands with the bed's cheap coverlet.

The eyes flashed from green to cobalt. And then to white.

Alan had to squint as it filled the screen like an explosion.

The horns coiled and bloomed black roses. The red bugs with dark skulls swarmed, ran across the horned bridge to the attacker's head, teemed down his face, stripping away flesh to pulsing cords of shiny muscle and highways of vein bundles. They moved voraciously down the body until he was as red as they were. He bent down to vomit. Alan fainted and the camera hit the ground.

The rest was static as Alan really passed out again.

Chapter Fourteen

Arcan put down the first photograph—yellowed and curling at the edges—and picked up the second. He was beginning to crave a cigarette, something with which to scorch his lungs and to occupy the fingers of his free hand as they trembled.

This other picture had been snapped at one of those deep jungle shrines. Arcan figured it was Nagas Wat, the place Harry mentioned long ago, from during the war when his unit got moved from Vietnam to Cambodia. The ancient temple was half-reclaimed by vines and velvety fungus, part ruin/part beautiful in a creepy, eldritch sort of way. Faces emerged in bas relief from black stone. Carved shapes depicted obscene rites.

(Well, obscene by Christian standards. No missionary positions here.)

Arcan remembered what Harry said once, during one of his rare visits home to the states. "What determines if these acts are pornographic? Is it morality? Or is it our lack of divinity which makes us condemn it?"

Arcan had just stared at him, unsure how to respond. He didn't know how he felt about the weird shit that Harry trucked home from the east. It was like this stuff didn't even originate on the same planet. His brother wasn't into the usual tourist trash. There were no smiling fat Buddhas or white elephants or jade belt buckles. It was all old, half-rotted like the interior of an abscessed tooth, all deeply carved.

Just like the walls of this shrine in the second photo. Where creatures both demonically hideous and celestially lovely simultaneously fucked and devoured be-garlanded sacrifices. The victims bore witless drugged smiles—or the vacuous grins of those who reach a kind of nirvana through the torturous orgasms of fatal ordeal. Some devilish chimera-styled deities sported jawed vulvas and ithyphallic tongues, their fantastic bodies almost redundant with genitalia explicit in every finger, every sublime curve and indecent hollow of anatomy, every exotically violent gesture.

Arcan studied the second snapshot, shivering at the graphic nature of the carvings. Recalling Harry's bemused comment as he'd brought home a long rice paper rubbing he'd charcoaled from a colonnade at one such site.

He'd joked, "You are what you eat."

It was intended as a joke, wasn't it?

Arcan thought of the Khmer hermaphrodite ejaculating into his brother's face and was immediately queasy.

(Arcan had come in his own victims' faces and mouths. But none of them had developed inner animals.)

No, the seed had to come from a god. Or from a god/goddess. There was nothing even remotely holy about Arcan.

Every time Harry came back to the states from the orient, he sported something new. Right after returning from his stint in Okinawa it was a set of superfluous nipples. A year or two later there were lumps in his chest, not cancerous, non-malignant bulbs of fat and tissue beneath the nipples. Another time there was a crease in each hand from some additional prophetic line centered in the palms. That had been during the same visit that Harry brought the charcoal rubbing home. He spread his hands for his baby brother to gawk at.

"What are those?" Arcan asked, touching them with wonder. The puckered skin felt weird: semi-electric in the ridges, almost squishily soft. Like some keloid scar tissue slowly dissolving into water.

"Time will tell," Harry replied cryptically.

During the last visit Harry dropped his pants and bent over, dog tags jingling around his neck. He'd been out of the service for years but he still always wore the dog tags, just like other folks never took off their crucifixes.

The nub he'd sprouted on his last trip—a bump at the base of the spine was all it had been then—had grown into a 10-inch tail.

"I roll it up and tape it when I get dressed every morning so it's not a problem in my trousers. Or with customs. But I dread the day when some official jerk decides to search me, thinking I'm smuggling Thai sticks in my butt."

Arcan was slack-jawed.

"Does it hurt?"

Harry carefully wound the tail back and secured it, pulling up his trousers.

"No, but sometimes when I shower, it sings to me," he replied in a hushed voice.

"Really?" Arcan asked, incredulous but knowing Harry would never bullshit him. "What does it sound like?"

"Like a nightingale gargling with a hummingbird's blood."

Harry revealed he'd converted to an eastern religion.

The Tylers had never been a religious family.

No shit.

"Buddhism?" Arcan arched an eyebrow, actually disbelieving his brother for the first time.

Harry chuckled, waving a dismissive hand. "No. I could never get into vegetarianism and contemplating my navel. You know that, bro."

Then he brought out museum shots of statuary.

"Shiva is sometimes depicted as hermaphroditic, yoni and lingham both present. The line between him and Kali sometimes blurs if you go back a few millennia. Was Shiva the Destroyer—Lord of the dance, haunter of cremation grounds, sometimes raving mad—a god, with both male and female aspects? Or was Kali so bloodthirsty that the faithful couldn't believe she didn't have a dick?"

"I suspect this is too deep for me," Arcan had responded.

He was abruptly uncomfortable. His brother *smelled* different. It wasn't any fragrance he could identify as a perfume. Nor was it a scent he could ever remember detecting on any woman he'd trolled. It also definitely wasn't masculine, wasn't *Harry*.

"This is the last time we're ever going to see one another." Harry told him then. "I'm going back to Nagas Wat. I'm going to stay there for good."

Arcan's heart sank. Harry was all the family he had left. He was all the family Arcan ever cared about.

"Why?" Arcan asked.

"I did some raunchy shit as a soldier. Not the least of which was raping that hermaphrodite. Well, that was no human thing but it was an important part of the place. I'm drawn back to that jungle and its people. I can't help it. It's why I keep going over there. I owe something to these folks, Arcan. A person's got to be shriven," Harry explained, his body radically altered from the way it had been at their mother's funeral, over 20 years ago.

Arcan pretended not to know what Harry was talking about. Harry clapped one of those changing hands on his brother's shoulder. Arcan felt the line in the palm's flesh whispering against bone as Harry said, "I know you've done bad things. I know you are doing them. I'm not judging you. I've got no right to. I'm just saying we all have our demons. Some of them—like mine—are of our own making, and others—like yours—aren't. This doesn't mean we don't still owe what we owe. When the time comes to make up for it, remember, Arcan, you've got to return to the source."

Harry stood up.

"I'm going to find salvation. *Atonement*."

He left and it was the last time Arcan heard from him until the second photo arrived in the mail.

This sentence was inked in as a caption to the picture.

I've gone to find atonement.

Along with it was a shred of an item cut from an English/ Kampuchea newspaper.

"Prosperity Comes To Village Near Phnom Kulan."
Best crops harvested since before the war.

Below that was a short blurb.

Members of a group investigating the existence of American POWs report a remote village returning to ancient Khmer customs.

It arrived the day after Arcan sneaked to Carmel Gaines' funeral. He hadn't heard from Harry since. He knew deep in his heart that this was it. He'd never hear from his brother again.

Now Arcan sat in the bedroom, baptized in darkness, only seeing the photograph with the light coming in the doorway from the hall. In the picture were a pair of temple priests in dusty saffron robes. He knew that many Orientals had small noses but these men appeared to have no noses at all—only nostril slits. Their very wide, thin mouths seemed to not have lips. It lent their faces—bisected with long slanted eyes—a serpentine cast. Bowing before this scene was a row of kowtowing peasants, faces respectfully in the dirt.

And what was that blur between the priests?

Dancing between them?

At first glance, could it be a part of the elaborate stone work?

At second glance, was it a twist of tropical light and archway shadow?

A tail swung, a censor smoking with incense at the end. Two pairs of breasts were as round and hard as any apsara's.

A damp womb glittered like a window shaded with testicles and penis. Hands were up, the palms with open mouths in the center.

Dog tags flashed around the neck.

Arcan slipped the photos back into the dresser drawer. He went to bed.

In a dream he had Delia pinned down in the forest. He grunted as he savagely jerked in and out of her. He was stuffing wet leaves down her throat to silence her screams. His animals were in full control, body replete with fangs and claws.

Delia changed.

She was Tawne Delaney from Galway's. Her strong arms came up to encircle his neck. Pendulous breasts rubbed against Arcan's chest. This was oddly arousing and he could feel his dick throbbing, seed about to burst.

Then she became Harry, transformed into some jungle goddess. The wide hips thrust up to his, dog tags jangling like musical instruments. The hands were up, palms melting into the faces of screaming women.

Arcan woke up with a start, jizm spurting out into the sheets. He grabbed his burning cock and then winced with the handful of sticky gloop. He wiped his fingers on the coverlet.

The ghosts were oozing from the walls and the window curtains.

He was out of cigarettes. He'd quit smoking again anyway. There was no use getting up just to light the match and let it burn down to his fingers. That was a paltry penance by anyone's standards.

Arcan sighed, stuck his head under the pillow, resigned to the fever and to listening as the ghostly women sobbed.

Chapter Fifteen

Tawne saw the man with his car pulled off onto the shoulder. He grunted as he worked to change a flat tire.

The man glanced up as Tawne walked up to him. She wasn't really *walking*. She was staggering down the highway. He saw the dark stains and holes in her T-shirt. A scraggly piece of tough bluish lungscrap hung a tendril out of one of the holes, like a shred of luncheon meat a sloppy eater had dropped from their sandwich. The man was a minor tech in the emergency room at the hospital. He knew gunshot wounds when he saw them.

He sprang to his feet at once. "Jesus! Lady?"

The bumper which had been hoisted onto a jack slipped. He jumped, startled as it almost fell. The jack was between notches. It caught on the notch below and the bumper held. He turned back to the injured woman. Her skin was brie-pasty, glowing like a lump of wet chalk in the dark.

He was thinking she must be in shock. He ran toward her, studying her eyes for signs of disorientation.

Charlee Jacob

And then he smiled, smiled . . . when their eyes met. Tawne hadn't even done it intentionally.

To the man, she seemed to float as she came up the road. Electricity was shooting along her back and up her legs, flowing out in a peculiar halo as it surrounded her head. Her hair lifted and spread out in the air.

She was no longer human. He believed very suddenly in goddesses for here was one drifting down to him in the moonlight. She wasn't in jeans and a T-shirt after all. She wore a pale off-the shoulder gown with silver sandals on her tiny feet. Her electric hair was in clouds of platinum.

He wouldn't even question it. He looked into her eyes and not only did he not see the oversized woman with the gunshot wounds he'd first noticed coming up the roadway, but his ability for rationality was lost. This was normal, wasn't it? There used to be a time when gods appeared to mortals pretty often. He'd read this somewhere and it had seemed to be a fable. But this proved it really happened.

Tawne was too weak to appreciate the adoration. Even in the kilowatt clutch she was cold. It was the sort of cold which always made her want to curl up and go into hibernation. Did vampires hibernate? Surely some werebears did. Wereanimals of Thoth did. Lying in a hazy, shifting lump in a cave someplace while a blizzard raged outside and snow drifted in, and a feral bridegroom rumbled alongside to keep her warm. He was a changer also.

She practically fell into the stranger's arms. She whispered hoarsely, "Lay me down and warm me, please."

Words drifted to her out of a complete void and she added without thinking, "Come to these deserted hips, this outcast breast."

She couldn't focus past the idea of getting off her feet and losing the chill. She projected out with desperation, hoping he liked what he saw. Obviously he did.

"Yes, ma'm," he said gratefully as he guided her to the back seat of his car.

This Symbiotic Fascination

She whispered, "Befriend my desolation."

"Whatever you say, Artemis," he replied. Or Diana or Ishtar.

It didn't seem to him as if he was doing anything she didn't want him to do. He began to unfasten the complicated dress, trying to fathom how what looked like a one-piece wrap-around style could unfasten and come off at the hips and legs with yet another part pulling up to reveal her chest. But he managed to get her naked somehow and she wasn't fighting. She was saying *yes, yes, contract, our contract* . . .

"Blood will be our contract," she said.

It didn't seem even passing strange that a goddess should utter such a fanciful thing.

Tawne felt the heat coming off his body but it wasn't a direct contact. It was as if she were trying to warm her hands when the furnace was in another room. This didn't improve much when he unfastened his trousers and entered her, his chest against hers.

Her legs swam around him as he kissed her mouth, her throat, her breasts with their still-raw wounds. At first he tasted an alien, lunar wine. It took a minute or two before he detected the blood and the gunpowder in burns. A flavor of fouled ruin flooded his mouth with sulfur and iron. The scraggly scrap of lung hanging from the hole had come off with the T-shirt but another squeezed out, wriggling like the lazarus of mortified finger-foods. He had just embraced this spot because it was so near the goddess's treasured nipples. He tried to pull back to spit it out. He couldn't see her eyes anymore but he could make out the curve of her jaw. It jutted out and was disfigured with welts that resembled nothing less than an Egyptian cartouche sculpted with the tip of a graverobber's profane digging tool. The nose ran with a gruel the consistency and color of the drainings from a plague bubo.

He screamed as he perceived the hairy belly of the beast

undulating under him. Both breasts had become the heads of animals, skinless but with muscles folded over the straining jaws, veined eyes bulging with the terror only a furious and wounded animal could manifest. He saw the lice in its fur.

Tawne never expected to chew into his shoulder. It had begun as a simple kiss. It was a way to warm her lips from the icy ache inside. His shudders were ecstasy, weren't they? Even as she shook in her own orgasm, letting his grind fill her up.

There was sudden warmth, a release into heat, but she didn't realize until countless swallows later that he hadn't been climaxing. He'd been struggling to free himself.

Eye contact had been broken in the clinch and he was fighting for his life. Her powerful arms encircled him. Her mouth was buried in the hollow of his shoulder. *Letting him fill her up. Contract signed, sealed and delivered.*

He stopped fighting. He slumped onto her as a child falls asleep on his mother's stomach. He was dead. Tawne had killed him.

She tasted gagging salt and metal. She pushed him off her as she hurried to pull her jeans back up and pull the T-shirt over her breasts. There! She was fully dressed again. Didn't that make it cleaner? She wasn't naked anymore so she couldn't have done that.

"My god," Tawne gasped, wiping her mouth hard with the back of her hand. "It's true."

She sobbed but was tearless. She'd never meant to hurt this man. The hunger took over without so much as a pardon me. She hadn't even known it was creeping up on her 'til it pounced.

He'd struggled like a wild man. Had it been so horrible when eye contact was broken, the image faltered and he saw her for what she was? She was overweight but, fuck, she wasn't that bad, was she?

"I feel like a damned rapist," she muttered. "Thanks for the boost to my confidence."

The event seemed like a dream. The moments had no proper sequence. She'd been pressed to another body, legs wrapped and hips thrusting, but it had been a light year of stretching toward distant suns from a point of intense gravity. It swallowed everything and gave no heat or light. She reached out from it only to have its gravity suck her back in. It was cold here and she'd yearned to leave it.

Now she was warm, his hemorrhaged life in her.

She'd had an orgasm while screwing the ugly man in Carl's image. Had she come this time? There had been a quiver. Then there was a staggering seismic shaking. Oblivion followed that.

Annihilation. Ascent and descent. Hell of a ride.

The gravity hole wasn't far from the tunnel with the light at its end. This must be the tunnel that folks with near-death experiences talked about. She'd reached for it, fluttering her hands. She'd reached with her thighs, hoping it would penetrate and impregnate her with human warmth. Finally, she'd reached with her mouth seeking a vulcanizing fusion. This was the stretch that did the trick. She'd swallowed it in flames.

"What have I done?" The sob was a series of hopeless cracks in her voice. Her eyes were dry, gritty. The answer came. *As if you didn't know.*

She squirmed in the back seat as carefully as she could. His body was on the floor and she didn't want to step on him. Then she pulled out his body once she was out herself, dragging it away from the road. She hoped it wouldn't be found too soon.

Tawne finished changing the tire. She looked over her shoulder constantly as the occasional car passed, praying there would be no more white knights. No one who would stop to help a lady and look into her eyes. Or who would see blood.

She drove into the city and parked just far enough that she could walk the rest of the way. She didn't want to park her victim's car anywhere near the brownstone.

Victim. The word had a dull ring in her head. She'd wanted lovers, not casualties.

She was on her block when the sun began coming up. At first it didn't even occur to her that this might be a problem.

After all, she hadn't really believed she'd be able to fascinate people into seeing her as she wanted them to. She hadn't honestly expected to be impervious to gunshots either. She never thought she'd crave and drink blood. (*Victim.*)

So why would she expect the dawn to be a threat?

Tawne's skin didn't burn as the orange rays shifted across the street. Her eyes didn't melt in thermonuclear exorcism. Her bones didn't crumble to dust. Everything was copacetic.

She was almost home when she saw the blood on her hands. It was left over from the stranger, right? She was a messy eater. It came from her wounds which she'd worried and dug into trying to find some pain she could claim for reality. There were speckles of it. She wiped them on her jeans and figured she'd dump her clothes in a good cold water soak as soon as she got into the apartment. Well, the T-shirt was a loss. She'd have to toss it. Holes. Powder burns. But a really good pair of jeans cost too many bucks to throw away when she hadn't been shot below the waist. Hey, she worked for a living.

The blood was back a moment later. It oozed from her pores, forming a connect-a-dot coating. She wiped her hands again. The pattern suppurated and was the same color as the reddest streaks on the eastern horizon.

Tawne's face was wet. She frowned as she touched her cheeks. "What is this shit?"

She peeked under her shirt and noticed for the first time

that her bra wasn't there. It lay in damp leaves and among rotting roots in the woods probably.

Blood ran out of her like sweat.

Tawne began to race the last half a block.

The light came over the low buildings. It spilled down the street, smashing open shadows. She could actually see their pieces fly in shrapnel, bits of dark bone and funeral threads. They even made a noise as they broke. They sounded precisely the way her blood did when it splashed the concrete.

Blood sluiced as Tawne fled, spattering around her in rain. She ran up the brownstone steps, crying. She'd never felt so corrupt.

Tawne's mother and father were there so she knew she was dreaming. Both parents had been dead for a couple of years. Dad had died from painful prostate cancer and had willed the family car to a pretty nurse. Her mother suffered some sort of overdose. The casket had to be custom built to accommodate Mrs. Delaney's large frame. Tawne remembered coming in to the funeral home and hearing the morticians making jokes about the extra large box.

In the dream her parents were standing on a darkened street corner. An American long-stemmed beauty strolled by and her father doffed his hat. Not many men wore hats anymore but he always had. He beamed with appreciation. A less than queen-sized queen was passing. Guinevere and Marie Antoinette. Tawne saw the crown of jewels on her head sparkle in the night.

Tawne's mother hung her head in shame for only a second. Tawne could see the thorn which had been pressed between the woman's breasts. It was as long as a two by four, the end of it sticking out the front, the sharp tip emerging out her back. She dribbled blood from both wounds. Her husband had done this, skewered her right through the heart.

Tawne's mother closed her eyes, sighed, then opened them again with a glint. She gripped both sides of her jowled face and began to pull in opposite directions. She was splitting herself apart!

"Momma!" Tawne cried.

The beautiful queen looked casually over her shoulder as Mrs. Delaney ripped herself in half, flab falling like sides of beef to the sidewalk. And a gorgeous woman emerged from the cast-off shell. There was the woman underneath that Tawne had always suspected lived inside her hated heaviness as well.

Tawne's newly revealed lovely mother and the queen shared a knowing look as Tawne's father babbled in flustered surprise. The American long-stemmed beauty began to laugh lightly, waving a perfect Princess Di gesture, the way the regal have waved from coronation carriages for centuries. And Tawne could see now that Delia was the queen. Delia looked back at Tawne's mother, smiling her royal approval as Mrs. Delaney slugged her husband right in the chops. He flew off into the night where Tawne couldn't see him anymore. But he was calling out, "I'm sorry, honey!"

Tawne's mother dusted off her hands. Elegant, small, white dove hands. She walked away proudly as the dawn had just arrived.

But Tawne noticed she was gaining a pound with every step she took toward the sunrise.

Tawne woke up on the floor of her apartment. She didn't recall coming into the building or running up the stairs. It satisfied her that she'd made it at all.

She must have gone into shock again. That was it. Then she passed out as soon as she managed to get inside her door.

All the blood had come out of her. It was sort of like being dehydrated. The way it felt to come out of a bad case of fever and diarrhea without a drop of moisture left in the whole body.

What was the vampire's credo? *The blood is the life*.

That was bullshit. Blood was only the fuel.

Tawne tried sitting up. This was when she started to panic. She couldn't move her arms and legs. She couldn't move anything.

Her head wouldn't move on her neck. She swiveled her eyes in their sockets to be able to get a look at herself. She couldn't see much because she'd fallen onto her front with her hand tucked under her face as if she were sleeping.

All she could see was a solid red. Solid because the blood that had orange-juiced from her pores was totally clotted. And since it had come from all her pores, and from every crease and hollow, she was wearing a shell of hardened blood.

Tawne tried to wiggle across the floor on her belly. No dice. It had also clotted her onto the carpet. As if a cat tossed a giant hairball and it dried overnight into a permanent fixture of the room.

She wondered, am I trapped inside this thing?

The sensation was claustrophobic on a major level. She had to get out!

Tawne tried to rock, hoping to eventually roll herself over after loosening the clot that held her to the rug. Was this what a butterfly felt like in a cocoon?

No, cocoons were soft as silk. This was rigid, stiff even as the hair on her head and along her arms had stuck to the blood, and the blood had welded to the carpet. Her jeans and T-shirt wrapped her in stiff armor. Her hands were balled fists with the fingers curled. The one to her face felt as if it were an extension of her cheek, a large growth from mutation that would forever keep her joined fist to face. Rodin's THINKER in crimson plaster.

God, not every night was going to be like last night, was it?

Tawne thought, I'm weak because I'm empty. I was weakened the first time when that trucker shot me. If I'd been alive, I'd have bled to death.

(If I'd been alive.)

Tawne couldn't help chuckling. It sounded flat against the floor. No echo and no force.

(If we had some ham we could have some ham and eggs if we had some eggs.)

Am I dead?

No, but I would be if I were alive, she decided as she tried again to gently rock free of her moorings.

At least she'd passed out in her living room where there weren't any windows. If she'd landed in the bedroom or kitchen with daylight doing a blitzkrieg through plenty of glass panes, what would have happened to her?

Tawne wasn't sure she wanted to know. This was bad enough. She tried to flex her leg, pulling the muscles behind her calf, bringing it back from the knee pressed to the floor. She attempted the same with her free arm. They might have been wearing casts of cement.

Well, she couldn't lie there until some cosmic insensibility made short work of her undead status. The smell of blood on her hand made her whimper. The next thought made her gag. It smacked of self-abuse and personal devourment.

No, Tawne reminded herself. It isn't my blood. It's the stranger's. The one I didn't mean to kill. I drank it and then it was squeezed out of me. Sucked by that old vampire-vampire, Aurora.

It smelled *good*. Better than freshly baked bread, than freshly brewed coffee, than sizzling bacon.

(Than sucking wounds the size of pancakes and all the hematoseptic sewage heaved up from the gastric pouches of ugly men.)

Tawne stuck out her tongue as far as it would go and

166

touched it to the slick hardened knuckles of her hand. Had she thought earlier that this reeked?

The fingers were close enough for her to bite. She did so, careful not to break the skin. Only to crack and crumble away the candy brittle of blood. It crunched like scabcovered nuts between her teeth.

Melts in your mouth, not in your hand. Her giggle sickened her.

Her stomach flopped. The nausea must only be psychological.

Alice In Wonderland and Eat Me, Drink Me. They had left out the third and most obvious. Eat And Drink Yourself.

She used the freed fingers to pry the layers from her cheeks. Then she pulled it from her throat and stuffed the rich scarlet pralines into her mouth. She next nibbled from the cottony arm of the T-shirt, inadvertently swallowing bits of the shirt with it. The threads tickled as they went down. She pulled gory layers of panocha from her breasts and torso, working down to scoop handfuls of it from between her legs, thinking *menses sunset* . . . When she could get up, she took a letter opener from the desk and used it to scrape lozenges of it from her back where her hands couldn't reach.

The warmth was meager because it was second hand. But it revived her. Tawne worked down her body like an insect consuming the amber that encased it.

Chapter Sixteen

The eyes flashed from cataract green to cobalt.

Then they went to white.

There was an explosion which was thermonuclear in scope.

Each time it was more than before.

This time Hiroshima of the underworld filled the camera, licking firestorm flames. It crackled and hissed, then faded to be swallowed whole by the night. Cinders hissed in the wet trees and the river.

The sides of the ugly man's head popped. The horns coiled out as they had the second, third and 30th time Alan watched the video. They bloomed black roses. But now the surrounding trees shed their bark as spirits stepped out. These beings were loose as a collection of bladders, balls of gelatin for heads and hands that drizzled bloody shadows onto the bank.

"No, wait. Who are those guys? They weren't there." Alan protested as he leaned forward. He was amazed he could see right through these additional creatures to the warped center of action. How was this scenario rewritten with every showing?

Red bugs with bright black skulls swarmed from the roses, working their way down the ugly man's flesh with a piranha fleetness that made Alan's face twitch. The bulbous tree spirits bent to snatch at pinkish gray bits that flaked off, missed by the bugs—children grabbing at morsels of Thanksgiving turkey that fell to the table as it was being carved. They opened the split udders of their mouths to stuff these in, revealing concentric rings of darkness in place of teeth.

The ugly man was eaten, his white bones exposed in patches of wicker basket ribs. A greasy smoke puffed out of him, unfolded crumpled wings and escaped. Whatever these carrion birds were that flapped out of the ugly man, they began to pick the insects off him with corkscrew teeth.

But the ugly man—extra ugly in this condition—wasn't through yet. He bent down to do the hurl thing. It wasn't blood and bile after all. It steamed in pulsations that crackled with negative energy. Corruption bubbles spat and yawned, filled with mewling, lipless mouths. It was alive and squeaking.

Inside the holes the bugs had chewed the sputum was busy clawing its way up from the ugly man's stomach. It scratched up the throat, scrabbled over the jaundiced tongue, leapt out to the large woman's mouth. It twisted to hold her lips away from her teeth, prying her jaws apart until they creaked.

The sozzly tree spirits began puking out the bits of the ugly man they had downed. These bits opened the ground up where they splashed in the mud. What crawled out of this rose like an animated gorge, like some non-life freak.

(It's long past time to faint, Alan. Long past time . . .)

The Alan Moravec holding the camera in the video should have fainted long ago, should have dropped the camcorder. The Alan Moravec sitting on the edge of the bed wondered why he hadn't fallen down again himself. He tasted sour ginger ale gas and held on, watching in stubborn terror, wanting not to watch.

What had been moments in the woods had become forever. This was what eternity was, viewed on an endless loop of change and changing terrors. It was a ceaseless unraveling that prolonged the crumble into dust.

The large woman choked as death sloshed eagerly down her throat to set up house in her spleen. The ugly man regurgitated out the force of unnature as his red face melted and the skull disintegrated after that, revealing what squirmed up from the ground. The horns became arms with hands that lifted to the sky, palm up. Enough already! Enough!

(With Alan clinging to the earth, clinging to the roach-infested carpet and begging out. Now? Now?)

Do I pass out now?

He knew the tape wasn't anywhere near this long. Why hadn't it run out? Why hadn't the machine stopped?

"Because it's an endless loop," Alan said out loud.

The camera dropped. The stars were spinning. At last last last. Oh, thank you. THANK YOU.

The Alan in the video must have lurched. Soon the camera would switch itself off as it always did eventually.

But the stars were spinning, white, swelling to cobalt.

Going to cataracts on green eyes. The film's intro in reverse.

They were still swelling. Still coming down.

(Now? Now? Do I pass out now?)

No.

Alan gasped and the air went into his mouth in a rush.

David Jewitt was trying to sleep. He didn't think he'd ever be able to sleep again. He couldn't close his eyes without seeing Janis and the kids lying on slabs at the morgue. Just as he'd last seen them. Looking down and getting dizzy because it was like looking down into sunset-splashed canyons.

It hadn't been difficult to identify their bodies. He'd been able to see them beneath the asphalt-flayed flesh, see the sudden fright that froze into what remained of their beloved faces. Not difficult to identify but impossible to live with.

He couldn't rest at all back in the lonely house on Magnolia Drive. He wandered from room to room, to the backyard to sit in one of the vacant swings. Back into the house to stare into the refrigerator.

You could tell a lot about a family by what they kept in the icebox. There was a casserole that Janis had made. It never made it to the oven and was now a fuzzy green. There was a piece of cake left over from Jorie's last birthday, hard as a rock. Isaac's medication was in carefully labeled bottles. These were mementos of them every bit as precious as toys and jewelry.

David wandered to the closet to look at Janis's dresses. He was unable to touch them. He couldn't let anyone pack them up either.

He'd taken to renting motel rooms to grab some sleep. But the decent places had too many decent people staying in them, reminding him of his nice, vanilla life—purged in steel, efficiently cremated and urned.

He started frequenting the awful places like this crotchnasty dive. The Bug-In, Bug-Out he referred to it in his own head. There could be no place less like the home Janis had made for him and the kids. So it was perfect because it in no way reminded him of what he'd lost.

David heard people screwing down the hall in rhythmic moans and chirping screeches. The cheap bed frame rattled as it bumped the wall.

Screwing. They most certainly weren't making love. No one who gave a damn about the other person came to a

171

joint like this to merge bodies and essences. To grapple sure, this was okay for that. To steal some momentary rut release, sure, and then run to a clinic for an antibiotic to kill whatever they might have picked up from the sheets or the toilet. Maneuvers here were without finesse, hormones at high pitch, not giving a shit who overheard or might be looking through a maintenance peek spot scratched into the mirror.

Hearing the couple was only faintly annoying. It was a natural, albeit animal, set of noises. It wasn't any worse than being on a business trip and staying in a Motel 6 next to the stockyards.

What was hard was hearing the movie the guy next door to him on the other side was watching. Full of godawful screams and the sounds of perpetual retching. Rising winds, monstrous roars and painful howls. Must be some George Romero spectacle on the cable.

Weren't there enough real horrors in the world without deliberately seeking more in jaded crap like that?

David and Janis had decided long ago not to let their kids watch any of that perversity. The two hours of nightly television Isaac and Jorie were permitted to watch were strictly supervised. The parents even banned cartoons because they were mostly violent trash. Five- and six-year-olds were too young to understand the angst of exploding cats. They did every imaginable cute atrocity but having Elmer impale the wabbit rectum first on a pike among other similarly writhing and rammed cartoon characters, and then sit below dining on Daffy Tartar while the bugsy rodent squirmed and bled. Vlad Dracul Fudd was bound to be an inspiration sooner or later for some demented horror freak.

David scrambled out of bed and called the desk. "Can't you tell the guy next door to me to turn down his TV?" he asked the clerk.

He was afraid to hold the receiver too close to his face.

It stank of fish and was sticky. Something obscene had been done with it by earlier tenants. He held his breath as he spoke loud enough to be heard through the phone held at arm's length.

"No," the clerk replied nasally. "He paid his 12 bucks same as you. If you don't like it, go to the fuckin' Hilton."

Click.

David sighed, replaced the receiver and hurried to scrub his hands.

He came back and pounded on the wall, hearing what honestly sounded like an army of zombies crunching cartilage and slurping crushed spine goo.

"Would you please turn it down?" David called out, trying not to sound too pissed off.

He sat down on the bed and held his hands over his ears. He laid down and pulled the pillow over his head. The sounds that came from the next room were grim. Impossible to shut out. Did they have to play it at full volume?

David got up again and pulled on his trousers. He padded in his bare feet down the hall, wincing as he stepped on a couple of roaches. They were big and crunched like Cheetos. He wished he'd put his shoes on first.

He knocked on the door, calling through it, "Hello? Could you please turn your TV down, sir?"

He waited a few seconds and nothing let up. He listened to shrieks, grunts and bestial percussion that made most modern metal music sound like church choir stuff. There was a string section that had to be made up of gut and sinew played with bows of whip leather. He hesitantly touched the door.

The door opened. The lock probably didn't work in this rundown trap. It had taken David three times to lock his own door.

The sounds stopped. Puzzled, David stepped into the room. He heard a whistle.

"Hello?"

173

There was white static on the TV screen. The video recorder's light blinked. A man was perched on his knees on the floor. His hands were clenched. His fingernails were bloody and had broken as he grasped the carpet, which in turn had torn away to reveal the concrete beneath. The man was inhaling sharply in a whistle.

"Hey, buddy, I didn't mean to startle you. Hey, are you all right?" David asked as he bent close.

He could tell by the man's bluing face that he wasn't all right. He sucked in air for an impossibly long time until David expected him to swell up and explode. There was a frozen stare of terror on his face not unlike those David had seen on the faces of his family in the morgue after the accident.

"Mister?" David whispered, astonished by how hot the guy was. Didn't he hyperventilate? Wouldn't he faint doing that?

The air rattled down his throat, fluting in a Pan's pipes through his teeth. Then the intake of air stopped suddenly with a sick, wet noise from within the man's chest. His eyes rolled up as he pitched forward, making another soggy sound as his face hit the floor.

Something flew from the man's shirt pocket as he fell. David knelt to pick it up. It was a woman's driver's license.

Chapter Seventeen

"Be seein' ya on the street, pal," Bill had said after Arcan was fired at Galway's. It was the kind of swaggering threat Arcan might have expected from one of Carl's cronies. It lacked in substance what it made up for in bravado.

Arcan didn't run into him on the street but at the grocery store. He turned the corner into frozen foods and bumped carts with the jerk.

"Well, if it ain't the slugger hisself." Bill snarled as he pulled his cart back and slammed it forward again, nearly knocking Arcan backward.

Arcan shook his head in disgust. What would he do next? Throw a candy bar at him?

"You know what I'm doin' here, asshole?" Bill asked as he pointed to the stuff he was buying. "I'm gettin' food Carl can eat. He's practically takin' it through a straw, ya know. Thanks to you. Soup and ice cream. Chicken fuckin' broth—no noodles even—and plain vanilla 'cause he can't chew no chocolate chips or butter pecan."

Arcan smiled, his wolf sticking its shaggy head out. "Too bad I didn't knock his teeth out. He could've chewed those."

Bill launched himself. The two carts were knocked aside and wheeled off down the aisle. Arcan ducked the left punch aimed at his head but took the right to his stomach. He doubled, teetered back, lifted his foot and brought his boot down on Bill's leg, hearing the fibula crunch. Bill howled as he hit the floor.

"My leg!" Bill shouted, holding it at an angle as he rocked back and forth. "You broke my fuckin' leg, you bastard!"

"All right!" some kid laughed, standing with his mother near the super glutton's pre-chewed lizard rectum TV dinners.

"Tommy!" his mother snapped as she pulled him away.

"Don't worry." Arcan told Bill as he stood over him. "You'll be able to eat most anything."

His wolf growled in his ear. *It would be easy to stomp this phlegmwad. Really teach him a lesson. He can go crawling back to Carl so they can whimper and lick each other's shattered bones. What d'ya say?*

It slavered. Muscles rippled beneath the surface, hard and eager. It moved to his face.

Arcan tightened his grip and shut his eyes. He made himself see a calming blue, smooth as water. The red dimmed, cooled, as the wolf withdrew. He turned to leave.

There was a woman with her back pressed to the glass doors of the frozen desserts case.

He thought, how appropriate for a cheesecake like her. He banished it.

She cringed and Arcan figured she was afraid he'd kick her, too. That he was, in fact, about to run amuck. He might even pull a gun and go postal through breakfast cereals and baby food. *Pick up on aisle fourteen . . .*

A stain was spreading on her well-tailored slacks. Urine ran down her legs.

"Jesus, lady," Arcan said to her. "It was just a little fight. I'm not carrying an Uzi, am I?"

. . . as he closed off the nagging suggestions of Deborah fucking up recitations of poetry as she squatted in a corner.

Then he recognized her. As the woman had already recognized him. When the wolf moved in his face.

Arcan expected her to scream. To become hysterical at the memory of his knife, his monstrous attack in the darkness of her bedroom. His sweating animals came back to her as if it had never ended.

As she must dream it every night. Even as Arcan dreamed it, along with every one of his other victims who haunted him. Because he haunted them, didn't he? His predatory actions had drawn them together for the rest of their lives. Days and nights.

But she didn't scream. His heart stopped. He stopped breathing as he waited for her to raise the alarm.

"Rape!"

my god

"Murder!"

Her cries would pierce his eardrums and shatter the cooler glass. But she only pushed against the doors, trying to enter the safety of the frozen glass by osmosis. Her eyes pleaded as they had before *please no more no more no more no more no more PLEASE!*

Then they were all there in the glass, reflected among the patterns of frost and vapor. He hadn't noticed them at first, since steam and ghosts blended well together.

How long had they been there? As soon as she recognized him. Or was it before that? Maybe they traveled with her.

No, Arcan knew they traveled with him. Women who had been murdered in spirit but whose bodies were left behind to cope.

She wasn't moving now. And when he stepped out of her line of sight, her eyes didn't follow him.

(She's with the ghosts. She's not going to scream.)

Arcan sidled over to Bill. He pointed to a wet spot where a bit of ice had been shaken loose to melt on the floor.

"You might profit by saying you fell there. You could sue the store," he said to the man who grimaced in pain.

Bill stopped glaring at him to glance over at the shiny dampness Arcan pointed out. When he looked back, Arcan was gone.

Chapter Eighteen

Tawne stood in front of the mirror and took stock of herself wearing her new vamping duds. All the erotic bloodsuckers in the books and movies wore them, making them look tough but lusty, predatory but worth letting them catch you. Dominator, dominatrix, making a bondage in which to keep prisoners of time and love.

The outfit looked like shit on her. The black leather miniskirt bulged around her wide hips, puckering above the muscles in her legs. The boots at least covered her thick calves but they made her knees look like grindstones. The low-cut bustier accentuated her waistline—or lack of one. And the sunglasses, well . . . Tawne tossed them out. She must make eye contact. Even when she wasn't actively doing that, the glasses made her look like a tourist in hell.

Right, maybe she could make them think this was the gorgeous death from their hottest groin-grabbing, wetness-emitting nightmares. If they could stop laughing long enough at this silly costume to fall under her spell.

Tawne stared furiously into the mirror. She had to see it for herself. What good was the power to fascinate if all *she* saw was lead and same-old disappointment?

"Change me," she commanded between gritted teeth.

She watched for any alteration no matter how fleeting, for that beauty which power must match side by side. There had to be a body that owned the right to have a mouth of desire and cruelty, a womb that was both kamasutra jam-kitchen and snake pit.

"Wait a minute," Tawne said. "I thought vampires didn't cast reflections."

Another myth bit the big one.

Dust was for the dead and unbeautiful. Not for the undead.

She went back to her focus, saying, "Change me."

No sleek, saber-toothed tigress emerged. No Kali Venus dripped honeywine and rust-colored cream. Her red hair didn't whip.

Tawne was not transformed, having emerged—folded—from the blood cocoon.

"I am not made beautiful in my sight," she said, sulking.

Tears froze back in her skull, hard as pearls in the ducts. But no tears flowed.

They stung an icy salt in her eyes which swelled, engorged in sleet. The eyes became balloons.

Would they explode? She was sure they would and waited for them to burst as they stretched past the sockets like one of those pop-eyed dolls. Still no tears. Couldn't she cry?

Did vampires cry?

The freezing liquid formed crystals she could see through, similar to cataracts but not blinding. They were multi-faceted and shimmered in a glacial veil. The ugly man had cataracts. Or was this what was in his eyes? Frozen tears? Tawne had difficulty picturing the ugly man as ever crying.

Then through the ice veil she saw Delia, posing in the mirror with long, sleek legs. The boots and bustier made Delia look like Wicked Wanda from the *Playboy* cartoon. All she needed was a cat-o'-nine-tails to crack and a room full of slavering men begging to be pussy-whipped.

Yes, Delia could definitely wear such vamping duds. They had been drawn from the erotic closet of blood fetishism specifically for a face and body like hers.

Right now Tawne was Delia, smoldering in black. She'd been stripped and rolled in the ashes of cremated Hindi brides to make it cling so perfectly.

"Do I look dangerous?"

Tawne narrowed her eyes and pouted with Delia's full red lips. She hissed and the mirror hissed back. She squealed with delight and pranced away to the book on her night stand. She opened it and read.

> I am the night,
> clothed in ghosts.
> I carry a crow's bone.
> The rose in my hair
> suffers not
> a trace of red.
> Black is never empty,
> just as spirits
> are never innocent.

She danced back to the glass. She saw herself for a moment but soon had Delia back. (clothed in ghosts)

Tawne liked the idea of being Delia. It sort of returned to Delia a measure of her life. As if the two of them shared it now. The way sisters of the twilight might.

It made Tawne feel less guilty because she'd bargained for her vanity while Delia's body lay broken and mutilated nearby. She couldn't have saved the Georgia peach anyway. She'd arrived and seen the murder already in progress, had

181

been transfixed with a netherworldy impotence which only the sight of an extreme act by a supernatural denizen could do. It would have taken a Beowulf to act against such horror. It would have taken a fuckin' archangel.

"You're a sweet gal," Tawne said. She distinctly heard the southern music of the other woman's voice.

Tawne shook her head so that her hair tossed. It was Delia's face and body but not her demureness.

> she was a bomb
> she was wild
> she was a thing
> of darkness beguiled
> she was the precipice woman
> and chasm's child

Page 12 of 'Immortal Inamorato'.

She'd memorized them all.

Such an untamed beauty could have anyone.

That was a rush. Tawne had never dreamed of having anyone she wanted. The men in her fantasies were always misfits. It would take someone not quite normal to love her, wouldn't it?

There was really only one man in her fantasies nowadays. That was the feral bridegroom. All others had been replaced by him. She'd gone to monandry. But despite the single spouse condition, he was still not normal.

Normal men wanted Kate Moss, Cindy Crawford, Claudia Schiffer.

Delia.

Not that the men in Tawne's dreams had ever been unattractive. They were barbaric, inclined to employing brute force. They were lycanthropic with the scrotal tattoos male animals got from running through bone-splintered midnight fields. And her single dream man wasn't the knight from most romantic schtick but the knight errant, the sort the maidens usually ran from—screaming all the way. He was able to love the strength but not the form. His ideal of beauty was callously deviated through no fault of his own so that he chose the thorn and not the rose, granite instead of garnet.

Oh, I'm here, baby . . . she thought, closing her eyes.

He had the uncanny ability to see beyond the material plane—even if his methods of achieving this sight were nothing short of autopsy.

It's the isolation that makes me this way . . . Tawne thought, wondering if she attributed this mental note to her raunchy soulmate or to herself. Waking moments had always found these revelations of deathlust damnable, drenching her with guilt and the sick fear that Christians have that their hidden fantasies will poopshoot them straight to hell.

Did it matter? There were no real men out there who had ever seen magic in Tawne. Even creatures of power like the ugly man saw the baboon. Even he had merely pitied her. And the violence was only the method of giving his gift. It wasn't as horrible as what he might have done. The secrets came in blood and bile which he'd given with all the thought of tossing a crust of bread to a starving beggar. *There you go, honey. Suck on that. It might not be all I can give, but it's all you're going to get.*

Now she had the power. The beggar strutted before the mirror with slim legs, with a waist a man could put his hands around. She had a face he'd commit sins to kiss. A man might even kill for a taste of such orange blossom saliva: betray his country to flames, sell his asshole to slavers, slash the throat of his only child. Cleopatra. Helen of Troy. Messalina. And Tawne. A queen at last.

She almost stayed there all night, wasting its few precious hours to look at herself. She wiped off the lipstick and put it on again. She parted the lips as she put the tiny cosmetic phallus to them, smiled, flicked her tongue to the

Revlon erection. She had only bought one lipstick: red. Vampires didn't wear fuchsia or mauve, did they?

She rearranged her hair a dozen ways to watch it glisten around her new face and throat. She undressed to see what men would see; then she dressed again—slowly. She did a striptease full of bumping and grinding, then played with the naked body after she'd gotten it stripped again. She pinched her nipples until they purpled. Delia's nipples were brown, not pink like Tawne's. She moistened her fingers on her tongue and then slid them across the delicate clitoris hidden in a fringe of pubic hair that was curly, not frizzy. She could only get one of the fingers into the vagina, it was so firm and tight. The look of euphoria on the face in the mirror thrilled her and made her wonder if this was what it would have been like to make love to Delia. It was certainly nothing like making love to herself.

Tawne arched her back, scratching at the taut buttocks until she seethed. She clenched the tiny elegant hands as she traced patterns on her stomach with the lubricants from between her legs. She batted the lashes around her icy eyes as she leaned forward to show the cleavage to herself. Tawne had always been big breasted. Delia's were smaller but better to look at. There were no stretch marks or bulging veins. She kneaded those breasts until she wanted to cry. Unable to do that, she laughed.

Tawne knew she must pull away. "I'm falling in love with myself here."

She shut her eyes and then opened them. The effort to close those eyes was a struggle. She'd been able to turn away earlier to get the poetry book. Ah, but she'd only just managed to see Delia in the mirror then. Now she'd been standing there for at least two hours. She was becoming trapped by Delia. By her own eyes of fascination.

"Heaven must be after dark," she said as she tried not to look into her eyes/Delia's eyes.

"Look at me and love!" the ugly man had commanded.

And, hot damn, this was all it took.

Tawne frowned, or tried to. How could she look at this object of joy and frown? But if she didn't, she'd starve. She would have survived dawn's light only to perish in her own.

"Wasn't this how Narcissus drowned?"

She forced her eyes shut again with a force of will she didn't know she possessed. It hurt to shut Delia out. It was like having someone steal the stars. She shut her eyes for a long time, counting to one hundred, counting to a thousand. She muttered, *one fuckin' eternity, two fuckin' eternity, three fuckin'* . . .

When Tawne opened them again, she was no longer Delia. She was lead. She was same old disappointment. She sighed and then held her breath so she wouldn't cry. She probably couldn't anyway but she didn't want her eyes to balloon again and ruin the careful make-up job.

Tawne had only been in a bar once in her life. It had been a humiliating experience in the loose '80s, back when all the panties were crotchless for accessibility and button-fly jeans frustrated the quick fumble.

Of course, Tawne hadn't been chosen.

Tawne went to the bar tonight and couldn't help being surprised at how many people were still doing the same careless sex hunt. As if there were no AIDS problem.

Do they think they're immortal? This thought struck her funny.

Surely most took precautions. She suddenly had a picture in her mind of a voluptuous woman in a chintz and French Provincial boudoir, holding up a crucifix to a handsome, caped vampire.

"It's okay. I have these on," he says as he opens his mouth wide to show tiny condoms on his incisors. "For safe sucks."

Charlee Jacob

Tawne took a booth in the shadows so she could watch without being observed.

She understood she'd have to be careful not to make the mistake she'd made with the cop at Swan's. She would see her heart's desire, pounce and get him out of there *mucho pronto* before anyone could interfere.

How many stories had she read about vampires and singles bars? With a pick-up and then a fuck 'n' suck scene? A million. It had reached a point of saturation and then suddenly one didn't see that sort of tale even in the cheap crotch-scaries available for a song and proof of age through the mail. As a result, she felt redundant being there, as if she were fulfilling some perverse 12-year-old's notion of Carmilla's night out. But where else could nouveau succubi and incubi earn their dark fairy wings and trench mouths?

(And every bell you heard meant that some horny vampire had just gotten their pubic purple hearts.)

Two men entered the bar and took a table not far from Tawne's booth. Carl Pruitt and Bill Tower seemed cheerful enough and were as loud as usual. Bill was clumsily staggering with a pair of crutches and a cast which wrapped the lower half of one leg. She was excited to see Carl. This was proof of kismet. If only he'd come alone.

"Damn!" Bill grimaced as he fumbled to ease himself into a chair. He couldn't seem to decide how to manipulate the crutches so he could lower himself to a sitting position. "I'm gonna kill that Arcan Tyler."

"No, shit." Carl nodded, trying to help his friend.

Tawne's eyes widened. Arcan did that to Bill? She had no doubt that Bill must have started it. A bright smile stretched like a satisfied cat across her face, rippling, then purring. She said softly, "Yeah. Arcan. Outstanding. I'll bet he had it coming."

"What are you guys gonna have?" asked the waitress.

"Pair of drafts, Laurie. And put a straw in mine, okay? I got t' take all my liquids through a straw," Carl said, grinning foolishly as much as he could within the confining chin cup.

"I don't need no straw," Bill told her. "No place on my leg to stick one."

Carl nudged him. "Hows 'bout 'tween 'em, bud?"

"You two boys been in an accident?" the waitress asked.

Carl shook his head. "Walkin' asshole-accident is more like it. Some guys just feel they got to prove their manhood by hittin' folks, ya know?"

The waitress smiled back at him and ruffled his hair. "Well, I'll bet he looks a lot worse. Am I right?"

Bill and Carl exchanged sullen looks.

Bill replied first, squinting belligerently. "Yeah. He looks like a chicken at a voodoo homecoming dance."

Carl laughed. "Right. That's why we're here and he ain't."

The waitress wiggled off to get their beer.

Tawne watched as a succession of beers came and went.

Carl left briefly to go the bathroom. Eventually Bill would have to do the same. Then Tawne could seize her moment.

Damn it, when was he going to go? He couldn't hold all that beer forever.

At last Bill groaned and reached for the aluminum crutches leaning against a spare chair. "Oh, hell. I've been dreadin' this. Gotta drain the dinosaur."

"Ain't that supposed to be drain the lizard?" Carl asked.

"Speak for your own equipment."

Bill cussed as he tried to guess the right way to push himself up from the chair and onto his crutches.

"Want some help?" Carl offered. "Want me to go with you?"

"No thanks, mommie. I gotta learn to dance this sucker myself. I'm gonna be on 'em for two months. Or until the grocery store settles the suit."

He groaned again as he began the strenuous chore of

circuiting the other tables and barflies to reach the men's room.

He won't be back too soon, Tawne decided.

She edged from the booth. She slipped up behind Carl's chair and tapped him lightly on the shoulder. He turned, wrinkling his nose when he spied her gigantic breasts overflowing the boundaries of the tiny bustier.

She leaned in and made sure their eyes locked. She felt the sting in kilowatts and static. She latched hold, orbs and orbits.

Carl was shocked. "Delia? Never seen you here before."

"Life can't be all work," she murmured, gently touching his bandaged chin.

"You look great. Really . . . *incredible*," he said approvingly as his gaze almost—but not quite—dipped to her cleavage. "Not what I ever thought in a zillion years I'd see you wear. You're always so prissy."

"All of us have an id, don't we, Carl?"

He was puzzled. "A what?"

She defined it for him. "A dark side. Alter ego. A buried monster."

He stumbled. "I guess so."

"Want to get to know mine?" she asked, teasing her tongue around the edges of her lips.

He smiled. "I thought you didn't like me. After you dumped that food on my head in the break room Friday. Ya know, over Ton a'Buns. I figured I'd never be able to get within six feet of you. Make that six miles, lady."

Tawne flinched. Delia did that for her? No wonder Carl had food stains on his clothes after she saw him in the stock room later. It must have taken a lot for Delia to come out of that protective shell to act on an outrage done to a woman she barely knew.

Tawne had stood still while this friend was being butchered. She'd bargained for her life while Delia lay twisted and mangled in a pipe.

She knew she was projecting Delia. She felt the form on her in skin and grace. She wanted to hold it, caress it, thank it. But there was just no way to.

"Do you know what doing something like that is a sign of, Carl?" Tawne asked him, not shrugging off her remorse but pushing it temporarily aside.

"What?" God, this yokel was stupid.

"Passion."

He nodded, and it was the way she'd always hoped he would look at her. His mouth hung open as he mentally undressed her (but without looking away from her eyes, a neat trick.)

She breathed huskily into his face. "Let's go."

Carl reached up for that breath and smacked at it hungrily with his mouth. She quickly led him out of the bar, noting the curiosity from some of the patrons who watched them leave. But not many seemed to care. Most were too drunk or too busy trying to field their own arrangements, feeling each other up under tables and leaning too close at the bar.

Bill limped back, having dribbled on his pants while trying to balance, teeter and pee at the same time.

"Laurie, where'd my buddy go?" he asked the waitress.

She shrugged as she picked up empty steins. "Left with a gal."

"He connected?" Bill laughed as he began the arduous task of sitting down again. "Was she a looker?"

"No, another bowser. Carl can't tell the difference when he's drunk. You know that, Bill."

It was well past midnight when they arrived at the park. It was also very dark. Exactly the way Tawne wanted it.

When Carl reached for her breasts, she almost fainted from happiness. Until he squeezed too hard. It wasn't painful but it wasn't pleasurable either. She grabbed his hands and forced them away. He was amazed at her strength.

189

"Not so rough, lover. I'm not going anywhere," she told him. "Just kiss me first."

Carl protested feebly. "Can't. My chin."

"Don't worry. It won't hurt," she promised as she stroked his cheek. "Look into my eyes and feel no pain."

But he was already looking into her eyes and feeling no pain. His warmth was light years away but his lips were soft and salty. The inside of his mouth was a separate living thing with his tongue a copperhead snake.

Tawne tasted the blood and broken bone beneath the bandages. It made her sigh, and Carl took this as a sign to drive his tongue deeper. They hurried to peel their clothes off. His body was muscled, his stomach a washboard. That wasn't a sock stuffed into the crotch of his jeans. When his erect penis bobbed its head, she stepped forward to clasp him to her—stomach to stomach. It rubbed her belly and crushed into her pubic hair. He pushed her down to the grass. She hardly protested.

Tawne whispered into his ear. "Yeah, I want it."

As soon as he entered, she had an orgasm from antici-pation. After all, this was Carl, the one she'd lusted after.

The moonlight came through the trees for only a few seconds, showing his lion's mane of blond hair. His chest glistened with sweat. His hands pushed on her shoulders even as he drove deeply with rough thrusts. She had a memory that panicked her as she saw him rocking away between her legs. It was exactly how the ugly man had looked when he changed, and it jolted her. That visage had been the typical Aryan Adonis. It had been Carl's body he'd plucked from Tawne's mind.

The moon retreated behind a fan of clouds. It really was Carl. His dick was no poisonous mushroom. It was big, slick and full of a heat that reached her oh, so slowly. Tawne reached up to squeeze him in an embrace but he pushed back from her, grunting. He was showing about as much regard for her as the ugly man had. His passion was just as impersonal. It was remorseless. He moaned, drooled and muttered pornographic endearments that didn't give Tawne what she needed. She didn't want only to be fucked; she wanted to be cherished.

"You got great tits, Delia. Great tits. Wow, your cunt's full of ice. You stick ice cubes up it back at the bar, baby?"

He grasped her breasts again and wrenched as if trying to open the escape hatch on a doomed submarine.

She begged him, "Hold me close! I'm so cold!"

"Huh? Oh, yeah, soon, baby, real soon," he moaned as he pounded her gracelessly. "You got me so hard."

She might as well have been clay. Or a blow-up doll, and he was doing an experiment to see how many pounds per square inch it would take to pop her.

Carl wasn't looking at her anymore. Eye contact had been broken in the darkness, making him unable to see. She could see in it very well, but she'd also looked away. She'd closed her eyes at the sense of dullness. She was really only tolerating the rest of this, disgusted by him. She was a body in the night to him and not even all of that. Just a pussy and tits.

But she was supposed to be in control. She'd engineered this screw, and it had to be more than this to please her.

"Hold me," Tawne insisted.

"Will you wait a fuckin' minute? I'm . . . about . . . there." He drove, wiggled and plowed.

The moon broke through again. Tawne grabbed him by the shoulders and shook him. "Look at me, damn you!"

Carl couldn't help but obey. She didn't attempt to make him see Delia or any other image of loveliness. She wanted him to see her. To know who he was with.

Carl shouted and tried to get off of her. Yeah, the coyote woman.

"Ton! What the fu . . . ?"

"Yeah, she wants it," Tawne said in a hiss.

She brought her leg across his back and flipped in a

wrestling maneuver that put her on top of him. He didn't even pop out of her. She put all her weight on him. She peered down as Carl flinched. He shuddered as if he'd seen something move in her face.

She felt it move—a man in her eyes, in her soulhouse, looking out.

Then Carl screamed outright. His eyes bulged and she could practically count the bursting veins around the pupils like an electric aurora. He drooled. There was a squelchy farting noise as his sphincter dropped a load of shit into the grass. His cock shriveled inside her.

In his eyes was something reflected . . . something hairy and grotesque. A weirdness with three doglike heads, two of them snarling foam where breasts should be.

Tawne looked down at her chest and didn't see this. And her skin might not be pretty but it was smooth.

How much more was this outrage going to hurt her?

She took Carl's chin in both her hands. She growled as she twisted her fingers in opposite directions.

The cup and bandages flew as his stitches ripped. She yanked the two halves of his wound apart like tangerine sections and then drew her face down to cover it. The blood exploded in her mouth as he shrieked against the bridge of her nose. She felt a throbbing heat which sang of furnaces and reactors.

Tawne didn't notice when the moon was covered again, putting the couple in darkness once more. She was lost in the heat of the blood and might have been anywhere this side of delirium.

When Tawne came to herself again she was climbing the stairs to her apartment. The heat was already gone. She was cold.

There was a feeble weight on her arm. She looked down. At some point she'd put on Carl's jacket to protect herself from the chill. Something pulpy dripped from the coat sleeve. She cried out and tried to sling it, the way anybody would try to shake off a spider.

It flung bloody strings but didn't come off. The heart was one tough muscle. She had no idea what she'd used to pin it there with because she didn't remember doing it.

She got into her apartment as fast as she could, grateful not to run into any of the neighbors. She unlocked the door and lurched inside, tearing the jacket in her rush to get it off. She wrestled the heart from the sleeve, finding it fastened to the material with shards of glass she must have picked up in the park. Tawne debated cutting the organ into chunks that would go down the garbage disposal. Maybe she could flush these down the toilet. Shit flushed and that was what Carl had been.

"I'm dreaming this," she muttered. "It's a nightmare."

In the dream the feral bridegroom offered her the heart pinned to his sleeve.

How had she come home from the park? Had she run on all fours?

Precious heat.

Tawne shivered, sat down at the kitchen table, and ate the heart. If anything had ever tasted better, she didn't know what it was.

But she was still disappointed. The genital climax had been over too fast. The blood was a better high. Carl hadn't been giving her a damned thing. He wasn't the type to give to anyone. He hadn't even put his arms around her. He'd put his hands on her shoulders to clutch for leverage. Now he was dead and where was the rest of what she'd expected?

He'd stared at her as if she was worse than the fat woman he despised. As if a grotesque fiend were straddling him.

He'd paid for that. Not that she'd really intended to hurt him when she lured him out there. But pain could reach a point where its consequences were uncontainable. Where the reflex of lashing out became supernatural.

This was empty. Tawne sighed in despair and was startled when she flowed out without warning. She breathed this pale gas out of her body and went right up the walls in it, then up to the ceiling. She kicked spirit feet in an effort to force herself back down. She launched through the floor instead and found she was in the Howe's apartment below hers. They were sleeping. She stared at them, smelling their heat. She was tempted to take them but she didn't think she could, with her body back at her kitchen table. She couldn't even control her direction.

Tawne didn't want them. It wouldn't fill her anyway. The Howes didn't look real. They were glass with blankets up to their chins.

I want out of here, she thought, and passed through the building, seeing brick inside out for the first time. She was over the street and people were walking on the sidewalk. They didn't see her: she barely saw them. Tawne was the occult creature but they were phantoms, going by like figures from a glass menagerie.

Tawne turned in the air and found that if she didn't fight too hard she could control her descent. She floated over to where a cowboy was walking his date. Tawne tapped him on the arm. A crack appeared, a webwork like one saw in old china teacups. It squirted. Intriguing.

He yelled as his arm broke for no reason at all. He fell to the concrete as his girlfriend started screaming.

An older man watched this from his car. He reached for a cellular phone to get help. Just a glass head through a window. The glass didn't even stop her as Tawne flew through it enough to put her mouth to his ear.

Tawne pretended she was a glassblower. She always liked to watch glassblowers anytime they had a booth set up at the mall. She blew and the man shrieked briefly as his head swelled. He fell back onto the seat, blood gushing from his ears, nose and mouth.

Tawne drew back, suddenly horrified at what she was

doing. Was it this easy? She couldn't feel the heat nor could she take nourishment from these people. She had to have her body for that.

Then why hurt them?

She drifted away, observing the pandemonium she'd created on the street. Not that there were many people out this late.

Had she ever been as light as they appeared to be? That was a funny question to ask someone who had always been bigger than most people.

Tawne had always been alone but this wasn't the question. She'd always been big. Now she'd crossed a barrier and had—what? Really *fleshed out*. She'd crystallized into that which didn't have to yield for it was nothing as passive as flesh.

She sped away, over houses and through alleys. She was shocked to find that there were other undead out there. Spread out across the city.

They saw her and glared at her suspiciously.

One of them jumped out from behind a parked bus. The action pushed Tawne's filmy spirit back, able to cling to nothing. He felt heavy and he trembled as if she was just as heavy to him, even if she wasn't in her body. It was the sort of gravity that must be thick when stars came too close.

"You're new," he burred. He held his hand up and dipped two fingers into his mouth, lathering them with saliva. He trailed this through the air in a musk of fatal DNA and hormones that left an indelible scent on his turf. "Don't feed here. These are my people."

Tawne promised not to. There was something about him that told her he was more powerful than he looked. His eyes had thick cataracts. He opened his mouth and a black mamba stuck its head out at her.

"Why are you here?" the snake demanded.

"I'm just floating. I've never done this before. I swear I

didn't come here to take your people. I'm not here for blood."

The snake spat venom at her and withdrew. The undead creature blinked, his frozen eyes clacking. "Why else would you be here? There's nothing left but blood."

He stank of it. It made rings under his armpits through his shirt and crunched in the crotch of his trousers like crusts of salt and semen. As if he'd been caught by the dawn a few times and never bothered to clean himself.

Tell me I won't end up like that!

Repelled, Tawne took off.

"Don't leave your body that way," he warned her. "Don't ever be vulnerable. The dawn watches all the time. From the horizon."

Tawne got back to the brownstone and slipped through the walls. By then she was windmilling her arms as she began losing control. She looked down at her body, still seated at the table, Carl's blood on her mouth, pieces of heart muscle between her teeth.

How do I get back in? I only got out by accident.

Just fall, she told herself. Let go and fall back in.

She did and opened her eyes.

"I didn't do this just so I could live forever," Tawne said, finding her tongue stiff, her lips rubbery.

Carl was dead. The buzz was short-lived. What kind of bargain had she made?

There was a touching but it didn't last long enough. The emptiness filled only with darkness and every moment became a colossal piece of time. She wasn't a glass of blood but she might as well be. She might as well be just the glass. The need never went away because only that yielding, passive flesh could be quenched. The dead felt nothing. The undead felt it but couldn't hold onto it.

Was it too late to join Delia in that cramped pipe?

Yes. Tawne was afraid it was. Shame. It was beginning to look better and better to her.

Chapter Nineteen

Saturday night. Arcan sat in front of the tube, growing disgusted with the creature feature's presumption of female innocence, as one feral horror after another slouched into the darkness toward some virginal cutie. He tugged on a plastic bottle of cheap tequila, biting a lemon as if it were a golden lip and licking salt from his hand as if tending to a wound the animal way—with the healing tongue. He didn't drink last evening. But after running into Bill—and that woman from his violently venereal past—at the grocery store, he'd decided to look for a worm in the swill. Something to bite in half with the teeth.

(He remembered the woman's name. It was Karen.)

Arcan didn't recall crawling down the hall to bed, but obviously he had.

No doubt running a gauntlet through two rows of ghostly women.

Now he dreamed. Again, reaching for nightmares, dreading them. Understanding at least partially how they held both the past and the future. It was in a heavily wooded glen, mist rising silvery, water moving nearby . . . surely a scenario borrowed from the Saturday night flick. He was standing amid the helpless victims. They were bound up sacrificially with silken cords. He was like some mythic beast arrived to be pacified, bought off with these offerings.

Each woman cowered, babbling softly in terrified prayer. Or in snatches of poetry.

Just the thought that it might be poetry infuriated him. They were jarring skreels of rhyme and meter which drove splinters into his brain. He leapt upon the first in line, then on the second . . .

. . . fangs cleaving downy flesh, crunching pelvic bone like candy jawbreakers and on into the jumbled morass within. The flavors of apples, hamburger, cabbage, pale custard, mushy bread: all variants that made up the contents of an individual's colon. There was the exhilarating stench of raw sewage and nutmeg, blood and rosewater douche, meat and retrograde in these innards.

Arcan experienced starbursts of a sickening groin hunger as he shook a corpse to pieces. Then he rolled in its wasted scraps, jerking off with fistfuls of gore.

Free! voices in him shouted. *Out! Out free forever!*

Spikes of maniac frequency rattled Arcan along his knobby spine. He was submerged in beastly pelts and canker sores, unable to exert any power in this dream. He might as well not have been a man at all. He floundered in lubricious viscera pouring from curved gouges as tight as rictal grins. He blew drowning bubbles of blood that snorted out through some animals prickly nostrils. The animal licked them back from its muzzle with glee, moving down the line of atavistic cunts.

But the damned bitches were murmuring. Prayers for deliverance until it was a shocking hum vibrating the mist. Or it was poetry in rippling droning waves.

This Symbiotic Fascination

Was there a difference? What was a poem but a prayer for deliverance: from loneliness through love, from ugliness through beauty, from the mundane through higher perceptions?

This was what the creatures that had taken Arcan over were doing: claws and fangs (or a knife which was a man's puny nails and teeth set to use by steel proxy) ripped the breasts, the wombs. They sundered the hearts and foggy whirlpools of all that chanted sentiment. Carved out the hated poetry.

For what possible use did a cat have for poetry as it shredded a dove in its talons? To give it understanding for flight? (Useless as tits on a bull.)

What wolf slapping its balls against wet carnage needed poetry? So it could enter a state of shaggy grace and worship some nun from a celibate distance?

What ghoul making sandwiches of graying clits between slabs of breasts needed poetry? So it could transcend the pungent filth of the grave it craved?

If Deborah thought this elevated prose would rescue her from the shifting thing she was, she'd been pitifully mistaken.

None of us is ever saved, Arcan decided.

The cat, the wolf and the ghoul inside Arcan wouldn't permit him any illusions. All they ever allowed him was a coppery taste, whether he wanted it or not.

On down the line of squirming females, souls and thighs spreadeagled for access.

The cat casually knocked out each of a teenage girl's teeth, observing with measured curiosity how each one fell, and how the little cheerleader cried out in spittled soprano.

The wolf stuck a rampant paw up Karen's cooze and flexed its claws. It remembered an old way to catch a monkey. Put out a jar filled with fruit and when the monkey reaches in . . . The wolf grabbed a sharply clenched pawful of fruit, to see how much he could pull out in a lump sum without getting stuck.

The ghoul whittled out Elise's eye and then popped it between his teeth like a ripe olive.

They cavorted in the jumble of steaming body parts, hallucinating with excess satiation. Killing at last, killing in the manner that Arcan had never permitted them to do. Finally Arcan thought, *Is this my dream or theirs?*

Yet this was surely what events would be if Arcan wasn't every moment holding them back. Not even letting them go all the way when they did manage to get loose on him.

The grotto in the woods became a total slaughterhouse, a jubilee of sweetbreads and spoiled clusters of mincemeat. Was it even possible to tear repeatedly until fragments became so small they virtually disappeared? The splash of blood and bursts of splattering fatty pockets became smaller in circumference with each rendering into the diminutive, becoming motes of a saturated darkness.

Whuff! Whuff! Free!

And yet Arcan—submerged and suffocating in frothy purge—could see that the ghoul had garments laid across its mold-encrusted arms. What the hell were those? Shining, soft gowns and masks, cloaks of damp silk? Had the ghoul collected their clothes?

No, the sacrifices had been delivered up naked.

The ghoul flayed the offerings. Sometime at the onset of this butcherfest? Easy as spooning poonpie, like sliding the casements from fine chunky sausages before pulling the tubes apart to fry?

The ghoul hung these from trees bowing at the perimeter of the glen. Juicy in the moonlight with jagged eyeholes and mouthholes, flapping arm and leg strings one could use to tie the raiments around them with. To do an Ed Gein jig if so inclined.

In the dewdrop, bloodspattered moonlight the beasts gorged, high on gut stews 'til they puked. Then they dozed.

Arcan's subconscious finally surfaced—as it were—in this nightmare. He stared at the menudo of gristle, ligament, organs strewn on the ground. Skins crucified on branches. He thought, *I never did this! I never did anything remotely resembling this!*

There was a cellophane rustling. Of taffeta flesh beaten in the wind. The moonlight was as bright as a ripe cancer sore. The flayed women in the trees climbed down. They crept through the mist. Like twisted mylar ribbons, like grotesque Hiroshima-blasted origami, they began dancing around Arcan.

He struggled so hard that the horror gradually dissolved.

Slop! Plop! Flop!

Mushy clots against his chest. Clammy as droolpaste pasta and snotballs rubbed against his skin.

Opening his eyes. Arcan saw Carmel Gaines sticking her fist into the back of her skull. What she brought out resembled one of those cold dog-testicle soups and spongy rice that he'd seen on the buffets of some Vietnamese restaurants.

Carmel applied this to the gray-church she was building on Arcan's bare chest. The squelch moving between her rotting fingers shriveled the kernels of his nipples.

"There is a sanctuary built upon the heart," she said, working relentlessly on her carrion cathedral.

Arcan sobbed. He tried hard not to look at the tiny windows where he knew he'd see miniature *womanly* faces if he did.

"You can't make me look." Arcan sputtered.

Carmel continued working the gangrenous clay.

"I *didn't* murder anybody and I *won't* look at them." Arcan insisted, trying desperately to lift his arms. But they were paralyzed, burned at his sides with the fever, sticking to his ribcage and hip bones. He tried to empower his hands to swipe the decaying slop off of him.

"All who have been wounded are welcomed there," Carmel said without benefit of soft palate or skullish echo chamber.

"God, I hate the smell of orchids!" Arcan exclaimed.

He managed to raise his fists by a few inches.

Voices in the damned Play-doh chapel droned, leprous Legos wriggling. Prayers or poetry or an orchestrated choir screaming soulless gospels from ant-sized mouths. But it wasn't until he heard the drums and smelled the fermenting orchids turn into sweet sandalwood that Arcan looked at the gray church.

At the queerly looped arch of the doorway where a shadow lithely undulated. An oriental spirit hauntingly familiar to Arcan was no bigger than a caterpillar. And yet somehow he could make out each distinctive attribute. Multi-breasted, tail braided with prayer beads, bronze bells around the ankles and a gold ring piercing the very tiny penis which dangled before a vagina the size of a stillborn kitten's nostril.

It suddenly seemed as if Carmel was molding a replica of a jungle temple, adorned with tier after lusty tier of erotica, intricate with orifice stuffing and genital juices. The dancer in the doorway tilted its head coquetishly. It revolved on a dainty foot, snaked its slender pairs of arms, flashed red eyes and sang from the mouths in its palms which opened wide all black. "Go to the source for atonement, return to the source . . ."

Chapter Twenty

The room was suddenly quiet after the man died. It spooked David with the first real moment of silence he'd had since checking into his own room four hours before. Even the people screwing down the hall dropped their commotion. Either they had reached their coital goal and collapsed into satisfied puddles or they had paused to listen, wondering what happened. There might be a psychic disturbance that went into the air when someone died.

(Sending up signals. *Can we have a moment of silence for the dead? You can touch yourself but be quiet about it.*)

David held his own breath for several seconds, waiting for something else to happen. Nothing did. The man face down on the floor didn't move, didn't spring back to life screaming "Boo! Fooled ya!"

David checked for a pulse. There was none.

He wiped his fingers on his trousers. He imagined he'd dipped them into a swollen plague bubo the size of a breadfruit. The resulting muck would be a disquieting cross between melted strawberry ice cream and gonorrheal jizm.

David walked over to the video recorder and ran the tape back to start. He pushed PLAY.

What was this movie that scared this poor guy to death?

There were no beginning credits. The scene was badly done, amateurish—for effect? It opened with two people getting it on before a river. The water surged beyond them like a crippled dragon, legless and dark.

"So where does the fiend come in and hack them to bits?" David wondered out loud, thinking of the noises he'd heard.

He recognized the woman. Her photo was on the driver's license which had come from the dead guy's shirt pocket. The man on top of her was scrawny and pustuled. The way they were going at it with the cheesy thrusts of such bone-ugly actors, it had to be some local porno production. Something like *Zombies Like It Raw* or *Corpses Do It Better*. Prosaic on Prozac. Made on a dollar and a half budget, and with the monsters made up with catsup and a number two pencil.

The man was lapping blood from his partner's breasts. David winced. The man sat up, smiled at the camera with the evil leer of a satanic child molester. And became some-one else. (A handsome devil)

It was a simple cinematic trick. David wasn't impressed.

The handsome devil bent and began vomiting red gore into the woman's open mouth. It splashed in elastic strings, crimson slinkies and roadkill spaghetti.

David's stomach revolted at slow 33 RPMs. *That* looked real enough.

The camera angle plunged. There was ground, then stars as the camera must have rolled.

FIN

The end.

David ran it forward, backward, fast and frame by frame,

trying to find more. But the whole production wasn't any longer than two or three minutes.

Where were the gut-wrenching screams? There had been some ordinary, brief retching but not the lengthy projectile pukes he'd heard from his own room. No rising wind, no eerie moans, no crunching bones with zombies and endless gouting dismemberment that seemed to fill the air as David sat on his bed trying to blot it out.

This couldn't have frightened this man to death. It wouldn't give a heart attack to a nun confined to a coronary unit.

He searched the room carefully. He didn't want to leave fingerprints.

He scratched his head. "There has to be another video."

If there was, David couldn't find it.

He stuck his head out the door to reconnoiter the hall. There was no one out there to see him as he tiptoed to the exit with the parking lot beyond. He put the driver's license and the tape in his car.

"Why am I doing this?" he asked himself. "I'm going to get in a lot of trouble."

Hell, David wanted to study that tape. It was all he could do not to sit there and watch it over and over, trying to understand what happened. It just cried out to be understood. However, there was a corpse in that room with horror rigid on its face. Well, probably. David had seen horror before the man pitched forward. Now David couldn't see the face. But he remembered distinctly what it looked like. David put the things into the trunk of his car, hidden beneath the spare tire. Then he locked it up. He went back to his own room and called the police.

He fully dressed and waited for them to arrive. He paced the floor, worrying about pilfering the tape. David wanted to hurry home to see it again. Wasn't it evidence? Wasn't the woman's driver's license evidence? Of what might have been a crime in progress, if not a home-cranked smut and glut flick?

"Why did I take those things?" he whined. "I've got to bring that stuff back in here. I've got to get the hell out, go home. I don't want to be a part of this."

He'd almost talked himself into running when David heard the police in the hall. He went to the door.

"Uh, hello," he stammered, feeling as if he'd been caught at something.

"You the man called about a dead body?" asked one policeman. He was a huge beagle-eyed fellow with a brassy name tag which identified him as Weigt.

"Yes, sir. He's right next door here. I didn't think to call the desk clerk. Should I have?" David fumbled as he led the way.

The officers made no comment as they followed him into the dead man's room.

The other policeman was very freckled with sunburned arms. His name tag read Pueller. Pueller knelt beside the body. "Was he like this when you found him?"

"No, sir. He was on his knees. He seemed to be having trouble breathing. He was gasping." David explained.

"What made you come in? Did you hear a disturbance? Fighting?" Weigt asked as he reached for the phone to call the desk.

"Yeah. I guess you could call it that. A disturbance, that is. No fighting. I was trying to sleep. He had his TV really loud. He was watching some kind of horror movie," David said and then thought of kicking himself. The television was on, the recorder switched off. But there wasn't a horror movie on. It was clearly in the middle of an old Marx Brothers flick. He changed directions, trying to keep his thoughts straight while the bigger cop talked on the phone to the clerk. Could he talk to the man at the desk and hear David at the same time? "Well, I called the desk to see if they would ask him to turn it down. The clerk was really rude and hung up on me. So I pounded on the wall. I didn't get an answer so I came over to knock on this man's door. It just opened and there he was. His face was blue and he was gasping. I went over to see if I could help and that's when he keeled."

Weigt hung up the phone and turned to his partner. "Clerk verifies the guy registered to this room checked in last night. Says there have been three or four complaints over the last 24 hours about the TV. He claims he called the room after midnight Friday and about noon today to ask him to turn it down. When the guy didn't answer, the clerk blew it off."

"He works night and day?" David asked.

"Owner," Pueller muttered. "Can't get anyone to work here because too much shit happens. The place has been robbed twice in the last month. There have been three rapes and a shooting in the same period. Not counting whatever this is."

David vowed not to check into any more dives for shut-eye. Home couldn't be any worse, memories or not.

He wished he could go home. He grimaced as he glanced at the dead man. What an awful sound the guy had made. His face had the dread of the grave imprinted on it. Maybe people having heart attacks always looked like that, as if they knew their time was up.

It frightened him. How could David have heard those noises coming from this room when they didn't match what he'd seen on the tape? Had this guy been watching it since the night before? Had he rewound it to watch it again, mesmerized? Making the other sound effects himself somehow? That was too weird.

Pueller snorted. "Hey, this motel doesn't provide video players. This is from the movie business across the street. Guy must have rented it. I don't see any tapes though, do you?"

Charlee Jacob

"Hey, buddy. You see any movies in here earlier?" Weigt asked David.

David's throat constricted guiltily. *Why did I take those things? I'm no thief. How do I explain the stuff is in my trunk without having them think I killed this man? What else could it look like? Why didn't I mind my own business?*

The body flopped on the floor. Bounced its chest against the carpet. Spasmed again until it tossed onto its back. The abdomen swelled and the shirt buttons popped off, the shirt flapping back. The two cops and David jumped away as there was the sound of tearing fabric, of wet sheets splitting.

The distended flesh on the man's revealed gut puckered, bubbles blubbering like the cheese on a baking lasagna. It boiled in separate bumps that then cratered in too many tiny holes to count. The bottoms of these splattered out, puffing maggot-sized mouthfuls of mozzarella skin as something minuscule clawed out of each one. Hordes of red insects began to scurry out of these craters, shiny black skulls no bigger than the heads of map pins. But David knew they were grinning.

There was nothing to do but retreat to the parking lot and call a meat wagon. They might even call an all-night exterminator. The police were too shaken to ask any more questions. It was obvious that this wasn't a murder but some sort of infestation.

"We may need to talk to you later," Officer Pueller told him. "Will you be staying here?"

David trembled. "Are you kidding?"

He gave them the address on Magnolia Drive.

"This is here in town. You live in town but you were staying here?" Weigt asked suspiciously.

David figured his grief was none of their business so he replied, "I had my house fumigated."

The paramedics brought out the body bag. David stared.

Would the plastic ripple from movement inside?

"Uh, what about the bugs?" Pueller asked them, eyeing it as if he expected the same thing. Could insects chew through it?

"We didn't see any," one of the paramedics replied as he hoisted his end of the gurney into the back of the ambulance.

The other agreed. "Not a one, boys."

"But there were thousands of them," Weigt argued. "They just came crawling out of his guts."

"Yeah, that was there all right. Bunch of gross little holes. Like some kind of pox only with all the boils popped. Maybe he had an allergy," replied the second paramedic as they anchored the gurney and its stay-fresh baggied occupant for the journey.

David got home about 4 a.m. He was badly jolted and exhausted.

He couldn't sleep in the bedroom he'd shared with Janis. He hadn't been able to do this since the accident. He collapsed onto the sofa and didn't go to sleep as much as passed out. Either way it was a loss of consciousness.

The fireplace facing the couch was cold. The hearthstones were sooty with flue-draft footprints. It would stay that way, not being cleaned so that it never resembled anything other than fire-and-air's animal. David probably wouldn't use it at all in the coming winter.

He and Janis used to sit before the fires, talking about their days and future. The kids toasted marshmallows there, white puffing out, blackening too-sweet flesh. There was a good chance that Jorie was conceived in front of that fireplace.

On the mantle sat three urns in flat, plain pewter. Modern man didn't decorate death as his ancestors did.

But now the urns were shaking. Was there an earthquake?

No, the urns were moving; nothing else was. Not Janis's Lladro porcelains lined up nor David's college running trophy.

They skittered and tapped.

David sat up on the couch and cried, "Janis!"

He grasped the sofa cushions in his hands and stared through the dark. A fire suddenly blazed among the useless remnants of wood, the light too white. The brightness filled the room for a blinding instant.

The sealed tops of the urns shook loose, flying into the air spinning like animated UFO toys. Red bugs with black skulls swarmed from the pewter.

The bugs loomed, telescoping in his perception until David could see they had little bodies in their clacking mandibles. Thousands of insects with thousands of small Janises and Jories and Isaacs in their mouths. Some carried just a leg or an arm or a head. But each doll miniature of his beloveds, in whole or part, was alive.

David woke up.

The room was dark, the fireplace hearthstones cold.

The urns didn't move. They were only filled with ashes.

David slept fitfully but wasn't rested when he finally got up at noon. He drank six cups of strong coffee. He unwrapped and tried to eat the rock-hard piece of cake from Jorie's sixth birthday party held five weeks ago. It didn't chew well but he was reaching to savor something of his child. A lost confection, the milk and cupcake smell of the very young.

David pictured red insects crawling from the urns. He spat the stale cake into the trash and put the rest of it under a tree in the backyard. Maybe the birds could eat it.

He guzzled the coffee and let it slowly burn through the lining of his stomach.

He decided to watch the video. Perhaps it would make some sense in the light of day.

This Symbiotic Fascination

There were no opening credits. He already knew that. But this wasn't really a movie. It might have only been intended as a trailer for a movie. There was no soundtrack. No synthesizer, bassoons or racing percussion.

The blood looked real. The woman was the same person on the license. She must have died. This was a tape of a murder, like one of the old rumored-to-be snuff flicks. No, the man changed and that was pure razzmatazz. The blood and bile were just damn good special effects—damn good for an otherwise amateurish sex-and-death piece. Boff-and-knock-em-off. The sort of thing meant to be shown at drunken bachelor revels and fraternity parties and small town splatter-sci fi conventions where the only guest speaker they could afford was the woman whose mother trained the dog that took the shit in the opening sequence of *Pink Flamingos*.

The camera pitched.

Stars.

Out.

David rewound it.

The fact that the man in the motel might have actually watched this sick sequence for 24 hours was hard to figure. *What did he see? What did I hear?*

David watched it again. The man humped the woman, slavered in the gory muck geysering from her chest. Then he changed into another man in a smile-without-fade-out. He vomited and she choked.

The camera pitched, rolled and was a late model Camry skidding on wet asphalt. One tire was blown to the rim, and metal rubbed sparks of friction. There were screams as the windshield webbed with fractures that sounded like an enormous walnut stepped on by an elephant with a crackckckck! Or the bones in a child's face finding the point of least resistance. Velocity and gravity jerked to a stop so fast that time bent backward.

The rest was white noise, gray flecks of raw tape without imprint.

David wept and watched it again.

Humping-screwing-fucking between broken legs in the mud before the mighty dragon river, blood on her breasts/ on his smile/in his saliva thick with threads of watercolors cherry-red, orange-orange, gangrene-green and sinus-yellow. Rainbow vomit full of dog food ribbons.

And the camera pitched.

And the Camry moved like a falling star through the night, turning, rolling, landing upright to glide on its sparks, to hover on them, to stop against the cement pylon. Jorie and Janis hit the windshield and bounced back, forward, back, cracking more each time 'til their rocking ceased. Isaac catapulted through it like a small torpedo, over the hood of the car, over the pylon, into the bushes that held him there until morning.

The scene switched back to the river. The ugly man and/ or his handsome devil replacement were gone. The woman's body was in the mud, eyes staring up, white as the moon where she wasn't covered in blood.

Unmistakably dead. Deader than door nails, than bodies falling on fire out of the Hindenburg, than Kennedy's being driven through downtown Dallas. David believed she was dead, that this was not special effects and it wasn't just a flesh wound.

Until she stood up and smiled into the camera. And became Janis, in a gown and hood of slivers of glass.

Chapter Twenty-one

Last night 10 women sat in a circle and looked into one another's scars.

Karen Strickland rocked in Elise Reedman's arms, certain she was still bleeding from a dozen places. She'd seen him. HIM. At the grocery store. He (IT she reminded herself as she recalled the moving of his features and the male animal stench) had fended off an attack by another man. But Karen had faded out, back into the glass of the cooler, had seen spirits around her that resembled her friends here in this very room. She hadn't cried for help. He'd gotten away.

Barbara Byrne occasionally ran her fingers along the edge of a book tucked into the flap of her purse. Elise couldn't see the title.

Marla Dennet hunched her shoulders and peeled green polish from her bitten nails.

Heather Bastilla and Celia Lehman had hands out in space, with just the fingertips touching. As if they were concentrating on the planchette of a ouija board no one else could see.

Julie Davis, Gina Brugaletta, Tira Kolumba and Ann Hunt watched as Karen wept, suffocating in their own silence.

Normally they talked at these meetings. It was stupid to come together and then only sit still, bound up and unable to communicate. It had been almost a year since the last one of them had met the serial rapist they shared in common. Silence was a stage that was expected at the beginning, not this late.

Talking was great therapy, but nobody was talking last night. Sometimes the room was full of too much pain.

Maybe it took a particular phase of the moon or special weather conditions. They would gather and what was missing put a strain on each of them. It was the same place that was gone from all of them. Since it didn't show on the outside. Elise assumed it was the soul. He'd stolen the soul from every woman there. Elise didn't know why he'd done that. She didn't know if he even knew he'd done it. It was a strange sensation, as if they could sense him nearby but not in their vicinity. They *felt* him close. No matter how often they turned suddenly about to find him, he wasn't there.

(Yet Karen had just seen him . . . in public, at the store. It must have been him. How many other shifters were there out there?)

How could they ever be whole again without their spirits? For—without souls—they really were lost and helpless. Elise had formed the group so they could reinforce one another, learning how not to be lost and helpless ever again.

That was what it took to heal. No one could have control over their lives if their souls were gone.

* * *

This Symbiotic Fascination

Elise carefully searched the Sunday paper next morning. Going through the city's newspapers was a chore she did faithfully every day. She even took papers from the surrounding towns. Looking for photos of men who had been arrested. Looking for his photo.

She watched the TV for local news but they recounted very few of the rapes and murders. She hoped to see his face between policemen, trying to spot him in crowd footage. It was frustrating because most of what they said on the air was gibberish.

She heard them babble, "More crime last night! More crime today!" Without reporting but a fraction of it.

He may have disappeared from the face of the earth for all she knew except for Karen's report. There were women raped every day but none of them described an assailant anything like the beast who had attacked the members of Elise's group.

It was a strain trying to read the papers and watch all the broadcast news since Elise had only the one eye now. It gave her severe headaches. She did this chore endlessly, absently touching a forefinger to the scar down her nose, feeling the ragged weal that had been a valley on the moon not long ago. The doctors stitched that cut but the mark was there where his knife had ripped. The socket itched behind the eye patch. Other places on her breasts and stomach twinged with weather changes. They gnawed each morning when Elise woke from the nightly reliving of it.

There wasn't a rape victim anywhere who wasn't a martyr, first to the crime and then to the world. Elise thought that if she heard *it takes two to tango* one more time, she'd resort to violence herself.

And that was the pitfall. The emotions which came after, whether he'd taken the soul or not. It came in predictable stages. The first was the silence thing. One went comatose, beaten raw and used until numb.

Second, one became petrified of their own shadow. The

215

days became grueling bouts of shadowboxing. This led to becoming defensive.

It was natural next to crave justice. And then came the religious zeal that offered healing and a sanctuary of forgiveness. The revenge cycle followed those.

Elise couldn't afford to give in or give up. She paced the floor, waiting for the papers to hit the sidewalk, chanting to herself, "Please just make it stop make it go away, make it end. Take the feelings, take all the feelings away."

Stage one was better. The ease of numbness.

Elise kept a scrapbook full of articles clipped on rape. She went to all the rape trials looking for him. She remembered the fiasco at the police station, trying to give a description to the sketch artist.

"His ears were sort of pointed," she'd said.

"Like that?" asked the artist as he put Vulcan ears on the picture.

"No, that's too much. They were like a cat's when he first grabbed me." She'd tried to explain. Recalling him beating and tying her up, rumbling like a cat, heavy as a panther. "His pupils were yellow."

Yellow doorways.

"When he first grabbed you?" asked Detective Cross.

"Yes, it must have been the lack of light. When he actually raped me, he seemed different," Elise had replied, moving her bandaged hands as if trying to illustrate his face in the air.

"Different how?" asked Cross.

Elise knew they had sent this female detective because they thought she'd be more comfortable talking to another woman. But Cross was no help at all. Who could help Elise as she attempted to explain that his shadow had shagged like a wolf's?

"The nose needs to come out here," Elise tried to tell them.

The artist altered the aquiline to a Roman nose.

"No, I mean *out*." Elise put her hand up and mimed a nose growing into . . . what? . . . a *snout*. "The jaws come forward, too."

She shuddered, smelling his breath of raw meat and bones again.

Detective Cross stared at the picture and commented blandly, "That looks more like a wolf."

Elise tried to nod with half her face wrapped in gauze. Yes, yes! That's it!

He'd looked like a wolf at that moment.

And after a half an hour or so, it had been different still.

"The forehead needs to lower. The skin was kind of gray . . ."

That had been the fiend with the knife and hungry jaws. His breath had been a graveyard.

"His head wasn't quite that long. It was like a squashed bullet."

Detective Cross sighed and wrinkled her brow at the crazy sketch. If it hadn't been for Elise's terrible injuries, Cross might have deduced that no crime had been committed because nothing looked like this. It was a waste of time and the taxpayer's money.

"Perhaps you need to see the doctor." Cross told her with a tight smile, meant to be sympathetic and patient. "I could call him. Could you use a tranquilizer?"

"I'm not hysterical," Elise snapped, even though she knew she was as close to being hysterical as she could be without babbling and trying to go fetal.

Somewhere in the background noise of the station, Elise overheard some jerk quip, "Call the zoo and see if we can get some animals for a line-up."

Another detective, Waters, whispered, "Shut up, asshole."

"What kind of lips did he have?" asked the artist.

Elise could barely say it. "None. He had no lips."

Cats and wolves didn't have lips. Ghouls didn't either. Just plenty of teeth.

The artist grunted.

The final picture looked nothing like him and everything like him. It was a ferocious cartoon, a monstrous caricature.

"We'll never I.D. anybody with that," Cross told Elise truthfully.

"Show it to the other women," Elise insisted.

"We can't catch phantoms, ma'am."

"Show it to them!" Elise had shouted, knowing it was ridiculous. It was a pathetic joke.

But the cops showed it to the other victims and each one had sobbed, saying, "Yes, that's him. That's him."

Now Elise was looking at different pictures. There were photos everywhere in her house, taken of Elise before the attack. They sat in silver and malachite frames showing the beauty she had been. She couldn't turn around without seeing one.

She'd almost tossed them out. It was painful to look at them. But in the end Elise kept them all, to make herself understand why she had to keep looking for him.

Chapter Twenty-two

Earlier in the evening Tawne stopped outside a club called LAMIA'S. She recognized it from gossip she'd heard when alive. It had tempted her then, after the word spread that this was where freaks came to party in the vampire style. Of course, Tawne had chickened out. Clubbing and she didn't mix well.

But she sure as shit went inside now. After all, she was the real thing, wasn't she? And maybe these guys were, too.

One look around told her that none of them were. They wore the duds in black leather and dark slinky stuff. Had coils of black kohl around their eyes. Wore their hair in straight shadow veils or in ebony ringlets. Red lipstick, men and women alike.

Tawne strode in, expecting . . . something. An embrace perhaps. To find her niche. For here were freaks by anyone else's standards.

But they just stared at her, six foot two and 270 pounds in short, tight midnight cow skins.

(How many of these people are bulimic to get so wraith-thin? she wondered, her own heart sinking.)

They did look magnificent, just as Tawne had always pictured the denizens from 'Immortal Inamorato' to appear.

A slender Lilith of a girl in kabuki makeup slinked up to Tawne. She cleared her throat. "It might be you're in the wrong place," the hungry-looking lovely said very politely.

"No, I don't think so," Tawne said defiantly.

"Don't you want the rock club down the block? BANG-ERS? This is a place for kindred spirits, sharing a common interest in . . ." The girl stumbled for a way to state it without being crude.

"Blood?" Tawne asked a bit acidly.

"Yes," she replied with surprise.

Two young men with cross earrings and ankhs across their fingers were whispering in the corner, glancing at Tawne. A woman with obviously blond hair dyed raven smiled with pity as she brought a glass to her lips. And what was it filled with? Cherry wine? Strawberry syrup?

"What's the matter? None of you ever see the real thing before?" Tawne said quite loudly.

The girl who had approached her frowned prettily and then stepped closer, studying Tawne's face.

"Yes, actually I have," the girl replied quietly. "They may not quite look as we like to think they do or as we make ourselves up to be, but it is an ideal we seek. It's like the difference between erotica and pornography. Both are about bodies and life forces, but one transcends the other's lack of grace."

Tawne glared, prepared to be insulted. "Is there a point to that?"

The girl blanched even paler than she'd dolled herself up to be. A man with face and arms so white they might have been marble—except that they were theatrical cos-metic—stood up from a nearby table and replied, "I believe what Cristabel is trying to say is that this is not your place."

This Symbiotic Fascination

"If a vampire isn't welcome at a vampire club, then don't you think you're hypocrites?" Tawne snapped.

The man spread his hands palms down, his fingernails painted scarlet and filed to delicate points. "We apologize for this exclusion. But I'm afraid you have to leave. You are shattering the illusion."

Tawne took in the darkness, the velvet drapes with satin tassels, the incense burners leaking ephemeral trails of smoke. A cross between medieval, Egyptian and sumptuous Oriental. Carved granite grotesques pilfered from tombs leaned from the tops of walls, standing sentinel against . . .

Against interlopers like Tawne.

Now not even the beastly were welcome. And if horror and hell wouldn't take monsters, where were they to go?

Tawne turned on a booted heel and left. She didn't know if it was to their credit or not, but as she departed she noticed that not a one of them laughed.

They sighed.

Tawne had wanted badly to scoop up that snobbish little girl at LAMIA'S and bite her to get warm. Not a clean little erotic nibble either but a raking carnivorous gouging. The kind that made a noise like fresh hamburger being thrown into a fan and which splurted like an accident with a tomato truck. Really show those dilettantes about ruining illusions.

Why hadn't the ugly man warned her it would be like this? Had he been the way he was for so long he'd forgotten about love and warmth (or had he given them up for lost causes?), and started enjoying having power over lives? It might have always been a power trip for him, and he'd never known what Tawne was searching for. "It's a terrible thing, loneliness is," he'd said. As if he sympathized. As if he could have pity. As if he *knew*.

Well, if he'd known, then why didn't he say something?

Why the hell didn't he tell her this was all there was?

(*Wait, it gets better,* the ugly man's battlement mouth seemed to whisper from a doorway.)

"How?" Tawne asked as she stopped on the sidewalk, people jostling past.

(*You're young. A fledgling. You still think mortal thoughts and aspire to mortal things.*)

She half-smiled. "And what do immortals aspire to?"

(*We do not.*)

She snorted. "Thanks a lot for nothin', Yoda."

The ugly man hadn't warned her about morning either. Had he assumed she'd seen all the movies?

Tawne recalled the two times she'd seen him. The sun was setting. There was light on rooftops and in patches on the street. Light at his very trouser cuffs. He hadn't bled, hadn't run away.

Could he be so old and powerful that he'd grappled with the dawn, beating her until she wouldn't mess with him?

Don't fuck with me, bitch.

Had they reached an understanding? Maybe he paid protection to the dawn mob.

His exhale was a deep bell, a horn sounding across water.

Tawne tipped her head back and exhaled, cried out, belching air. There were no bells in it.

She heard laughter. The word *fledgling* said with a pimpled tongue.

A block later Tawne saw a tall teenage boy on the steps to his house. He was drunkenly bidding goodnight to his friends.

"Bye, guys! See ya tomorrow!" He waved, then shared a syrupy kiss with a pneumatic child. "Thanks for showing, Chloe."

"Yeah, great party. Chaz." The girl grinned as she nibbled his upper lip.

A CD playing through the window was cranking down

to fading cowbells and drums. Tawne smelled beer and pizza.

"First to weave, last to leave," piped a boy with a coiling dance step complete with sinuous hand gestures. His baggy jeans slipped, revealing a gorgeous waistline. Tawne wanted to stick her thumb in his navel and pull out a plum.

"Need help cleaning up before your folks get home tomorrow?" Chloe asked Chaz as she rubbed his butt. "I could come by about 10."

The tall teen flushed to an auric orange and gold. "Sure. If they see this, I'll be grounded 'til graduation."

"No problem. I'll skip my morning classes."

She got into a car with some other kids.

He let out a gust of relief. "Thanks for not telling Lisa about Chloe."

He and the wave boy slapped palms. Then wave boy staggered off down the street. The kids in the car were still singing. It echoed as the auto turned a corner.

Tawne nodded. This kid was half her age and had already enjoyed more than she ever did. She waited until she was sure all his other guests were gone before she knocked on the door. He was bleary when he opened it but still grinned. She made immediate eye contact. "Excuse me, is there a party here?" Tawne said in Delia's southern silver. But in her mind's eye she was a younger Delia, fresh-faced and irresistible.

"Uhm, it's over," he replied, little valentines pluming from his ears as he fell into instant love. He was wearing his father's after shave. It smelled of Persian limes and sea foam. Tawne sulked prettily. "I missed it? I had trouble slipping out of the house. My mom's really been on the rag lately."

"That's too bad," he said as he obviously tried to place where he knew her from.

She sparkled and held out her hand. "I'm Delia. I'm a friend of Chloe's." She figured it would be better to be associated with the new girlfriend than with poor Lisa who didn't even know she was on the way out. Always go with a winner. "Could I maybe have just one teeny weeny beer so it's not a total loss?"

He beamed graciously, stepping aside for her to enter the house. "Anything you want. Just name it."

He gave her a beer and Tawne put it down without tasting it. She asked him for one slow dance before they would make love. She tried hard to feel his heat as she nestled in his arms, her head on his shoulder. This boy was summer if ever there were such, so alive he was incandescent.

Perhaps if she could have some of that warmth through this simple touching, she wouldn't have to hurt him after all.

David ran screaming from the house on Magnolia Drive. He shivered and sweated on the lawn for about an hour in the darkness. He'd rushed outside, shocked to see that night had fallen. When had that happened? While he'd been watching the tape.

When he finally decided to go back in, he first went around to the back to switch off the breakers to the living room and den. This would shut off not only the lights but the television and video recorder as well. He feared that if he went inside and they were still running, he'd never be able to pull himself away again. He would rewind and watch, rewind and watch until he died. Like the man in the motel had died.

And what had that man seen? Not Janis and the kids. He'd had his own nightmare drawing out, graphically extrapolated along an unpredictable curve. The reason he'd watched it for 24 hours was to see how it changed and developed. It was impossible not to want to know—to *need* to know—what would happen in the next showing.

David sneaked into the now silent living room. The tape had ejected itself when the power went out; David removed it, turning it over in his hands. There were no runes that marked it for a demonic thing. He carried it into the bedroom and took a crucifix from Janis's jewelry box, pressing it to the plastic. Nothing happened. He put it on the table, picked up the woman's license he pilfered from the dead man's motel room and left to find the address on it.

It was about two in the morning when David came to the brownstone. There were a few drunks and druggies on the sidewalk. He stared at them waiting to see the face of the ugly man or the blond man the ugly man had turned into. David would always be looking over his shoulder, afraid this bipolar transmogrifier would be behind him.

Watching the video summoned up demons as surely as any circle and incantation. And if the folk tales were true, why—if you didn't put them back right—they plagued you 'til they got you.

David studied the brownstone and wondered why he'd come. What did he expect to find there? He knew it was the only connection he had with the enigma of the tape.

(And why do you care? Why not just throw it away? Or mail it anonymously to the police and forget about it?)

Because it has me by the balls. Because my dead wife appeared on it, dressed in a windshield. Because the woman who transformed into my wife lives HERE.

Or lived, past tense. If anything on the tape could be believed, then the woman was dead at the end of the video.

David slipped inside the building and looked over the names on the mailboxes in the first floor foyer. On the third floor was a Delaney, Tawne S. The name on the license. He began climbing the stairs.

It was an old building. The owners were trying to keep up appearances. The banister and hallway had recently been painted ivory. There was a new rust colored carpet laid on the stairs. He almost didn't see the drops of blood, the threads of blood, slickered up the two flights—or down?—strings of it as if a huge leech had trailed a scarlet slime.

It must be paint. Somewhere upstairs was an apartment painted red. It had spilled on the stairs. Otherwise the tenants would have noticed. Blood on rust carpet. The landlords would have cleaned it up.

No one would have noticed. It was a good match. David only saw it because he'd seen a lot of blood lately. So much that this could easily be paint and he would still be certain it was blood.

He followed it up the two flights. It led him directly to the Delaney door. He knocked lightly.

(She's dead, you fool.)

So? Does that mean she lived alone?

(Yes! Yes, this woman was *alone*!)

He knocked louder, glancing around nervously. He was afraid of disturbing the neighbors. They might phone police.

He'd already stolen evidence from one place. David didn't want to be caught breaking and entering.

He took his Visa card from his wallet and wiggled it between the door and jamb to slip the bolt. He'd seen it done in the movies. He was upset when the card broke in half. He took out the penknife Janis had given him last Christmas, using it to probe the lock. Now he had no choice but to get inside. One half of his VISA card was in there. It identified him. If police came here looking for the dead woman, they would find it.

There was a dark cherry smudge on the brass knob. David felt metal nudge, heard the click. He opened the door, easing himself in, pawing for a light switch on the wall.

(Don't be afraid. She was alone and now she's dead. There's no one else here.)

He nearly tripped over a space heater in the middle of

the floor. There were other space heaters everywhere, glowing hot.

It was October 3rd in Texas and not cold at all. There was a chill to the air that was early for this time of year, but not enough to warrant this much toast.

David glanced around. The air conditioning vent was blowing softly. The central heat and air was probably a chilled water system and a boiler. The tenants had no individual control over the climate in their apartments. If a person was cold-natured, reptile-blooded . . .

But . . . this many heaters? There were two in every room, including the bathroom. The place was an oven. Who could be that cold?

David quickly searched the place. His heart was in his throat, certain that somebody was going to walk in any moment. He couldn't see how burglars had the nerve to go into any stranger's house. He was sick with fear.

In the bedroom closet were large-sized dowdy clothes. By the narrow bed was a worn book of poetry sitting open to this poem.

> The ghost exposed
> manifests a backbone,
> and vertebrate's mongrel
> all redded and rosed
> noses abroad
> like a fierce hologram
> whose hard dreams
> have given it life.
> Unmelting seams
> crackle in the frost,
> revealing the throwback future
> for moments.
> Then these become lost
> in lethal tracks
> without history or omens.

Charlee Jacob

On the vanity were 12 empty cans of diet cola in a pyramid, an unused tampon inserted in each wedge opening. At first David thought she was just a gross housekeeper. Then he realized this was intended as sculpture. Scrawled across one can was the signature of the artist. It wasn't signed Tawne Delaney.

In the bathroom was a shopping bag from Galway's filled with newly purchased cosmetics. Bright red lipstick melted in the blast from the space heaters. Queen-sized black silk stockings had been rinsed and were drying on the shower rod.

In the kitchen David looked into the refrigerator and found graying cold cuts, curdled milk, fuzzying fruit, microwave pretzels and wizened fried chicken.

It reminded him poignantly of his own fridge, full of food. Things unfinished left by the dead. There were red stains on the woman's kitchen table. A man's jacket hanging on the back of the chair had one sleeve crusty with blood and stiffened shreds of meat the consistency of undercooked menudo. Flies had been at these gobbets and now their little ricey babies corkscrewed across the leather.

David was about to leave when he spotted the stains on the living room carpet. Not much, just bits of rust clinging to the rug fibers. The carpet itself was strangely barren in places as if it had been nibbled by goats.

He picked up the half a VISA card and departed, closing the door behind him.

It had been a wasted trip. He hadn't really found out anything. There had been no books on demonology. There were no dismembered children's bodies in the closet. No photos of the dead woman posing with her arm around Henry Lee Lucas. Nothing special at all.

David walked toward the stairs. Someone was trudging up them, head and shoulders visible above the landing. Long red hair swung at hips too wide for the leather mini she wore. Her enormous hands ran fingertips along the banister.

She saw him and frowned. (Haven't seen you before, Mister.)

But David had seen her. On the license. In the video, struggling, pumping, orgasming even as her broken legs crackled with heat lightning. Choking to death on the weird upwardly-mobile vampiric purge. If the ugly man had gone from blond hunk to head like a giant asshole, it might have been a monstrous dysentery.

David felt his own bowels shift at the thought, at the sight of her and the knowledge of what had slid down her throat in vermilion clumps. He tried to keep cool. Just stroll past her as if he wasn't shocked or terrified or even vaguely curious. She was alive, that was all. It was only a movie and she had pretended to die in it.

Not only a movie.

He looked down at the rust in the carpet. Bloody video/bloody apartment. And there was the bloody woman.

Tawne eyed him suspiciously. She coughed to make him look up. Then she made contact with a chilly sizzle of volts.

She was still ruffled after the slow dance with the tall teen. The flavor of his heat had faded. She felt a vague sorrow at his passing. The dance hadn't been enough after all. A shame. Poor Chloe. Lisa would get over it once she'd heard about her rival. And Tawne would be over it in about half an hour, hopefully.

If only the boy hadn't pulled away from her at the last moment with that *look*. As if seeing Godzilla very close up and able to count the mashed humans of Tokyo between the colossal fangs. As if seeing something other than the beautiful Delia—or even Tawne herself—caused his mind to downslide toward a gibbering madness. Thus were fine moments spoiled.

Tawne couldn't resist turning on the glamour for this guy.

David didn't blink. He gulped, taking in this woman's beauty. Slim and dark and . . .

Tawne withdrew Delia, letting him go. She shrewdly watched his doubletake and then his quiet, quick retreat.

She mused. "So what was he doing up here, huh?"

Visiting friends at 2 A.M.?

He didn't look like a thief. He looked like a businessman, middle-aged and mousy. She didn't believe for a moment he could be a cop.

"I don't like the way he looked at me," she said to herself. Meaning before she laid Delia on him for that heartbeat or two. Even though it wasn't as bad as whatever the teenage boy or Carl or the guy fixing the flat tire had seen. "He looked at me like he'd seen a ghost."

Tawne unlocked the door and saw a sliver of shiny plastic inside the room. She picked it up. There was part of a number on it.

He'd been here. His warmth lingered, tinged with pheromones of fear.

She gasped. "He knows about me."

Tawne should have realized it from his reaction. She should have hauled his butt back in here to find out who he was and exactly what he knew. Fix it so he couldn't do anything about it. She was so vulnerable these days. And for all her nights to be.

But if he was a cop, there would be other cops after him. How many knew? Or if he wasn't a policeman, who was he working with?

"If he's a cop and thought I was dead because they found my car out with Delia's, he'd have said, *hey, we thought you were dead. I need to ask some questions.* He wouldn't nearly piss himself like he'd seen Cujo and scurry off."

She decided that, at this point, it wasn't important who he was. Only that he'd broken into her place and feared her. Feared her before she used the split second thrall job on him.

What was important was that Tawne leave here and not come back.

Chapter Twenty-three

The ghosts were slowly circling the bed. They passed through the wall on the right side of the headboard and re-emerged from the left side to go around the cape horn of the footboard. As they stared at Arcan, their sheer faces clearly beheld his animals.

Arcan sweated beneath the sheets. His limbs were weighted, trapped beneath the nets of blankets. A window was open but the cool air did nothing to refresh him. The ghosts were ovens of pain, heating rising off them to feed his fever. Carmel Gaines had stoked coals visible front to back in her skull. She swerved from circling his bed. She ran to the walls and began pounding on them with her fists, striking with surprisingly solid sounds for a wraith. The others followed her as they often did, spirits of little volition who needed to be led by someone who possessed two ounces more horror than they did.

They had to follow someone who was truly dead.

No sounds came from their open mouths. He should

have at least been able to hear their gasps for breath, their moaning and weeping. There was nothing but the pounding against the walls until the house shook.

"I'm sorry," Arcan whispered in the tiny, helpless voice that slipped from dreams. "God, I'm sorry."

The apology didn't make them stop pounding. It couldn't make them vanish. Maybe they couldn't hear him any more than he could hear them. All he *could* hear were their fists against the walls. They meant for him to hear that. In his sleep Arcan tasted the flavors of uncooked spongy meats sprayed with assorted perfumes, sharp as witch hazel on his tongue. He tasted whip leather and lingerie, the cheap rayons and expensive silks alike in texture on his mouth muscle. He tasted knife steel and the terrors that sheathed a body like poisoned rainwater.

He woke murmuring *sorry* as he realized the pounding persisted even though the ghosts disappeared. Arcan peeled damp sheets off himself as he swung his legs out of bed.

"Just a minute!" he shouted to whatever demon was knocking on the door at—he looked at the alarm clock—6:30 A.M.

Morning and not morning. The sun wasn't even up yet for Hell's sake. Arcan staggered to the hallway, cursing when he stepped on a piece of glass he'd missed when cleaning up from the other night. He sat on the arm of the couch and lifted his foot. He plucked the sliver out and squinted at blood oozing from the gash. He walked on the heel and the other foot to the door.

Arcan kept only a low wattage bug light on the porch. All it did was turn the night a dark urine yellow. He could barely see the whore with her short skirt, distended cleavage, and enough makeup to stand by itself. Were sluts making housecalls now or had the Jehovah's Witnesses started traveling undercover?

"Yeah, what d'ya want?" Arcan asked menacingly.

A split second turned on a dusky dime as her face slowly came up. He recognized Tawne Delaney, her eyes strangely pink around the lead gray irises.

"Arcan, could I please come in?" she asked.

He stepped aside. "Hmmph? Sure, what's up?"

He had the fleeting notion that all her clothes had been stolen at the laundromat, and she'd been forced by modest necessity to wear this stupid get-up.

"I have a big favor to ask," she told him directly.

It was one of the things he liked about Tawne. She didn't bullshit.

"Name it," he said with his hands on his hips, one foot balanced on the heel. Droplets of blood trickled itchingly down the arch.

"I need a place to stay. It's a matter of life and death."

He motioned for her to sit on the couch. He took the chair, propping the cut foot up on the coffee table.

Tawne saw and smelled the red. She wanted to kiss that foot. But the drive wasn't anything she couldn't handle. She'd fed well tonight. She hadn't been nearly shot to pieces on top of it so she had nothing to compensate for. Besides, Arcan was different. She couldn't look at him as someone who would never be missed. (She'd miss him.) Nor could she see him as someone who had enjoyed all they were worth and were fair game for the feast.

"So what happened? You get evicted?"

"Not exactly." She rubbed her chin. She'd tried to think up ways to state her case on the way over but she wasn't satisfied with any of her explanations. It had taken her more than an hour to break into Galway's so she could find out where Arcan lived from the employee files in the computer. He wasn't in the phone book. She probably could have flown through the walls to get to everything faster but she was afraid to leave her body unguarded. The mall had security officers. The undead she'd seen the other night had warned her about leaving her body, and she intended never to do it again.

Arcan scratched his nose, not impatient at all. "You don't have to tell me . . ."

"It's not that, man. You have a right," she replied.

". . . 'cause you can stay." He couldn't believe he'd said that. A woman? In his house?

(She'd be like a talisman. The ghosts would see her and think they had blundered into the wrong haunt.)

As if to say it was okay and needed no furthers, Arcan stood up and switched on the TV. See? We're at home here already. Channel 7 News A.M. was gearing up. The President's face was fading out. First story dust.

"A body found Saturday night at the Mongoose Motel has been identified as that of former Channel 7 reporter Alan Moravec. Natural causes are currently being given as the reason. He was 34."

No account was given of his piece done on Friday. They didn't even say anything about *Mean Streets*.

The screen displayed tape of the river. Men were pulling a body from a pipe. Tawne knew it had to be Delia. She closed her eyes and ran her hands across her arms, felt her face with her fingers. *No, Delia is safe inside me. She comes out from time to time to love and be loved.*

". . . the Culvert Killer again. The woman's body has been identified as that of Delia Hall . . ."

Safe . . . inside . . . from time to time . . .

Tawne's eyes snapped open when Arcan started to moan. It rose, quavering like a tornado warning warbling through a dangerous wind. He looked lost, as if he couldn't for all the world understand how it had happened.

(Had he secretly been in love with Delia?)

"I did it!" Arcan screamed, grasping handfuls of his hair. "I really went and did it! I've lost it! I've never not remembered after!"

Tawne dashed to his chair and grabbed his hands before he could do major damage to his scalp.

"What are you talking about?" she shouted.

His hands clenched as he still reached for himself. He was pinned by her but unaware of it. He stared as the crew put the mangled body on a stretcher and loaded it. Police were picking through the area looking for scattered body funk: severed buttons, a stray nipple, anything.

They were interviewing a thin woman with owly glasses. She said, "I brought my Sunday school class out on a field trip. It was two of the kids who found her."

The ghosts stepped from the walls, wary of Arcan.

He sobbed, seeing them coming out from the drywall and plaster the way floaters suddenly surfaced in lakewater. "I actually murdered one outright. It wasn't Delia's fault I got fired."

"Good grief, Arcan. You didn't kill Delia," Tawne tried to explain.

"I did. I did. You don't know about me," he whimpered.

The cat and the wolf rolled over inside him, laughing their feral laughs, bellies full, fur unnaturally slick. The ghoul was grinning and grotesque. Arcan would never be able to keep them under again. Not if they could come out and he not know about it.

Friday night, the news said it might have happened. What was he doing Friday night? Was that when he got drunk and stoned, trashing the house? Or was that Thursday night?

Only his animals and the coroner would know for certain.

"I know you damn sure didn't kill Delia." Tawne said sternly. She shook him until he looked away from the television. The cold in her hands shocked his skin.

She saw them crouching in Arcan's face, eyes glinting out at her with suspicion, hostility, cruelty. As if they saw a beast they ought to know but hadn't encountered before.

Not everything in the chains of caves came close enough to be distinguished.

The soulwindows to Arcan's body house were certainly full. His face moved subtly, then stopped. He was trying hard to control them even if he did believe he was no longer able to. Tawne frowned down into his eyes without making the link.

What was it Nietzsche said, about staring into the abyss 'til it stared back? Wet fields and dangerous alleys.

Fenris.

She looked up to try to see what Arcan was seeing when he turned away from her. There were shadowy women with imprints from Arcan's crouching howlers on them: mutilated genitals and faces, sheer layers of blood and sliced flesh making the chiffon and lace on profane nighties. Only one among the revenant women was obviously, truly dead. The others were only dead-in-part as they accused him. Victims that made Tawne's few look amateurish and barely touched.

(Did the man fixing his tire, Carl, and the tall teen lurk somewhere for Tawne? Or had their deaths been too sudden? They had only had a moment of fear as they looked at her and saw . . . whatever they saw. The focus had been on heat, not torture. Tawne wasn't sadistic. As long as she didn't count the cowboy whose arm she'd broken and the man in the car whose brain she'd softened into waxy flan with a glassblower's breath. But she hadn't been in her body then. Perhaps cruelty was easier during astral projection.)

"I'm sorry," Arcan whispered, sick with himself.

My god, he knows the dark. Has known it all along. He knows it better than I do.

This knowledge came ultimately from the same source as Tawne's. From a point of despair.

She put her face inches from his. "You didn't kill Delia." He protested. "I did. I blamed her for losing my job. I even fantasized about killing her. I *dreamed* about it."

And he'd dreamed the animals were loose, running amuck, wallowing in absolute shred-bingeing. Had it been a warning or was he so deeply submerged by them at the time that he couldn't tell that it was really happening?

But that was last night—Saturday night's nightmare. On Friday he'd had Delia pinned in woods, stuffing leaves down her throat.

They'd found her body in the woods.

"I killed her." Arcan whispered solemnly to himself in terror, in disgust.

A thin smile played about Tawne's lips. "No, I saw it. I know who killed Delia and it wasn't you."

"You're just saying that. I did it. I've been fighting them so long just to lose." Arcan sighed, utterly wretched. "I tortured and raped her and finally killed her."

"Delia was tortured and raped and murdered—but not by you."

Arcan shook his head, unconvinced. "You lie."

The animals evolved in angles here and there in his face. They were disguised as a tensed jaw, a twitch of the eye. His voice rumbled.

Tawne expected him to turn into a werewolf in front of her while she gripped him in her hands. But he couldn't because he wasn't a werewolf. There could be no manifestation. She almost wished there could be for the satisfying sake of seeing the freakish mutation in another: misery loving company. Arcan couldn't physically change outright. Not beyond subtle feature alterations produced by the animal minds over human matter.

But Tawne could. She could and would change. And she did, making him look into her eyes and then willing it, sensing the ripple and shock as she became Delia.

Arcan howled, trying to wriggle away from her. Then he stopped and melted, pleading, whispering, "I'm sorry."

"Does this look dead to you?" she asked in Delia's voice.

He shook his head, puzzled.

"You didn't kill Delia." She let the image fade.

"Tawne," he said, inhaling sharply. "Tawne."

"I let you see that for a reason, Arcan," she told him. "Something happened the other night that killed Delia and changed me. I saw what happened to her and it almost did to me, too. You weren't there."

"I'm a monster," he said simply.

"Join the club," she replied.

Staples of light punched through the living room window.

Tawne felt the contact. Blood came through her pores where dawn touched.

"Jesus!" she snapped and darted away, alarmed. "Shut those!"

Arcan quickly closed the drapes. He turned back and saw red smears down her arms and on one cheek. Red flowered through the black hose on her thighs.

"Are you okay?" he asked.

She nodded. "As long as the sunlight doesn't suck me dry."

He was a blank. He'd seen her in the daylight many times, when they worked together at Galway's.

"Some of the myth stuff is right on; some is crap. Sunlight really is harmful to vampires, I guess," Tawne replied, feeling her lips shape the V word, looking for the impact in his eyes.

Arcan was trying to decide if she was crazy or had changed drastically since he'd last seen her. She'd become Delia and then switched back. There was something in that, wasn't there? He carefully pulled the drapes, overlapping them anywhere they didn't seem to be secure enough. His hands trembled. Not erratically, not until they must shatter, but as if Arcan was *almost* in perfect control.

"I only have one room without windows. That's the *batroom* in the hall. The one with the big bedroom still has

239

one small window. I guess I could get thicker, darker curtains," he said.

Tawne smirked. Arcan realized he called it a *batroom*. Slip of the tongue? He apologized.

But he was thinking of adolescent blondes with long hair tickling the cracks of their asses as they hung all over his father, gazing luridly down into Deborah Tyler's grave. Lamia visages, vestiges of life giving almost as good as they got. Vampires who would probably take a little boy to bed and expect him to perform like a fully grown slave when less than a dozen years ago those breasts had been his milk bottles.

Licking that life force with cat-rough tongues and scratching at you, all the time scratching, confusing passion and litter boxes, trying to cover up something offensively male about you. That was where the smell of dust came from—their claws. When they wept and wiped their eyes, it clotted between their fingers, making them feel inelegant, fussy, asking, *do you still find me beautiful? Do you still find me beautiful as I slowly unscrew this useless heart from your chest?*

Vampires. Was it possible that Tawne could be like that?

She gradually withdrew down the hall as dawn filtered grayly through the thin curtains, pursuing her in poison fog. It probed, spreading across the floor and walls in leisurely white stains. She likewise moved backward without the haste she'd shown when the sun first touched her. She kept one hand along the wall, slightly behind her, feeling out for the shadows and dipping her fingers into the dark to keep herself steady.

There was nothing mincing, pretentious or false in Tawne's movements. She wasn't like them. They were sinuous, indecent, debauched in snake robes. The silly outfit was something they would wear but it was misleading on her. Wrapped in leather was no Lilith and no punk. It didn't matter that Arcan had seen her change forms.

Changing forms was merely an extension of darkness. Tawne had done it to help him, to make him see that there was something out of the ordinary here. She'd done it so his psyche—wallowing in the belief he must have murdered Delia—would be able to take notice out of its misery.

Tawne glided backward. She felt the press of the advancing steam of light. It wasn't like any sacred fire scorching her creatures at bay. It filled her with a sense of impending weakness, a pool of dampness just below the entire surface of her skin, waiting to erupt.

Two mornings ago, the light had struck her so fast that Tawne was taken by surprise. If there had been any gradual swelling, she hadn't noticed it in her panic. It might not have been there. Maybe this was worse because it was the second time and too soon. Then she'd lost all of her blood. Did it get worse each time? What could be worse than losing all one's blood?

Motes danced like infinitesimal gyroscopes. She knew she'd better run into the bathroom and close the door, seal out the day. She was fascinated with the way it moved, slowly yet completely filling up the room. Gaseous. Radium. Not that she couldn't get away from it. It was as easy as outrunning the stumbling dead.

She knew Arcan was watching. Tawne imagined what he thought. *Why did I answer the door? I could be sleeping.*

It was lucky for her he'd answered. She could be on the street right now. She never could have found total concealment in the 15 minutes since she'd gotten Arcan out of bed.

They heard a sound. A sort of breath. The lightest of wings.

There were moths outside, energized in the dawn. Softly fluttering beyond where Arcan had patted the curtains together. Their small bodies cast shadows onto the windows, becoming spots along the carpet and walls. Neither Tawne nor Arcan expected them to strike the window. They didn't weigh enough to do that. Unless, of course, they did it by the hundreds.

A bird confused and blinded by their number rammed into the glass, shattering a weak pane, ripping the curtain. It jerked convulsively on the floor, moths caught in its feathers. The sun followed the bird through the torn drape. A dart of light speared Tawne.

Her skin swelled so fast the leather in the skirt and boots creaked, straining at their stitchings. The bustier popped as her breasts heaved out, glossed with blood. One eye—the only part of her face stabbed by the sun—caught the dart and seemed to explode as the window had. Blood poured from it in a frothy gouge. She clutched at it, screaming with astonishment, trying to fold it back into the socket and only succeeding in mashing the detonated tissue against her cheek. She spun in the same place in the hall, as if she'd been skewered there.

Was there sentience in the dawn? Could it make the moths do this?

(It knows me.)

(*She* knows me.)

(We're at least acquainted. We met the other day but didn't exactly hit it off.)

"Shit!" Arcan cried, leaping over the coffee table. He landed on the cut ball of his foot. He sprang into the hallway, putting his body between the woman and the light stiletto. He caught Tawne in a half-tackle and dragged her into the bathroom, slamming the door behind them.

He gasped at the exploded baked potato of the eye and the gory outsized marshmallows of her breasts. He wet a washcloth in the sink. When he turned back, she was laughing.

"It's okay," she assured him. "It'll heal. I hope."

Arcan couldn't help trying to clean her wounds. He dabbed the cloth at her cheek where blood and gooey globs of pupil smothered them. He couldn't believe she was able to sit up. He tried to clean the bloody breasts but couldn't bring himself to touch them.

"I guess calling the doctor is out of the question," he said. "I don't imagine the folks at 911 have a chapter for this in their field manual."

Tawne grinned. "It doesn't hurt."

"You're kidding."

She added more soberly, "Nothing ever hurts."

"Nothing?" Arcan asked, his eyes widening, remembering her scream. He knew from his own past experience, however, that it was possible to scream and rant and roar without any physical pain being present.

Tawne began licking the blood from her hand. She huffed. "This is damn embarrassing, you know?"

She wasn't actively oozing anymore. Her tongue lapped as she cleaned her fingers like she'd just had the best chicken dinner ever. She touched her breasts to smear the fingers again, lifted them to her lips with the delicate grace of a tabby grooming mouse grease and shit from its fur. He knew that maneuver. He had a cat inside himself.

Arcan flinched as he discovered this was arousing him. Tawne shook her head at the idea of having an audience for this bizarre activity. She looked up at his frank stare and smiled. "Don't ever let pieces of yourself go, Arcan. Each of us needs it all. Never waste a drop."

I have to do this, she told herself as she continued to re-consume the teenager's blood. *I'll be weak if I don't I'll have to replace it, and the only person available is Arcan. I won't hurt Arcan.*

She tweaked balls of gore from the large quartz of her nipples and wrung it from her long hair.

Arcan wasn't disgusted at all. Should he be? When the ghoul had tasted blood and flesh?

To him, Tawne had always possessed marvelous strength. Now it was magnified. She was no longer a woman to him for he hated women. She'd become a terrible goddess. Kali, of death and death's special beauty, Her (or Her hermaphroditic consort Shiva's) shrine was black with red floors. Germanic Hel, Sumerian Ereshkergal, Greek Artemis-Hecate, Aztec Ilamatecuhtli. The Egyptian goddess-guardians of the 21 gates of the Underworld. Goddesses of the Land of No Return. One could love them even if he couldn't stand mortal women.

Arcan closed his eyes and corrected himself. *No, only your animals love her,* thinking *of victims shrieking beneath sacrificial knives and tusks, on primeval altars of bone and satin—hard unyielding bone and soft, soft satin.*

He smirked as the beasts shrank back. *No, they most certainly didn't love her. Anymore than they could stand Harry after he'd come back from Cambodia changing, smelling different. This was one attraction Arcan couldn't put off on the monsters.*

Arcan watched her take back the effused blood. The socket filled, at first a red giant sun of an eye. It shrank back to the size of the other, its lead-colored iris swimming into view like a continent rising from a red ocean. Arcan's heart beat so fast he thought he'd lose his balance. The arousal didn't make him want to harm her or to impose his will on her. What did he want, then?

She took the washcloth Arcan used on her face and bit into it, letting what blood was in it drain into her mouth, her lips quivering around the droplets. Afterward she stood up, stronger but able to tell that the sun flooded the whole house now. All save this little room.

It was the only safe place to hide. "We both know secrets about each other we didn't know before." Tawne said. Her breasts were still fully exposed in the torn bustier which hung like a flimsy vest. She made no attempt to cover them. "If you turn me out now, I'll die. If you have to because you can't stomach this or can't take it on top of your own troubles, I can understand. Just please let me hang 'til sundown. Tell me. I never checked before. Does this city have an underground sewer? If it was good enough for the phantom of the opera . . ."

Arcan grabbed her naked shoulders to tell her it was okay. Before he could check himself, he put his arms around her neck, pressing his forehead to hers. She was an inch or two taller than he was. He marveled at how cool her brow was, how cold her breasts were against him. They were cold enough to chase a fever off. She didn't pull away as he leaned into her and embraced that coolness. The desperation as he folded her close didn't tell Tawne she could stay; it begged her to stay.

Tawne also put her arms around Arcan. Excitement and sorrow mixed, making her half-crazy. She hadn't needed to trick him with enchantment. He was with her knowing not only that she was too plain/too large Tawne, but also knowing what she *was*. It was too good to be true, but it was also crushing. Had she gone through all this only to find someone who might have loved her anyway? Someone her undeath didn't matter to?

Oh, and didn't it matter? Arcan knew the darkness, was a man of beasts, had his own personal anti-fan club of ghosts. Was he her feral bridegroom? He had to be. Loving in shadows. Calling to her from them.

They unlocked foreheads and simultaneously offered a kiss. Arcan tasted blood on her breath and was thrilled by its slick ice. His tongue pushed back across hers, intrigued by the truth that this blood was second hand. He brought up his hand and briefly squeezed one of her broad shoulders, sticky with plasma and her own saliva. He could feel her muscles locked and equal to—greater than—his own, like two wolves finding one another in a forest after dark. The sweats from all his nights of reliving his horrors and crimes dried up. He no longer thought he'd catch fire.

Tawne felt the tombstone-hard erection pressing against her groin. She felt the flood of his heat pouring over her, starting at this center. It was sustaining her. She didn't need to find warmth from his blood. It wasn't light years away. It was right there. She slipped her hand into Arcan's pajama bottoms and grasped the cock. A bolt of intense heat coursed like a bolt of lightning, up in a shock to her shoulder.

Arcan moaned and slid up her short skirt. He forced the ends of his fingers through the crotch of the sheer pantyhose. She was wet but not with traditional female lubrication. She was bloody, down her stomach, thighs, buttocks. Everywhere she hadn't reconsumed what had flowed out. The sun had made her erupt blood in all places. She leaned back against the door with her legs apart. He drove in, gasping at the chill, shuddering as it rendered him even harder, seeming to freeze his erection into permanence. There was definitely no mistaking Tawne for a living woman.

And when her body became ape-hairy, her face obscene with leaking hieroglyphic swellings, Arcan held her tighter and kissed the striated membranes of her dog lips.

Inside the bathroom in the center of the building, neither of them heard the moths outside, thudding against the roof and walls.

Chapter Twenty-four

It was a fine day for a bust. Sunshine was always better for weddings, funerals and arrests. Detective Rob Waters and Denise Cross were at opposite doors. Their guns were drawn, flat in their hands with the muzzles pointed up.

Waters hoped they hadn't hurt the kid yet.

Eight-year-old Brad Sullivan had been snatched out in front of the Catholic school two days ago. The ransom note had arrived at his parents' home within an hour of that. The SWATS were coordinating, watching the planned drop-off point where an attaché of grands sat as ordered. Other cops were watching the hotel on the block where the pay phone call made by the kidnappers had been traced to.

But Waters had this hunch. He remembered the Mandy Rankin kidnapping five years back. She'd been 10 and was now deceased. Shot through the eye after the pay-off. Stolen in front of the same school.

That pair of perps had been arrested. Joe Gordon died

in prison two years ago, knifed by another inmate. Wendel Parker was on death row, waiting while they went through appeals to see if he'd get the injection.

Parker had a brother who was 13 when the Rankin kidnapping happened. Now Willis Parker was 18 and not in school. He was out of work and living in the shack his father had left the brothers when he died drunk seven years ago. It was the same house where the Rankin girl had been held prisoner.

The lieutenant wouldn't listen. He thought it was too much of a coincidence. Besides, Willis Parker had no priors, not even juvie ones. The lieutenant believed this was gang-related shit. There was gang activity in the neighborhood that hadn't been there five years ago. Hell, there was gang shit everywhere these days.

Waters had been there when they found the girl's body in the closet, sitting on a stack of *Hustler* and *Soldier of Fortune* magazines. Her head leaned back against the wall. A raincoat hanging on the rod had dangled across half her face, stirred by the bullet disturbing the air.

Waters was drawn to the place and drove past it several times afterward. Morbidly fascinated as if Rob saw *something* but couldn't quite tell what it was. He'd get a rush, chills, like a kid sneaking past the local haunted house.

The shack was tumbledown enough to be a haunted house. The children in the area threw rocks through the windows until Willis started coming outside, confronting them, and then . . . asking them inside.

Would you like to come inside?

He'd invite them with his snotty drippy voice, his toothpick hips, and his wrists thicker than his hands.

The kids stayed away in droves then.

Waters secretly wished some swaggering gangster would do the world a favor and perform a drive-by on that sucker, but no one ever did. Willis Parker had given Rob the creeps when the kid was just 13. And that was enough to cause the detective to think such uncharitable thoughts about somebody who had never broken the law. Apparently he could give the bad folks in his own hood enough shivers that they left his ass alone.

Waters had this hunch and only his partner would listen. He hoped he could trust her on this one. Denise was a dynamo cop who wasn't afraid of anything.

Or so he'd always believed. She might just be afraid of poverty the way she was taking gratuities from the local drug squires and shaking down a few poor hookers for more than their pimps took. Had she done this for years before anyone caught on? Rob couldn't believe it was true. Denise lived a simple life style. She seldom went out when off-duty. She wasn't into fancy clothes or jewelry, and she didn't want an expensive car. She was the Spartan type, a good soldier. She'd been married once but had divorced the guy after he was arrested on a single D.U.I. She had that kind of no-excuses rigid uprightness.

Maybe she had a sick mother somewhere.

Why else would Denise Cross do an about-face like this?

Waters hoped he could trust her one more time before he had to turn her in. By the end of the week he should have all the evidence he needed: bank statements, photos and recordings. And a battered 16-year-old prostitute named Darlene who needed a bit more coaxing before she'd testify. She'd come across as soon as Rob could make her understand she'd be protected.

At first Waters had been too stunned to believe it. Shit, Cross had medals. She'd saved his life more than once.

He looked at his watch, at the second hand shadowing the quarter past mark. He wondered which of the two men was inside. He was sure there were two kidnappers. Willis, of course. And Lloyd Tillins, an ex-con with burglary and assault priors who crashed there occasionally. Friend of brother Wendel. One was gone picking up the ransom.

The seconds were at the halfway mark and ticking

toward noon. Waters and Cross had agreed to one minute past arrival. Slowly up to the front and back of the house. What would Cross be thinking? Waters knew what was going through his mind . . . that he'd dreamed about this place. He dreamed about a body in the closet, face back and looking up to see that closet rod and the narrow walls. Like it was the dumbwaiter dropping someone into hell. Spectral hands coming from the dark on the way down to wave good-bye.

Would you like to come inside?

Time. Waters kicked in the front door and hoped Cross was doing the same at the back. He thought he heard her do it, but it might only have been the echo of his own kick. The entire shack shuddered along its dry-rotted plain wood frame. The door bounced off the wall and came back at him. Rob kicked it again and sprang inside.

Good god, Waters thought nervously as he landed on the moth-eaten braid of an oval throw rug. To think there was a time when he'd rather have Denise Cross at his side (or his back) than anyone else in the whole department. If only the crap he'd found out she was up to wasn't so blatantly criminal, he might be tempted to shut his eyes. Lots of cops did a little graft just to get by, and it didn't keep them from serving and protecting. If only it was just some petty shit that hadn't hurt anybody so he could turn his back.

(Denise should be coming through the kitchen about now. The screen door would swing back silently, or maybe thrum like a dulcimer.)

There was a small parochial uniform jacket on the living room floor, beige and kelly green, the colors for St. Anne's. It was crumpled and torn at the shoulders as if it had been ripped off. Nearby were the little trousers and the shirt.

They were keeping Brad Sullivan here. Was the kid still alive?

Waters sniffed, expecting the signature scent of death to be in the air.

There was a mural on the largest wall. Waters didn't recall that being there five years ago. It depicted a full moon with craters defining a face with eyes rolled up to the whites and lips bowed down in the strain of an epileptic seizure. An oriental carpet flew through the weird sky of this moon, perfectly patterned, unfurled. The Aladdin seated on it was a portrait of Willis himself. Waters was amazed at the detail in the carpet's mandala, the boy's look of sick fear as if the journey wasn't his plan.

Rob had no idea that Willis Parker had this kind of talent.

It was all drawn in crayon. The detective smelled the wax, the lingering childhood aroma of Crayola.

He heard footsteps, slow and sneaky. Cross was moving up through the hallway between the kitchen and the dining room. A strange set-up. The house had been renovated a decade ago after the old kitchen was ruined in a grease fire that also burned Mrs. Parker to death. The garage had been rebuilt into the new kitchen with the money from their mother's insurance. Cross would enter through the door on the left. Waters swiveled the other direction, to the right, toward the bedroom. The barrel of his gun was no longer pointed straight up but was trained on the door closed in front of him.

He put his hand on the door and pushed it open, standing just to the side.

The bedroom was messy and stank like a sewer. There were a few blood stains on the mattress where the sheets had been clutched and twisted away. The mural on the wall behind the headboard was of a woman standing in flames, her hair blackened down to the scalp, her mouth open in an insane scream of pain, teeth exploding out like kernels of popcorn. She held a frying pan in one hand, or was the cast iron fused to the flesh of the fingers melted into a flipper? Her dowdy dress and apron were a fog of fiery tendrils, exposing skin beneath, cracking open like crevices in a volcano.

Very graphically rendered. The ruined body had the shiny slick texture of the real thing. The artist had layered on waxy pinks and yellows 'til it seemed that fat poured from the fissures of her torso.

Mommie Parker.

Someone jumped up from behind the bed and fired at Waters. Already leaning away, the detective saw the flash, brighter than the crayon sparks on the wall, heard the fire-cracker report of a cheap small caliber hand gun. Amateurs. Christ. It had to be Parker because Tillins would know better than to use a .22 pop pistol.

It was Parker. Shit, with all the gang business in the neighborhood, couldn't he have bought something better?

The young jerk ducked back behind the bed. Waters shouted and moaned, letting him think he'd hit the cop. He threw his body against the wall to make a decent sound-ing thud, then quietly stepped back into the doorway. He shot Willis Parker between the eyes when he jack-in-the-boxed back up for a look-see.

Idiot. This was too damned easy.

Waters moved in, saw the crayon pictures on each wall. One depicted a rumba line of corpses, bodies in varying stages of decay, complete with maggots and flies. Each one sported a boner, decomposing flesh trailing in banners or scabs flaking over running green sores. Even the dead women in the line had boners, bouncing like a third im-perfect leg beneath the flapping shreds of their breasts. And there was Willis, sketched bent over a rail of bones, his backside presented as each cadaver took its turn.

Another wall was drawn with lines in deep perspective until it appeared that there was a long hallway stretched back for miles. It was illustrated with dark and moulding brick, slimy in the mortar. Here and there—and here and there down for miles—spongy tips of tentacles protruded, gesturing out, with tiny twisted faces embedded in the end of each. There was a shadow shaped like a man, stretched across the floor and cast against one wall, as if he had only just set foot in this corridor. The minutiae was impressive, from the little rat skeleton to the doll's head (or the baby's head) to the oddly flopping rodent that was half ferret and half manta ray.

The fourth wall had a gargoyle face coming out of the dark done in grays, charcoals and blacks. The face was of brother Wendel with about a hundred hypo needles sticking out of his skull, his mouth split into a grin with prison bars for teeth. Fucked up. Waters stepped around the bed, gun still trained. Parker's body was naked from the waist down. It was sweaty with shit caked around the anus.

Waters' shoulders sagged. The body was face down—as it was on the mural with the line of corpses queued up for a poke. He couldn't see if there was shit and blood on the penis or not. The fecal reek gagged him. The exit wound in the back of the skull was trailing clots of gray brain matter in an almost mandalic pattern of spatters.

Waters didn't regret one bit having shot him, thinking about the Sullivan boy. He wished he could do the same to Tillins. The SWATS would get him first. They might already have.

"Well," Cross said behind him, slipping her own piece into the holster inside her tailored blazer. "When I heard you scream and that thud, I said to myself, old Rob's at it again. Fake and splatter."

She smiled grimly. She walked around the bed to the body.

Waters only had eyes for the closet door, thinking of the Rankin girl and of history repeating itself. That closet fairly pulsed with haunted energy, on the same wall as the fucking dead and covered with turgid stiffs. Rob wanted to believe the Sullivan boy wasn't dead in there. Perhaps he was just scared.

Detective Waters moved to the closet door. "Asshole," he muttered as the knob turned in his hand. "Son of a bitch. Cross, you want to call an ambulance?"

He looked inside. Pictures, crayon drawing of hands showing fleshless tendons, veins, da Vinci anatomicals. Well, Gacy painted but he never had as much talent as this twisted ganglia. Even the fingernails were perfect down to the half moons, cuticles, ends ragged from biting or from clawing at brickwork they were chained to.

"Why? Willis doesn't need it. Neither will you."

Rob began to turn. Cross had picked up the .22. Flaky piece or not, properly aimed and at close range, it did the trick.

They would logically assume Parker had shot Rob and that Cross then shot Parker.

She fired and Rob Waters fell back into the closet, looking up, those crayon hands waving good-bye.

Denise heard the rattled breath and saw the naked child cowering under the bed. He'd seen it all. His hand and wrist were dripping shit.

He was in shock but he could talk later. If she wouldn't let Rob Waters ruin her life, she wasn't going to let this kid do it. She felt the .22 in her fingers and thanked her lucky stars that she didn't have a maternal bone in her body.

So much for that flashback in her life. Denise replayed it when she wanted to feel invincible. Morning at the station had been anything but bolstering. Since Waters died, she was certain the other detectives were looking at her sideways although nothing had been said to indicate that her partner hadn't died at Willis Parker's hands.

It might have been because the lieutenant hadn't sanctioned their going to Parker's house in the first place and it resulted in a detective's death. It might have been because—for all his faults—Rob had been right about Parker's connection with the Sullivan kidnapping. Lieutenant Guntz didn't like being shown up, especially since, if he'd let them go in when Waters spoke up about his theory, the kid might still be alive. As it was, no one knew if the boy had been killed before or during their raid.

Denise hadn't been assigned another partner yet. She didn't expect to get one.

As for the crap Waters had against her, that was lost in the shit detail because he hadn't told anyone. And little Darlene suffered an unfortunate overdose, brain cells fairly igniting with so much heroin.

Denise looked into her face as the girl sailed out on the final rush. Darlene's eyes were enigmatic. Denise wanted to ask her. "What do you see?"

Cross had never gotten on well with most of the men in the department. They thought she was too gung ho. Her instincts were too primal to be fully human. She knew they were planning to stick her behind a desk next week. They had been waiting a long time to do this; now was their chance. It looked bad that the police so purely fouled this case. The Rankin kidnapping might have been five years back but the news dug it all out. Police had fucked that one up also. This time everyone was killed but Cross. They needed a scapegoat.

She'd fight that in her style: full frontal assault. No other officer had as many commendations as she did. She hadn't joined the force to sharpen pencils. She'd joined because it was the only place a woman could be on the front lines. Well, they could on a limited basis in the American military, but there were only so many wars. The streets were the only places where blood roared, adrenaline ruled and power slid freely like saliva up and down the throat.

Denise pulled up to the house on Magnolia Drive. It was a beautiful neighborhood. The houses weren't too close together, were brick with white driveways—no oil stains—

hedges and chrysanthemums in abundance. This would probably be her last real work before Lieutenant Guntz took his chance to ground her, promising, "It's only for a while until we can get you a new partner."

Neighbors had been complaining of noises the last couple days. Screaming, grinding music, crashing and mashing. The TV was up too high but the owner wouldn't answer the door when they knocked to ask him to turn it down. Normally in a neighborhood laid out like this one, a little television noise was only a minor annoyance. But even Denise could hear it from her car with the windows rolled up. He really had it cranked. It might be one of those horror novels on tape, and it was the stereo cranked up to full volume. It sounded like car chase scenes from a dozen different cop movies, voracious raptors storming through fun parks and slashers running amuck at pajama parties all going at once. No wonder the neighbors complained.

Not that detectives went out on petty disturbance calls but this was special. The computer spit out that the owner of the house—a David Vance Jewitt—was the citizen to report Alan Moravec's body, late of the Mongoose Motel.

It was a nagging item, that video player in Moravec's room rented from the movie store across the street. There were no tapes found in the room though. Moravec's car in the parking lot had a video camera in it but no tape. He'd been a newsman. He must have had a tape in it and had rented the machine to view it.

Knowing the late Moravec's penchant for sick violence and senseless overload, what might be on such a tape if it existed could be pretty bizarre. Had he filmed something that anyone in particular didn't want made public? "Hey, mister! You're an asshole!" And Moravec was an asshole. Any one of a number of people who had been subjects of derision on his news spot would have motive to kill him.

It might have only been an innocent video but if somebody recognized him, they might pilfer such a tape, hoping it had a certain underground potential.

Could this Jewitt have called police but pocketed the video, planning to sell it to tabloid TV? They could do one of those stupid mystery shows. *Newsman's body undergoes bizarre infestation. See the exclusive footage of 'Mean Streets' final gross-out coup. How does the lynching at the country bar link with his death? Is there an alien connection? Did Elvis stage his own death to go underground as a hit man for the Southern Mafia? Was Elvis given Moravec's contract by a bunch of disaffected rednecks?*

Cross had seen the final *Mean Streets* about the dog and the cowboys in Red's Stomping Ground. Not her cup of tea. Juicy but juvenile. Any potential Alan Moravec might have had for real evil was drowned in his mediocrity.

He'd died under strange circumstances. She'd read the autopsy report. She'd talked to officers Weigt and Pueller about black-skulled bugs digging their way out of the dead man's chest and guts. The internal damage had been fantastic—whole organs metamorphosing into pure drain cleaner.

Walking up the sidewalk to the neat porch with its ornamental swing and wrought iron fretwork, Denise felt energy itching in her hands. She popped her knuckles white to alleviate it. She heard noises roaring inside as she put those swollen knuckles to the door.

Next to the door was a big picture window, lacy curtains filmy through which she spied movement. She saw a man and woman embracing. The woman was in a sequin gown and the man was struggling. Denise pressed to the glass, straining to see through the lace. It was like trying to see through a veil but she could tell that blood was literally being slung as the man flailed his ripped arms. He was trying to pull his face from the woman's.

Detective Cross pounded on the window. "Hey, police! Halt!"

The woman casually turned her head toward the window. Her face sparkled, painted in glitter. Even her hair shone, braided and woven with diamonds. Blood dripped from shimmering lips.

"Shit!" Cross shouted and kicked the door down. She drew her weapon and jumped through the entrance.

Blood squirted like warm cherry Kool-Ade being forced from a water pistol. It geysered everywhere from the man, spraying the walls, ceiling and floor.

"I said halt!" Denise yelled as she aimed at the woman. But they were too damned close. How could she stop the woman and keep from hitting the man? Not that she gave two cents whether he was carved or not, but she was supposed to ask him some questions.

Did it matter? His clothes and skin hung in strips as if he'd narrowly missed death through a paper shredder.

What was the woman doing to him? Denise saw no weapons. The woman was only kissing him, holding him tightly against her body, stroking him with her hands that must be covered in diamond rings, rubbing herself against him—the spangles in her dress tinkling with every passionate movement. Did she have razor blades in those hands? Was the dress made of ground glass?

Denise warned her. "Step back! Let him go!"

The woman did step back.

Well, not exactly *step*. She seemed to irradiate away from him, glittery face serene, mouth open slightly in the pose of the half-kiss. And then she collapsed into a formless scattering of sharp glass shards. Into scintillant pebbles of the sort Denise saw at traffic accidents with windshields shattered and twinkling under roadway flares.

The man leaned on his feet for mere seconds in the direction she dissolved, as if threaded to her memory by a spare webbing of capillaries and cords of nerve bundles. Denise darted forward to catch him but he fell onto the glass before the detective could reach him. He twitched, further grinding himself, then lay still.

Denise looked warily around the living room. She stalked the rest of the house, pistol drawn and ready to fire if she saw anything bright.

Where was the woman of the sequin dress and glitter-painted skin? Denise knew she couldn't really have dissolved into so many blue white chips. She found no one. She came back to the living room. The television was on but the screen was blank. White noise seemed not so much to hiss from it as to crunch and crackle in high-pitched, very short sound waves. It came to the end and the video recorder clicked, whirred its whining tickering back and then clicked a second time as if to announce:

> We're ready again.
> Ready to commence.
> What are you waiting for?

The woman had been there, beautiful and shining, and now she wasn't. All that remained were granules of pulverized slicing glass. And a body lacerated beyond description. It was likely that of David Jewitt. Dental records would prove it.

Denise hit the PLAY button.

The couple in the darkness rode as she watched, not recognizing either David Jewitt, Alan Moravec or the woman in sequins. The ugly man sat up, snapped the woman's legs and looked then into the camera. His eyes bolted right to Denise Cross.

He became Denise. With grenades for breasts, the rings piercing the nipples with brass. Her hair streamed away from her face and her mouth filled with rubies. Rob Waters writhed beneath her, blind as King Oedipus, one of his eyes in her navel.

(Denise caught her breath as she watched . . .)

The video Denise leaned back and yanked out the rings. There was gray explosion, harmonizing with her red howl. And then—like the old song sang—it was raining men. Hallelujah.

(Denise watched and began to smile. She ran it again, smiling slyly.)

There was a knock at the door. Denise snarled at being interrupted.

She'd been so deeply in tune with the video. Every alteration was fascinating. The story meant so much to her personally. And to have some jackass come to the door? It was probably one of the neighbors. Well, she had a use for them. Good use. They should have waited it out. They should have packed up and moved away.

She strode to the front door. It was still open from her having kicked it in. A postman was waiting patiently on the porch.

"I have a package here, postage due. Forty-two cents," he said.

Denise smirked as she produced her badge. "Come inside."

He blanched when he saw the shredded wheat carnage. He clutched his gut as if considering losing his breakfast, and rammed his legs together like he was afraid of shitting his pants.

"I want you to look at this tape found here at the scene. I know this is terrible and I do apologize. But you can see there's been a murder. I think the persons displayed on this tape may be suspects. I need you to try and remember if you might have seen them in this neighborhood before," Cross explained, trying to appear courteous. "What's your name, sir?"

"Ron Spooner," he whispered, trying not to look at the splattered red walls—the body—God! had that been a man?

"Mr. Spooner, why don't you sit down here. Please?

Thank you. I know there's blood on the screen but I can't wipe it off. The forensic team has to be able to see everything before a speck of it can be cleaned up. You'll have to see it through the blood. I'm sorry. There's so little time. We're dealing with maniacs."

He nodded rigidly, perched on the edge of the sofa. There was blood there, too, blood everywhere for god's sake, and he didn't want to sit in it, get it on his uniform. He didn't want it to touch him.

Denise hit PLAY and then stood back to watch the lights and images slide across his features. She looked at his face as she had studied Darlene's face after Denise forced the overdose on her, and the way she'd studied Rob's after she shot him.

She wanted to observe this guy's reaction. It ought to be fun. She'd certainly been having a good time watching the tape before he'd arrived.

The video opened with the man and woman rutting on the river bank. The postman frowned, blushed, his fingers curling in his lap.

The ugly man sat up, broke the woman's legs, and looked into the camera. Something oozed out his nostril in a thickly spun rope of vivid red, black and yellow rings. It slithered over his chin and onto his shoulder, the coral snake tongue darting. It went down his chest where each wiry hair stiffened and began to wriggle, opening eyes along each thickening tip. The skin of the ugly man's face toughened, slicked, and his mouth split all the way back to his ears which flattened into diamond shapes.

Denise wondered what the postman was seeing as he snorted with contempt and disbelief. She saw what she'd seen before. She'd sensed from the beginning that his interpretation would be different. That he would hate it just as she loved it. Objects of power weren't intended for everyone. The tape clicked. The postman jumped to his feet, shoes splashing in puddles of David Jewitt's blood. He was sweating through his uniform. "Sorry! I didn't recognize nobody!"

He edged toward the door.

"Sit down, Ron. You'll have to see it again. You have to be absolutely sure," Denise said, walking with him, staying only a foot from him.

"I'm positive! I don't want to see that again. I've got to finish my route," he complained.

Denise pulled her service revolver and brandished it in his face. Had what he'd seen been worse than that?

"I told you to sit down."

He did. She pushed him from the edge of the sofa's seat to sitting with his back against it. The look on his face was priceless as the bloody-wet upholstery smacked him.

"Get comfy, Mr. Spooner. So you're receptive."

She hit PLAY. The ugly man sprouted serpents, became a serpent on whose body roiled, coiled and boiled snakes. Every inch of him moved as he rocked on top of the woman. As for her, lying on the bank, her breasts flattened and became a thin back with bony shoulder blades. The pubic depilated and then rounded up into buttocks. The head spun to press to the ground face down, becoming male and bearded. A crown of thorns squirmed in bas relief from his hair and forehead sharply.

The postman moaned, his eyes darting to the gun Denise held. He pulled a chain up from under his collar, grasping the silver crucifix and muttering a prayer.

"Tell me what you see, Ron."

He tried to shut his eyes. They fluttered open as if tugged by invisible wires. He might be repulsed but he had to see.

There wasn't a speck of gore in the scene except for tiny droplets emerging from where the thorns pricked the bearded man's brow. Some people were shocked by visions of unspeakable mangling, revolted by slabs of the meat of children—treated as if it was only so much veal. It took some folks enormous amounts of plasma and entrails to give them a single honest shiver, desensitized by the over-load of modern society. And Ron had been sickened by the sight of Jewitt's cheese-grated flesh, yet it was nothing he would ever have seen in any of his own nightmares. There were others, like Ron, whose inner terrors were simpler, medieval, fundamental. These were people who still be-lieved in black and white, in a grail, in Geraldo Rivera and the presence of Satanists everywhere.

But he couldn't talk about it. How could he utter such filthy words? That in a vision from Hell he watched Satan commit the ultimate obscene rape of Jesus? The river bank was burning. The river itself was on fire even as it screwed and undulated behind the sodomite couple. Heads and hands struggled, reaching up from the smoke and flames, blistering and bubbling around the sacrilege. How could he say it? It was blasphemy even to watch.

Ron moaned, "My eyes are damned."

And his brain was damned for receiving such pictures from his eyes.

"I *said* tell me what you see." Denise impatiently smacked him in the teeth with the barrel of the pistol. He shouted as the front ones broke, blood cascading out of his mouth.

He told her, crying, wiping snot from his nose and gory spittle from his swelling lips, begging his Lord for forgive-ness for having to be the instrument of voyeurism for the Devil. He slobbered until Denise wanted to puke just look-ing at him. But she listened. She stood there with the gun pressed to the bridge of his nose, letting the tape finish and rewind. She hit PLAY again by stretching to reach it from where she stood in front of the couch, keeping the gun on him, letting him know she'd blow out his brains if he tried to run.

He was made to watch again and couldn't sit still.

"Tell me what you see," she said, knowing it was esca-lating, getting worse.

He shook his head. "Can't," was all he could reply. "Can't."

She struck and cursed him, beating him as he began raving but wouldn't talk sense. He must belong to one of those churches that talked in tongues, she decided. All that came out of his mouth was gibberish. And whatever it was, it was bringing out all the stops of his timid little faith. He was more afraid of what he saw in the video than he was of her.

Denise shouted, "Tell me! Tell me!"

He was self-destructing over what he saw, and that had to be the most unusual thing Denise had ever encountered. So he saw the worst thing he could think of? You told yourself over and over *it's only a movie, only a movie* . . . and that worked for most Americans, right?

He screamed, a single oscillating *ave* of a shriek that hung in the air like Latin. Denise heard the crack of bones stretching to their bursting point. His wet skin tearing was almost as loud as when it split outright shortly after. A snake as thick as a man's arm slowly worked out of the hole in his chest. It unhinged its jaws and fastened canal-iculated fangs onto his face. They penetrated from the top of his balding scalp to just below his nose. The postman's own mouth opened to scream a second time—broken teeth from when she'd struck him with the pistol hanging by a few shreds of gum—and it made the sprung head seem almost twice as long. The wounds gouted in red that turned red-yellow-orange. Then the venom ignited his blood.

Denise laughed nervously as she moved back in a hurry.

The man's sparse hair caught fire, his clothes puffing into oily flames. These spread quickly to the sofa, tufts of fluffy stuffing erupting like cotton candy soaked in gasoline.

Denise retrieved the tape. She glanced back once when she reached the front door as the polyester carpet caught, fibers melting to release choking toxins. She thought for a moment she could still see herself on the TV screen, pulling the pins on the grenades of her breasts.

Only the eyes weren't hers. They were the ugly man's.

Chapter Twenty-five

He called Tawne to enter the shadows. She ran to him (on all fours, on two sturdy legs, with wings) as she always did. He was moving toward the mouth of the cavern. There was a pale shaft of light from something like the moon making the opening of the cave visible to Tawne for the first time in this series of dreams. She glanced up but couldn't find the moon. Where did the light come from, then?

He was coming out to greet her, face visible for a moment.

It was Arcan. Of course it was.

He'd always been her feral bridegroom. His body was different. It was slickered with blood and covered in fur. Only his face was human.

It was all that needed to be human.

The sun was setting. It was already getting dark in the living room which solidly faced east. But in Arcan's bedroom at the west end of the house, the rays pierced through horizontally, parallel with the floor and ceiling. It was why Arcan chose that bedroom instead of the other one which—like the living room—faced east and would have been too bright for a man who liked to sleep late.

Tawne slept, curled up in the bathtub, its porcelain no colder than her skin. As big as she was, she had to assume a tight fetal position to fit into it at all. The bathroom floor wasn't long enough for her to stretch out in. Now it was almost time for her to be safe. She could go out and fill herself up.

Last night she'd found a guy about to enter a bar. She'd slipped into Delia and went with him to his car, taking his heat willingly given at first, then having to hold him down as he suddenly was terrified of her and fighting for his life. Then she hurried home to cuddle with Arcan on the sofa, forgetting the horror on the man's face and a bestial reflection in his eyes. They watched syndicated reruns of *The Night Stalker* taped from the Sci Fi Channel. She'd indulged in his warmth, and Arcan was relaxed as he'd never been before.

How had they become lovers? It was a mystery to both of them but neither was willing to tamper with it by trying to examine it too closely.

They made love on Arcan's bed. She imagined he was covered in fur and that was why he was so warm. Only her feral bridegroom could ever heat her up enough. And she never dreamed he was seeing her as other than she saw herself.

Still it was strange. When they held each other, Arcan wouldn't touch her breasts with his hands. He caressed the muscles in her arms, tickled her thighs with his fingers, ran his palms over her sturdy hips. He buried his face between her thighs and made the heat so intense it was painful. He sighed into her hair as he entered her. The sweat dripping from his face onto hers sizzled like lava as he put his opened lips to hers, probing every inch of her mouth with his tongue. He crushed against her, chest to chest. But he wouldn't touch her breasts with his hands. Was that odd?

Tawne stood in front of the full length mirror on the bathroom door. Arcan had put it up for her yesterday. He'd smashed all the others. She thought she understood why, knowing what it was like to hate what you saw.

She stared at the oversized, plain woman and wondered why Arcan loved her. What did he see in those doughy features? He saw beyond them to the thorn and granite beauty that was his ideal. Because he was fenris, the shaggy consort who loved what others couldn't fathom.

Tawne squinted and stuck her tongue out at her reflection. It wasn't the sort of face that one expected to see love animating. Did such a face deserve joy? Or was it fated for pain alone? How many big women were on the illustrated covers of romance novels even though they probably made up a large percentage of the readership? When had Jackie Collins or Judith Krantz ever written about a glamorous heavy-set woman conquering fame and bedrooms?

Tawne changed into Delia. Okay, let lovely Delia, sweet Delia bask in the happiness instead of her. Delia had the body worthy of poets. Tawne didn't know if Delia had ever been in love or been loved.

Looking like that? She must have been.

Ugly people might have sex but love was the prerogative of the beautiful. So the whole world taught in every movie and portrait, each verse.

Well, not every verse. Tawne thought of a poem in the book left in her abandoned apartment. She knew it by heart, she'd read it so often.

> she bends toward the mud reflection
> seeing nothing,
> seeing the thick defect of herself
> praying for a lover

from any prince of faults.
the hand that cracks the glass
cracks her heart,
touches with the devil's pity
her cheek of scabs,
the primordial ridge of bone
in her relentless unbeauty,
slime woman finds mercy
as the sump parts
with the Iconoclast's smile,
slime woman has a valentine.

Was Tawne slime woman? No, she was the coyote woman. Close enough for night work.

Not exactly Lord Byron but it hadn't been intended for Venuses. The new wave of dark fantasy poets had other ideas, not necessarily evil just because they were nightdriven.

Of course, it might be that Tawne would be disappointed there, too, should she ever cross paths with those poets. They might shun her just like the clubby vampires had.

But Arcan hadn't shunned her. He hadn't seen whatever horror the other men beheld in her either.

She looked at Delia smiling in the glass, happy to the point of tears, glowing even if it was glacial. Hoping this would never end.

"My valentine," Tawne said coquettishly, watching Delia's lips form the words.

They were out of sinc like a badly dubbed line in a foreign film.

"I am the slime woman," Tawne said next. She could feel herself smiling widely. "I am the coyote woman!" she shouted and then let loose with a jubilant howl.

This didn't match the reflection. Delia wasn't smiling now. Tawne leaned close. So did the image.

Naturally the image leaned. It was herself, wasn't it?

The lips moved, the reflection of Delia sadly shaking her head. The mouth worked silently because Tawne wasn't speaking.

Delia! The real Delia is trying to speak to me!

What was she trying to say? What would she have to say to Tawne at all? Tawne couldn't read the lips. It was just so much grimacing to her.

The image was slow, sleepy, eyes half-closed with drowsy lids. As if Delia were trying to empower it to communicate from a great distance.

It stopped and the reflection didn't move again until Tawne did. It dropped its sculpted jaw in surprise, perfect white teeth parting, pink tongue dabbing at the full lips nervously. Blinking those exquisite eyes with lashes like fringed shawls.

Tawne was trapped in the image again, hypnotized by herself. If Delia's spirit had been trying to contact her a few moments ago, then that was finished. Tawne had searched it so hard for meaning that she'd fallen under her own spell again.

"She walks in beauty like the night
of cloudless climes and starry skies . . ."

Feeling for all the absolute universe that there was nothing that existed but her face.

How long would Tawne have been there? Emptying out with love, with a self-devouring narcissism? How long would she have been trapped if Arcan hadn't walked into the bathroom, turned her around (and away from the glass), piercing it? Draining Delia out to replace it with Tawne, red hair streaming as he embraced her?

They heard it again. Thudding on the roof and against the outside walls like rain.

Arcan went outside and Tawne went only to the doorway. It was as far as she dared go for a few more minutes. The living room was dark enough. The sun was down so far.

Moths were hitting the house. Kamikaze—divine wind—summoned by the dying light. They were so thick, it was hard to see what sunlight was left, so heavy that the air smelled dusty with them. They splattered against the walls and windows, single-minded, suicidal, trying to get at Tawne.

Not that they could have hurt her if they could get inside.

But the sunrise and the sunset were sending their message.

Chapter Twenty-six

Elise felt the sunset the way that only early autumn could make it feel. It came through a window with the blinds up, turning the glass colors that were identical with turning leaves. The same colors washed over her skin, making it appear flushed with reds, jaundiced with yellows. It was warm but it was a drowsy heat, weighted with faint fall cool all around. It weakly pierced the chill as it gave way to twilight. Autumn's sun was self-conscious, less self-evident than the summer sun.

She saw a connection, as if it and she were losing their power and were aware of it.

She tried to help the women in her therapy group—and herself—to realize that strength could be theirs again. It wasn't necessary to be afraid. If the world and the police couldn't protect them, they must find their own power. They could have souls again.

But Elise was afraid of being alone. It was something she'd never experienced in her life before the attack. She'd always been beautiful. There had always been someone there to share her life with. The sense of belonging had been natural to her. She'd never before known what it was not to be included.

She picked up her brush, the tiger eye handle gleaming in the sunset. She unfastened the clips that held her long hair up. She wondered if it would look so bad if she began wearing her hair pulled over one side of her face. To cover the eye patch. Or she could wear it over the other side to conceal the scars along her cheek and nose.

What the hell, she thought, why not just comb it over her whole face and look like Cousin It from *The Addam's Family*?

Elise knew a lot of strangers saw the patch and thought it strange that she didn't get a glass eye. But there had to be enough tissue left to hold one in. The doctors had been very sorry. There just wasn't sufficient flesh left. It was a miracle the assailant's knife hadn't penetrated her brain, considering how much muscle and bone from the cavity of the orbit had been gouged, not to mention the entire tunic and the appendages: eyebrow, eyelid, the conjunctiva and the lachrymal apparatus.

Except to Elise. As if she was supposed to know what those terms meant. Mucous membranes and tear ducts et al.

There were new techniques that were very expensive, but Elise's insurance had run out. She wasn't rich; she was only a secretary. There weren't any programs to help her rehabilitate and renew her lost flesh. Just a flimsy *we're terribly sorry this happened to you; that's life*.

Elise used to be one dark-eyed beauty. Now she was a dark one-eyed beauty.

Beauty. Elise sneered. She combed her chestnut hair and then watched it fall. Strands of carnelian and amber came alive falsely in the sunset. She saw a glint of sharp metal. She stood closer to the mirror to see, using her fingers to pull back hair, looking for it hiding along her scalp. She stepped back so that the light would strike it again. Show her where it was.

There, a few gray hairs. She was only 27 years old. How could she have gray hairs?

A year ago there had been no gray. A year ago she hadn't yet been raped.

Elise re-applied her lipstick. One corner of her mouth was slightly skewed by the scar tissue along the nose. She seemed to be eternally smirking. But she rarely smiled now. She saw enough of her old smiles in the framed photographs, pre-assault, lined up along her dressing table.

· The lipstick was creamy and thick. Suddenly it felt like a smear on her mouth of something utterly foreign and unwanted. Spittle and semen. She wiped it off with the back of her hand.

I'm still a woman. I like my mouth better with more color. I have a right to it. Am I going to let him cheat me out of everything?

He's already stolen my soul. What more does the bastard want?

Elise put it on again, imagining that the otherness of it was nothing more than a sweet, lingering kiss.

She was surprised by a knock at the door. She glanced at the clock. It was too early for Karen's arrival, to give Elise a lift to the session.

She picked up her pistol and walked through the house with it. Elise peered through the peep hole to see who it was. Maybe it would be the police at long last saying it was over, that the beast had been caught.

No. Not with the description provided by Elise and the other victims. What had the detective said? Oh, so softly, not meaning any disrespect, but, "We can't catch phantoms, ma'm."

Elise's heart sank when she saw it was Cole. She opened the door for him. There was a woman with him.

He was embarrassed as he said, "Hello, Elise."

They both saw the gun, hanging limp in Elise's hand. Their eyes widened. The woman put a hand to her mouth in alarm.

Too much, Elise thought. But then this woman might think it was feminine of her to look vulnerable. A lot of men liked that. At least some women thought they did. Still shrieked when they saw mice and snakes, and still expected to be protected.

Protected. If she'd said the word out loud it would have tasted of rust. But—merely thought—it sank into Elise's brain like a knife sliver.

"Sorry," Elise said. "Can't be too careful."

She stepped back and let them come inside.

"Uh, Elise, this is Linda, my . . ."

Big pause, fumble. The young woman flashed a big, fake smile, then squinted at Cole when he didn't finish the introduction.

"Fianceé," Linda said for him.

Didn't waste a whole heck of a lot of time, did you, Cole? She's so pretty, too. Too. Two eyes. Too much smooth unfaulted faceline. Too too.

"Congrats," Elise replied coolly. "Let's hope you never really need him, Linda."

Linda's eyes narrowed again, her mouth set in a hard line. Cole turned very red.

Say something, you coward. Tell me I'm wrong.

Elise hadn't been trying to be mean. She really wanted to warn this poor woman not to see just Cole's boyish good looks, muscles and apparent manly assurance.

He'll treat you delicately like the doll you are. Until you get broken. Fine things are only good to collect as long as they're unmarred.

"I hope we didn't come at a bad time," Cole said. He was already looking around the room so he wouldn't have to look at Elise.

"No, Mel Gibson is picking me up in five minutes but other than that . . ." Elise said, smiling, feeling that scarred corner of her mouth ride up even higher.

"I . . . uh . . . just stopped to get my mother's vase. I sort of left it behind when I . . . er . . . moved," he dithered, so uncomfortable that Elise was surprised he didn't start tugging his trousers from the crack of his butt.

Elise wanted to say, "I thought you gave that vase to me. Yes, it was your mother's but you wanted me to have it. Along with her wedding ring. I didn't get to keep that either."

She saw Linda was wearing the ring, the same one Cole put on Elise's finger when he proposed. When had he sneaked it off of her? While Elise was unconscious in the hospital? Had she actually given it back to him?

Instead Elise said, "You know where it is." Her voice was as flat as walls, flat as stainless steel on an operating table.

"Be right back, Lin," Cole said too softly to his fianceé.

And he scooted from the room. Down the hall. To where Elise kept the vase in the bedroom. A room they once shared. The same room where she'd been attacked while Cole was working late. It would give him the shivers, wouldn't it? Going back in there? As the darkness seeped into the room, remembering finding her. Blood everywhere, her body hanging half off the slaughterhouse bed. He'd tried to call Elise by another name. By several other names. All friends of hers. So positive was he that this couldn't be Elise because it no longer looked like her. It wasn't possible he'd ever kissed that mutilated face, licked those chewed nipples until they hardened, put himself between those red-slathered thighs.

Elise had answered to each of those names he'd called her because at the time she'd lost all sense of herself. She didn't know what her name was anymore. She hoped only that he knew and would help to put her together again. Hoped Cole would save her.

Linda tried not to stare at Elise but she couldn't help it.

"Have you set a date yet?" Elise asked, trying to make conversation.

That false smile again. "Christmas." The smile turned up at the corners as if tugged by scar tissue, forcing it to do what didn't come naturally.

Linda looked at her with revulsion as if Elise were a leper. The scars were obvious. But, the rest, should that be obvious, too? And Elise knew the other woman was feeling sorry for her, yes, but Linda was also trying to imagine herself being victimized that way. And thinking, no, never. NEVER in a million years. There had to be something wrong with you for that to happen.

"Christmas is a good time," Elise replied. "Take real good care of yourself, Linda."

Linda flushed. "What's that supposed to mean?"

She asked with a snap in her voice, but not too much of one. She restrained most of it because you just didn't talk crossly to people who were sick, wounded or crazy.

Crazy. Yes, this makes me a little crazy.

"Because Cole's a shit, honey. He's a weak bastard who'll stick by you only as long as it's good for him and you can shine on his arm."

"Bullshit," Linda said. But her eyes wavered. She stayed several feet from Elise. Getting too close might make her liable to catch something. All the while with that pitying look of horror that one gave any legless wonder on the street.

"Did he tell you what happened to me?"

Linda nodded hesitantly.

"Be careful. Always carry a gun or something you can defend yourself with. Take some martial arts. Don't feel safe and careless in your own home. Get a guard dog. Whatever. Don't let this happen to you, even in miniature, without all the scars on your body. Even one scar would be enough for a jerk like Cole. If you want him, that's your problem. Just make sure he'll always want you or you'll be in a for a world of hurt."

Linda was breathing through her mouth as if there was a funny smell in the house. *It's not contagious, girl.* Afraid to share the same air with Elise. *I'll bet she's a real delight touring the children's burn ward.*

"I can take care of myself."

Elise sighed. "Boy, does that sound familiar."

Cole came back down the hall with the vase tucked under his arm. He wouldn't meet Elise's eyes.

Elise's eye.

"Th-thanks," he mumbled and the pair left.

"Have a nice life," Elise said to the air.

Her shoulders sagged as she went back into the bedroom, closing the blinds against the night. She turned on every light, training them into a spot before the mirror. Then she took off the patch and unbuttoned her blouse, gazing at herself until she felt tears coming. Elise looked hard until the sight of herself was all there was, and the tears dried without ever falling.

Chapter Twenty-seven

It might have fallen by the wayside.

It could have been burned in the fire and lost forever.

It could have fallen into the wrong hands.

Correction: this thing destroyed the wrong hands.

That was precisely what the glitter woman had been, a manifestation of that destruction. So had the serpent. That, too, was destruction. And the fire.

There was smoke rising behind her as Denise drove away from the house on Magnolia Drive. It lifted as if supplicating black arms with black veils tied at the wrists, trailing with each pleading gesture.

She heard the sirens shortly after. There was something satisfying in their screams, unearthly but full of mortality at the same time. It must be what hell sounded like: full of wailing sirens like police cars racing to murders and riots, fire engines streaking to babies burning to death, paramedics hurrying to clamp severed arteries and fibrillate stopped hearts. What was hell after all but a most dangerous city of the dead? Any other city was only made up of those who waited to die.

Denise was the right person for this tape. Hers were the correct hands. An object of power like this came along once in a millennium. It wasn't for instant mass destruction like a nuclear weapon with a misery index registered only upon survivors. This was for inducing novel terror. There was no better way to study the human mind than through what terrified it.

Denise loved fear, cherished its smell on others, was pumped by its presence to be stronger and faster. What was the big deal? This society thrived on it. It was evident from Roman bread and circuses to Twinkies and *I Witness Video*.

Five hundred years ago she'd have shaved her head and pretended to be a man to become an Inquisitor. A thousand years ago she'd have been a Toltec indulging in human sacrifice. Two thousand years ago she'd have been a gladiator or would have tortured saints into disavowing their Christianity. (Those nasty Romans again.)

These days she became a cop. Not that most cops were in the business for the same reason Denise was. Most of them were like her late fool partner, Rob Waters. Full of altruistic motives, full of a simpering savior mentality. She knew an opportunity when she saw it. Fighters needed to fight, soldiers sought battles, the hungry had to prowl.

There was something on the tape; there was something *in* the tape, hungry and prowling. Able to make you see; able to make you think you saw. Changing as soon as that ugly man looked into the camera and into your eyes.

It was sentient and it knew what it was doing.

He certainly did. The ugly man was one wily son of a bitch.

Son of a jackal. She admired that in a man.

Denise watched people on the street as she turned corners toward the police station. Women were wheeling babies, business suits hustled to meetings, druggies with cracked engine blocks stared blankly at a carnival world. She wished she could sit each of them down and observe their faces as the video unfolded its story for them. She had no doubt that each would have a different horror and ghastly epiphany, suffer a different but unavoidable fate. That she could eat just by watching.

"Tell me what you see."

They wouldn't have to tell her. Pretty soon they would show her.

Damn, but that made Denise feel good. Her head buzzed, thinking so fast she could barely keep up with it. It careened with nor-adrenaline steadily pumping. All the synapses of her brain flicked, clicked, connected. She couldn't wait to show this video to Lieutenant Guntz.

Better than cocaine, amphetamines or any dusty designer jewel that provided a rush and a veneer of power. Those were too short-lived and flash-in-the-pan fake compared to this. This was real and had her on a rocket.

Just how had Moravec come by this? She assumed this was the video he'd rented the VCR to see. It had to be because he was dead from odd circumstances, chest and guts drilled out of by grinning death's head bugs, red bodies and black skulls.

Denise would bet a dime to a dollar that Moravec saw red insects on the tape.

The postman talked about snakes and old snake-Satan, and out popped a serpent from his head *sproinnnnnggggg!* like coils of paper from a two bit joke can.

David Jewitt had seen—what? A glowing angel of lights? Of heavenly shrapnel? In a gown of ground glass?

Denise had seen her own breasts become grenades. Well, her nipples were feeling pretty hard right now.

She turned into the parking lot and saw Guntz's car in its reserved spot. She picked up her purse with the tape at parade rest within. She got out of her own vehicle. She slammed the door shut with a smile, imagining she was shutting the door to another life. The ugly man had virtually promised her power with that steady look into her eyes. Far more directly than he'd looked into their eyes. He could tell who and what she was.

The way she couldn't be deceived by who and WHAT he was.

Cross marched directly into the lieutenant's office.

"You see this Jewitt character?" Guntz asked her.

"Sure did," she replied, trying to downplay it for the moment. Keep herself tight and level. Not show her hand too fast. "He handed the tape over to me. I've got it right here. He was watching it when I got to his house. So, yeah, I've seen it."

"And? Well?"

"You've got to see this. Looks like Moravec's handiwork all right. If you took some of his sicker stuff from *Mean Streets* and multiplied it a few times," Denise said, trying to sound deadpan, shrugging but wanting to snare his interest. "Jewitt was pretty sheepish when I confronted him. What could he say when it's right there on his TV screen? Not exactly a home movie with the kids opening presents and the wife basting a turkey. His family died a few weeks ago, by the way. Car accident."

"Go on."

"I know I should have arrested him on the spot. He said he was feeling guilty about the tape. Didn't know why he stole it from the scene yadda yadda yadda. That bit about his whole family, sir. The depression has him geared. Plus we know he saw whatever Pueller and Weigt say they saw. We know where he is, right? He needs to see a shrink but it's not like he murdered Moravec. Just pilfered a souvenir."

Guntz reflected. "Hmm. Is the tape kinky? Think Moravec was going to use it on his show?"

"Kinky, yeah. No way he intended it for *Mean Streets* or any other television, not even cable. He was into something you have to see to believe." Denise whistled through her teeth for emphasis. "Quite a cast of characters. A certain outspoken member of the city council if I saw him well enough. He didn't have his head up. Visible drug use and blatant violations of both the state's sodomy laws and juvenile codes. One possible homicide, but I'm not sure. It'll take some scrutiny. We'll try to identify the scene—it's outdoors, sir—and then possibly look for a body. I think we might want some others to view this as well from the git-go. See who they may recognize that we don't."

Guntz sat straight up, rubbing his chin as if whiskers had just sprouted an inch. He extracted a cigarette from a pack in his shirt pocket and lit up. "No shit?"

Denise watched the lighter flame the tip to a red glow. She thought about houses on fire, of men and snakes on fire. She didn't allow herself to grin as she smelled bacon, chicken, hair frying.

The phone on the desk rang and the Lieutenant answered it crisply. "Yeah? When?" He puffed smoke out his nostrils with each word. He rolled his eyes slowly to meet Denise's. He hung up and touched his finger along the side of his nose like Santa preparing to bungee up the chimney.

"Jewitt's house just burned to the ground. Two bodies inside."

It was a moment world. No big deal. He knew Denise had been there. He'd sent her there. Shit happened.

"Two bodies? Jewitt had no company I know of while I was there," Denise said, shaking her head. "It hasn't been more than 40 minutes since I left. Maybe an hour. Someone must have rolled up right after I left."

"Maybe an associate of this Moravec looking for the tape."

She'd hoped he would suggest that.

Denise nodded. "Maybe the coroner should take another look inside Moravec's body. I think we should view the tape first. With anyone who might be able to I.D. some of the personalities in it. Guys from Vice. Homicide, too."

"Maybe I should see it first."

"Sir, it's a regular feature film. A lot of morbid detail. It would take about two hours for you to see the whole thing. Then another couple of hours for anybody else. That's four hours. Sounds like at least three people may have been murdered over this thing. I can have it set up for you, Davis, Long and Warsaw in five minutes. Semple, too. He headed that task force last spring on the Belial cult that was cranking the kiddie porn. He may see someone's face or backside he knows. What do you think, sir?"

Denise could have chosen anyone from the department. As far as she was concerned, they were all pricks. The names she pulled were men who were likely candidates to handle cases of the type she was suggesting. They were the very men Guntz would have selected.

"Do it." Guntz pushed his chair back from his desk and stood up. He was florid, wondering what taboos had been shattered that he'd not already seen, what fleshy sins had been committed that were new in his book.

Denise had carefully touched his curiosity without making him suspicious.

As for Davis, Long, Warsaw and Semple—they fairly leapt at the chance. They assembled in the muster room where the equipment was. Guntz normally had the same in his office but the VCR was out getting maintenance. The men were conversing in low tones, giving Cross the look they always gave, condescending to one not in their mighty dick club. Wondering why Denise was the one to stumble on such juicy stuff. Soon they would know why. They would grovel with the knowledge.

Guntz was tersely filling them in. Since Moravec's death hadn't previously been considered a homicide, neither Davis nor Long had known anything past the man's brief obit on the tube. Warsaw and Semple were familiar with the

Mongoose pit and the porn place across the street from it. But there was nothing else for them beyond having heard the bug rumors from the two uniforms. No one really believed that Pueller and Weigt had seen what they claimed. The coroner found no shiny crimson carapaces, no bug shit, no eggs. Not even a roach motel partially dissolved in stomach acid. Just lots of wormy holes in the torso from neck to scrotum.

"Ready?" Denise purred.

Guntz closed and locked the door. The men took their seats.

"Sir, we might kill the lights. The film was shot out of doors at night and it's grainy. It might be easier to see, especially since we're hoping to make I.D.s," Denise suggested because, oh, the dark was much better. Once it got rolling, it would tend to incubate their fears. The images would be solid in the dark, alive in it as indeed they had to be to consciously manifest change, alter their script to match some secret DNA in the souls of the viewers.

The lights went out and Denise felt a thrill course through her. She hit the PLAY button and could have sworn the static snap of contact wasn't mere friction but personal lightning.

The man and the woman coiled from the screen, bodies entwined on the murky bank, the river moving behind them. Their skins seemed too soft and yeasty in the night.

"Say cheese," said Warsaw blandly as he viewed the humping and groping.

Semple was nodding. "Gotta be a Dittmar production."

Warsaw agreed with a half smile at the technique. "Yeah, definitely Dittmar 'cause . . ."

"Those people are so ug—*leeeee*!" Semple and Warsaw shouted in unison as they slapped palms.

The two men chuckled as the homicide guys broke up.

"Pipe down." Guntz leaned forward in his chair and craned his neck. Had he already seen something out of the ordinary? His eyes narrowed as he studied the screen.

Maybe he just liked big women.

The man in the film bent at an odd angle, his back moving like a piece of flexible duct. He was sucking the woman's breasts. Guntz saw a suggestion of blood. Yes, there was blood on her chest. There was a sizable wound.

The man sat up and broke her legs, heaving them over his head for the deep thrust. The gleam of white exposed bone was so phallic, Denise shivered, fantasizing about lowering herself onto that gleaming knob.

The ugly man leaned away from the woman as his hips continued their rhythm. He mugged the camera. He looked at Denise.

She realized, *he's looking at me. Me*.

As if to say to her, "All for you, my fledgling."

He passed through her vision and into her head like a sharp kiss at the third eye. Denise's nipples plumped as she beheld him becoming her.

Yeah, but what did they see? This was what she wanted to know. Warsaw gasped, his fillings visible far back into his skull from the wan television light pooling into his open mouth. Semple jumped to his feet. Davis shouted something, brief but furious. Long fell out of his chair completely. Guntz's face went white. Even in the darkened room Denise could tell that all of the color had drained from the lieutenant.

One beat. Two beats.

The video went to a hiss and she knew there was no more picture.

"Something fucked up," she muttered as she turned away from observing them to quickly run the tape back. "There's a lot more. Must be a glitch. Sorry. There."

She didn't even have to watch them to feel their surprise, shock, outrage, whatever. There wasn't an officer in the room who didn't have blue fire in his veins at the moment.

"Wait!" Guntz snapped. "What the hell was that?"

"Special effects," Warsaw whispered to convince himself. "He became a corpse. He was oozin' all over her . . ."

"No, he was on fire . . ." Semple shook his head groggily as he swallowed to get down a nasty lump. "Fire and spiders . . ."

"Horseshit! That was Jeremy Lauder. Assholes let 'im out of the nuthouse already. He'll kill again. I told 'em. He wasn't crazy. Never was. He was evil!" Davis yelled.

Long wasn't saying anything. He was slowly climbing back onto his chair, hand over hand from the floor as if it was entirely too tall for him. He kept his eyes trained down.

This was working fast.

"That was my kid up there," Guntz murmured. "My daughter, Lisa. That ain't even possible. She's . . ."

He stared at the blank screen as his voice cracked. "She's . . ."

Denise depressed PLAY, and the dark, the river and the motion started over.

Guntz looked sick. "She was just a baby."

Few at the station knew much about Guntz's daughter, save that she was younger than the average child suicide.

Denise opened her mouth and tasted the sour sweetness on her tongue. Fear and horror like sweat and fats. The five men stood or sat, eyes locked in the orbits of their dry sockets in the direction of the screen. They barely breathed. Breath moved in and out of them like water over shallow footprints on a sandy beach. She didn't have to see the television to know that soon the ugly man would sit up. He'd look at them. He'd fix them with his stare and his smile. Fix them real good.

Denise's breasts ached. Every part of her body ached, blood pounding in tension she savored. The ugly man must be sitting up, the river moving blackly beyond him like a beast slouching toward a sleeping village. He must be sitting up because the expressions on the men's faces stretched back to reveal shiny gums.

Charlee Jacob

They didn't move when the white noise came. Didn't budge as Denise rewound the tape and played it again. The air was redolent with the fact they couldn't move. They were frozen, muscles paralyzed, jaws locked in a rictus. It rendered the air delicious. Denise could see their breaths cold-icy-pluming in foggy gusts even though the officers were sweating. It stank. The scent of it raised the hair along her arms, prickling each nerve ending with a spark, combustible in vast stores of napalm in her veins.

The couple thrashed on the bank. The ugly man sat up, broke the woman's legs as he poked between them. He was all pimples and bristly hair. His eyes were ancient. His smile was a keen scythe that cut right through the darkness, straight through the film, through the glass matrix of the screen, through the misting ether in the room, through their theoretical hearts. Cleanly.

Uncleanly.

Hell broke loose. Denise liked that phrase.

Detective Warsaw screamed. His skin was stiffening in patches, then falling slack as a too-big garment, especially baggy at the armpits and groin. It grew rigid and then slackened again until it appeared to be inching over the length and width of him. It mottled with purplish knots, hung in spotty soured milk-oozing pockets, split and dripped a foul gray slime. He screamed again, the sound gurgling as the cartilage of the larynx mushed and disintegrated, necrotic phlegm curdling around his loose teeth. Warsaw was dead on his feet. He'd seen the ugly man as grotesque corpse, and now he was rotting and aware in each hurried, humid display of decay. Warsaw reached out a gummy hand to the other vice detective but the ends of his fingers burst like bubbles of fondue cheese.

If Semple screamed it was lost in the roar as his skin ignited with a whoosh inside his suit. He didn't burn the way the postman had. Nothing caught fire around him, not the carpet nor the chairs nor the other men. They remained untouched in his vicinity, even though the fire was so hot as it exploded from his torso that his glasses melted right off his face before the fire flashed up to consume his head . . . the proverbial spontaneous combustion. The sprinklers didn't even come on as the smoke never seemed to reach the ceiling to set them off. The fire spat as it consumed him, bright cinders and hoary living embers landing in a rough circle around Semple's feet. Each of these sprouted eight legs and scuttled back to spin glassy webs in the smoky spaces appearing between Semple's blackening ribs.

(Fire and squirmies: the most common phobias? Denise tilted her head. If she did this a thousand times, how many people would see and manifest burning and something wriggly?)

Detective Davis pulled his service revolver from its shoulder holster. He began firing at point blank range into the face of serial killer Jeremy Lauder as the psychotic killer suddenly appeared in front of him. The maniac had somehow been released from the nuthouse and beamed through some demonic hyperspace to threaten the cop who had put him away. Blood and bone splattered as bullets struck, bored, shattered and splashed.

"Die, you fuck!" Davis shrieked, his mouth twisted with hatred for the bipolar freak of nature who had brutally mangled and defiled more than a dozen people.

The pistol fired until it landed on empty chamber after empty chamber. Davis's finger spasmed click-click, his eyes popping as he saw Lauder stepping toward him, those steroid mutated muscles reaching for him. Lauder's face was just a pulp of asymmetrical skullbone and raw wet matter. The maniac clutched Davis, forcing him to the floor. He punched down with one massive fist into the cop's groin, knuckles heaving all the way to the spine. He then reached down into the hole and yanked out a fistful of lower intestine, spewing shit through the nicks. Lauder proceeded to stuff this down Davis's throat. It was debatable whether the detective bled to death or strangled first.

(Denise inhaled the stench, thinking of the fools of the 14th century, spending hours daily crouched over latrines, deliberately snorting wafts of reeking crap and piss in the belief that fetid odors held the power to keep them safe from the plague. Denise wasn't seeking protection. She wanted this black death. Semple's smoke made her eyes and sinuses smart, rolled her stomach. And yet she was stronger, stoked by the fears of these men.)

Guntz was on his knees, begging an eight- or nine-year-old girl to forgive him. She was naked and impossibly thin, twigged at the joints like an anorexic. There was blood between her legs though she was clearly too young to have begun menstruating. She pulled off his glasses and began to scratch his eyes out, ribbons of cherry licorice down his cheekbones. She plowed furrows with her birdlike hands, claws ending in curved iron. The lieutenant didn't even struggle. He only wept until his eyes were gone and then he blubbered her name endlessly until that capacity had left also.

"Lisa," Denise crooned after Guntz's voice fell silent. "Lisa."

It was a name of agony like nectar.

Where the girl came from didn't matter. She came from the same place as the serial killer. From where the glass angel at the house on Magnolia Drive had come from. The snakes and spiders and red bugs. From the video tape. From the ugly man looking into their eyes.

From the ugly man. Hunting souls like eggs on Easter morning. Cracking them open when he found them to lap with rubbery lips at all the good runny yellow.

Long crouched before his chair as the floor rippled under him. It fissured with hairline fractures that resembled obscene bearded mouths in the carpet. These buckled, elongated into trenches, canyoned down until Long was stranded on an island of floor.

How far down? Denise stared across the edge and could see no bottom. She could see the strata of linoleum and sub-flooring and building foundation, concrete, earth, fossils in layers, trickles of ground water.

No end.

"Oh God I am sorry to have offended Thee mea culpa mea maxima culpa it has been six months since my last confession holy Mary mother of grace quite contrary how does your garden grow with silver bells and cockleshells and please I just want to go home now . . ." Long muttered, drool shiny across his chin.

Sinewy ropes of tissue pawed up from the circular crevice, winding up like eldritch vines over the central column that held up Long's harbor of floor. They were wet, colored with hues Denise had never seen before. They shot out of the shaft like loose power cables, twitching with uncontrolled voltage.

Something—part of something—followed these up, was the main body or the edge of a massive creature, jerking with rows of sharky teeth and bramble talons. It sniffed at Semple's charred grease and at the bodies of the others. Ripe, smelly, easy for a carrion eater to find. It rolled in their blood, dragging them over the side with a few of the appendages as Long clutched the chair so hard he bent the cheap metal back.

"The Lord is my shepherd I shall not want and I have walked in the valley of the shadow of death with it snapping at my heels and I fear the evil that stretches beyond the stars we see and please please PLEASE!"

Denise recognized the concept from a story she'd read as a child and that Detective Long must have read, too. The Great Old Ones, wasn't it? Cthulhu stuff? How interesting that only one of these officers had selected a fictional being as his personal demon. What if the *Evil Dead* had appeared or the Cenobites? She chortled over the idea of meeting Clive Barker's Pinhead and maybe going for a spin on the pillory. Were the Old Ones going to come through one by one to rule the earth now?

"That is not dead which can eternal lie," Denise repeated from what she remembered of the Mythos. What was the rest? "And with strange aeons even death may die."

All right! Come on up! Let's rock! Denise laughed and shouted the phrase again, certain it would strengthen Long's monster-god.

The blob and limbs surfaced again, latching onto Long, squeezing him until bones snapped and scarlet mush came out with shattered skeletal ends. It dragged him down into the pit, the convoluted frame of his metal chair dangling for a moment before toppling in after them.

This was what Long had expected, wasn't it? The fact that he didn't struggle or make a noise after he stopped that annoying praying didn't lessen the energy put out in roentgens by his terror.

And ah! Denise's breasts were hard. Solid! She ran her hands over them. She detected lumps in symmetrical designs, in bas relief runes. Come on! Come on into the world!

But the limbs of the abyss shriveled away, never reaching for Denise. Not emerging in gargantuan evil to destroy the races of the earth. Steam gushed from the crevice like a great sulfuric fart and then went to the hiss of the tape.

"Shit," Denise said with disappointment. Wouldn't that have been something? She could have looked into the dreaded face of Cthulhu that drove people mad, and she could have said, "Tell me what You see."

Her bones creaked. Denise plainly heard them, audibly as the tape went to unrecorded space. The pain. PAIN. Gorgeous gibbering near-death experience pain. As muscles wrapped around those bones were stretched, tendons extended. The skin became supremely tight, each flaw and sun crease smoothing snugly as it was pulled.

Heat—Denise's blood boiled.

Rigid breasts, rock-solid tits.

Denise barely managed to pop the tape from the VCR, her hands shaking with voltage all blue in the dark. Her tongue swelled in her mouth as if she'd drunk seawater. Knee joints popped like dime firecrackers. Her knuckles itched so much she cracked them. Then she saw how long those fingers had become.

Her blouse tore, the jacket ripping sideways at both shoulder seams. Her pantyhose stretched to the maximum and then shredded.

Denise imagined the Incredible Hulk in the old series bursting snot-green from his clothes. She squealed even as she unlocked the door, stooping to squeeze under the six foot, eight inch frame.

The cops in the outer offices had heard the commotion and finally reckoned that it wasn't just some prisoner being ornery—a druggie seeing orange godzillas stomping along his mainframe. A couple of uniforms ran toward her. Denise covered her face with a too-long hand, curling drainage pipe fingers over her skull. She pointed with the other hand at the ghastly interior of the muster room as if she were in shock. They might have stared at this distorted giantess if it hadn't been for the smoke drifting from the room. That and the stench. And the noise as the floor and the earth beneath the floor clamped shut again, fissures sealing, edges coming together again even if less than perfectly. The uniforms ran past Denise.

She moved away fast, grinning as she tried to cover her face. As if anyone might absurdly recognize this bulging lump as the formerly sveldt Detective Cross.

"Hey, you there!" some rookie shouted as he stepped in her path.

Her arm and shoulder rippled, jutting like stone monoliths being pushed up from magma. They jerked out pectorals that were out of all proportion with the other side of her. They pumped into a crazy braid of muscles, sticks of dynamite, shields of hammered steel. She raised the enormous arm and brought it down like a club. He didn't break and fall as much as he dissolved, worn to silt. She had to adjust her stance because the weight of it threatened to throw her off balance.

Denise ducked a bullet as another officer fired at her. She squatted in fullback style as she butted him, pinning him to the wall with the grotesque arm. His head cracked back into the plaster, the hole it made quickly filling with a wellspring of blood and gray brains.

People screamed and dove under desks, into restrooms, heaving chairs and telephones at her that bounced like harmless cottonballs. Denise scraped along the wall, leaning into it to hold up her lesser side, the heavier half reaching a maximum when the capillaries along the maxed-out skin began leaking.

With each burst of panic that radiated her way, Denise was ionized. The muscles on the other side began to pulse and pump. The arm and shoulder swelled, hardening to the approximate proportions of the first. It made her roar with laughter to look at it. The gym was never like this.

A burglary dick came around the corner and fired. Denise felt the bullet bite, passing with a jagged nibble through her slab side. She caught him in a bearhug and squeezed until he went doughy in the center. Bones rearranged to either side of this bizarre compression, breaching his skin on one edge with the organs on the other.

Her own weapon had been lost when her holster came off her expanding form like a flailing bra strap. Denise tried to pick up his gun but couldn't get her sausage roll fingers through to pull the trigger. There were two or three more bullets fired her way. They stung, chipping muscles in ineffectual bits. It was like trying to cut a diamond with a nut pick.

Denise clubbed anyone stupid enough to try to stop her. Cops were like other folks. If they could puke at a murder scene, they could damn well scream and hide when they saw a monster.

Denise was ecstatic with every crushing thud and soggy fruitsplit of heads. She grabbed a prisoner by the handcuff chain and threw him against two more advancing officers. At least one of his hands severed in the steel cuffs, pulled off as easily as a doll's plastic limb.

"Fledgling?" Denise chuckled as she thought of what the ugly man had said in her head. "Some fledgling."

She had to break down the door. Not because it wouldn't open for her but because she couldn't fit through it. Denise sprang down the front steps and to the pavement, her feet thundering.

Chapter Twenty-eight

Tawne's howler was dying in the cavern. She couldn't see him; she was out where the light which resembled moonlight was. But there was no moon. His breath rasped, his heart weakening to a terrifying slowness. His teeth scraped on rocks as he crawled.

She was losing him as a sound came from the moonless sky, of chimes in a temple where much blood has been spilled. Chimes for the dead.

Did he cry out for her, just once? Tawne scrabbled to the cave's mouth.

"Arcan?" she called into the dark echo.

His fingers came out from the hollow as she reached forward. They almost touched.

Tawne either woke in the bathtub she was curled up in or she merely shook—for did the undead sleep or only close their eyes and dream? One didn't have to sleep to dream. Schizophrenics did it. It was labeled as hallucination, but it was the same thing.

This Symbiotic Fascination

Sitting up in the tub, Tawne wondered if she would live forever. Didn't she heal when wounded? Such regenerations could make one effectively immortal. Just like the bulk of folklore whispered and the Hollywood hype snickered insidiously into the ears of every child who feared death.

She'd asked the ugly man that question but he hadn't really answered. He'd deliberately been vague. All in all, as a mentor he left a lot to be desired.

Tawne had only been in this state for a few days so she didn't really know what to expect. She still thought as a mortal human did. As if she'd undergone a brain transplant that put her mind into the body of a dog. But she still considered slow dances, lipstick and satin sheets—things a dog had no use for. Hollywood had done a few of those stories, too.

Those others she'd seen on the street who prowled their territories with midnight monomanias had been what they were long enough that they had lost all semblance to humanity. How long would it take before this happened to her? Decades? Centuries? How old was the ugly man?

(Old enough to find a way to fool the light. Old enough to stand in the sunset with its rays reflecting off his cataracts without those eyes exploding.)

The ugly man bemoaned loneliness but his hollow words were mimicry. There was no human spirit or complicated intellect there, only hunger and abstract cruelty. A cat playing with a mouse, a cat with a short fucking attention span and one ultimate goal: to feed. He wasn't a stage vampire bored with the chase and suffering cosmic angst. Decadence was a wholly human concept. Survival was universal, requiring no broad range of emotional potential.

Tawne still had all her emotions. She found it hard to imagine fading into a one-dimensional feeder, hunger braced only by cunning. The years she'd lived seemed like a long time for they were everything in her experience minus less than a week. Those years had been lived alone.

Tawne thought about the dream. What if she lost Arcan because he wasn't as she was? The dream was prophetic. This was how it must end eventually. He might be her feral bridegroom but he was mortal. Cats died. Wolves died.

(What did ghouls do? They died and were eaten by other ghouls. Recycling darkness.)

No, it wasn't funny. When Arcan was gone—even if 50 years from now—that would be it. There could never be another.

Tawne sat in the kitchen and watched as Arcan puttered around the stove. He was cooking a late dinner for himself. She didn't need to eat nor did she want to anymore. One human trait gone: gluttony. One down—what to go?

The smells of frying hamburger filled the air with cremated garlic and pepper. He was burning it well done. Onions in the same pan were turning a caramel color in the grease. Standard bachelor fare. Tawne was only mildly surprised her lover didn't prefer it rare.

No, that would be too much like what the ghoul would have.

Watching Arcan do these little domestic things made Tawne ache even more for him. She adored him by such trivial acts as these. They were homey, normal. Like a family.

Could Tawne have babies? She doubted it. That had to involve functions of the ova, menstrual cycles and fertility periods which belonged to the living.

When she considered it, it might actually be better they couldn't produce babies. She could imagine coming into the nursery for the 2 A.M. feeding only to discover that her husband had reverted to his ghoul self and was eating the infant's liver.

Could the two of them really be a couple when he was

bound to age and die while she went on? And on . . . ? It was like the soap opera tear-jerker about the healthy lover devoted to the terminally ill lover. Make the most of your time, shut up and be grateful. It was better to have loved and lost, right? Gather ye rosebloods.

Mortality was a terminal illness. Sent by the cancers of the day in the form of slow deterioration of the nervous system and anatomy.

An hour ago, right after sunset, Tawne and Arcan had gone outside to shovel the litter of that day's bombardment. Tawne pushed the broom while Arcan held the dustpan. He'd tried lifting them by the armfuls but the moths' wings made him sneeze. They lay in heaps in the yard like snow drifts, some still faintly rustling. They fell down from the roof and stopped up the gutters that ran along the eaves. The two raked the yard, making many piles that might have been leaves in the dark but weren't. They stuffed about 20 or 30 hefty bags with them, then lugged them to the curb for the garbage men. Neither Arcan nor Tawne commented on the fact that there were no dead moths in the street or in the yards to either side of Arcan's.

It was lucky the house was screened from view from the rest of the neighborhood by a lot of oak trees. What would people think, seeing hordes of moths attacking the old Tyler place?

Mortality was sent by the day. Only the night offered forever. The folklore and Hollywood claptrap said that. Tawne wouldn't have given such drivel a second thought before last Friday night—except in her dreams. And while reading and rereading her favorite book of poetry.

But now? Well, some of the hype had proved itself.

This is the only happiness I've ever known. How can I give it up?

Tawne needed this; she needed Arcan. To be alone was cold.

He held the knife and picked a tomato from the counter.

Its skin was shiny, freshly washed with beads of water rolling across it. He held it, red and plump as a breast. He looked at it curiously. It was like a breast which had been skinned 'til it was red. This was experience. Been there; done that.

A skinned breast felt just so in the hand. A flash of the old fever burned his wrist, sizzling down through his fingers holding the knife.

The hamburger was done. Fingers. Breast. Knife.

His fingers trembled. The hand around the tomato squeezed slightly and he half-expected to hear a woman moan in pain.

Arcan closed his eyes. The tears were because of the smoke. He decided to let the burger cook until it no longer resembled meat. He cut the tomato in half, focusing on the myriad seeds through the pulp.

It has seeds, he thought. Vegetables have seeds, breasts do not. It is a vegetable, not a breast. Just seedy vegetable.

Arcan nodded to himself.

But it also has pulp, the animals managed to whisper from where he'd banished them. A breast has pulp, too. Spongy and yummy.

Arcan quickly looked away from the tomato to Tawne sitting at the table, her red hair streaming over her shoulders. The urge subsided. The hatred and rage mellowed. He smiled at her. He'd not seen the ghosts even once since the first morning she'd come to stay.

Tawne was lost in thought. He could tell by the set of her strong jaw and the creases in her forehead.

"What's going on in that head of yours?" Arcan asked as he switched off the stove. The burger was black enough to suit him.

She glanced up and asked, "How would you feel if I offered you eternal life?"

Just like that. As if it were an invitation to a Sadie Hawkins dance.

He didn't even blink. He turned back to the counter and began to cut the tomato into thin slices.

"No, I don't think so," Arcan replied softly, in control.

"Why not? We could be together forever. Or, if it isn't in the cards and what we've got going fades—hey, it happens—you'd still be fit and young," she told him, wondering if this was true or not. The legends didn't know everything. They were wrong about the mirrors. "But I don't believe this'll fade. Neither one of us has ever had anyone before. Look at us. What an unlikely pair. This must be destiny."

Who wouldn't leap at the chance for the elixir of life sought by every poet and emperor since time began?

Or some such crap. *When you're in love, suddenly it's not crap anymore.*

Arcan was adamant. "No."

He took the meat out of the pan with a spatula and placed it on the bottom bun he'd prepared on a plate. He put the grilled and greasy crusts of the onions over that, slices of tomato over the onions. He put on the top bun, smeared with plenty of catsup. Then Arcan picked it up with both hands and examined it. Seeds. Vegetables had seeds.

Tawne had a lot of power and was offering it to him. He could have it. Immortality and power. Strength that couldn't be denied.

I know what I'd do with it. In the end. In the beginning. I know what the animals would do with it.

Those beasts were jumping up and down inside him with their excitement. Yes! Yes! Go for it!

Pulp. Squeezing 'til the poor woman moaned.

"No," Arcan said louder, more forcefully. No to Tawne; no to the animals.

She was amazed. "Why not?"

How could he refuse. How could *anyone* refuse?

Tawne hadn't refused. She'd dived off the edge of her

life after it with both feet. She'd even asked for it, making herself look as miserable and needy as possible to appeal to the ugly man. Not that it had been hard to do.

Arcan told her, "I can't because of guilt. Because of Carmel Gaines and Elise Reedman. Because of a bunch of women at a rape therapy center who've seen my faces. Because of what I can barely control now."

(And because of dreams of unspeakable carnage. Dead pussies, bitches and Liliths everywhere in the squeaky mist. Female forms of cats, wolves and ghouls?) He took a big bite of the hamburger and it nearly choked him. It chewed like a mouthful of ashes. It was dry as dust except for the catsup and the juice from the breast—the tomato. This ran red from the corners of his mouth.

Tawne sighed deeply and began to quote the title poem from that favorite book. It was easy to slip into such a little habit, used to being alone and not having people around when she did such a bizarre thing, quoting poetry to express an emotion she could not otherwise get out of her. It should have embarrassed her, but she didn't even understand that she'd said anything.

"Immortal inamorato, gothic scarecrow. Solomon of the space shrewd years. Pan of the dark fruitful. Osiris of downfall creation stillborn. Who wants you? Your naked hand strikes me vigorous. I am stark and surrounded. The dark flicks to blank where you as a prophet stuck your blind bone to my wet animal. Who wants you? The one who hears your hoof-foot tap. The one who wears your fall of blood at a wedding destined for the frost."

Arcan frowned, snapping his head up until the back of his neck creaked. Poetry. His mother had done that. (Who wants me? . . . Who wants you?) If ever there were a symbol of weakness and treachery, poetry was it. It didn't speak plainly and was meant to manipulate the emotions.

Maybe Tawne wasn't exactly as he believed her to be.

This Symbiotic Fascination

The animals tumbled inside him. *Kick her out at sunrise! Watch her shrivel and bleed!*

No, go to sleep, he thought to them. There's nothing here for you to eat.

They made love once.

Tawne traced the scars down Arcan's back in old furrows. They looked like the scars an angel would have if the wings had been brutally amputated. There were scars on his chest, belly and arms. Everywhere. They didn't look as if they had been made by barbed wire or sharp glass. Or by razors as the scars on her wrists had been made.

These were from fingernails. Tawne touched the streaks and canals. They were hot and felt good against her. She wondered at the violence that must have made them. She touched them gently and licked gently, thinking she could never get enough of Arcan's beautiful scars.

She knew on some level that she ought to be embarrassed that Arcan's violent past might be important to her. That she could fuck a man who had done revolting things to other women. That she could be enticed by the musk of such a monster whose crimes should have made her automatically hate him.

But she felt no shame. A wolf killed; fenris was a wolf. It was the nature of the beast no matter how uncomfortable Arcan seemed with it. How could a wolf hate what it was? She wasn't any different from any other woman who mooned over the virile mystery of the bad man in any number of movies and books, even as she supposedly cheered the hero on. How good were heroes in bed? Were their dicks as big?

Not that Tawne wished any violence on those poor women. Women were all sisters, weren't they?

(Arcan claimed he'd never killed anyone.)

Of course, Tawne was horrified that those women had

303

been raped. Damn it, why did the sexual violence of it have to reach her so much?

Am I ashamed after all?

Worse, am I one of those—or was I in my life before— murder groupies who would eventually have found a mate in prison? Would I have sought to be a pen pal and even a wife to some night stalker and be on all the talk shows about how I knew he really had good in his soul?

But Arcan did have good in him or he wouldn't be in so much torment over his crimes.

In the dreams, fenris had given Tawne a heart to eat. There was the smell of carnage in the cavern. These were a wolf's sacraments.

(Arcan was studying the scars on Tawne's wrists. He hadn't really noticed them until now. Unlike his, hers were self-inflicted. Deborah used to thrust her hands through the window. He was confused. Tawne was strong but capable of this weakness? When he looked into her face he saw another soldier of darkness, trying to exist with a creature emotion she knew she'd be better off without. There was nothing false or too soft in that face. Was she only testing him? The animals within did this all the time. It drove him crazy. He kissed her and cooled his fever there. He vowed to give her the benefit of the doubt for now.)

Maybe this was what Harry'd meant by finding atonement at the source. That Arcan—who had always detested women—could only be saved after finally loving one. And that she must be a woman removed from the traditional stereotypes of femininity . . . as different as a goddess with a dick or a god with a twat.

Different as night and day.

Tawne put her head on his chest. She might have fallen asleep there. All she did was what vampires did when they closed their eyes: she dreamed.

She was creeping toward the cavern, hearing chimes

from the moonless sky. Hearing his voice from inside the cave.

Did he cry out for her just once? *Why didn't you save me when you had the chance? Didn't you love me?*

She was alone after that, unable ever to find another like him. There was only one fenris.

The fingers quivered out from the hollow as she reached into the cave. They almost touched. These fingers were arthritic and bloody, the hair on the backs of the hands a withering white. His voice had almost no breath left in it. He managed to sob like an old, old wolf. "Why didn't you save me when you could?"

Tawne opened her eyes. The two of them lay together on Arcan's bed, hot arms and legs braided with cold ones. The room steamed from the heat and ice coming together. It was good to be with him. Arcan saturated her and made Tawne greedy. People killed for less.

He'd cried out for her in her dreams. One day he'd die and she'd be alone again. This was what all her dreams had led her to. Her meeting with the ugly man . . . planned. Yes, planned to bring her to this crossroads that would bind them forever. Was it so much to ask? Arcan was only afraid of that first step because it was a doozy.

If it was Tawne's fate, then it was Arcan's fate as well. She bent her head to his bare chest, hairy and sweet with his perspiration. She bent to it and bit.

Arcan gasped in shock, shuddering as she drank fast, his blood burning with bubbles of air. She'd startled him before he could react and she had the upper hand. She drank deeply and swallowed. Gulped. Then pulled back, coming up to reverse the process.

He stared up at her in that brief moment when she moved from chewing down to his heart to parting her lips in the obscenely emetic kiss. She realized how horrible she must look, enormous bloated face and body swimming up to him like a killer whale. Tawne decided to soften the image to lull him. She took on Delia, beautiful, lithe, the hunger only a sexual intensity.

Arcan screamed, in fury, in terror, the Lilith of nightmares descending on him. Breasts like something rising dangerously from the thorny nest to lure travelers and eat children, eat little boys from the penis outward. Lamia lovelies all cunt and claws. He tried to rise up, angling a weak fist which he managed to land on her china teacup jaw.

Tawne pushed him down. Easy, really, considering he had a hole in his chest. Why was he looking at her like he'd never seen her before? The image in his eyes was one of grace and desire. Not like the—whatever it was—she thought she glimpsed reflected in the man changing his tire, Carl, and the tall teenager she'd hoped to be able to win without torment. Arcan was looking at her now as they had when the mask dropped. She held him, suspending her face above his, coiling and uncoiling the lining of her stomach, arching her esophagus, turning it all back to vomit it, processed with her own codes back into his mouth.

Tawne's belly convulsed in the only action that approximated pain for her. She had grabbed him by the wrists and held him fast to the mattress as he began to fight. Arcan choked and gurgled out what she poured into him, getting some of it down anyway because there was just so much of it that some of it had to go down.

Arcan struggled to maintain a hold of himself, a balance that was mortal and disciplined. But it was slipping as Tawne gouted blood, bile and ether. He wrestled under her sizable bulk, his face terrified and betrayed. His animals moved there, twisting feral shapes of snarling fear, hissing and howling and shouting blasphemies until the gore drowned out his capacity to make any noise other than choking.

What was Tawne doing to him? He'd told her he didn't

want this. She was doing it anyway, just like a woman, a damnable fucking woman. How could he ever have let a woman into his house? It might not be politically correct but she was *killing* him when he'd said no. Didn't no mean anything?

(Yet a part of Arcan strained up to meet her. He'd fight that! The hell with it. He couldn't do this . . . he knew too well what it would mean . . . what it would do . . . it would result in butchery.)

His animals flashed in his eyes, moving in his face, and it startled Tawne to see them so clearly as she pressed her mouth to his. She could barely see Arcan there at all. But animals couldn't comprehend intent, recognizing only states of agony and states of pleasure.

"I'm trying to save you, Arcan," Tawne sputtered in globs.

(I'm trying to keep you.)

The process was horror but Arcan would have a body of iron after. Her breath was meat; it was spoiled and disgusting. And she was disgusting, devouring something she loved, inflicting a torture that she knew very well for she'd undergone this.

Tawne begged him, "Lie still, honey. Lie still."

Could Arcan even understand what she was spitting? She thought absurdly of the old trick of the dummy talking while the ventriloquist drank a glass of water.

Tawne wished she could cry, that she had tears. Then she would give them to Arcan with the blood and the rest, to show him how sorry she was. How she understood. It was love. Because of the dream, she couldn't allow Arcan to refuse.

"Arcan, I love you." Blood wads spewed.

"Love you . . . could never really hurt you." Hawking slobber and stomach festerings.

"Lie still." Love bitter as gall.

Then they could go on with the business of eternity.

Charlee Jacob

He'd understand once he was there. When it was over. And she wouldn't lose him because he'd be there and not among the chimes for the dead. Tawne would save him and he'd never have to ask her why she hadn't.

Arcan bucked, knees coming up on either side of her, kicking at her with his feet, trying to rake and disembowel her with his toenails as if he were a puma fighting with rear claws. But he was only a man after all and didn't have claws. He bucked and gradually melted beneath the blood vomit onslaught. He twitched, strangling feebly.

Arcan went limp. Had he died?

Tawne pulled away, dripping, wiping her mouth with hands she'd held him down with.

Arcan was still. He was slowly losing his heat. That wasn't an item a living person would notice in mere seconds. But Tawne wasn't a living person and was sensitive to human warmth. His heart wasn't beating. No breath flowed through the clogged and clotting mouth and nostrils. She'd murdered him.

(With love, for love, this was different.)

Tawne must believe in dreams, mustn't she, when those dreams had been right about Arcan being her fenris? She'd never guessed it before in all the time she'd worked side by side with him at Galway's.

What happened if this didn't work? What if the ugly man had this power to give, but measly Tawne Delaney of a few days immortality didn't? Then Arcan was lost to her. She'd fucked up royally and wasted what precious years she might have had with him.

Tawne got off the bed and stood on the other side of the room with her arms wrapped around herself, hunching her tall frame. She was so cold.

"Arcan?" she whispered. She blew a ring of fog.

No response. She groaned and hit herself with an enormous fist. "Oh, stupid, stupid, stupid!"

His eyes opened. He climbed off the bed, clearly in a

trance. Well, she'd also been in a trance at first. She didn't even recall leaving the river bank.

Arcan might have been in a stupor but he was lithe as a cat, all the parts working with a wolfish grace.

He was a sticky mess. He looked as if he'd been smacked in the mouth a few artless times with a tire iron. The hole in his bare chest glistened a crimson wet which he pondered, touching with ginger fingertips. He coughed, hocked out slimy ruby chunks, spat until his throat cleared enough he could breathe . . . breathing because animals breathed—never considering that it might not be necessary.

"Arcan?" Tawne repeated gently, softly, a little afraid.

He spun on the ball of one foot as if realizing she was there for the first time. He glared, jerked back as she stepped forward and reached out to touch him.

"It's okay, Arcan."

He hissed. The hair on his head and all along his body stood on end.

Tawne saw that he hated her. He only saw her as a traitor.

(It'll be all right. He'll see. He'll come around when the shock wears off. He'll still love me.)

Arcan ran from the room. Tawne heard him speeding down the narrow hall on bare feet, punching walls on either side as he ran. She heard the front door being jerked off its hinges as he fled into the night.

He'll still love me.

"No, he won't," Tawne told herself, wishing for those tears.

The ice in her eyes felt as if it would explode as they filled with sleet that couldn't flow.

Chapter Twenty-nine

As he ran, everyone Arcan saw was a fire. Afire. On fire. The trees, the animals, the ground glowed. The women blazed.

Arcan knew it was night. It was night, wasn't it?

Could he have lain so long after Tawne traitorously turned on him that it had become day?

No, it wasn't day yet. But could night sparkle like this?

It was as if everything in the night that bore flesh or breath or any form of life spark had a light to it. And the things that didn't were dark.

Was Arcan dark? No life spark there at all.

How could he have ever loved her? Or any woman? How could he have mistaken her pretense for strength? Look at him. He'd given her everything to indulge in her cool flesh. What did he have to show for it? A red wound in his chest showing how he'd died for his pleasures. There could be no forgiveness, only oblivion for what he'd felt for Tawne.

Arcan ran down the street. People cried out, scattering

to get out of his way. They stood in the parking lot of a convenience store and pointed. They stood inside the store and pressed their faces to the glass doors. Seeing him, a man drove his car into a fire hydrant which exploded into a waterfall.

Arcan was only now coming to his senses enough to realize he had no clothes on. *The emperor has no clothes the emperor has no clothes the emperor* babbled in his head, a litany that hissed and howled and meowed as the animals found this hilarious.

He had to find a place to hide. Someone was bound to call the cops. He didn't know what would happen if police showed up. He didn't know what to do. The dark neighborhood houses were thinning out toward a busier commercial area with stores and restaurants. That would be disastrous. There would be more strangers, less cover. He turned, the hard street under his feet. An asphalt surface ought to tear bare feet, shredding the soles as he skidded to change course. But it didn't. There was no pain. Did he run on pads now?

Arcan couldn't simply turn and go home. She was there. Jezebel. Messalina. Lilith.

He'd never stood a chance. He should have known when she said the poetry. That was a clue, a slip of the lip.

Had he really thought Tawne wasn't like other vampires? She was covered in blood, wasn't she? She said yes when he said no, didn't she? She entered his house, his life, and his life was gone now, wasn't it? What more did Arcan need to convince him? He was naked, ruined and couldn't run home. *She* was there; he could never return.

How had he thought this would be different? She seemed to cool his fever, even driving his ghosts away. But it was a lie. And he was seduced—into what? What new horrors could there be that Arcan had not already known?

Oh, there can always be new horrors! the animals cheered with delight. Should have impaled her with a table leg. Broke

Charlee Jacob

up the wooden stake furniture and put one in her heart and another up her ass! Should have grabbed her by a tit and tossed her to the sunrise . . .

Arcan leapt over a fence from the sidewalk. It was about five feet high, and he cleared it as easily as hopping a puddle. Not bad for a man with a ragged hole over his heart. He could still hear commotion down the street, beyond the last twist of corner as people shouted about the maniac on crack all bloody and foaming cherries at the mouth who had run *thattaway,* no *down there,* gotta *call 911.* By the time they had it figured out, he might have gone straight the fuck up.

Arcan slipped across a yard. It was better in the alley than on the asphalt. The street had no light. It was dark. It was dead. It was like running over nothing.

The alley glowed. It had light. It was wet and field-soft like what the wolf would enjoy, what the cat would love to prowl in. It was natural and grassy, rutted and full of interesting rotting garbage.

A dog began to bark. Arcan trotted over to it and put his face right up against the fence where the dog scampered and snapped. He hissed into its steaming muzzle. It shut right up after whimpering once. Its ears flattened back, tail tucked between its legs.

Arcan hurried through the next yard, so damn fast on his feet he couldn't believe it. The grass was brown and wet, flashing gold from the muddy earth. He jumped another fence, smelled redwood in it, smelled the whole forest where the redwood trees had been cut down.

He caught a glimpse of a woman in the house of that yard. He saw her in sections through the horizontal slats of lavender Levolor blinds. Just winks of her, sparkling among her dead bed sheets and dead walls, turning the pages of a book. Her face smiled as her eyes tracked left to right across the sentences. He could actually hear her turning the pages. They were brittle through the wall, dry leaves stroked on the corners by her oiled fingertip. It was an old book. He read Emile Zola's *Nana* through the slats.

Arcan began to shake. He was naked and cold. Like Tawne was cold. She'd taken away his fever forever. He felt frozen gooseflesh turned inside-out.

Then he discovered he was hungry. It was like before when the animals would take over, each one sniffing out their particular share. But this was stronger. This was worse as they yammered all at once. His senses magnified. He'd had the animal's attitudes before tonight but not their keen hearing, their special sense of smell. Now he smelled this woman through the wall like the flame in a scented candle, like an all-night deli with a case of freshly sliced meats. He had to have that.

Arcan stepped back to give himself distance to run. He drew his legs up and propelled himself through the window. Glass embedded in his chest wound, in his hands and arms outstretched to protect his face, splintering in his testicles like cloves studding apples. The light from the lamp beside her bed reflected off the glass shards in his penis. It erected and the glass popped out of it like quills released from a porcupine.

It didn't hurt. He felt ice and misery and hatred for this woman, but there was no pain.

She screamed as the window exploded. She dropped the book and cringed as the blinds ripped the bolts from the wall. His legs tangled in them for a mere three seconds before he cast them off like paper chains. She didn't have a chance to get out of bed and run before he avalanched on top of her and sucked out her heat. He didn't even tear her out from under the covers. He threw all his weight on her and bit into her face.

His mouth was a tornado. Did she continue to scream? Could she? Arcan didn't hear it. He knew only that one moment he was cold and the next he ignited like a wick. He gulped her blood and found fever as he swallowed. He couldn't believe he'd ever fought fever. Had he really held Tawne hoping the fever would go away? Arcan ripped the woman to pieces. She wasn't alive anymore but he disjointed her, snapping parts from a fryer hen. He strung these around the squares and turrets of her bedroom furniture. At first the loops were as bright as gaily draped Christmas bulbs. But she was dead and the spirit was leaving. As soon as it was gone, the aura left. He folded a loop of her intestine, watching it twinkle, then darken.

Lights out, the cat growled, wolf howled, ghoul babbled. They were jubilant. *Lights out, bitch*.

Arcan struggled weakly beneath them. He was asleep. He was having a very bad nightmare. He dreamed he'd jumped through a window, stuffed the pages from an old book between a woman's jaws, and then fucked her heart to death. He wanted to wake up. He shook himself and heard the animals roar in triumph. He saw the haunches and gut menudo they made of the woman, and he moaned. All was lost.

The beasts had been out and he'd been out of control. Arcan would never have control again, would he? No.

If *life* was a series of wearing shackles, struggling and bleeding into the blunt links of the chains, of screaming in the feudal bonds, and then of breaking them to pass them on down to others—then what was *death*? It was appetite. It was no chains at all. It was inescapable evil.

Arcan grew cold again, the temporary warmth from the woman leaking out.

He heard a sob. Was there someone else home? A child! He smacked his lips and then shuddered again. He tried to push back the vicious gluttony. (. . . and was it a *female* child?)

The wolf's loins were already hardening at the prospect; the ghoul was running the tip of his tongue along the points of his sharpest teeth.

Arcan searched the house. He went down the hall and

into a second bedroom. He ripped the mattress from the bed. There was no child under it. He tore open the closet. Nothing hung from it but a few old coats. He smelled mothballs. He ripped each drawer from the dresser and smashed his fists through the wooden bottoms. There was no child hiding in any of them. He went to the bathroom, tore the shower curtain down ring by ring to find no one behind it either. He ransacked the towels in the linen closet, pissing and shitting on them. He broke every dish in the kitchen and dumped the contents of the refrigerator onto the floor. He was frenzied. She had to be there somewhere, sobbing, terrified, pink cleft intact and awaiting impalement by a monster so rigid he disemboweled with each thrust.

A young unbled lamia to initiate him into delicious new horrors, virile in the emancipation of his animals. There would be no more senseless soul-searching restraint. They wouldn't be hobbled and gelded by this fool who hadn't wanted his tongue, his teeth, his belly, his vengeful cock. His instincts.

Where was she? This tiny squeaking baby mouse for his cat to douse its whiskers with. A yielding lamb for the horny wolf. A child to be passionately consumed in marshmallow marrow by the ghoul.

Tear the floor boards up . . . see if she's hiding under the house! Knock down the walls! She must be hiding between them . . .

Arcan put his fingernails in his cheeks, felt his flesh pop as he clamped and raked down.

"Stop!" he begged. He didn't want to kill a child.

There was no child anyway. What a relief. There was only the sob again.

He pulled the tasseled cover off the bird cage. The budgie shrieked as he rattled the thrumming curve of its walls. He stuck his hand in and pulled it out in his fist, stuffing it wholly into his mouth. He wasn't fully satisfied by the crunch of its hollow little bones.

"Stop!" Arcan begged. But he didn't articulate well over the dusty feathers.

A sob. Arcan saw the woman's face emerge timidly from the dark. Did she have a twin sister? Hidden in a closet and now trying to sneak away? No, he'd checked all the closets out, anywhere she might have hidden.

She'd come from a secret room. Where the child was still hidden. They would both pay for that with the rest of the night, in tatters and shreds and the most unholy of discreations.

"Stop it!" Arcan pleaded, his voice cracking. "Stop it!"

Carmel Gaines put a thin hand on the woman's translucent shoulder. The brains that were hard in corrugated runnels from the front to the back of Carmel's skull had no heat in them. There was no living light there. The cold in her eyes—that was in the eyes of all the ghosts as they emerged from the plaster—that *cold* was merciless.

There were men's clothes in the woman's closet. She had a lover or husband who might be coming to find this. The longer Arcan stayed, the greater the risk this man would catch him. Arcan dressed in some of the clothes even though they were too small for him. He didn't bother to wash first so that the material stuck to him as the blood dried. He sat in the bedroom with the pieces of his victim festooning the walls and furniture, and he waited for this man to arrive.

"I have to try to let him kill me," Arcan said to himself.

Surely this man would when he saw what Arcan had done to this poor lady.

He struggled hard to make himself think of her that way. She was an unfortunate woman who had never done Arcan any harm. She wasn't a bitch or a whore or a Lilith even though the animals were furiously putting these words into his ears.

The man would go crazy and attack Arcan out of a natural knee-jerk reaction that the butcher would do the same to him.

But would the animals let Arcan sit there and give himself up to justice? More than that. Could Arcan be punished by this man? By anyone?

A cat could be dispatched by blows or gunshots. So could a wolf. So could a ghoul. Well, probably a ghoul could be. A ghoul wasn't a supernatural creature—just a carrion eater.

Arcan reconsidered this. When he'd read about the hashish drinkers, he'd also read about the Arabic ghuls, demons that ate corpses or small children. A ghoul wasn't a man. It was one of hell's animals. Arcan didn't know if it could be killed with blows or gunshots or not. The cat and wolf could be. Best two out of three.

But he knew that a vampire couldn't be shot. Tawne had been shot and the wounds had healed. And it couldn't have just been bullshit because his own chest wound from her attack was already non-existent.

Arcan glanced at the ghost of the woman he'd killed tonight. Among all the other spirits, she was the first in their banshee ranks whom he'd killed with his own hands. Carmel Gaines had been a suicide—one he was responsible for because he'd driven her to putting that gun in her mouth, but still not one of his own actual murdering. And the women who were only partially dead didn't belong in her category either. Her total rupturing between body and soul was his, all his. Arcan wondered how many more would join her before his animals were put to rest.

This nameless woman hovered near him, sobbing like a child. Her face and head were whole—although Arcan hadn't left them that way—but her body floated beneath the head in pieces, the limbs twisted loose at the joints.

They swirled around the puzzle of the torso.

She didn't want him to stay and wait for her man to return. She knew he would kill her man. Arcan wouldn't be able to help it. The man would attack and Arcan would defend himself. Even if Arcan tried to lie still and absorb the damage, eventually the animals would retaliate. They would probably pounce the moment he entered the house, smelling him as an easy meal.

Arcan stood up and left the house. The ghosts followed. Even the new one. She wasn't going to haunt the walls where she'd been killed but was going to haunt Arcan. She had to follow. She couldn't help it.

Arcan turned to her and shrugged. "Okay, so I can't let him kill me. But I won't kill him either."

Had she sighed with relief? Arcan couldn't tell. Could so many chunks sigh?

He was still bloody but since he was no longer naked, he didn't draw as much attention. There were fewer people on the streets anyway because several hours had passed. It was late.

The animals argued, *No, no, the night is in its prime . . .*

He ran on all fours. He loped close to the buildings. A few people glanced his way but they looked down, not at the same level as if he were standing upright to move. They looked down as if seeing a strange wild dog. No one saw him clearly. But he didn't like their faces. Arcan began to go down alleys instead of wide open streets. Arcan's shadow was folded over, too short here and too long there, knotted across the arch of his back.

It was an animal's shadow. It jumped easily over garbage cans, flew across dumpsters. Arcan was frightened by it.

There was still a sliver of him inside the feral thing he'd become. He was afraid and convinced that he had to do something to change it before even that bit of him was gone to the animals. If there was just a fragment of Arcan, then there might be a chance. Not for survival, but for atonement: that thing which only humans sought.

"Ah

"Tone

"Ment," his own voice sounded out the syllables.

But what shape could it take? It wasn't as simple as forcing himself to give up violence. Tawne had seen to that. And he couldn't ask some invisible god for forgiveness and salvation. He and his animals were way past this. What shape could atonement take? The only shape (shapes) left him.

Arcan was cold again. He would have to sup a second time. So soon. He'd already just done that.

He'd better do it before he reached his destination. It mustn't be an act of desperation then. Not when Arcan would need control so he could use it to terrify, to convey an object/abject lesson. When he got there, it had to be accomplished slowly and cruelly. With bestial finesse with *him* using the animals for a change.

Provided this was even possible. If it backfired, it would be a bloodbath.

So, eat now. Do it. Faaaaaststst . . . don't know how long we can hold back.

Arcan stopped at the black mouth of the alley he was in.

"Thanks, buddy," an old man was saying to a cabbie.

The old guy huffed and puffed his rail-self out of the taxi. His gray-green raincoat hung loosely on him. Arcan smelled a mixture of white wine and fillet of sole, citric shaving lotion and a colostomy bag. The beasts weren't finicky about this last. What wolf didn't know the smell of shit on its dinner?

The taxi rolled away. The old man turned tiredly to enter his hotel. The animals pounced, slashing his screams across the windpipe at the onset. Then they dragged him, spraying blood but wild-eyed and conscious, back into the alley.

The sick old man's warmth was like rocks in the sun.

Arcan shut his eyes and withdrew while they feasted,

telling himself that, "This is only a sharkstop on the road to salvation."

The ghoul giggled, thinking this was funny. Then it laughed out loud when the man's shitbag burst.

"How soon will I be shriven?" Arcan whispered to himself as he clung to the wall.

He became very quiet as he neared a window where he heard the women talking. He hadn't wanted to risk being seen by those inside the building. He hadn't gone through the door. He climbed up the outside wall, thinking he'd be like a gecko with adhesive disks on its toes. He'd seen this in a Dracula movie once, the vampire gliding silently up the stone wall. This was brick. Close enough.

But it wasn't a glide and it wasn't easy. Arcan was unable to hold on to any shape that even resembled human for long. And apparently wolves weren't great climbers. The cat helped but even those claws scrabbled, breaking off in raggedy points. His shaggy weight slipped, grabbing purchase where he could, hauling himself up a few more inches.

Three floors up was a long way at this pace. Thank God they didn't hold their meetings on the sixth. Would he have made it had they been that far up? Yes, but probably not before dawn. And his claws would have been worn down to the shoulders.

Arcan remembered being back in school when all the kids cringed at the mention of even one fingernail being bent backward. Now all of his bowed, wedging in brickwork until they snapped off, flying in chips past his face.

He peered into the window and heard the group, saw them sitting in a circle. Ten women.

He'd known they would be here this late. They couldn't bear the idea of being in their homes where it might have happened to them. Of being alone and vulnerable with their memories of him. When this group met they stayed half the night, holding each other's hands as they pondered their scars. Wondering how much longer the night would hold terror for them.

Arcan slipped again, talons catching in the mortar. His blood didn't soak quickly into the brick but trickled down, slow in the cold. His weight dipped down toward gravity. He certainly weighed more than any cat unless it were a fully grown tiger. How much did wolves weigh? His hairy flanks shuddered as he braced with his feet, hugging the wall. He reached for the sill, muscles pulling, shoulders bunched like fists.

He could see Elise Reedman through the window. Her eye patch was hot white and scalded him. Arcan growled. He jabbed his arm through the glass, then hoisted the rest of himself over the jagged sill. It sliced along his buttocks and thighs. But that was of no consequence except to further shake up these women.

Whether Arcan was slashed to the bone or not, Heather Bastilla screamed at the sight of a large animal crawling through the window it had just shattered. She yanked an object from her purse in the same breath. That purse had been open in Heather's lap and she'd been steadily pulling tissues from it to dry her eyes with. She pointed the object in a black and blue blur, firing. The other women screamed and grabbed pistols, tasers, and mace from their bags and pockets. There were bursts of fire, stings and clouds of gas. Arcan just smiled through it.

He knew them all. These were the ghosts in the flesh. Out of their haunts and right where he could torment them.

Here I am, Harry, he said to himself. *At the source.*

Celia Lehman was yelling, "Help us, somebody!"

Arcan remembered Celia. She'd been wearing a granny gown because it was November and colder than usual for Thanksgiving. There had actually been snow on the ground, not too common for this part of East Texas. The flannel had chewed dryly. The ghoul definitely preferred lighter fabrics.

"There's no one here except maybe a cleaning crew," Elise chattered. She fired from four feet away and it struck Arcan in the chest. He didn't even flinch.

If there was a cleaning crew, then they were running out the door by now—or hiding. They heard so many weapons go off at once they probably thought it was a gang war.

Someone kicked at him, flying through the air. He caught the foot and shoved her against the wall. Julie, that was her name. Not a black belt yet, are you, Julie? She knocked teaching certificates off the wall and landed on her shoulder on the floor. She sat up, a great deal more dazed than he was.

Another rushed forward with a wail, pressing her gun against Arcan's skull and firing to aerate the bone. The bullet echoed in his ears, thrummed against hard matter, and went out the other side without rattling about too much in the brain.

Arcan grinned.

She blanched, her finger freezing on the trigger, gun back a few inches from the recoil but coming forward—slowly as if he had a force field to push it back with.

"Shoot again, stupid. Shoot me dead at point blank. Then watch nothin'," he said as he spread his hands, shaking his head so that some of what leaked out of the head wounds flew.

"You bastard!" she shrieked, firing a second time. She tasted his blood as it spattered her face. She probably thought it was her own blood. Karen, she was. Karen Strickland. She was the one he'd seen in the grocery store when he had the fight with Bill. She was the one who definitely couldn't have children after he attacked her because Arcan had left with too much of her uterus under his nails.

He repeated what he'd said to her in her bedroom a year ago, "Time for the cradle to fall."

Just in case she had any doubts as to his identity.

Karen's jaw dropped in horror. Arcan reached up and curled his fingers around her weapon, wrenching it from her until he heard bones in her hand and wrist snap. He spun her, pulling her backward into an embrace she could barely move in.

The women were backing away, sobbing, crying, babbling. Trying to get to the door. But Arcan sprang to it with Karen in his arms. He could feel the springs coiling in his legs as he made it in a single impossible leap across the entire room.

"Isn't anyone glad to see your long lost lover?" he cooed. It was a litany in diphthongs and throaty R's. Very catlike.

Looking down, he could see that his hands wrapped around Karen were a man's.

(No, they were the ghoul's. A ghoul wasn't a man.)

The women knotted together, backs to the wall near the blackboard. Clinging to each other, faces ghostly. Not solid at all. He could see right through them. This made Arcan uneasy. The animals growled. Animals didn't like ghosts. He had to assert himself. He had to shape his salvation. For he was back at the source and it was only here could he find it. Harry'd said so and Harry ought to know.

Arcan sneered. "Thought I was dead, huh? 'Cause nobody'd heard from me in a while? Thought I'd left town to maybe go hunting in New Orleans?"

Elise almost seemed to be smiling at him through her fear because of the way that scar tugged her mouth. She put a hand over her eye patch as if it throbbed.

He'd seen it throbbing, hot white.

"I'm dead," Arcan whispered and bent down. He licked the throat of the woman in his arms. Karen whimpered, shrinking under his tongue.

The vein in that throat pulsed, rich and warm, with a

drum in it doing a solo which pounded in Arcan's ears. It rattled through his brain that bullets had burrowed through.

She would have to be the one. Sorry, lady.

Arcan bit that tympani vein and it clacked into his mouth.

Several women called out Karen's name. But none of them moved more than inches. They were so thoroughly afraid. And incomplete.

They didn't rush forward to help Karen just as she hardly struggled. She hung limp in his arms, quivering, like a rabbit brought down only shakes and twitches as the wolf tears it. The rabbit knew its place. It had a role in life. And in death. The heat in her felt so good. Warmer even than the first kill in the house and the second one with his shitbag.

Was this because Arcan had been shot? Tawne had said she was weakened after being wounded. But it was okay. He was already healing. He could feel the holes meshing edges, cells weaving new fabric in his chest and head and wherever else he'd been hit by these pitiful bitches.

(No, not bitches . . . this was atonement time. Those were words the animals used. It made women easier to hate. But Arcan didn't want to hate them. If he gave in to that, there would be no stopping him.)

He couldn't help it. He moaned loudly with pleasure as the heat flooded his mouth with rust and copper—all precious metal. He drank greedily, savoring while seeing them from the corner of one eye. The brain dripping into that eye didn't make it difficult at all.

They were crying messily, hiding their faces. Their heartbeats were a panicked roar. Arcan's hearing was so good he could hear single eyelashes falling with their tears. Could hear the arteries in their necks as their blood seemed to whisper to him. The animals listened, straining to speak back to each and every throat.

Karen Strickland faded to quiet as the vein collapsed. The ghoul wanted to eat. Arcan pushed him, submerging him, fighting to keep him from sinking his teeth in to dig for more.

Arcan snapped his head up and howled at the women. "Look at me!"

They had no choice but to obey. He felt the spark the traitor had told him about in detail. His eyes flicked to each one and it connected. It passed away moments later as he moved his attention on, feeling it connect with the next woman and the next. They gasped, screamed, saw him change, more than just his face moving. Each creature emerged—not a little bit as when he'd attacked them as a mortal man.

The cat was huge, fur full of kilowatts. Its whole body moved as if it were a single gesticulating hand. The wolf was gross with a crooked foul erection that made the linings of their mouths ache with memory. The ghoul was ulcerous, his belly enormous with tiny feet and hands visible. These pawed him from within as if he were about to give birth to something monstrous. His gash of a mouth opened and drooled blood. Arcan flickered the connection back to this one, to that one, to Elise's one eye. He let them see him as each thing and as Arcan, then back again. "Get the idea? Know what I am? Well, you'd better know it for a fact. Make no mistake about it. The world isn't safe, ladies."

Arcan laughed at this. The ghoul laughed. A lot of things tended to strike the ghoul as funny.

They cowered but no one looked away.

"Your puny mace and itty bitty guns are crap." Arcan stuck a finger into one of the wounds—the skull part which had the best share of holes—and examined the finger after he took it out. The blood and brain had already stopped oozing. He put the remnant of it in his mouth and smacked. "You can't kill a vampire with that shit.

"Go ahead, call the cops and see how hard they laugh. They didn't think much of you when you couldn't describe me before. What will they say when you tell them you shot and tasered and all that stuff? And I didn't even have the courtesy to fall down? You're a bunch of hysterical cunts and tomorrow night I'm gonna come back here and have another one of you. Just like I had this bitch."

Arcan shifted the drained body in his arms so that he could take Karen's head in both hands, snapping it viciously. It crunched, stretched elastically on the ligature of the neck, split the spinal cord, and nearly came off. He lifted Karen by that head and tossed the body at them. It knocked Heather and—what was the other woman's name?—Gina down like bowling pins. *Strike!*

Arcan tore his shirt with a slow rip that was huge in the almost silent room. The cotton, stiff with dried and fresh blood, parted to show them the wound Elise had made in his chest. It was practically healed. He was mending faster than he had a few hours ago. The wound Tawne made over his heart took longer than this to close.

He strode over and snatched a woman. The kid, Marla. The cheerleader he'd had after the big game. He grabbed her and thrust her splayed fingers into that chest wound, then up and into the head holes. He dropped her to the floor. She was trying desperately to wipe those fingers clean on her jeans.

"What does it take? A wooden stake? A silver bullet? A flame thrower aimed by the Pope? See you tomorrow night, whores. Draw lots among yourselves or let me pick. You all look pretty tasty. It doesn't matter. And don't bother trying to hide. I know where you live. I'll always know where you live and I can follow you anyplace you go."

Arcan ran to the shattered window and jumped out.

The women rushed to it and stared as he ran off on all fours to be quickly lost on the dark street.

Arcan heard them crying again. The facts were sinking

in about the nightmare they shared, discovering that not a one of them was asleep. Didn't they dream him every night? Yeah, but never like this. They never would have imagined him to be like this.

Arcan wondered, if this doesn't do it, what'll I do?

(What'll I do, Harry?)

He could feel the woman he'd just killed. Her pale spirit clung to him, and he couldn't dislodge her. She bobbed against him as he ran, like a baby monkey holding onto its mother, like a shriveled idiot twin attached at the organs.

Chapter Thirty

Denise Cross looked at her deflated self and sobbed. She'd shrunk back to her former human dimensions.

She'd been huge and exhilarated. Pumped on fear steroids culled from fools who trembled and painted with their piss the monsters they feared most into the video frames. That kind of stuff could make you rowdy.

The air went out of the bulk, the muscles wizening. With each step on concrete, bubbles of her fizzled as she dwarfed, Gog and Magog became Thumbalina. She felt like a goddess stripped of her powers. It enraged her.

Denise had squashed people, flattening them with one/two strikes. The sidewalk had cracked beneath her feet. She'd chopped a steel lamppost as she ran past, snapping it like a toothpick. This was why the ancients feared giants.

And it was gone, just like that? A mere drug she had to crash from?

No. Denise probed her arm with her fingers, felt her shoulders. There was more muscle than she'd had before the transformation. It wasn't as noticeable as when she'd been slamming pedestrians downtown but it was there. It wasn't all gone. The skin was smooth, belonging to the woman Denise Cross. But that which lay beneath it was hard.

Like her nipples.

She hurried home to view the video again. The ugly man sat up, sat up, sat up. Looked right into her eyes. Smiled the smile she had to grin back at him in greeting, in mutual recognition.

Denise, baby?

He murmured in her head.

Denise, baby, fledgling. You know. You KNOW.

He became her each time he sat up and looked into her eyes.

Denise got out her make-up kit. She used only the browns and olive greens. The tiniest amount of black eye-liner for tracing. She painted the moons of her breasts to resemble the pineapple pattern on a pair of hand grenades. The shape wasn't right, of course, but the idea was unmistakable when rendered. She admired this in the mirror, squeezing them. The shadows were powdery against her palms.

Something was missing. Oh, right.

She rummaged through her jewelry box until she found the big hoop earrings. They weren't brass but gold. This was okay. They had wires at least instead of studs. Studs would never have been wide enough for Denise's large nipples set into the sizable circles of her areola. They were too gaudy in gold to be paramilitary. That would have required a buffed, flat finish. But the rings in the video sparkled, invited to be touched, grasped, teased. These would do nicely.

She used a pair of pliers to stretch the wires a bit. Filed the ends to needle sharpness. Then Denise grasped the right nipple, squeezing it between her thumb and forefinger, piercing it from right to left with the wire.

It surprised her that it hurt so much. As hard as they were, she'd thought there would be no pain at all. The blood trickled from each side where she strung it through, funneling over the eye shadows 'til they caked like mud from battle trenches.

A small amount of whitish liquid bubbled through the berry ducts. At first Denise thought it was pus but it had to be fat. It couldn't be milk. She wasn't lactating, was she?

The wire was pulled through and then turned so that the hoop hung down at the proper angle. She fastened the back and then stuck cotton to the seeping holes.

Denise pinched the left nipple, wincing in anticipation of pain, and jabbed it with the second sharpened gold wire. Her clitoris burned from stimulation. She imagined herself as she was in the video after the ugly man became her. Rocking on top of Rob Waters, onto the death hardness of him, coldly erect but helpless. That made it better. Denise pulled the wire through and felt the fibers in the nipple tear as they parted. By the time she fastened the wire shut on it, she was shaking all over. The room blurred in shadows of yellow like citron and white like aspirin, the way it always did when she had an orgasm. She moaned huskily, thighs pressed tightly together. She was still pinching the nipple, and it bled much more than the other one. She'd have to repaint the grenades with fresh shadows.

Denise examined this in the mirror, flicking the rings with satisfaction.

"Cool. What a pity Halloween's weeks away," Denise said, smirking. "I could carry a knife in my teeth, stick an Uzi up my butt, and go as the prop box for the next Rambo film."

She was going to need another video fix soon. It was too much of a rush without wanting to indulge it again. Magic was made to be used and abused. This had come into her hands and hadn't destroyed her because Denise and it were the same.

The ugly man summoned her with his eyes. She heard him in her head. When she flexed her new muscles, he was deep inside, flexing his.

Chapter Thirty-one

Elise thought the pain behind the eye patch would never stop.

Karen's body was on the floor.

"I'll call the police," Heather said as she tried to walk to the door to go out into the hall. There was a pay phone near the stairs. Her legs didn't want to hold her up. There was a high red in her cheeks. A vein slowly pulsed, outlined sharply in her forehead.

Elise calmly took Heather by the arm to stop her. "No."

"What?" several of the women whispered in shock.

Was there to be no help? (Had there ever been?)

"We mustn't call anyone," Elise replied. "We have to talk."

"What's there to talk about?" asked Julie. "Karen's dead. We have to call the cops."

"What would we tell them? How would we explain how he killed her? How would we describe him? They always want a description. I'll bet no two of us would say the same thing. We'd look like idiots, just like we did last time. Only this'll be worse. You remember how it was, don't you? We can't catch phantoms. I can't go through that again."

Celia's voice was thin. "But it was the same man."

There was hoarse assent around the room.

Barbara moaned. "We can't just let him get away with it."

And yet Barbara's face was full of futility, as if she knew as she said it that there was nothing else they could do.

"Damn right it was the same man. But not the same, see what I mean? No way was he like that when he attacked me. He's changed. He's—more—than he was last time. That's what makes it worse," Elise told them.

Celia argued, hands fluttering. "But he said he's coming back."

Elise laid it out. "I'll bet he will. We could call the cops and tell them what we saw. That would get some strange looks, you better believe it. But that won't keep him away. I mean, he got to most of us in our homes. Would you rather have that happen again, when you're alone? And he's like *this* now?"

Celia protested. "But the police can protect us. They'll give us guards."

Elise laughed harshly. "They could protect us from that? Would their guns work better than ours did? Besides, they wouldn't believe it. We saw a vampire? Whose going to credit that shit? Look how he changed, how he killed Karen, that jump from the window, I mean, sweet Jesus, we told them last time how he seemed to look like animals. What did they say? That they could never get someone on that kind of description. That they could do a line-up from the city zoo! And even if they managed to get a suspect, we couldn't say that crap in court because then we'd get laughed *out* of court."

Elise was worked up, furious about how they had been treated. Adrenaline had her striding back and forth across the floor. The other women watched her but weren't able to work it off as she did.

Elise continued. "They're not going to protect us. Oh, they might give us a guard for a few days or a week. Then we'll get the *manpower drain* speech, and the cops will be re-assigned, and *then* he'll get us. One by one. Whenever he feels like it.

"But he'll probably be back tomorrow night, like he said. Where would we go? I don't have the money to relocate. Shit. He found us here, didn't he?"

There were softly muffled sobs, shoulders hitching, twitching with recollections of his touch, his clammy mouth and sour seed. Elise knew they were watching her. Did they think she was the strong one? Then how come she didn't feel strong? How come she couldn't feel strong?

"So what do we do? Just wait?" Tira blurted, fingers stiff. There were old scars of round blisters visible on them, on the wrist going up to disappear under the sleeve. Cigarette burns spotted her like a jaguar. She always wore high collars and long sleeves to hide where he'd burned obscenities on her throat and arms.

Elise watched the round circle scars on Tira's fingers stretch as Tira whimpered. "I don't want to end up like her." Tira pointed at Karen's body.

"Look into the mirror," Elise replied without meaning to be cruel. "You're two heartbeats shy of it already. We all are. He has our spirits. We won't have control over our lives until we get them back."

The women glanced at each other nervously. It wasn't something Elise had said to them before. Did they look skeptical? It was a bizarre idea, borne out of tragedy. Out of hysteria.

"This is why we never heal," Elise said. "That's why there always seems to be a piece missing. It's because there *is* a piece gone. Does every rapist do this to his victim? One thing's for sure—this one does."

They began to nod. They searched themselves for it and clearly came up empty-handed.

"Guns don't work. That's obvious," said Heather, holding her own weapon in her hand as if it were an alien artifact. "I shot him myself. I saw Karen shoot him point blank in the head. No way that's normal."

And he was an animal when he crashed through the window, Heather added mentally but couldn't say it.

"Sort of tends to lend some credence to his claim, doesn't it?" Elise replied bitterly.

They wondered what death tasted like in the mouth. And for how long? Just because the brain was gone—snapped at the spine and devoid of sending any more messages—didn't mean there couldn't be some semblance remaining, something that ached and suffered by degrees. It was in Karen's face, in the eyes that were wide open.

Could they die if he had their souls?

(Karen looked pretty dead.)

Elise frowned. *Well, we're all pretty dead, actually.*

There had been 10 women in the group before Karen was murdered. Now there were nine. Elise thought that nine might be a mystical number.

It had better be if they were going to live.

The tree of life. That was it. Nine was the number of the tree of life.

"So," Elise said to the others, "what do we do here? Stakes and crucifixes? There must be lots of books on this. The backs of cereal boxes. Whatever."

Barbara shrugged sheepishly. "I've read a few books. I really got into it for a long time. Stories and novels about vampires."

Barbara lowered her head, ashamed.

"Did you stop reading them after you were attacked?" Ann asked.

Barbara shook her head with a silly smile. "No, that's when I started," she admitted.

Elise was fascinated. "Really? What was the appeal?"

Barbara laughed self-deprecatingly. "They're incorruptible. They have this beauty that endures when everything else rots."

Tira snorted and seemed to lose her breath. She pulled off her concealing sweater. Across her breasts and down both arms had been burned the words *lamia, Lilith* and *vampire*. She looked at Karen's body and burst into fresh tears.

Tira said, "This is how beauty endures."

Elise sighed. "Stakes it is. If he really isn't a vampire and he's done this incredible mass hypnosis thing on us, a stake'll still kill him. Piercing the heart has that effect, so I'm told."

"But where do we get them?" Gina asked.

Marla smiled weakly. "At the hardware store."

Ann shook her head as she tried to light a cigarette. Normally the therapy room was a non-smoking area. But as badly as she was shaking, there were no objections. "This sounds too easy for what we saw here tonight."

"Don't worry, honey. It won't be easy," Elise assured her, then grasped the other woman's hand to gently guide the trembling lighter to the tip of her cigarette.

Ann took a raw inhale of hot smoke, and her eyelids half closed as if it were pure cocaine.

"Shouldn't we get holy water, too? I mean I've seen them do that in a couple of movies on the cable. It's supposed to burn 'em like acid," Marla suggested. She'd been the youngest of Arcan's victims. Marla had been just 16 when he attacked her two summers ago. Her false teeth rattled in her mouth as she spoke, the wolf having knocked out the real ones.

Heather smirked. "It's not like we can get that in liters at True Value."

"There's a church down the street," Julie suggested.

"There is?" Celia asked. "I've always driven here from the other way, I guess."

"Yeah," Heather corrected her, "but it isn't Catholic. It's Baptist. No holy water. Leastwise, I don't think so."

"We'll use whatever we can get, objects with physical weight, tangible and sharp. That'll kill him no matter what the hell he is," Elise said. "I think you all should go home now. I'll call the cops about Karen. But I'm going to tell them I found her like this, okay? We'll meet tomorrow night to wait for him. Otherwise they'll send us home with a token piece of shit uniform who'll sit all night in his car outside our homes, eating bear claws and joking *yeah, that's him!* every time a stray dog crosses the street."

Barbara agreed with her head bent and eyes closed. "I'll be here tomorrow night. I can't run anymore or wait for some white knight to vindicate me."

"Me, too. I promise," said Tira. She took the cigarette from Ann. She touched the burning tip into the dot on the "i" in the word *vampire* across her chest. There were gasps as the women heard the hiss and smelled the flesh char through the scar.

Ann took her smoke back and touched it to her own hand. She winced but didn't cry out.

The cigarette made its way around the circle, each woman burning herself with it once as a vow to return.

They left. Elise was alone with Karen's body. She closed her single eye and focused on the empty socket. She drew on the astral record of the missing optic. And—as always when she did this—she swore she could see with it.

Not in bursts of insight. There was nothing of the future. But in thunderbolts that were flashes of his jagged blade.

There was movement inside her where the knife had been. She felt motion, sentient shadows in her scars buried deep beneath the white puckers and crimson streaks. These took the place of her missing soul. Elise felt them when she took off her blouse and looked into the mirror at home.

She could see them coming for her when she saw within the empty socket.

They were there for every victim to one degree or another. No more than a dark spot out of the corner of the eye for some, a partial eclipse of the sun for many, total night for others.

Elise wished she could hide right now in a room with a mirror, like she always did when she was especially depressed. She wanted to strip, to stare at her crosshatched skin until tears flowed. The shadows moved, unhindered by a vigilant soul, calling to her to come view the pattern of the night on herself.

Were the others going to do that tonight when they got home? Masochistic flop-sweat?

But Elise couldn't do that now. Maybe she could never do it again. She and the others were going to have to fight for themselves. And if they survived the next 24 hours, things might not be the same.

The shadows might not have a hold on them anymore.

Chapter Thirty-two

Arcan curled up in a sewer under the bus station, hearing animal rumbles of diesel overhead. It was a cramped space but there was a large pavilion over where the buses parked and loaded. Even in broad daylight, it remained safe from the sun. The fumes from the exhaust didn't bother him. But the spirit of the woman Karen still clung to him, light as a crepe paper banner. He closed his eyes and tried to sleep as Tawne (that traitorous bitch) appeared to do when folded into his bathtub.

It was impossible to sleep with Karen's wrinkled, deflated protoplasm rustling against him like a newspaper being blown across a drunk in the park. She cried softly into his fur. Interesting that the ghosts of the women had Karen with them but here she was also in this aggravating second form. How many pieces to a spirit were there?

Arcan's stomach hurt.

He wasn't supposed to feel pain. Tawne had told him that.

Charlee Jacob

But the pain was there, evasive and probing. The shirt he'd taken from the closet of the first victim hung on him in strips. Through it he looked down to examine himself. Something moved just beneath the surface in nubs. As if there were fat worms inside.

Or fingers.

Arcan knew she was there. The woman who had been reading *Nana*.

Not all of her was there. It was only finger-enough of her that he felt her groping blindly within his stomach. Like the boy swallowed whole by a tiger in some story he'd read years ago, eaten alive and battling to get out. But she hadn't been eaten whole. He'd only devoured pieces.

Arcan corrected himself. His animals had done the deed.

These pieces were apparently not happy where they were. They also wouldn't let Arcan close his eyes.

There was a blossoming hurt a little farther down. He took off the ruined trousers and stared at the curve under his belly. It puckered along the line of guts concealed by flesh and muscle. It blew a bubble not unlike the color of pink chewing gum.

This was the haunting gift from the old man he'd dragged into the alley. It was the colostomy bag.

It filled and gurgled all day, even as the woman reading *Nana* pushed fingertips from within, and Karen rustled and wept.

Chapter Thirty-three

Tawne couldn't taste the man anymore, the one she'd seduced with Delia's image at the git-n-shit a couple of blocks away. She'd lured him back here to drink him dry in Arcan's bed. Tawne was afraid to be away from the house long in case Arcan returned. What did it matter if there was now a dead man in the bedroom? No one would be sleeping there anymore. Arcan wouldn't be able to because of the windows.

If, that is, Arcan ever came home. There was a man murdered in his bed, where the two of them had made love back when Arcan still loved her. Where Tawne had to strip the sheets and blankets that were full of puke and gore from her having done the change on Arcan. She had to do this before she could even think about going out to hunt for herself. Couldn't exactly bring a guy home to that, could she? There was a corpse in there almost as cold as she was, its eyes bulging with shock and going milky white.

If Arcan did come home to see that drained and ravaged shell, what would he think?

Of course, he'd be home, she assured herself. He had to: He needed to be safe during the day.

Making love to the man-who-now-lay-dead in the bedroom hadn't even been slightly sweet. Tawne couldn't find his warmth because it didn't compare with Arcan's fine heat. All she could think of was Arcan as she pulled this stranger's erection into herself while he looked with passion at the beautiful Delia. Tawne thought only of Arcan as she let the stranger spend himself, thinking of Arcan as the man suddenly began to fight and she had to really hurt him to keep him from screaming. Of Arcan as she drank and reached for just one good moment that never came.

Arcan was gone and she'd been so stupid. Even with the dream, there was no excuse for what she'd done to him.

Perhaps there was no excuse for what Tawne had done to anyone lately. She appeared strong, had always seemed to be with her big meaty hands and thick shoulders. But Tawne was weak after all. She'd given her life for one meaningless vision and then had given Arcan's life for another. How fucked-up could anyone get?

Tawne stripped to stand naked before the full length mirror on the bathroom door. She stared at every ugly nuance and at each inelegant lump. She willed it to worsen until the reflection stopped, the arms lengthened bluntly until squared knuckles brushed the floor. The thick flesh shagged out as the forehead shortened and the face became a snout with wide canine jaws.

"Ooga booga!" she exclaimed.

Thoth's dog-headed ape. That was what the ugly man had called her.

Wasn't Thoth the god that weighed the hearts of the dead in order to judge them?

The dog's black nose ran from one nostril and the baboon body scratched its private parts. With a little effort, the dog's head became that of a coyote. Coyote woman. Coyote baboon. *There* was an image to chew your own arm off over. Ooga booga howl.

How would Tawne's heart weigh? How would Thoth judge her merits and sins? How had Delia's heart been found? Surely not wanting. If not pure, it had at least been caring.

Tawne concentrated to banish the deformity in the mirror.

"Okay, enough of beating myself up. How's about an image worthy of love? I need some hope and inspiration here. A little Righteous Brothers' music please, maestro."

Delia's image. Who else had she ever known sympathy from or a moment of sincere sisterhood? Most people weren't that generous. Even her downstairs neighbors had only been kind after Tawne's suicide attempt.

It always boiled down to death, didn't it? Only when folks came nose-flat against mortality did they finally act in whatever manner proved their stuff. Tawne considered how she'd acted as Delia's body lay crammed into the drainage pipe.

Tawne hugged the other woman's reflection tighter, fearful to give it up. Not wanting to see in her own face how she'd screwed up her life and now had messed up even her death.

The image rolled like a heat mirage. It rippled.

"Tawne."

She heard it distinctly.

"I must have said it to myself."

To label Delia's appearance with her own name.

"Tawne, honey."

The full perfect lips moved. Hers hadn't.

"Delia?" Tawne finally whispered, stepping closer to the mirror. The reflection didn't do the same.

"Don't use me anymore."

Delia's face was very sad. The lustrous eyes had tears in them. But Tawne couldn't cry anymore.

"What did you say?" Tawne blurted. She shook. This was a ghost, wasn't it? A ghost was speaking to her. She tried not to be afraid. Tawne was a supernatural creature, too. What was there to be afraid of?

But what could Delia's spirit possibly have to tell her? She leaned close, putting her ear to the glass. Since becoming a vampire, Tawne's hearing had sharpened. Delia's voice, however, was soft and seemed to come from very far away. The mirror was cold, a frozen pond. The voice was an eddy of pure warmth. She could feel the summer drawl in Delia's breath.

"Don't use me to hurt people," the ghost said, her eyes streaming, hair wild with grief.

Then Delia was gone. The image became flat like a poor photograph. Tawne let it fade, staring briefly at the dull lump of a woman with Thoth's ape just below the surface.

Where was Arcan?

Tawne stood on the porch. She'd paced it a few hundred times. She must have worn a groove into it. She anxiously squeezed her hands together, stopping at intervals to stand motionless, hoping to see him coming through the oaks in the yard.

She hoped he hadn't done something careless to get himself thrown into jail. They weren't murky dungeons anymore. They probably had windows these days. And if they didn't, if he was taken later to be booked or questioned, he might have to pass windows and light. That would be her fault.

If he fought the cops like a tiger, and they shot him and captured him and found how he was *different*, would they lock him up in a secret place to study him? Like those aliens the feds were supposed to be holding in Hangar 18 or E.T. Lala Land or wherever? They would torture him and watch him. Maybe starving him, maybe giving him lab rats and rhesus monkeys so he could get just enough to keep him going. So they could stick him with one more needle filled with drain cleaner, fire one more experimental black Rhino bullet into his brainpan, burn him with one more ray of sunlight.

Tawne laughed nervously. "Get a hold of yourself, girl. He'll be okay. I was okay and I didn't have the first idea what to expect. He does 'cause I told him. He'll be fine. He was a tough bastard before this. He's gonna be a pro."

He'll be good at this, she almost said but it turned to shit in her mouth.

"He has to come home soon," she repeated to herself.

He didn't. It wasn't too long before sunrise. A couple of hours. Damn. Where was he?

"I'm responsible," Tawne said.

And then she forced it, breaking the physical lock. Tawne left her body and felt herself float up, down, out through the trees bordering the yard. She'd told herself she'd never do this again but she had to find Arcan before it was too late.

There were cop cars all over the fucking place just a few blocks away. She saw them from overhead and flew down. A man was on the sidewalk outside the house. He was in shock.

"You hadn't been fighting with your wife, had you?" a cop was asking him.

"No, I told you. I just got home from work. I manage a restaurant that doesn't close 'til two. Then I have to do the bookwork, the cash receipts, make up the deposit for the next day. You can check with my employees. I found her like this."

Tawne streamed through the house, saw pieces everywhere. The blood stench was thick. The limbs were like shards of broken glass to her.

Charlee Jacob

"Looks like she was torn apart by animals, doesn't it?" one detective was asking another.

"I ain't never seen nothin' like this. And I've seen some shit," the other replied, looking green around the gills.

It stank but it was amazing how little blood there really was. There was more meat than anything, in tooth-marked scalloped strawberry ribbons, draped over curtain rods, wreathing lamp shades, garlanding hanging pictures. Pieces of a woman's head made Tawne marvel how such damage was possible without a hammer and bone saw. Jaws separated, skull in a puzzle, even the tongue in an ashtray.

Tawne caught a scent. Animal musk. Animal piss. She'd smelled this on Arcan and knew he'd been here. But he wasn't here now; this murder had been hours ago.

She left and flew over the city. *Arcan, where the hell are you, lover?*

Red flashing lights. A couple of cruisers, an ambulance, an unmarked car. There was a body in the street and two in a house. Bullet holes through the walls had caught a hapless little girl sitting on the floor in front of the television. Her brains decorated the screen as images of cartoon characters slid across the curds. Her brother sat with his head back in a recliner, three eyes staring up at the ceiling. An undead lingered nearby with its nose wrinkling, sniffing. Blood everywhere at this one. Not a trace of Arcan in the air.

Tawne caught enough from the conversation to know this had been a drive-by shooting.

But less than half a mile from here was a body of a shrimpy elderly guy. Ripped from stem to stern, as if a cook had de-boned and deveined him and then had started to butterfly him for frying.

"He was registered here at the hotel," the patrolman was telling a detective. "Guy putting out the trash found him."

"I want to talk to that guy."

"I just saw him running to the john to throw up again. Been doin' it ever since."

"Can't say I blame him. I smell animals."

"Sir?"

"Animals. Smell that? Wild smell. Not that I can figure where they came from. Pack of dogs maybe. One thing's for sure. A man didn't do this to him."

"A man couldn't have done *this* to him."

Tawne smelled wild, too. Wild Arcan.

"Look at that. Dogs couldn't have done that," the detective said, indicating the alley wall of the hotel. Shit had been smeared across it.

"Looks like a word," the cop said, stepping back to examine it, putting the beam from his flashlight to it.

"*Lupus.* What's this? A wolfman joke?" The detective spat.

"Actually, sir. I think it says *Lucas.*"

Tawne left. What time was it? The witching hour had passed ages ago. It wasn't ripe anymore. The stars weren't as aggressive as they had been. She didn't see colors in the east yet but they couldn't be too long in coming.

Tawne didn't see Arcan along any of the streets. He wasn't running through the alleys. She even turned toward the river, thinking maybe his animals would head for the wooded areas. That's when she saw more police cars. Red lights flashed everywhere. In some old business school. A body had been taken away. There was a little blood but not much. It was the Arcan smell that kept Tawne from leaving right away.

She hovered at a third story window which had been smashed. A woman with a white eye patch was talking to another detective.

"Yes, poor Karen. Alone. If only we'd been here."

"So no one saw the killer, Ms. Reedman?"

"No, I only came because no one was able to contact her

to let her know we'd canceled the meeting. I figured she had to be here."

"At 3 A.M.?"

"We're all nighthawks. Most of us don't sleep well anymore. This place was a safe haven for us. I don't know where we'll take the group now."

"Could you spell your first name for me?"

"E-L-I-S-E," she said. "Think it's the Culvert Killer?"

"No. Not that the Culvert Killer doesn't do some hefty physical damage but this isn't his M.O. And there's always a lot of blood in the area. Almost none here. Culvert Killer tears 'em up more, too." The detective paused and looked at the woman as if he realized this was hardly tactful.

Tawne didn't need to see the body to know this had been pretty bad. But there were no meat smears on the walls or the floor so maybe it hadn't been dismembered like the other two.

Elise Reedman. Tawne would have gasped if she'd been in her body. Arcan had said this name before. The woman was one of his victims when he'd been into the rape thing. Tawne had seen her face among Arcan's collection of ghosts. This was the rape group he'd mentioned.

Three in one night. He'd been busy. Tawne never took more than one in a single night. Not counting the two men she'd injured while in spirit form. That wasn't hunger, only curiosity.

But Tawne had never been an especially furious person. She never had a fast metabolism. Arcan was the lean and intense one. He probably burned it off as fast as he could get it.

Bullshit. Vampires didn't burn anything. They didn't have metabolisms.

Still, it had to be due to differences between Tawne and Arcan. She'd never been physical. She'd never had the urge to hurt anyone save for the occasional left hook to some loudmouth's jaw. How often had that happened? Only three, maybe four times since and including high school. Usually cruel jokes made her withdraw into herself even more.

Arcan had a long history of violence.

What was it he'd said when Tawne offered him eternity? No.

(Why?)

Because of what I can only barely control now.

But the dream told her to do it. It came from her lover's own future agony. The dream had compelled Tawne to act. Three in a night and he might only be gearing up. What would he do with all traces of his humanity gone?

"I still have mine," Tawne said to herself but with little self-congratulatory conviction. "I can limit myself to one a night. Eventually I'll learn to take a little blood, only what I need to get by. I won't have to kill anymore. Just let me get the hang of this."

Right, Tawne was humane. Didn't make 'em suffer.

Except when they looked at her and obviously didn't see Delia anymore. And maybe they didn't see Tawne anymore either. She'd seen something reflected in the eyes . . . a hallucination that hadn't matched what she saw of herself when she looked down at her body. Then they went quite insane with terror and she had no choice but to squash 'em good, finish them. Maybe with a bit more fury than was kind because it hurt so much to be stared at like that.

(Oh, well, and there were those two guys during the first flight. Broke a guy's arm with a touch and pulped another's brain with a breath. Not that she'd really meant to hurt them. It was the spirit form. Now it was all she could do not to stick a spirit finger into that white eye patch and jerk it around the socket to see what would happen.)

Tawne forced herself away from the window. As soon as she noticed she was getting too close to the woman, forefinger out in a jab. She sailed across the street. No, Tawne let folks die in a beautiful embrace, at the height of orgasm, even slow dancing with them first. Or at least she would have let them die that way. She remembered the tall teenager's stricken face, and the way he shrieked so hard he tore something in his own throat. Something crawled across his pupils 'til she was sure he'd gotten a load of bugs in his eyes . . . because that wasn't her reflection . . . it *wasn't*. He was seeing Delia, gorgeous, lithe, every woman's dream of how she wanted to look. At least according to Madison Avenue.

Whatever. The bottom line was that Tawne didn't willfully rip people to pieces.

"This isn't doing me a bit of good. It's mortal thinking again."

The need to rationalize was strong. To find meanings and destiny was an irresistible quest.

"Vampire, know thyself."

Well, she could already heal herself.

(*Fledgling*, the ugly man scoffed in her head.)

After instincts were laid aside as the excuse for everything, didn't responsibility for one's actions count for something?

"It was the dream. Arcan cried out to me. He was old and dying. He sent a message back not to listen when he said no," Tawne told herself.

If the undead didn't believe in contacts through time and from beyond the grave, what was there?

Rose and yellow on the horizon. Tawne almost froze in midair and then spun herself in the direction of Arcan's house.

Something seemed to be running on the world's rim. It had full skirts and many veils, unwinding in bolts of silk.

Fanciful. Tawne was only trying to see a woman there. As if one female entity perched on the edge of the sky could make the entire night turn back.

Hurry, girl, just in case.

Over her shoulder, Tawne saw dawn coming. She could

hear the trees rustling. Had the dawn seen her yet? Was the undead right who told her that Aurora always watched?

The creature running along the horizon was a woman. She had bright red hair, the color Tawne's would have been had it not been so dull.

No, it wasn't hair. Her head was on fire. The flames danced in all directions. And the face seemed to be looking right at Tawne.

Tawne went through the oak trees on the front lawn that surrounded the house. They were still in plenty of darkness. There was only a little light on a few distant rooftops. Tawne passed through the walls of the house and entered her body with a jolt.

It was a couple minutes before the moths started splattering soft wings against the windows. As she crawled into the bathtub, Tawne heard a strange yipping sound. But she was into another dream with her eyes closed before she could identify it.

Chapter Thirty-four

The women had been waiting since just before sunset. Rush hour had passed, making it easier for the two cars they piled into to find parking on the street across from the business school. There were still scores of people thronging the sidewalks, shopping the smallish boutiques, walking down the block for evening services at the Baptist Church, eating at the cafes open for late suppers.

If this were a month ago, it would still be full summer, and the sun wouldn't be setting until about eight o'clock. If a month later—when did Daylight Savings Time end? It would have been dark by six. The night would have already seemed too damned long.

The nine women sat in the parked cars and fidgeted as each played out a personal death scenario in her mind.

Tira wrung her hands in her lap. "Wonder when it'll be."

"Depends on whether he makes any other stops," Elise replied dully.

They had seen the news. The police were linking two

other deaths with Karen's. All in a night's work for a vampire. Or a werewolf. Or whatever this crazy fucker was.

"God, I'll die if I have to wait here 'til after midnight. Think he'll come as late as last night?" Marla moaned in between the clacking of her loose dentures.

Elise shrugged. It didn't surprise her that every one showed. No one fled.

They had burned themselves with the cigarette as a sign of faith. Despite all the scars they had, they allowed for one more to bind them to this action.

The round blister on Elise's hand still hurt.

At least half of them might have been on the next plane to either coast or out of the country altogether, if they could have liquidated their few assets quickly enough. At least two might have committed suicide rather than face this night. Elise knew she'd considered both options, especially the latter.

But for Elise, it finally boiled down to the fact that she might be able to run, but she couldn't hide. That old tired movie line. This *was* suicide. At least she could fight for herself. This was how the others had seen it, too.

I'll die if I have to wait here 'til after midnight.

What if the bastard didn't show? It would be an effective method of further tormenting them. If not now, my god *when*?

(Anytime, baby. Soon as I get hungry enough.)

A cold front had pushed down from the north. People hustled by in woolly sweaters and lightweight coats. A few stared at the two carloads of women, quickly turning away. When it was dark enough, after the shops and restaurants closed, it was hard to see the women's faces. They kept no lights on inside the cars and the mercury vapor street lamps were next to useless for seeing into dark vehicles. They illumined the streets well enough, even if the glow they cast was sort of purple. Anyone standing directly under such a light had skin the gray-yellow pallor of a host of liver diseases. Even the building—normally kept blazing all night for the groups which rented classrooms for transcendental meditation, diet hypes, huckster success seminars, rape therapy—was stone cold. Because of the murder on the third floor last night.

Someone thought it was dignified to close shop in honor of the dead. They didn't even hold classes that day. The management promised it would be back to business as usual by Monday. They gave Ms. Reedman's group keys to a different room for their use by then. But the owners were considering a building curfew by 11 P.M., not allowing special interest groups to use any of the facilities after that time, no matter how much they paid for the space.

The sidewalks cleared of most people by 9 o'clock. By 10, it was pretty lonely out there. Everyone had gone to the places in the city where theaters and clubs were. By 11, two of the women started to cry, one in each car. They snuffled behind their hands. Elise saw Gina's shoulders heaving in the car ahead. In her car, which held five of the nine, Tira wept almost silently. Her burn-spotted fingers were pushed up against the tunnels of her nostrils as if to stop her from even breathing.

By midnight, they almost nodded off.

All of the women in Elise's car screamed when a loud thump on the hood startled them awake.

"It's him." Heather hit the horn and the headlights at the same time.

The women in the other car screamed, too. Everyone stared out with wide eyes, expecting to see a slavering monster rocking over the engine.

"Wake up, bitches!" the shaven-headed punk yelled from curbside as he slapped the hood again with the palm of his stud-gloved hand.

"Lookin' fer some action?" The taller, fish-lipped Nazi with him laughed as he grabbed the crotch of his jeans and squeezed.

Elise rolled down her window.

Tira whispered in shock, "Elise, what are you doing?"

Elise crooked a finger and crooned, "Come here, hunkie."

"Ooh, a one-eyed babe. You a pirate queen lookin' fer Cap'n Hook?" The first geek drooled as he strutted over and leaned down.

"Yeah, for Captain Meathook," Elise smiled, snaking one hand into her purse.

He grinned. "I got yer yo-ho's right here."

Elise grabbed him by the collar and shoved a canister into his face. She depressed the button and sprayed his eyes full of bright green dye.

"Randy!" he screamed to his friend for help.

"Hey!" Fish Lips cried, pulling a knife from his jacket.

Elise was vaguely surprised. She thought all punks these days carried guns. She kept spraying, hearing car doors opening. She let him go.

Barbara snarled. "Get out of here, assholes."

There were a few solid thuds. The knife clattered to the sidewalk. Fish Lips was wailing from having his wrist broken. His hand dangled at a sick angle and he was bending over from having been kicked in the groin.

"Can't you see you're interfering with a stake-out?" That was Julie's voice. "Get out of here before we really bust you."

The women made very little noise as they brought mallet heads down onto the two wriggling teenagers.

"Hey, we're goin' already! Jesus, don't kill us, okay?" Fish Lips sputtered gastric juices and cradled his arm. He was finding it hard to stand up after the punch to his balls but he managed to stumble a few steps back.

The first skinhead whined. "I can't see nothin'."

He was positively phosphorescent under the street lights.

Ann snapped, "There's nothing to see."

Another thud. After the two left, the women looked nervously up and down the street. Could *he* have seen? For that matter, had he sent those jerks?

No, they were too useless and stupid to serve a thing like him. "They might have had cockroach breath but they weren't exactly Renfields," Barbara commented.

He would have done better to sneak up on them himself once he saw they were dozing.

"You okay?" Celia asked.

Elise nodded. "What time is it?"

Celia looked at the luminous dial of her watch. "Quarter past 12."

"Ladies, we must stay awake," Elise said pointedly. "If that had been him . . ."

They agreed. They checked the street again for any kind of shadow. They sniffed the air for a dog, the closest they could get to a wolf smell. They shuddered when the wind tapped at the street signs.

"Maybe we shouldn't sit here anymore," Julie suggested. "I mean, we're kind of obvious out here."

"We could park over behind The Pepper Grill and stand watch in the doorway," Tira said.

The Pepper Grill was around the corner. It didn't face the front of the school but the same side with the window the killer had broken through. The grill had a large *al fresco* section with a wide tarp over it. It was black under there now. The women walked up to it, climbing over the low wrought iron fence that decorated its boundaries. They could barely make out the chairs stacked on top of the tables at the outer edge.

It was as good a place as any to watch from. Several sat down, knees shaking too much to hold them up for sentinel duty.

By 1 o'clock, Marla had to go to the bathroom.

Barbara snickered. "You can't leave. There's no place open."

Elise indicated the darkness. "Try the corner near the door."

Marla was horrified. "Outside?"

Celia smiled. "Winos do it all the time."

"We promise not to look," Ann said.

Marla blushed and slipped into the further shadows. They heard her ease her jeans down. This was followed by a hissing splash. She muttered "Damn!" as she struggled to get her jeans up.

"Never meet the devil with a full bladder," Heather told her as Marla slunk red-faced from the corner. Gina laughed out loud.

Barbara grabbed her arm. "Shhh! Look!"

At first they thought one of those small East European cars was speeding up the street. It wasn't in the street; it was on the opposite sidewalk close to the walls. And there was no engine sound, no tires or lights. It was lower, slouching and angular. A scarf fluttered across its back, trailing behind.

It would have made them think of the Tasmanian Devil from the cartoons, in high gear and about to pounce— except that the noise was all wrong. There was almost no noise at all. The shape was constantly changing. It stopped and sniffed. The wind was blowing toward them so it couldn't pick up their scent. It looked up.

It had far less of the man in it tonight. It sat up on its back legs and put paws against the wall. A third limb they had thought was a scarf, but which was shaped less like the other legs and more like a human's arm, scratched at its back.

Elise discovered it was really shaped like a woman. She clutched at her eye patch, thinking, *it's too small, a blow-up doll with most of the air out of it.*

The animal stretched, pulled itself like taffy, and the back legs lengthened by at least a foot. Its jaws cracked open and a long black tongue panted out.

"Ah."

The women looked at one another under the tarp. Had that been an animal sound?

"Tone," it whispered from across the street and carried back to them in the breeze.

It definitely wasn't an animal sound.

"Ment," it finished and then began scrabbling up the side of the building.

It didn't look much as it had the night before. There was a bag under its belly as if it had a tumor; the bag bobbled soggily.

Arcan had been fast, beyond any speed he'd known in life. Beyond what Tawne could do. When she ran from the light, it wasn't much over a human's speed. But this? Was it due to his new state or because of the animals in this state?

Arcan's toes scratched to find grooves in the brick. His claws pulsed as they jutted out and then retracted almost fully as they scraped against the masonry. The wrinkled plasmic Karen thing moved, stiff as taffeta.

He'd had to take a child when he woke at sunset. He saw the little boy at the bus station. The kid had been sticking the toe of a sneaker into the slatted grate, staring down into the depths for dropped money. The boy blinked stupidly when he saw the dark form climbing up toward the top, looking away to search for his mother. "Momma, there's a doggy down there."

Arcan popped the grate for a split second and dragged him down. He broke the kid's neck immediately so there would be no screams to rouse any of the hassled, unob-servant fools who missed the snatch to begin with. As he dined, he heard the mother as she noticed the boy was gone.

"Roy?" she said quietly enough at first. Her voice rose more in annoyance than fear. "Roy!"

She sounded like a bitch.

"Wait'll I get you home, Roy!"

I saved you from her, kid. Saved you from her fingernails and her damnable poetry and stretched out gummy cunt. You're not going at all gently into the good night. Because, what's so good about it?

Then Arcan was forced to sup again, only a couple of hours after sneaking away from the bus station. That wasn't much more exciting. There was this little old couple sitting on a swing on their front porch. They held hands, looking very much alike. Grandma's sagging tits were nearly identical with Grandpa's paunch. The old guy hummed a Tommy Dorsey band tune as the swing carried them back and forth, chain creaking the way their bones did.

Now Arcan felt the child with him, crawling around behind his testicles, looking for a womb out as if the kid thought he was going to be born again. It made Arcan's scrotum pull up and cramp. He could feel the elderly couple's 60-odd years of memories together surging through his brain, felt their arthritic hands trying to reach one another from opposite sides of his head. The woman who had read *Nana* was poking Arcan in the guts, trying to get out. The old geezer's colostomy bag scraped against the bricks as Arcan arduously pulled himself up foot by foot. He winced in pain, shivering as the bulk jiggled, suggesting his intestines were about to unravel.

Not that any of these things were really a threat to Arcan. He'd figured out they couldn't hurt him. Just as the ghosts hadn't really been able to do anything to him but haunt. And these were simply hauntings, that was all. More physically manifested than the fractious images of mere spirits, bringing a degree of their own physical misery with them. This was what separated the two. It had really confused him before—with the two Karens.

Arcan's dead wouldn't leave him alone. The more his animals killed, the worse it would get as the weight and

torment piled on, and each corpse sought its way out of
Arcan Tyler.

Talk about carrying the world around on your shoulders.

. . . and in a shitbag.

An entire talon yanked out as it caught on the brick
stubble. It didn't merely shatter to spew fragments. It came
out an entire thorn, the ball beneath the digit bloody as it
sputtered past his snout. The cat spat at it and the ghoul
blasphemed in several archaic languages.

Arcan slipped, back legs swinging away from the wall.
He drove his remaining claws in as hard as he could in
order to hang on, the talons going into brick like mountain
climber spikes on a sheer rock face. The wolf yelped, snarling as he managed to draw his haunches up under him,
putting his pads against the cold wall. The cat's sharper
trenchant talons inserted into brick groove, and he scrambled up again past the second bank of windows. It had
been the cat that allowed Arcan to climb up the night before.

The regrowth of the claw was already molding, curving.
The muscles of his limbs moved in a kind of oil, carved
from butter. But his fur rubbed the wall, talons granulating
even if they did re-appear almost immediately. He was
right below the third floor ledge. It had taken a lot less time
to climb than last night. Perhaps it was because Arcan was
more animal now.

Arcan was surprised there was no light.

They would wait in the dark. Yes, why not? What did
they have? An impressive arsenal of guns filled with silver
bullets? Would state-of-the-art red lasers dot across him as
they aimed for his heart, making sure at least one of them
hit it?

He tensed as he wrapped a paw over the edge, letting
the ghoul's fingers slide out enough to give him grasp. Arcan hoisted himself farther. He felt the boards across the
space where the window had been. It never occurred to

him that the authorities would board up the window he'd shattered. There was probably crime scene tape across the door.

Those cunts aren't in there, the ghoul muttered.

Of course not. The ghoul giggled. He'd scared the crap out of them. They were hiding under their beds and inside moldy closets, reliving in Technicolor paranoia the wolf's dick, the cat's subtle hiss, the ghoul's foul mouth.

They didn't come. Arcan sobbed. He'd meant to make them see how they must destroy him. There was no other way.

He'd overdone it. They would never release him now.

The Karen thing flapped across his back and coiled around to claw at his face. The fingers of the woman-who-had-read-*Nana* managed to briefly puncture his stomach lining before it re-knitted. The shitbag rubbed too much against brick and started leaking from one brown crease. The child shoved against the balls-under-pressure, causing Arcan to double as if kicked in the nuts from the inside. The old couple barely touched each other across the gulf of his brain, and for a second Arcan heard roaring trumpets, clarinets and maybe Gene Krupa himself beating the hell out of the drums.

Arcan lost his grip. The animals fell, spinning in the air, bouncing against the wall to knock out a couple of bloody fangs. The cat managed to pull them together to come down on its feet. It splashed in a three-point landing with fish-and-humus reeking juices splattering the cement in yellowish brown. Damn that skinny old guy in the raincoat.

The animals shook themselves, static on the edges of pelts and the points of teeth. The images of women closed in from across the street. The ghosts, swarming like hornets. Their auras were reds, oranges, hot whites.

The wolf bared its fangs and the ghoul snickered. "Twatburgers. Nice of you to deliver."

The cat was easily prepared for confrontation, smelling

them now. It knew these weren't ghosts. These were thriving, sweating mice with fear stains in their underwear.

The three animals merged, then took six steps forward so quickly they seemed to lurch on still feet. Heather pulled a crucifix from her bag. The cross was as big as a torch and twice as blinding. All the women took rubber mallets, drilling hammers, and wrist-thick gardening stakes from bags deep enough to hold the entire array of inquisitor's tools from strappado to rack.

A shred that was still Arcan felt a flood of relief. He wanted to stand with his arms wide and let them overwhelm him.

His animals joined to produce an earsplitting roar instead. It stopped the women in their tracks.

"God," Tira said, dropping her vampire-killing tools in the street. "I can't go up against that."

Marla fell to her knees just 10 feet from him, her legs buckling. She began to pray, dentures clicking. "Our Father Who art in Heaven . . ."

He grabbed her in a single blurring leap. He crammed his hands into her mouth and yanked her jaws apart. The dentures flew out with blood and spittle. Two of the women vomited at the sound of the teen's face being torn in half. The women began to run away.

"No!" Elise shouted after them. She continued forward, the large economy-size cross purchased in bulk with the others at Sacred Heart Books and Gifts clutched in both hands. She swung it like a baseball bat as the thing bent to lap at Marla's meat river, spewing from the tunnel of her throat to pool at the junction of the upper and lower mandibles. "Come back!"

Elise brought it against the side of the beast's head. She tried not to see the face of the wrinkled woman thing that sprang from its back. It was too much like Karen. The stench of shit leaking from the bubble under the beast's gut made her dizzy.

She struck a second time, hearing metal sizzling into fur. The beast didn't shriek but merely fell away, clasping burns that melted into feral skin. She waited for it to attack her but, amazingly, it didn't.

She heard a murmur so faint it was almost lost in the crackle of burning hair. Elise . . . Elise. . . . Elise . . .

She didn't know if it came from the twitching thing that looked like the dead Karen on the beast's back or from the beast itself.

Arcan tried to stay. He fought to stay so he could be SHRIVEN. But the animals panicked, wrenching control away to sweep him down the street with them. *Wait!* he cried in his head. *This is it! I have to die tonight! You are the source!*

He fought for control, struggling to make the animals remain to take their punishment. He wanted to be a man inside the creatures but he couldn't make his legs stand. They were in full flight, hissing and seething as pus lathered from the crosshatched score of hot holy metal imprinted in his skull bone.

"Did you see that?" Elise turned, gesturing with the bent cross. "It works; it burned him. We can do this!"

Barbara and Celia crept back slowly, staring down in horror at Marla's ripped face, snot and saliva bubbling back in the throat. They crunched scattered teeth under their shoes. Marla's arms and legs jerked as if she were still alive. But she couldn't possibly be alive like that, could she?

They knelt, feeling her quivering heat pass through the asphalt. They couldn't leave her. Not if she lived.

(But how could anyone be alive like that?)

Elise touched Marla's hands, then toppled backward as the chest suddenly heaved. Suction and clot and bleeding vacant gums flapped, unable to close, unable to breathe. Green sinus juice splashed outward as the river at the junction of the splayed jaws was a frothy blue. Marla's eyes opened and shut once as if blinking. As if trying to wake up.

Then she was dead.

Heather screamed in rage, taking off down the street after the beast. Did any of them still think of it as a man? Did they remember that he'd sort of had a man's shape when they first saw him?

"Come on, damn it!" Heather shouted, and Elise stumbled to follow her.

One by one the women started running down the middle of the empty street after him. Tawne was coming up on foot the other way and saw the harried procession. She didn't see Arcan but she smelled him and the strong carnage. Someone was dead or was at least badly injured and pumping lots of heated red blood out. It made her tingle to smell it, leaning toward its scent. It made her aware of how cold she was.

"He's here," Tawne said to herself, dizzy at the prospect of seeing Arcan again. How would he react when he saw her? Did he still hate her?

Tawne spotted the traditional Van Helsing shit in their hands as the women charged past the closed businesses. That could only mean one thing: they knew what Arcan was and were going to destroy him. She'd come here hoping to find him. She might just end up saving his ass as well. Then he'd surely forgive her.

Everything would be all right between them again.

Arcan was helpless as the cat, wolf, ghoul loped down the street. They turned from one back into the other and then to a mixture of forms, trying to shake the light from their eyes, burned onto their retinas in crucifixion after images. The wound in their head seeped, without healing as it should have already begun to do. There was a corner up ahead they could swerve around to lose these cunts. But something was wrong. They were slower. Where was the speed which should have taken them far away by now?

Tawne started to yell out to Arcan. If he was near, he'd hear her. But did she dare? If the women knew what she was—if they knew what to look for—then they could just as easily try to dispatch her. That is, if the stake business wasn't as much bullshit as the jazz about not reflecting in the mirror.

The throbbing in Elise's empty socket was horrible. Knifing thunderbolts.

"Damn, look. He's just standing there." Heather pointed with the cross in her fist. "In front of the church."

The animals scratched, snarled and pitched an unholy fit to get away. They were at the corner. They could go around it and be lost in no time in the weave of filthy alleys and raw steak shadows. But he had stopped—the man inside. He had re-asserted himself and there they were, trapped with the pack closing in behind them.

"When will I be shriven?" Arcan managed to say through the slash of feral mouth and rows of thick teeth.

He'd never been a church-going person. That organized righteousness was for sheep. But he understood sin and knew the animals were scared. The cross burned them. And they didn't like this building. If he could get inside despite them, this might work as planned. Maybe this night wouldn't be endless. Arcan tried to walk toward the steps. But the animals pulled at his arms and legs, making them unstable for individual movement. He jerked like a marionette.

Two women stood not 25 feet from him. They watched to see if he would whirl and attack or if he'd continue on down the street. They were shaking being so close to him. One was Julie, the woman he'd sliced the breasts from, dragging her into her bathroom by her hair to force her to watch as he flushed them down her toilet. He didn't remember every particular of what he'd done to the other woman. So many mouthfuls of soft flesh, so much acidic sweat.

Charlee Jacob

Footsteps echoed up. The other women were out of breath, anxious to tear him to pieces.

The animals were a cold tide, icy waters he was slipping beneath. Foam effervesced from his jaws. The ghoul chattered obscenities. Arcan would never make it. He couldn't fight them.

Then he saw her on the steps of the church. Her face was blackened with powder burns, the mouth a ragged cavity. He knew without having to look what the back of her head looked like.

There was no back to her head.

"There is a sanctuary built upon the heart," said Carmel Gaines. She held out her hand as she slowly descended the steps in a cloud of blood-mist.

The cat screamed. The wolf shrieked. The ghoul wept as they felt the electricity in that hand. The fingers linked with Arcan's, soft as Play-doh.

The Karen thing was cellophane against the back of his neck. It whispered into his ear gently, urging him to go with Carmel.

He let the ghost lead him inside. It was all Arcan could do to remain on his feet when the cramps came, doubling him over at the gut and scrotum. The animals had gone insane and were whipping about in a frenzy to get loose. The orchid perfume on Carmel's spirit gagged Arcan and suffocated the beasts.

He saw people sitting in the pews, heads bowed. They weren't solid like the women running down the street. These were the ghosts, shifting until their faces were a blur. Not all of them were women. Now there were two old men and a little boy.

Inside him and sitting in the pews.

Carmel led Arcan past, holding him up, bearing him on his wobbly feet as the animals twisted his arms and legs backward at elbows and knees. She held him so close he could smell the black gunpowder and sundered meat in her head.

The ghosts in the pews murmured without looking up as the couple passed. A bride and her epileptic groom.

Carmel gently tugged Arcan to the floor before the pulpit. All of his limbs spasmed. His eyes rolled to the whites. He tried to lie down on his back as he heard the group coming through the door. He wondered if they could see Carmel.

No, she was there to help him, to comfort him as he took back control for the last time.

But the women crowded inside, hunting him down. They cringed once past the door. They couldn't see the assembly but each felt the presence of a personal fetch in a flood of intense electricity. For a moment they thought they were sitting in the varnished pews, gilt-edged black gospel books in front of them.

Elise gasped, reaching out half blind. There was something long lost nearby. She heard a wolf howl and saw the beast on the floor of the pulpit. She saw the Karen thing shrivel like a useless umbilical cord and fall away.

"There he is!" Elise pointed and ran up the aisle, trying not to look right or left. There was nothing there. There were only shadows behind her patch. A thunderbolt in steel.

The liquid bag of lumps at the beast's gut detached and rolled, drying and puffing fecal dust. It was the effigy of a small tumbleweed. Elise stepped over it.

The women banged their mallets into the sides of the pews as they followed her.

"All who have been wounded are welcomed there," Carmel said as her too-soft hands kneaded Arcan's chest.

His arms and legs pounded violently against the floor. His head came up and slammed backward, came up to slam back again until his skull fractured. His brain was shaken, trying to fuse, rupturing again before it could heal.

The animals panicked but Arcan wouldn't let them go. He thought he was only rocking a little now, in slow motion. The woman who had read *Nana* no longer prodded his stomach to get out. The child curled up behind Arcan's balls to doze. The old man in the raincoat no longer churned waste. The ancient couple embraced as slow dance music burbled through Arcan's ears. He was dreaming this. It was really rather soothing. Even if he did hear animals screaming far away in what must be a packing plant slaughtering pen.

Someone dropped to their knees next to him, moving through Carmel like stepping through a viscous rainbow. He felt a heavy object on his chest. In a stained glass window Arcan saw a Madonna figure change into Harry, into the hermaphroditic Shiva, dancing smoothly in fragile pieces colored with metal oxides. Saying "I went to find salvation and atonement. I have become these things. These things I *am*."

Tawne ran to the doorway and was thrown back. She jumped up and hurled her body in a standing broadjump to the entrance. A wall of force flung her onto her ass in the street.

She couldn't get inside. Why not, when Arcan had gone in? She ran to the window and clung to it. She saw women running down the aisle. The same women were sitting with their heads bowed as if praying or waiting to be blessed. Arcan was in a tantrum on the floor, kicking so hard that the stained glass rattled in the windows. The women began pounding him into blood pudding but he didn't strike out at any of them. He continued to roll in a seizure but never lifted a claw to defend himself.

Just like in the movies.

No, it wasn't like the movies at all. Tawne whimpered in defeat. You didn't feel yourself losing someone when it was the movies. You didn't feel eternity's cheat in the fucking movies. That was Arcan in there, not dying of old age in a cave. Not even where she could touch his hand. He was out of reach completely beyond where Tawne could save him.

She also saw what looked like an eastern styled deity or maybe some bizarre Chinese concoction. It danced in mid-air above the altar, part beauty/part convoluted horror. It seemed to reach down for Arcan, lightly staining the fingertips of one hand with his blood while smearing him in its bronze tears with the other hand.

Now what the hell did that have to do with any of this? It coiled braceleted arms, knotting and unknotting the sublime muscles of its stomach as it swayed coiled hips. Then it disappeared.

Elise struck the blow that burst the beast's heart, blood exploding across her face. It stung her single eye like freezing liquid nitrogen. It dyed the patch crimson. It cascaded across all the women as they lifted their mallets and beat him or stabbed with the stakes used as knives—not even trying to pound them in. They wept and laughed and screamed as every pain he'd given them passed from their hands into his body.

Arcan jerked and shifted. They could see every nasty creature that ran or flew or dug through dung heaps in these shapes. The last form was the man-lump. They expected it to crumble to dust but it didn't. It lay battered the way a butchered beaten body does, scarcely recognizable as having been a person. But, yes, they could see he'd been a man all along. From the very beginning.

Tira plucked out his eyes. Celia crushed them beneath her heels. Elise watched them pop and felt the sentience in every scar she had. And then she felt the shadows drain out of her. Elise held up her hand and stared at the haze of light around it. Was that there before? Had it been there and disappeared after he attacked her?

Tawne's moon face looked in through the window, watching the people in the pews vanish.

"Incorruptible," Barbara said strangely. She shook her head.

She began to giggle hysterically. After a minute she stopped and buried her face in her hands. Then she pulled her hands away because they were slimy with his blood.

"Are we safe?" Gina asked meekly.

The other women couldn't answer. They began to stagger back down the aisle to leave the church.

"No," Tawne said at the window. She slipped back so they wouldn't see her as they came outside. "No, you're not safe."

Chapter Thirty-five

Tawne didn't know why she didn't take the women then. She was frozen with grief. Arcan had been only a few feet away and she couldn't do anything to help him. She had, as a matter of fact, been responsible for his death and then this second butchering of him.

He'd walked into the church. He'd gone down before the pulpit. He'd allowed them to do this to him.

"How would you feel if I offered you eternal life?"

"No, I don't think so."

Flatly.

"Why . . . ?" .

"I can't because of guilt. Because of what I can barely control now," Arcan had explained.

He now controlled it without question.

But this didn't mean Tawne should let these women go unpunished. They murdered Arcan!

(No, I did that.)

He was gone forever. He was lost to her. This was what it felt like to be scooped out.

Damn the ugly man. He'd known she'd never have comfort. He'd known what she was looking for. His way wasn't a release from the loneliness. Tawne was worse off than before.

Was the ugly man somewhere nearby? Did he watch Tawne and see everything she did? He laughed at her fuck-ups. He howled as he watched her watching Arcan die.

"When you seek the powers of the night, you get darkness. And the dark is what it is," she seemed to hear the ugly man saying. His silver cataracts glinted, balls of mercury poisoning clear water. "If you expected something else, it's your own fault."

All our advertisements to the contrary . . .

There was a haze in the east. If Tawne didn't hurry, she wouldn't make it home before Aurora charged. She was only a couple blocks away and she was fast, but all it took was a spot of light on her skin for it to crack.

Tawne ran. The trees and bushes were swaying. The air hummed with the sound of very soft wings. The moths had been alerted. Their goddess called. They clung to the bark, wings folding and unfolding: brown, black, gold, yellow—like a pile of raked leaves come to life.

Tawne never noticed before how fall colors were those of someone turned inside-out. The rusts pumped from a heart balanced on a sleeve. The browns and bronzes were culled from liver and ligament. Bare trees mocked bare bones with warped limbs. Balls with sockets slimed wet to decay fast when exposed to the air.

A person inside-out grew cold. They were open to pain that only being flayed alive was second to.

Tawne was inside-out.

When she was only a block away, the sunlight creased over the rooftops and spread through fences, dotting the ground like heat-seeking missiles aimed for her back.

Something flapped around her face until she couldn't see. It didn't really have any force, being only a tight mist of moths settling over her.

She spun, batting at them. They parted a little and she saw a woman running up the street in a line perpendicular to the horizon. She trailed wisps that were so bright that Tawne couldn't bear to look straight on. Photosynthetic veils swirled around the woman and her head was on fire. The scabbed and crusted mouth spilled lasers. She was chasing Tawne with torch eyes riveted on her.

The moths closed rank again, laying across Tawne's face in a blinding smother. Their wings sliced at her pupils with the force of hundreds of paper cuts as they plucked at her eyelashes with their feelers. They flew down her throat and crawled up her nostrils, working their mushy way into her ears.

"Get off me!" Tawne roared. The volume of her scream startled even her as front windows on the houses on either side of the street bowed and then cracked.

Tawne covered her head with her arms and continued on up the block. The woman with her head on fire was right behind her. She could feel the silken hems of the woman's skirts throwing waves of heat at her. Tawne couldn't see much as the minuscule razor slices at her eyeballs mended and were cut, mended and then burned with another series of dusty incisions. She swiped at them, hoping she was still headed toward home. Tawne stumbled off the sidewalk, feet turning on their sides like in some old Jerry Lewis skit. There was soft grass under them so she jerked back to the right until she felt concrete again. The moths were thick as a wall, the worst they were capable of. But the point must have been to make it possible for morning to reach her. So it was enough that the moths slowed Tawne down, even if by mere inches.

Someone cried out from a doorstep, a neighbor out to get the morning paper. Tawne and the crazed creatures went past, leaving a tattered pile of wings on the sidewalk and lawn. The woman with her head on fire did no more than caress the neighbor's cheek with fleeting warmth. The neighbor couldn't see her.

Dawn caught up with Tawne, was running smoothly alongside her like a sunny jaguar, a lithely muscled body only burned from the neck up. And her face didn't really look touched by fire: it smoldered and cracked as if from intolerable internal combustion. The eyes puffed out like rose cinders, magma burst from the cheeks and forehead— around the lips—in pimply volcanoes.

Through the oak trees in Arcan's front yard and Tawne was bleeding from the light, almost giving up when she heard the yipping.

Through a red mist Tawne saw the coyotes sitting on their haunches. Were these going to attack as well, summoned by Aurora? If they did, this would be the end. Tawne would never stay on her feet with a pack of them hanging on, there were so many. How had they ever gotten there without someone seeing them come through the city?

They didn't attack. They sat and watched, yipping like pups as Tawne lurched onto the porch. Tawne leaned heavily against the door as moths dove in loose formation, swooping under the patio cover, fluttering in her face with their wings soaking up the blood that juiced out of her. They crumbled as she mashed them by leaning all her weight against the door.

Tawne squinted and shielded her eyes from the light. She reached back, feeling her fingers across the wood to find the knob. The dawn-creature leaned in as if to kiss her. The breath moved forward in a gust to roast Tawne's face. Light radiated lambently out and pierced one of Tawne's eyes like a heated brand. A burned spray of blood geysered from the socket. Tawne actually shrieked, feeling a pain she hadn't thought she was still vulnerable to vor- texing back into her skull.

This Symbiotic Fascination

Tawne's hand fumbled, slipping greasily on the brass, and then wrenching it clockwise. She ducked under the fiery embrace and fell into the open doorway, tearlessly sobbing, hitching her breath from a mortal memory of what crying was like. Tawne slammed the door with her foot. Veils and skirts of light caught in the jamb and winked out because the living room was still dark.

The door bounced back open as Tawne crawled across the carpet toward the bathroom. She left shreds of herself along the rug, scraps and a few fingers and toes. The moths flew through, turned bright by the light through their thin wings. The light itself was a leprosy, a disease of scabs and failed flesh. Tawne saw several yellow cabbage moths—acting in tandem—carry off a trifle of her brain they had drawn out through the cavernous eye socket. She tried to yell but choked as her tongue split in her mouth.

The woman with her head on fire stepped through the door.

Tawne dragged herself on her elbows into the hallway, scudding onto her face as elbow joints suddenly went soft, mushing into the hollows of her arms. She rolled through the bathroom door on hips plasticizing into liquid polymer. She moved the door shut with her side, leaving gummy tapioca on the wood. Moths caught in the door twitched.

Tawne was drained dry and frozen to the tile. Why hadn't she passed out yet? The first time she was unconscious long before this much damage was done.

It's because I'm stronger now. And I'm older. Yeah, a whole week older. Think I'll reach two weeks?

Tawne thought, *I'm inside-out.* She'd have laughed but she couldn't even get a rattle out of her throat. She was scared. She managed to look down at herself with a bare incline of the head. *Yes, Virginia, there ARE seven layers of skin.*

Moths floated through the hallway, flickering flame-like

with the morning through their wings as they went from room to room. The woman with her head on fire whispered outside the bathroom door, "Tawne. Tawne." And the way she said it in burning mandolins, it was almost the goddess's name.

"Let me in," said Dawn. "Die in my light."

It sounded like the same offering Tawne would make to one of her victims. The kind of thing she'd say with a few lines of 'Immortal Inamorato' and a request for a slow dance.

"Get out! Get out of here, you nasty things!" someone was shouting.

Tawne wondered if she was doing it herself but it was beyond the door. Something stiff slammed the walls.

"Get out of here! Weird! I thought moths were nocturnal . . ."

The moths rustled away from the door, back down the hallway, making no more noise. What happened to the coyotes? They didn't yip anymore. It grew quiet except for the sounds of someone knocking on the bathroom door. "Ma'am?"

It wasn't the voice of the woman with her head on fire.

"Ma'am? You in there? You okay?"

The knob twisted.

The neighbor gasped, setting her trusty broom against the wall so she could kneel down next to Tawne. The woman's hair was in soft sponge curlers and her skin smelled like Dove soap.

Tawne mumbled, trying to articulate.

"What's that, honey?" The woman was almost crying, seeing how torn up Tawne was, wondering how moths—no matter how many there were—could possibly have done this. She leaned down next to Tawne's mouth to hear what she was saying.

Tawne had just enough strength left to bite that fresh-scrubbed face.

This Symbiotic Fascination

* * *

Tawne's howler was dying in the cavern. There was no moon but there was a light. His breath rasped, teeth scraping rocks as he crawled.

"But you're dead," Tawne said in the dream, the neighbor's blood warm in her veins. "You're already dead. It's all my fault."

Did he cry out for her, just once? A sound came out of the moonless sky.

Tawne protested. "This isn't right. You're lost to me."

Why didn't you save me when you could?

His fingers came out of the hollow.

Didn't you love me?

"Yes, Arcan! I loved you!" Tawne shouted as she reached forward. They almost touched.

The fingers jerked out in a hand stark with pimples and eczema, grabbing her wrist and twisting it.

"Fledgling!" the ugly man cackled from fenris shadows.

They weren't chimes for the dead but a bell. It was the ugly man all along, and he didn't mind that she knew it.

"Shit, you were *soooo* easy!" He laughed.

He knew what Tawne wanted as he held her in his arms in her fantasies. He appeared twice in the flesh, the first time to get her attention with bait, the second to spring the trap.

No wonder he'd been in the light at sunset. He wasn't a vampire, although it sure had been simple to make Tawne one.

"What's the matter? Hasn't it been glorious making them see you as you wanted them to?" he asked slyly.

Reflected in the silver mirrors of his cataracts, Tawne saw the beauty of Delia and then the swarthy horror of the beast. He hadn't even let her have that, really.

"It's always better being loved for who you really are, isn't it? So the yahoos claim." The ugly man chuckled.

"This is not my dream," Tawne mumbled, denying it.

"Such are contracts in blood. I'm your bridegroom. Always cry at weddings. Don't you?"

"No, you're not. Arcan was him. Who are you?"

But she felt stupid for asking because she knew who he was. He was the one who granted wishes and closed the ranks between the living and the dead.

Chapter Thirty-six

The eight women limped back to the two parked cars and were dropped off at their homes to collapse into deep sleeps.

Barbara called Elise about 4 o'clock in the afternoon.

"Hi. Did I wake you?"

"I'd just opened my eyes about three seconds before the phone rang."

"I think we ought to get together. The school gave us keys to another room, and we should hold group."

"I agree."

Barbara sounded far away. "I can't believe I used to read those books and think it was . . ."

She trailed off without finishing her statement. But Elise knew what she meant.

"I understand," Elise replied quietly.

"Elise? Do you think there's anything in this world that's painless?"

"No, honey. I don't."

"Do you think there's anything incorruptible?"

It was Elise's turn to pause.

"Maybe," she replied hopefully.

They straggled in around 8 P.M., anywhere from 15 minutes before to 25 minutes after. Everyone was freshly showered with shampooed hair and scrupulously clean fingernails. Every part of them that could be reached with ritual soap and water was used to excess. Something had gone down the drain. Burdens. But they still looked tired even if most of them had slept more than around the clock.

"Where's Elise?" Heather asked, jiggling her key ring as she unlocked the door to the new room on the second floor.

Julie shrugged. "She should be on her way."

Celia yawned. "Maybe she crawled back into bed."

Someone was stomping up the stairs.

Ann gestured languidly. "There she is."

But it wasn't Elise. The fortyish woman had her head up and seemed mildly surprised to see them. She asked, "Is this the rape therapy group?"

Most recognized her from the police station. Tira nodded.

The woman glanced up the next flight. "I thought your group met on the third floor?"

Gina cleared her throat. "We used to. One of us was murdered up there two nights ago."

The women bowed their heads momentarily as they remembered Karen. Barbara noticed a glint in the woman's eye when she was told this.

"We're meeting down here now," Heather said unnecessarily.

"Oh, sorry. I'm very sorry." The woman smiled with a warmth that was a trifle too sincere. "They should have made the connection when they sent me. I'm Detective Denise Cross. The station sent me over."

"I knew I'd seen you before," Barbara said, recalling how the woman had seemed kind when questioning the victims but was really cold as a stone.

Denise opened her billfold with the gleaming shield.

"Are you here about Karen Strickland?" Celia was surprised. She couldn't be there because the police caught the rapist.

"No. We have a new department that works with citizens groups. Trying to inform the public on defending against crimes against persons. I'm sorry. This was obviously not the best time for them to send me over. I thought they contacted someone a week ago to set this up . . ."

"Elise? Ms. Reedman's not here yet," Celia told her. "She's the group founder."

The detective smiled again. "That must be who. I was supposed to show a new tape on rape prevention and coping with personal trauma."

Denise recalled the name. She'd told the Reedman woman *we can't catch phantoms*. Trying to appear sympathetic but angling to make her feel even lower. Denise had no use for the weak.

Tira laughed out loud, then slapped a hand across her mouth in embarrassment. Must have been the 'coping with personal trauma' bit. She shut her eyes and blurted a hasty apology.

Julie explained. "We're kind of on edge."

Cross was smooth. "I can imagine."

"Come on in," Heather said, and the ladies filed in after her. "No reason you can't do what you came here to do."

"Why, thank you." Cross grinned and took a VHS tape from her purse.

She unbuttoned and slipped off her jacket, hanging it neatly over the back of a chair. The butt of her revolver gleamed dully from the shoulder holster, strapped over a green blouse which hung in folds, loosely tucked into her skirt waistband.

"Shouldn't we wait for Elise?" Barbara asked Heather in confidence. She hadn't liked the cop before and she liked her even less now. Cross bore too many smiles, too much sincerity on the lips with none of it twinkling in the eyes. Just like some men who asked a woman out to dinner and then attacked.

"Elise may have gone to bed. She thought we should see this or she wouldn't have set it up." Heather patted her friend's shoulder.

Barbara shot the cop a mistrustful glance. "Then why didn't Elise tell us about it?"

Heather sighed patiently and bit her lip.

Barbara huffed, feeling stupid. "Shit, *really*."

As if with all that had gone down the last couple days, Elise would've had free time to think about anything as mundane as a chat with the local constabulary. And it wasn't as if the woman was a stranger who might only be posing as police.

Many of the rooms in the school had screens and video players for aid in teaching. Denise popped out a tape marked "Eighteen Column Instruction" and slid in her own, which was unmarked save for a few drops of blood on the black plastic.

"This runs about 20 minutes and is a whole new concept," Cross said, half-turning to the group after they had rearranged the student seating into a semi-circle. "When it's over we like to think you can defend yourself against virtually any attack."

Tira giggled again. "Bet we could show you a thing or two."

Ann gently nudged her. "Shhh."

The detective nodded toward Tira amiably. The little lines framing her eyes were sharp; they weren't laugh lines. She leaned forward a bit too much as she said, "I certainly hope you will. The department has been showing this quite a lot lately. We're pretty darned proud of it. It's been getting surprising results in Dallas and Fort Worth. But it's getting grainy after being shown several times a day for the past month. So—uh—would it possible to turn out the lights? Will that bother any of you ladies?"

So solicitous. Barbara squirmed. *That* was condescending. "Will you hold our hands if it does?"

"Barb!" Celia whispered loudly.

"I'm sorry." Denise Cross tilted her head as if she couldn't imagine what she'd said. "I didn't mean to offend anyone. I just meant that some folks don't see as well in the dark.

Barbara flushed. Why was she being such an ass to this person? "No, Detective," she said, blinking. "I'm sorry. I apologize."

Barbara stood to go to the back of the room. She hit the switch and tried not to shiver as the place suddenly seemed colder.

Denise felt the revolver snug under her arm as she put the magic on the screen. The women shifted uncomfortably as the murky river bank churned under the couple. Was this a simulated rape? It was hard to tell. It didn't matter. If the people who put this together were going for blunt realism, they succeeded.

An ugly man on top sat up, flexed impossibly, coiling boneless to suck at the big woman's massive breasts. He yanked up her legs, breaking the thighs so audibly that the therapy group jumped in their seats. He looked into the camera with green and metallic eyes in paroxysm mirrors.

Denise ran her tongue over the inside of her mouth, across hard edges of teeth and the backs of spongecake lips. She covered every hollow and ripple of the gums, walls, corrugated roof. It was a meat and bone taste, self-devouring and sensual. She watched each woman and the disgust on every face. She smiled as all of them crossed their legs defensively, bunched their hands into fists, gritted their teeth into barricades.

Oh, they would be sublime when they got started. Their scars fairly glowed in the dark. The man who did the numbers on them was an artist.

The tape fuzzed out.

"Oops. Minor glitch, ladies," she assured them. "Just a sec while I run it back."

Denise fussed with it as if it were fixable with mumbles and the passing of hands. As if they knew the difference.

"I know the opening is rough. But I swear there's a point to it." Denise ran it back and felt everybody in the room tense with the two forms on the riverbank.

Barbara was wrong. The room hadn't grown colder. It was hotter. Sweat trickled behind her ears.

The ugly man sat up.

Sat up.

Sat up.

Sat up.

Sat

Up.

And he was the man. *The* Man. Whose face shifted into the inhuman. Who, the last time they saw him, even twisted his body into the inhuman.

A cat-wolf-ghoul stared into the camera. His eyes were bloodstones, green slabs spattered with red, veined with scarlet. He looked directly through the camera at them. At Celia, Barbara, Ann, Julie, Heather, Tira, Gina. His lips were pulled back into what must be a bestial leer. As if to say . . .

See? You couldn't kill me. I was already dead. I told you that, you filthy douche bags bitches bloody cunts.

The camera pulled back. The large woman under him became them. Celia saw herself being raped. Barbara saw herself being defiled. Julie watched as he sliced off her breasts. Tira saw him with the cigarette burning words into her bare flesh.

Denise swallowed their horror and let it pump her up. They were tailor-made junk food and the calories were swelling. Cross knew what she saw in the video . . . herself atop a rotting but priapic Rob Waters. Her tits were ready to explode the entire fucking forest. What did they see? Think she didn't know? She'd chosen them because she knew precisely what they must see on this tape. They had no choice. It was the evil of man: their real hells.

Denise quickly rewound and replayed. The women didn't move. They stared at the screen and shook until the floor practically erupted with it. Their chairs vibrated under their butts for chrissakes. Denise was going to revel as never before. Already her underwear was wet all the way through the crotch of her pantyhose. That was where hell burned. Her breasts were mountains of iron ore, sore where she'd pierced the nipples.

Come to me come to me come to me come oh I'm gonna be so BIG.

Denise gasped as the tension surged through her pores. What would these victims do? Ignite? Go nova? Or disintegrate into shrieking, helpless muck? Blue fire in their veins . . .

See? You couldn't kill us, the animals grinned as they glutted, gutted and gouged.

"Yes, we did," Barbara hissed, leaping from her chair.

Celia jumped up so fast she knocked her seat over. "We got you, asshole."

Denise jerked out of her reverie. She glanced at the screen. *What were they seeing, dammit?*.

In the video, Rob Waters had her by the throat.

Denise swung around, drawing the gun from her holster. A chair struck her in the shoulder, knocking her backward. The revolver spun across the floor.

"Are you one of *them*?" Tira screamed as she reached for another chair.

Heather, Julie and Ann grabbed their huge bags and

were digging tools out from the night before. Denise scrabbled to her feet, shocked when she saw three-pound drilling hammers, mallets and sharpened stakes—all covered in dried blood.

"You're one of *them*, aren't you?" Tira accused her, determined to get the cop to admit it.

One of whom? Denise wondered. Whatever sweet masses of muscle had begun to fill out her body now deflated, shrinking up like endangered male genitals. Her victims— her *cows*—weren't terrified. They were pissed. Her hands came up to ward them off.

Gina cried, "Look at her fingers!"

In the wan glow of the screen gone to static, Denise saw her long, extra-jointed fingers from partial transformation into hulk. It was the way they had been at the station. They were slowly shortening.

"She's one of them. She's changing just like he did."

The women charged. Denise yelled, her voice very high pitched. It was the noise of a tiny hollow-boned animal. She ran for the door. Blows rained down on her from every side. Someone drove a sharpened stake through her back. Its tip emerged near her collar bone. They beat her down to her knees.

This wasn't how it was supposed to happen. Denise looked up in confusion at the screen. The tape rewound itself and was replaying. There was no river bank, no mud, no big woman naked and spread-eagled. There was only the ugly man, cataracts winking dead stars as he stared at her. This had been power intended for her. Denise Cross was the only one who hadn't been a victim of it. These bitches had been victims. It was in their faces, in their protective body language huddled into their chairs like whipped children. She'd known how to use it.

Denise tasted blood in her mouth, felt it pooling in both ears, snaking wetly through the crease in her skull from a hammer having crashed against her head. There was sharpness as she was stabbed in the thigh and hip with one of those damned stakes. But she couldn't look away from the ugly man on screen.

Denise had one chance and that was magic. The power still remained in her hard breasts, the only place left strong. She had to hurry before one of these women stabbed her in the chest.

Denise tore open her blouse and grabbed the loops of her hand grenades, gleaming camouflage in the screen's light. The ugly man nodded. The answer in his eyes was positive.

She clutched, determined to explode herself and these damn whores to hell. Denise jerked the rings as hard as she could, waiting for the thunder after the three second pause.

But nothing boomed in her ears except her heart as the earring wires ripped out her nipples. Denise grabbed both bleeding breasts in her hands and screamed. She stared in disbelief at the ugly man's face as he sneered at her with contempt.

"Liar!" Denise shrieked as the tape went to gray static.

There was another sharpness in the middle of her back, hard and heavy. And then her heart wasn't booming in her ears anymore.

Chapter Thirty-seven

Elise looked at her watch. She was late for group. She got out of the cab and fished some bills from her purse. The driver accepted, then quickly pulled away from the curb.

A woman stepped out from the shadows. She said, "I'd like to talk to you about joining your group." Elise didn't think she'd ever seen a more emotionally wounded female. There was more hurt in the big woman's eyes than she'd seen altogether in any three of the ladies in the therapy group—living or dead. "Sure. Come in." Elise extended her hand, ready to take one of the other's unusually large ones in her own. Touch was important in giving comfort. The big lady stepped back, stammering, "There are others there. I—I can't." There was a great bottomless pain in her face. "Please, can't I just talk to you first? For a few minutes?"

Elise's heart went out to her as she joined the woman in the dark.

Tawne easily threw her to the ground and pinned her there. She stared down at the canals and splinters of hard tissue. This woman had once been very beautiful. What lived in this face now was torment and a fierce loneliness. Tawne was tempted to let her go.

Almost.

Elise gasped. "Who are you?"

"This is about Arcan Tyler." Tawne replied.

"Who?"

This former beauty hadn't even known his name as she pounded a stake through his heart.

Elise lost her breath when knocked over. She tried to scream after she saw the rage in the big woman's face. Then the face *moved*, changing subtly. It froze her to the bone, remembering her attack nearly a year ago. How his face moved.

The woman slapped her, jarring the air out of her again before she could fill her lungs. Then the woman descended to smother her.

Tawne couldn't look down as she left the alley. She wiped her mouth but couldn't look at Elise Reedman's face, another wounded not unlike herself. She'd suffered a lot before Tawne got her. This attack was probably only one nightmare in a series of them.

Tawne didn't feel she'd vindicated Arcan or herself. Yeah, one nightmare in a series.

There was a light on the school's second floor. The others were up there. She crossed the street to go in the opposite direction.

The ugly man stepped out from a doorway. "What about *them?*" he asked, broken teeth too soft in his mouth.

"What *about* them?" Tawne retorted, wishing she could vent her anger on him. On this nasty trickster, not fenriswolf but fenris-worm. She knew she couldn't.

He laughed and turned his head on the invertebrate neck. He hissed, "Fledgling. Novice."

His mouth was full of rows of tiny teeth as flaccid as wax.

Tawne turned her back on him and walked away.

"Be seeing you," he promised.

How had she gotten home? It wasn't important. After Elise rinsed out her mouth and then washed the hideous cavity over her heart, all she could do was ponder why she wasn't dead. The wound should have killed her. She ought to have bled to death. There was a great quantity of blood on her so she must surely have lost too much to live.

The crater was pulling together. Threads of flesh knitted into nothing as much as the scars she already had.

What happened? There was a big, homely, sad woman with thick red hair. And hands so big that, once in their grasp, it wasn't possible to escape.

What was it the woman said? Not with any real meanness. The threat was too tired. "There's nothing worse I could do to you."

Elise climbed into the shower and slowly rubbed shampoo through her chestnut hair. She spat out more foulness. She rubbed her body with the towel, discarding it when it got too wet, picking up another. She turned the heat way up. Might be an early winter coming; it was already so cold.

Elise looked into her mirror at the reflection of the chest wound which was almost gone. She stared at her image, feeling for the sentient shadows. They had to be back. They were gone after the group killed the beast and the women regained their spirits. But now? Something was missing. Or . . . something had been added.

All around the room, throughout the house, were old photographs of Elise from before last year's attack. When she'd been lovely.

Elise focused on the valley scar down her cheek, by her nose, and lifting the corner of her mouth in that perpetual sneer.

It was all gone. She unwrapped the towel. Her body was smooth and flawless.

The socket didn't throb. There was no darkness there behind the patch. Yes! She could *see* the darkness behind the patch.

Elise quickly removed it and gazed at the exquisite dark eye, full-lashed.

She wondered why she wasn't crying for joy.

When she turned away from the mirror and looked down at her scars, she could put her finger into the space where the eye had been. Then she wished she could cry.

Elise turned back toward the mirror, looking until the ugliness vanished.

Later, Tawne also sat before a mirror. There were cloying powdery scales from moths' wings everywhere. There was a crusty swathe of gore from where she'd dragged herself across the living room carpet the morning before.

There was a woman's corpse in the bathroom, spongy soft curlers more or less intact around the bleached face. Tawne hadn't been able to hypnotize the woman so there had been quite a struggle. Tawne had been weak but she'd won because she'd been so hungry.

(There was also a dead man in Arcan's bed who was starting to smell because it had been two nights.)

Tawne was in the spare bedroom. Arcan had told her his brother used to sleep there when he visited town but that he hadn't been there since moving to Cambodia almost a year ago.

It would soon be morning. She dragged in the long mirror from the bathroom and set it against the outside wall next to the window. She sat on the floor in front of it. Her eyes were hard, encased in grit and icicles.

Taking Elise Reedman wasn't feeding. The blood was returned, processed to infect. She wondered at the pointlessness of that gesture. Tawne would stalk no more, would seek no more stolen heat. The real heat would come soon enough.

"Lookin' like shit, lady," Tawne said as she slumped before the mirror. She added mentally, *deserve to*.

She looked at her graceless mass of lumps. She tugged and snorted with distaste at the dog-headed ape. She tugged again and became a slimy, very decomposed corpse with frigid, snowy eyes.

Then she became a reeking mound of shit, steam visibly rising in the reflection.

She heard yipping and drew back the curtains. The yipping turned to howling. It was the coyotes, some up on hind legs with their paws on the window. There were dozens in the yard, hundreds perhaps. It was still dark. They weren't summoned by the sunrise. Tawne wondered if they surrounded the house.

No, she could see where their lines ended. They weren't trying to get in as the moths did at sunrise and sunset. They just wanted to see Tawne, howling so she'd look out for them.

There was a sound in their howling. "Tawne! Tawne!"

She glanced back in the mirror and saw herself with a giant coyote head, body covered in mangy fur swarming with fleas.

"Hey, Coyote Woman!" they howled, then began laughing until they sounded like jackals.

Several people began to move through their number. Carl Pruitt was there, and the man who had been changing a tire. There was the teenager she slow danced with, the guy from the bar, the guy in the bedroom. They had bloody stumps for arms and waved these toward the window.

"Rather chew 'em off than wake up with you, Coyote Woman!" they cried.

It was the ugly man's voice. Well, it would have been hard for him to roust a bunch of dog-headed baboons. So he'd settled for an all-points bulletin to the local little wolves. Tawne didn't care how he'd made her victims appear. He was full of tricks.

She closed the drapes again. And stared hard at Coyote Woman in misery. Until she changed into Delia.

Tawne hadn't tried to, but there she was—lovely and kind. The hair was wilder than Tawne would have summoned. The reflection called her name softly.

Tawne replied, "Hello, Delia. I didn't use you tonight. You asked me not to, so I didn't."

Delia smiled. "But you may use me now."

Tawne nodded, smiling back. She let herself bathe in the beauty of this desirable image until she desired it herself. She stared into the fascinating eyes and fell.

"We'll do it together." And it was Delia's voice, Tawne's voice. Spoken in the hypnotic weave. If Tawne could have chosen a face on Death as It came for her—pulling back the hood to reveal Its identity—It would have been Delia's.

People had looked into this as Tawne impersonated Death, going under enchantment. This trap was what Tawne wanted now, to wear her chosen face for Death. Without it, she couldn't do this. When morning came, she must be able to resist the call to self preservation. Otherwise she'd run. It was basic instinct.

But trapped and in love with herself as Delia, and she wouldn't be able to move.

Tawne knew the sun was coming up when she heard the first moths hit the house. The howling stopped at the same time. Did the coyotes leave? She felt Delia with her in more than just the image so perhaps this finally chased the ugly man away. It didn't matter. She couldn't turn away from the reflection of the eyes in the mirror to pull back the drape again.

More moths struck the house, so many it sounded like an avalanche. The way silent snow sounded rolling down a mountain.

"It's you and me, babe," Tawne whispered, her own eyes

Charlee Jacob

dry and cold. She thought of lines from 'Immortal Inamorato' a last time.

> I will follow you between the stones,
> eating the bitter bloodroot with gratitude,
> for I have loved you all of my death.

Tawne struck out with her fist, grabbing a handful of curtain, smashing the window. Moths swarmed through, dancing, thought by many cultures (along with butterflies) to be the souls of the dead. The neighbor called them nocturnal and yet morning summoned them here, as did sunset. What did it mean? Were day and night connected all along? Could they merge?

Tawne couldn't move; the image smiled. Moths came through the opening and rested on her body to quiver. Their wings opened and closed as light filtered inside in pinpoints.

(Rising from the horizon.)

It gleamed across the walls in brittle angles.

(Running down the street, head-on-fire.)

It flooded in slowly, shining.

THE TRAVELING VAMPIRE SHOW
RICHARD LAYMON

It's a hot August morning in 1963. All over the rural town of Grandville, tacked to the power poles and trees, taped to store windows, flyers have appeared announcing the one-night-only performance of The Traveling Vampire Show. The promised highlight of the show is the gorgeous Valeria, the only living vampire in captivity.

For three local teenagers, two boys and a girl, this is a show they can't miss. Even though the flyers say no one under eighteen will be admitted, they're determined to find a way. What follows is a story of friendship and courage, temptation and terror, when three friends go where they shouldn't go, and find much more than they ever expected.

__4850-7 $5.99 US/$6.99 CAN

Dorchester Publishing Co., Inc.
P.O. Box 6640
Wayne, PA 19087-8640

IN THE DARK

RICHARD LAYMON

Nothing much happens to Jane Kerry, a young librarian. Then one day Jane finds an envelope containing a fifty-dollar bill and a note instructing her to "Look homeward, angel." Jane pulls a copy of the Thomas Wolfe novel of that title off the shelf and finds a second envelope. This one contains a hundred-dollar bill and another clue. Both are signed, "MOG (Master of Games)." But this is no ordinary game. As it goes on, it requires more and more of Jane's ingenuity, and pushes her into actions that she knows are crazy, immoral or criminal—and it becomes continually more dangerous. More than once, Jane must fight for her life, and she soon learns that MOG won't let her quit this game. She'll have to play to the bitter end.

___4916-3 $5.99 US/$6.99 CAN

VOICE
OF THE
BLOOD
JEMIAH JEFFERSON

Ariane is desperate for some change, some excitement to shake things up. She has no idea she is only one step away from a whole new world–a world of darkness and decay, of eternal life and eternal death. But once she falls prey to Ricari she will learn more about this world than she ever dreamt possible. More than anyone should dare to know . . . if they value their soul. For Ricari's is the world of the undead, the vampire, a world far beyond the myths and legends that the living think they know. From the clubs of San Francisco to a deserted Hollywood hotel known as Rotting Hxall, the denizens of this land of darkness hold sway over the night. Bur a seductive and erotic as these predators may be, Ariane will soon discover that a little knowledge can be a very dangerous thing indeed.

___4830-2 $5.99 US/$6.99 CAN

HEXES

TOM PICCIRILLI

Matthew Galen has come back to his childhood home because his best friend is in the hospital for the criminally insane—for crimes too unspeakable to believe. But Matthew knows the ultimate evil doesn't reside in his friend's twisted soul. Matthew knows it comes from a far darker place.

___4483-8 $4.99 US/$5.99 CAN

THE DECEASED
TOM PICCIRILLI

Something is calling Jacob Maelstrom back to the isolated home of his childhood—to the scene of a living nightmare that almost cost him his life. Ten years ago his sister slaughtered their brother and parents, locked Jacob in a closet . . . then committed a hideous suicide. Now, as the anniversary of that dark night approaches, Jacob is drawn back to a house where the line between the living and the dead is constantly shifting.

But there's more than awful memories waiting for Jacob at the Maelstrom mansion. There are depraved secrets, evil legacies, and family ghosts that are all too real. There's the long-dead writer, whose mad fantasies continue to shape reality. And in the woods there are nameless creatures who patiently await the return of their creator.

___4752-7 $5.50 US/$6.50 CAN